THIS HYENA IS GOING TO HEAVEN

THIS HYENA IS GOING TO HEAVEN

GRACE KING'ARA

iUniverse, Inc.
Bloomington

This Hyena Is Going to Heaven

Copyright © 2011 by Grace King'ara

This is a work of fiction. All of the characters, names, incidents, organizations, and dialogue in this novel are either the products of the author's imagination or are used fictitiously.

iUniverse books may be ordered through booksellers or by contacting:

iUniverse
1663 Liberty Drive
Bloomington, IN 47403
www.iuniverse.com
1-800-Authors (1-800-288-4677)

Illustrated by Michael Githui Muthiga of Fatboy Animations

ISBN: 978-1-4502-8710-4 (sc)
ISBN: 978-1-4502-8712-8 (dj)
ISBN: 978-1-4502-8711-1 (ebk)

Printed in the United States of America

iUniverse rev. date: 04/01/2011

The Author Dedicates this book to the Author of Life

Once Upon a Time

❧

Once upon a time, there was a little jungle kingdom in a place called Samburu. It lay on the equator in a land of sunshine called Kenya. Every morning, the sun journeyed from east to west. She caught her breath on everyone's head at midday and then hurried west to paint the horizon with magnificent colors. The animals believed she slept on a rainbow. The next day, she caught a tunnel under the earth and made it east again in time to wake up the birds that then woke up the rest of the jungle. Time was told by the position of the sun and shadows.

Lion was king, Twiga the giraffe was pastor, Tortoise was the fountain of knowledge, and Hyena cleaned bones from the king's palace. The mysterious Vulture knew everything about everyone, but no one knew anything about her. She was never a part of anyone's life, yet she was never apart. Parrot reported everything that happened to everyone. Lizard was consulted on all news about man. Humans did not mind his presence in their jungle as long as he fed on the flies they hated. Snake was rumored to be in the hush-hush business of stolen eggs. Monkey had something spooky going up his tree; he was suspected of witchcraft. There were many other businesses in the jungle, but this story does not want to be about work.

1

Almost all the animals were Christian and God fearing. On Sundays, they worshiped God under the sacred tree, a giant umbrella of dark green leaves rumored to be older than Tortoise. Nobody knew how old Tortoise was. He just was. Everyone's great-grandmother had met him, and some guesses included a century!

The king had decreed that no animal should kill or eat another on Sunday. It was therefore safe for anyone to go to church and socialize with neighbors.

Sadly, nobody ever invited Hyena, and he was too shy to go alone. He had no friends. Sometimes he eavesdropped on Parrot or Lizard briefing the king just to keep abreast of the news. But he felt ashamed afterwards. Human news was juicy, such as when they used animal stories to teach their cubs in school, or when they were all freaked out about the mad cow disease. He planned to ditch eavesdropping soon and behave with integrity, but every time a juicy piece was reported, he postponed his transformation. After all, no one believed he was capable of integrity.

Frustrated and lonely, he lost motivation even to clean himself. He believed he was ugly and could not wash that away—and he suspected that everyone agreed. His front legs were longer than his hind legs, so sometimes he put his hind legs on higher ground and pretended to be a handsome, straight animal like Lion. His dotted coat was dirt in color, and something always dripped from his mouth after scavenging. These days, the queen and the princess wrinkled their noses when he passed.

Hyena lived in the servant quarters of the palace. It was a burrow in the ground that the king had commissioned Warthog to dig in return for one week's amnesty. During that time, no animal was allowed by law to eat or harm warthog, even if it was not a Sunday. That was how the king paid his wages. The Green House was the royal lair of King Lion. It was a long, flat stretch of the greenest grass. Little squares of tall grass provided sleeping quarters for members of the first family. In an oval office, the king held court and received important news from the jungle reporters.

Hyena's den was nice and warm. Sometimes the royal cubs pulled pranks on him by throwing bones in the hole that landed on his head. He got out and chased them around, even though the queen was always watching and suspicious. King Lion was kind, fair, and down to earth. Sometimes he cracked jokes with Hyena but only when the queen was not around. Queen Bora believed royalty was not to mix with every scavenger out there.

One day, the whole jungle had left for church except for Hyena. Hyena believed in the unseen God, but he prayed only for others, never himself. This particular Sunday, he chose to pray for the first family. There were times he wanted to pray for himself, but he was not sure God cared to have a pet Hyena. Perhaps when he cleaned up, quit scavenging and eavesdropping for integrity, God would love him. In the meantime, he prayed for God's favorite creatures, just to show God he was not jealous. He understood and forgave everyone. In his opinion, it was hard for anyone—even God—to love a scavenger like him.

Dear God, he prayed, kneeling in his den, his nose in the sky. *This is Hyena, but do not concern yourself with me. I am calling about the happiness of the royal family. The king favors the princess, which hurts the prince. He ought to roar by now, but he doesn't—and he can't be king till he roars. The queen favors the prince. It hurts the princess so badly she eats her own weight in food. The queen also thinks she is smarter than her husband. God, if you trust the nose of a hyena, I smell something sinister lurking around her, something that reeks of witchcraft. I don't know, God, seeing as I am only a scavenger, but something's not right in the royal household. It is spiraling out of control, and you might want to reel it in. Amen.*

If anyone cared to know, Hyena called himself an atheist, sometimes agnostic. He had no idea what either of them meant, but the shock effect on the Christian animals was worth it. If they were too high and mighty to invite him to meet their God, he wanted to believe in something they hated—or at least pretend to. He kept telling himself he did not care, but deep down he did. He wanted desperately to be someone's friend.

Soon the sun was overhead and he was still alone sitting in a shrub hating his life. He recalled the most embarrassing day of his life, when Pig had invited his family to a party. It was supposed to be his happiest … until his family was disgraced.

The hyenas had arrived several hours earlier than agreed. He and his macho cousin had immediately jumped into the mud pool where piglets were playing and bullied them to tears. He remembered with heavy guilt how they had bullied the innocent piglets, splashing them with mud till no one could tell what they were.

Meanwhile, Hyena's adult relatives had eaten everything in sight. Though only one family had been invited, the entire clan had tagged along. Pig and Warthog had politely tried to feed everyone, but the hyenas had asked for more and more helpings till all the food was gone. The other guests were yet to arrive.

The hyenas had made unbearable noise, stealing bites from one another and fighting over leftovers. Although it was Sunday, they had attempted to eat their hosts when no more food was available. That was when six elephant brothers and Rhino arrived. Grasping the situation quickly, the elephants tossed every hyena over the fence, but not before Rhino had poked a hole in every one of their behinds. He still remembered everyone running home with tails tucked between their legs, flat against their bellies. He had barely escaped a poke by hiding under the long legs of an arriving giraffe.

Parrot told everyone in the jungle what happened, and the hyenas were ostracized. They had never been invited anywhere since. Well, that was not exactly true. Good old Warthog had invited the clan to church one day, but they had turned him down cold. Now he wished they had not.

Every Sunday, Hyena watched other animals groom themselves, hug their families, and walk together to church. Whatever was served there, everyone came back happier and friendlier. Something in his spirit kept urging him to go, invited or not. Perhaps God himself was inviting him. A few Sunday's later, while praying for the royal family he snuck in a tiny prayer of courage for himself. Then he tiptoed to church unnoticed. In that way, if he did not like it and never wanted to go back, he would not have to explain himself to anyone—not that anyone cared, but he was trying to keep the faith.

Once Upon the Devil's Mountain

❧

S nake's real name was Black Mamba. He had been told he was the fastest snake in the world. His venom was toxic enough to kill anyone of any size, even an elephant if he wanted to. But he had never needed to harm anyone ... at least not yet.

Black did not believe in the unseen God. In his opinion, it was blasphemous to claim that some God whom no one had ever seen, smelled, or tasted had made him. According to his ancestors, snakes came from one mighty egg laid by a giant female rock god on the Devil's Mountain. It was somewhere in Eastern Kenya. The rock was shaped like a half moon with two horns. Standing under her on the very bottom of the earth was the male rock god, Axis. His head was the other half moon. The visible female half-functioned as his eyes. She had the upper lip, and he had the lower. He had a human body, the muscles of a fighting bull, and the tail of a giant snake. Snakes believed it was Axis who held earth in two strong arms so it did not tilt or overturn, pouring everyone into the abyss.

Once upon a moment, the male rock god shot up to join the female in a rocky embrace, causing a great earthquake. Millions of rocks were strewn all over the world. That was how rocks were formed. In that moment, the two half moons became a full moon head, complete with eyes and a mouth.

The mouth released a giant egg that had been forming in the female for 666 moons. For another 666 moons, the sun warmed the egg daily on its way west. One day, millions of hatchlings burst out of the shell. Two of every kind of snake scattered all over the world. Male and female, they hatched out—except the Brahmin snake. Only one female came out; the egg had no more space to grow her mate. That is why all Brahmin snakes are female.

Afterwards, Axis went back to the bottom a frustrated god. His precious snakes had failed to evangelize the jungle, and all the other animals belonged to a cult called Christianity. The dreaded Christian sect was like a virus spreading across species, from humans to domestic animals and finally to jungle animals. Once it caught, it had no cure.

A furious Axis shook a fist, and a large portion of earth sunk, forming the Great Rift Valley. This was where the infectious faith was most intense. In one little jungle called Nyandarua, the animals had even predicted the exact date of the end of the world. No one else mortal or spirit was privy to that information.

In another bout of range, Axis swayed sideways, spilling some of the earth's water, which collected into many lakes. Lake Nakuru was owned by a very tall, pink bird called Flamingo. Her legs were longer than her whole body. She had webbed feet and a brain smaller than her eye, but she could fly, walk, swim, and even sit down.

Lake Victoria, a humongous freshwater lake, collected in a place called Kisumu. It spilled over to the lands of Kilimanjaro and the Ruwenzori Mountains of the Moon. The waters were owned by the biggest python, called Omieri, the most revered priest of Axis among the snakes. Some humans were rumored to accord him deity status, but then anything was possible with humans. They were even harder to predict than God.

The majestic Mount Kenya sprung up in the same chaos. Black thought it was a confused mountain because it had snow on its cap, which was closer to the sun than its bottom. It would have made more sense if the snow was on the bottom where it was shaded by the forest. The famous mountain of Kenya was owned by huge elephants. But it was the hushed up Devil's Mountain that was infamous.

Everyone had heard whispers of the scary mystical place covered with ancient rocks and shrubs. A lost animal stumbling upon the mountain immediately released his bowels out of fear. But the spookiest part was when the urine defied gravity and flowed uphill instead of downhill! This was enough to freak out even King Lion. Once uphill, it was impossible to climb down. Some force kept pulling uphill. A kicked stone rolled right back up. Survivors of the encounter had fur that stayed upright permanently. Others had lost their minds. A carnivore had turned into a herbivore and now ate grass. A dik-dik had eaten a jackal, and a domestic sheep had bitten her human master's bottom off. Herds of humans had been heard screaming out there, but no one knew if they were coming or going.

The only way down Devil's Mountain was walking backwards with one's eyes closed in order to avoid meeting any eye of the rock. She had them hidden all over her body. Every 666 minutes, she opened one, and anyone who caught it with his own became blind. Mole and Bat could attest to that if anyone could get them to talk. Survivors of the haunted rock never remembered their ordeal—or if they did, they never told.

Underneath the rock was a very deep cave abandoned by human witches thousands of moons before. It now served as a transit center for demons. When someone died or embraced The Name, the demons that must then leave his body rested in the cave until they could be reassigned. No one knowingly set off to go there. A resting place for demons was no resting place.

No animal wanted to appear to know much about the place lest they were dubbed devil worshipers. Suspects were immediately ostracized. One was Vulture's aunt. Her eyes were a bit off color. Even Snake thought she had the evil eye. Anyone whose stomach remained bulged during a drought also caused whispers of devil worship. The Christians were notorious for denying such bulging evidence. They said their unseen God could provide good health in all seasons. Snake decided something had to be loose in their heads. Both the followers of Christ and the followers of Axis suspected the other of being a satanic cult. As far as Black Mamba was concerned, the score was even.

Snake's ancestors had taken pilgrims to the Devil's Mountain, tasted the air, and liked it. But none had ever revealed what happened during the pilgrimage. They just slithered around as if they possessed an important secret. Some never came back. There was something out there, and Black wanted to unravel the mystery. Perhaps they had gone right ahead to snakes' heaven without experiencing death. He would like that.

The Devil's Mountain was also rumored to be the headquarters of The Mass, the most feared secret sect in the jungle world. Only the very elite were members, and no one knew for sure who they were. Christians thought The Mass was a code name for devil worship and that Axis was the very devil. Black Mamba did not care what they thought. No one sought out The Mass. They approached whomever they found worthy of belonging and then offered him membership. This kept many in secret expectation. It would feel good to be chosen for something, even if you were going to turn it down. It meant someone somewhere took notice. In this jungle, rumors were more often true than the truth, so Black had kept an expectant heart, and it had paid off.

The Mass had sent him a voice, just a voice. He had heard it again last night. But first he had to straighten out his good-for-nothing son, Nyoka. It was time he knew their god Axis.

THE FIRST FAMILY

ↂↄ

King Moran believed in God. He was a confessed baptized Christian. But whenever he closed his eyes to pray, he fell asleep. He suspected a sleeping demon, but he did not know how to cast it out. He knew he should pray first thing, say good morning to God, but when the rays of the sun hit, he got busy trying to focus. Soon the sun paused overhead, and he took a nap. The queen fed him dinner, and the evening rolled into the night. He was snoring before he said goodnight to Jesus. God would understand. He was a king, too, and matters of a kingdom could be very involving. When he had said he loved him and had gotten baptized Christian and proper, he had meant it. Surely God knew that without a thousand reminders.

Sometimes he blamed his blond mane that was extremely long. When the sun was overhead, he got too hot and napped completely motionless for anywhere from a few minutes to a whole day. Once in a while, he would swat the flies that buzzed around him with his tufted tail or just let them be. After all, he was king. No need to kill his subjects unnecessarily, even if they were flies. His thoughts drifted back and forth this afternoon as he dozed. He got up quickly when the queen, her sisters, and her female cousins returned with a kill.

King Moran was taking another of his legendary naps in the palace and thinking how much he loved his Queen. She had the combined beauty of all the females in the world and their temper but boy did he love her! She also had too many rules about propriety, some made up as she went along. For instance, he liked Hyena, but she needed extra air when he was around. He smelled. The king had lost many good helpers because she disliked them for unpredictable reasons. But he was determined to keep Hyena. He cleaned up bones better than anyone, though he was a little on the ragged side. He was also good for the first cubs of the jungle.

The King swatted a fly...oops, he had killed a subject! Then he raised his eyes towards the distant horizon. A sleek brown feline approached. Her sisters and the sunset were behind her both in positioning and beauty. "That's my Queen!" he said proudly to the flies he had not killed.

She was a God-fearing wife and mother with a cute touch of paganism. There were moments she talked about evil eyes and witchy hooves to be careful about. Superstitions were bad for his family and his jungle, but Queen Bora came from a superstitious family. Her great-grandmother was a witch, and her grandmother had a little brush with the occult, just a little consulting with an ancestor. She had been told that her granddaughter would marry the king, and it had come to pass! Her mother was a prayerful Christian who lived with them even now. She did not condone any of the old rituals and called them abominations. But it was the grandmother who had raised the queen and left her mark in her. Secretly, the king admired the combination of heaven and earth in her, as long as it remained entombed there.

He had forbidden any witchcraft in his jungle. Nevertheless, one strand of his mane kept itching when she looked at him a certain way. He had a creepy feeling she was delving in a little on her own, perhaps to fix their son, Simba. He was long past the age he should have roared. Four sisters and six female cousins of the queen lived with them. The four sisters walked immediately behind her royal highness. The cousins walked in a circle around the royal sisters. They fed and protected the first family but the queen always carried in the kill. Only she had the right to feed her husband the first bite. The numerous cubs from the extended family were snickering behind Simba's back and roaring just to bully him. One of these days, the king decided, he was going to pray about it. That is as soon as he was through with the most pressing matters of the kingdom.

King Moran arose to let the queen feed him his first bite as was custom. This had to be the best kill ever. She was the best. She had to be and he was sure he was not thinking with his stomach! Even the flies that followed him everywhere seemed to respect her by keeping their distance.

The prince and princess sprung up with their babysitter and headed for the kill. King Moran thought the princess was very pretty with a long body though a tad toward weighty. Her mother thought she ate and slept too much for a princess. He doted on her and sneaked her extra bites when the queen was not looking. He just loved the way she snuggled into his long mane. The queen was more affectionate with Simba. He was every inch a prince, handsome, agile, charismatic, and firmly decisive but without a roar. The last time he had tried, he had sounded like a female kitten. He could not be king if he did not roar. Perhaps it was time to consider his twin sister—a *Queendom* instead of a *kingdom*. The females did all the work anyway, but that was a thought that could trigger Armageddon. The king decided he had not even thought it.

THE IRON FANG

∞

Black Mamba the snake ruled his family with an iron fang. They lived in a little, collapsed, grass and mud, human hut, but it was home. He liked his wife, but he was not sure of that love business. King Cobra had decreed that snakes must have proper families—one snake, one wife, and they should look after their hatchlings. In the good old days, a male met a female, made eggs, and everyone went their way leaving the eggs to get a life. The hatchlings came out self-sufficient, and they never needed love—whatever that was under the sun. Did the sun not provide all the love a snake needed through her warmth? But a king's decree was a king's decree. King Cobra considered himself enlightened and did not tolerate absentee fathers or mothers in his kingdom. They were free to leave Samburu or comply.

Black watched his wife lying in a corner with all ten hatchlings coiled around her. They were all female and blind as bats. Not that he had anything against blindness or bats, but whatever had caused this misfortune was not from his side of the family! They were also too small! He never touched them or went very close, but he could tell they did not resemble him or his wife. The eleventh was a son, a replica of his father, but Black thought his son was as weak as a worm. Nyoka was curled alone in a corner. At least that was a sign of strength. He did not want his son sniveling around his mother like a tiny hatchling, but Black suspected Nyoka did exactly that the minute he turned his back.

His family was taking this love and quality-time business too seriously. He was beginning to like it too, but he was fighting the weakness. He was a tough, cold-blooded reptile, not some hugging, kissing, warm-blooded mammal! Still it was nice to come home to someone, even ten blind females whose paternity he was starting to doubt.

He remembered the day he got married. He had never seen her before, but he had smelled her. The scent had struck him like thunder as he sunned himself on a stone. He had gotten up and followed, ready to go the end of the earth. He suspected she was aware of him all along. Whenever he got too tired and slowed down, the scent remained in the same intensity, as if she had slowed down to wait. After almost a whole day, she had allowed him to catch up with her. He had followed tradition and examined her health status by flicking his tongue all over her body before asking her to marry him. She had flicked out her tongue at his face and sweetly hissed a yes. Two witnesses had taken their names to King Cobra's court, and their marriage was legal.

The snakes were part of the Samburu, but they had demanded their own king. King Lion had agreed, mainly to assert himself at home because the queen had opposed it. Sometimes she thought she was the one running the jungle. He also just hated hissing affairs. King Cobra liked to imitate King Lion, who believed in family. But Cobra had gone a step ahead and made it law. That was how Samburu snakes had ended up married and raising families.

Black had never asked his wife where she came from or where she was going. Neither had she volunteered her history. Mostly snakes were just eggs that had gotten a life, end of story. They had no nuclear or extended families before now. She also had no name. He had named her Swift because of the way she moved, and she had liked it. Swift was the same size and looked exactly like him.

Black considered beating the truth about the hatchlings out of his wife but thought better of it. She looked as viciously aggressive as he was and better exercised. There were battered husbands these days, and he did not care to be laughed out of the jungle. Still he suspected the hatchlings did not resemble his side of the family, even if he had not met his family. Surely his relatives and ancestors looked like him! He decided not to pursue the matter. After all, his "daughters" were hatched in his compound; that ought to make him their father. He had the hiccups just thinking about it.

Swift studied her husband, who kept glancing at their son Nyoka. He was their only flesh and blood, but she loved all eleven of her hatchlings. She had not bothered to name the ten sisters. Even if she had, she could not possibly tell them apart. They were identical, clones of one snake. When Nyoka insisted on names, she had given them one to share amongst themselves—Darklay. Partly because they were dark in color and partly for the dark secret that was their life. She had no courage to share it with her husband just yet.

Black had told her to watch their eleven eggs till they hatched. One evening, she had been distracted as she watched black ants carrying loads of food bigger than themselves in a very long convoy. Fascinated, she had followed to see where it all ended. In the meantime, someone had stolen ten of her eggs, leaving only one. Fearing the wrath of her husband, Swift had frantically searched for more eggs, anyone's eggs to replace the stolen ones. At last she found ten perfect little eggs that someone had left and carried them in her mouth. They were tiny, but she had decided they would do.

The tiny eggs had hatched earlier than Nyoka, who took three full moons. She hoped her husband would never know the difference. But ten identical hatchlings resembling neither of them had to be suspicious. Heck, he wanted to be a father, and she had made him one as best as she could. That ought to make her a good wife— whatever that meant.

She loved her husband but resented the way he treated Nyoka. She turned her gaze on Darklay. They liked to eat ants and termites and bury themselves in moist soil. She wished they were bigger. Whatever their species, they had saved her marriage for the time being, and she was ready to love them whether they were earthlings or aliens. They were now her responsibility.

Nyoka wanted to play with his father, perhaps some wrestling. His sisters had such fun with their mother, but Black had forbidden such immature behavior. Nyoka was unhappy. His father never touched him in affection, or anyone in the family for that matter. Sometimes he wished he could go away, any place with his mother and sisters. Then he realized he did not know his mother either.

Where did she come from? Did she believe in Jesus or Axis? She gave a lot of physical attention but said nothing about herself. All he knew was that she and all her hatchlings said yes to their father and told him what he wanted to hear.

"Get ready, everyone," Black announced. "It's time for church. Nyoka, watch the house while we are gone."

Nyoka was hurt as usual, always left behind. His father feared he might believe something in church. He wanted him to know only Axis, the god who held the axis of the earth.

"Why do you let mother and my sisters go to church?" Nyoka asked his father one day when the mood was safe.

"We have to keep up the appearances, or someone will think we are devil worshippers," Black had replied. "But I do not want my son contaminated with that faith. It does not matter what females believe." Nyoka had thought that was a very sexist remark, but he held his tongue. He loved his mother and sisters, and they were just as smart as any male. For the first time, he wished Black was not his father. This was very bad love.

The Voice had warned Black to keep up appearances. It spoke to him every time he followed the dark and wide path, away from the straight and narrow that led toward church. The Voice was loud and clear, but Black did not see anyone. He was not even sure if it was inside or outside his head. He had no external ears like other creatures, but The Voice was clear. At first he was afraid. Then he started anticipating and even going after it.

"Great Mamba, The Mass sees you. The Mass honors your faith in Axis." Those were the first words of The Voice that first time. Last evening, he had dared a conversation with it.

"Who are you?" he had asked.

"I am The Voice of The Mass."

"What must I do?" Black had pleaded.

"Wait. Keep up the appearances, for you are chosen. Your wish is about to be granted," The Voice had promised before fading away. Black had nursed one wish all his life: to have legs. Big legs like Giraffe, perhaps even many legs like Millipede. He had kept his heart expectant, and *The Mass* was choosing him. But now more than ever, he must go to church. The animals were suspicious of anyone who did not go to church. Not that Christians ever trusted snakes, but no need to give anyone a reason to point a paw. Nevertheless, he would not let his son Nyoka anywhere near those poisons.

Yellow Is Not Just a Color

❧

Yellow Eyes was a smart demon. He knew they had Black Mamba. The Mass knew of his innermost desire. The Mass always knew. After all, they planted self-sightedness. Sometimes he occupied the body of the quiet vulture. Then he could be anywhere, quietly listening to anyone, just pecking around. The vulture was actually a Christian bird, but she had once secretly visited Chameleon the wizard in a bid to contact her dead mother. Chameleon had given her a mantra of two words to chant: "Yellow Eyes." Within minutes after his name was called, he had left the cave in the Devil's Mountain where he was hanging out waiting, since Aunt Vulture's mum had died. He disguised himself as the dearly departed mother. Yellow had known her and everyone before her for thousands of years. He had always been a part of that family and knew all the right things to say—some that only the vulture and her mother knew. And now he had legal ground to enter and torment Aunt Vulture. She had even called him by name. Once again, he had a permanent home till the wretched vulture died. He could come and go as he liked. He also brought seven friends along for house sharing. If he was out on an external mission, he needed the indwellers to keep house. Left vacant for a moment, these mortals could hear J. C.'s knock on their door, and once he was in, Yellow was out. He was not taking chances.

Sometimes Yellow left the body of the vulture and remained in spirit form. To Black Mamba the snake, he was simply a voice. Voice was power. Mortals were prone to believing they were hearing from God without confirming which god. Yellow thrived on their lack of knowledge. Deep down, they all believed in the unseen God but chose not to acknowledge him. He had left his fingerprints all over them when he made them.

At the moment, his best gate was their discontentment. They worried more about *how* and not *why* they were made. Once a mortal was discontented with his entire self, he was ready to be manipulated, a weapon of mass destruction against the kingdom of God. Snake wanted legs. All snakes wanted legs deep down because they once had them. They had suffered from missing limb syndrome since the garden of God. Yellow needed more of such creatures to stop and destroy Samburu animals. The Mass had enough problems eradicating Christianity from Kenyan humans without animals catching the incurable virus.

Under the Sacred Tree

ᏻ

It was the Sunday Hyena finally prayed for courage and tiptoed to church unnoticed. He hid at a vantage point under the sacred tree where he could observe without being observed. One by one, the animals came. Every side of the tree was the door, save the path reserved for the pastor and the royal family. Hyena thought the peacocks were the most colorful. Snake's wife and her ten strange daughters were there to show off their new skins, or so Hyena thought. As soon as they were suitably noticed, they left. He looked sadly at his own shabby, dotted coat of fur. It was comforting to see Monkey partly uncovered, his bottom exposed.

Everyone stood quietly and waited. Pastor Twiga arrived wearing a collar made from a slice of banana stem. He was the tallest animal in the world, and his presence never failed to wow the brethren. His wife, Gloria, walked gracefully beside him. Her fur coat had brown blotches separated by light colored hair. Twiga's blotches were bigger than Gloria's because he was older. Their necks were so long that their small heads seemed closer to heaven than earth. If they had claimed to hear some heavenly jingle bells, smaller animals like Rat would have believed them. Scores of animals passed undetected under their long, endless legs.

Gloria was named after the glory of God. Her pastor husband had named her himself when he baptized her, and she loved it. She was slightly shorter than him, and her two horns were smaller. Twiga had three horns, but the middle one was not hard. He was born with two and developed a third later. Twiga was the love of Gloria's life. Whenever he preached, she stood next to him praying silently, interceding for his message. Sometimes she nuzzled the scar on his upper lip in encouragement. If his message dulled a little, she started a cheer, which the congregation picked up, boosting his ego. She was a true pastor's wife.

Twiga and Gloria were on call day and night. Luckily they had learned to nap while standing. They never worried about food because nobody else was tall enough to eat the sweet leaves on top of the trees. The only threat was when the elephants came calling and yanked the trees out from the roots. The giraffes were the tallest of earth, but Elephant was the strongest mammal this side of heaven. Twiga and Gloria fasted routinely, even going for long periods without water. The stomach held no power over them. They could visit the brethren anytime, anywhere without worrying what they would eat or drink. Their eyesight was the best there was. They could see the farthest animal, even when he could not see them. No one could have asked for better qualities in a spiritual first couple. Having no children of their own, they were contented to parent the pets of God.

As Hyena watched the giraffes, he liked his own body a little. The pastor's front legs were more elongated than the rear, just like his own. His dots almost resembled Twiga's blotches. Perhaps they were even related somewhere in their ancestry. If God could choose an animal that bore any resemblance to him, perhaps he was not so bad looking after all.

A big gasp swept through the congregation when the king and queen arrived. Snuggled between them were Crown Prince Simba and

Princess Simbora. The cubs were delightfully playful with everyone. But sometimes they made funny faces during intense moments in church causing some disruption as the queen tried to subdue them. Today the royal family seemed withdrawn, preoccupied with something. The prince was especially out of it. Hyena feared they were still worried about Simba. He wondered if God had heard his prayer; he wanted Simba to roar.

The king waved a friendly greeting and gave a nod for the pastor to begin. Dove led a chorus about birds of the air who did not sow or reap, who never stored anything away in barns like humans because the heavenly father fed them. Weaverbird weaved in more lines as the chorus progressed to a climax. It was Hummingbird who hummed them into the worship, transporting them to a heavenly realm. Mrs. Zebra was way up there, her massive head tilted back as her body swayed back and forth. Hyena dared not sing in case anyone noticed his presence. Besides, he did not know the songs.

One of these days he would make his own music for the unseen God. One day, they would be friends instead of acquaintances. Everything was going smoothly until the praying mantis said a very long and repetitive startup prayer. Warthog snored loudly, embarrassing everyone. Luckily his own snores woke him up. The pastor was ready to begin.

He preached about heaven, hell, and the judgment day. Hyena was fascinated by heaven, a place of incomprehensible beauty and splendor. Good animals went there when they died clad in new bodies that remained forever young. Ugly emotions like hate, fear, defeat, sadness, loneliness, jealousy, and low self-esteem were banned. There was no dirt, sickness, or death up there. Hyena understood no scavenger on board! He planned to start eating nice and proper like Lion. No wonder God had made him king.

"But God will do away with stomachs!" Giraffe warned. "Let no one be plotting to eat anyone up there!" Many shouted "Amen!" amidst laughter. Everyone knew someone who desired to eat them.

Snake, who had remained behind when his wife and daughters left, now shot up and stood on his tail. This kind of blasphemy made his fangs grind.

"Why can't I keep my stomach there?" he demanded. "I only really eat dust!"

"Because there will be no dust in heaven," Giraffe replied politely. "All streets will be made of gold!"

"Should he not stop biting humans?" Mrs. Zebra shot out of order, to point out snake's sins. The congregation started mumbling.

"We will sort this out later, Sister Zeb," Twiga replied calmly, not wishing to embarrass her. Gloria was about to frown at Mrs. Zebra but stopped herself on time.

"Believe me, humans do not taste as good as dust!" Black Mamba shot at Mrs. Zebra.

"Brother Black, your venom kills humans! It is a sin to harm the image of God," Twiga said and regretted it immediately. He did not want to be sucked into an argument and alienate anyone, even Snake. The church was meant to be a thicket of love since God is love.

"Tell them to keep their big feet off me!" he hissed. "Have you any idea how much those humans weigh?" He slithered out indignantly, having no interest in heaven or any other galaxy. Then he remembered The Voice and regretted immediately. He was supposed to keep up appearances. But it was too late. He was too angry to stay.

This time, Gloria did frown at Mrs. Zebra, but in one of those female sign languages. Mrs. Zebra caught on fast and started a chorus, "Oh God is good." The pastor needed a moment to recover and work up the mood again. Something had crash-landed them back to earth and they needed to ascend again. The mysterious vulture left from the back as quietly as she had come. The mood started rising as they praised. Nothing evoked the presence of God better than praise.

Hyena mulled over the idea of heaven and a new body that stayed clean without being washed. A "shake and wear" body! Washing was such a drag. He closed his eyes and roamed his mind to heaven. An angel hyena, face cuter than Tiger's, wings prettier than a peacock and the majestic soar of an eagle. This Hyena was going to heaven! But having no stomach was not an interesting thought. He had hoped that whenever he was good, God would allow him to eat a human here and there, perhaps an angel … he would love to taste an angel—wings and all!

His nose hit a stone on the ground, and he realized he had dozed off for a moment. A fly entered his nose, and he snorted. A tick bit him somewhere he could not reach just as the pastor asked everyone to pray for the animal next to him. He had no one next to him, so he prayed there would be no flies or ticks in heaven. Then he felt selfish because God made them too. In retraction, he prayed there would be mouth-free ticks and flies. Angels could be bitten all over the place!

"The only way to get to heaven," Giraffe continued, "is to love the Lord your God with all your heart and mind, and your neighbor as yourself. And you must never eat or harm humans, for they are made in God's image. Those that have done it must repent. Some have even eaten dead humans whose causes of death were unknown. God calls that an abomination! Human meat is not to be desired or sniffed, even in your dreams!"

Hyena salivated at the mention of dead humans. This was his most favorite food ever! When he was young, he and his cousin had run away from their clan to be near humans. His cousin had been captured by them and never seen again. He had stopped hunting humans then, but if a dead one turned up, he was not making any promises.

"Does anyone want to ask Jesus into his heart today?" Twiga asked, making an altar call.

Suddenly, a strange warmth engulfed Hyena. He sensed the presence of God. More than anything, he wanted to become a pet of God. He decided to come out of hiding and ask them to pray for him, to ask Jesus into his heart.

As if on cue, the mysterious Vulture came in again. She had watched Hyena from far, his contrite face, that look of surrender, and winked at the spirit of disruption in Mrs. Zebra.

Just as Hyena was about to stand up, Mrs. Zebra went shyly forward to confess something. Last week, she had kicked a human who had come up behind her. She was afraid humans had acquired an exotic appetite for her milk and she was not some sorry cow!

"I kicked the human with my hind leg, and all his teeth flew out! I think I killed him. Will I still go heaven?" she asked timidly, paw in mouth and a nervous toothy grin. Giraffe assured her that protecting herself or her calf's food was not a sin but her responsibility.

"It is best to steer clear of humans," Giraffe expounded. "But if cornered in your own habitat, you have a right to defend yourself because suicide too is a sin. Remember, humans are not God. They too were made from dust. But though we were formed before them it was man who named us, like he is our godfather. God also chose to show us what he looks like by making them in his own image. It would be immoral and surely in bad conscience to hurt, kill or eat the image of God!

If a demon could fall in love, Yellow knew it would be with Mrs. Zebra. Thanks to her, the moment of a contrite heart had passed for Hyena and all his insecurities had resurfaced. The vulture Yellow was hiding in shuffled out, this time squeezing through some animals and "accidentally" stepping on mouse who shrieked loudly. Yellow liked going to church, but only to stay informed. He hated having to close his ears every time they mentioned the J name. It made him tremble and fall on his knees supplicating to one who was not his master. His vulture house must think she had a combination of Malaria and sleeping sickness. He liked that.

Who was I kidding? Hyena thought. *I could never possibly be as pious as Mrs. Zebra, Owl, or even Tortoise who sits as if God is sitting on him!*

Mrs. Zebra walked back to her place next to her son. Her nose remained in the air, cultivating an aura of piousness. Her real name was Milia, but everyone called her Mama Zeb after her son. He never left her side on Sundays. When Zeb was born, Milia hid him from everyone for three days, including her husband, Punda. She wanted him to recognize her face, voice, and smell before anyone else's. As soon as he patented on her, she introduced him to his father and stepmothers.

Zeb spent a lot of time with the rest of the family, but everyone knew Sunday was mother and son day. Milia wanted to instill good Christian morals in him before he joined the bachelor group and planned his own family. She hoped he would not end up a polygamous happy-go-lucky like his father who had married many other wives after her. All the same, theirs was a close-knit family. If any of them were lost, they all joined forces to look for him. They also slowed their pace when grazing or walking to accommodate the elderly and the weak. They were a good family, real Christian-like, but she was the only one that professed the faith.

Milia had a massive head, which she translated as endless wisdom. That was why some were jealous of her when she participated intelligently in church. Perhaps she should ease up a little. Not many creatures could handle a smart female, especially when God was clearly using her to pinpoint sin in others for their own good! She was furious that the other Christians did not ask questions of their own but simply tried to silence her with their stares and snickers.

Her coat of fur had shiny black and white stripes of no particular pattern. This confused anyone who thought of her as food. From far, they could not tell her shape or her distance. The stripes did not cover her belly but formed beautiful triangular patterns on her legs.

A small mane of short, erect hair completed her attire. Her foal, Zeb, was a miniature replica of her, but his stripes were different if one looked very closely. Every zebra's stripe pattern was unique to the owner. The pastor said the uniqueness was the signature of God.

Mrs. Zebra rubbed her son's neck with her own and swatted flies for both of them with her tuft-ended tail. Zeb looked embarrassed, and it irritated her. She was setting an example for him here. Kids!

It was time for a song of adoration. Six birds of paradise sang their hearts out, calling upon the Lord who was worthy to be praised, in order to be saved from enemies. Mrs. Zebra thought it was most appropriate. She closed her eyes and sang along with her neighbors but not for the same reasons. It was such a beautiful song that most animals felt heaven bound. When they sang, "We are standing on holy ground, and I know that there are angels all around," tears flowed freely, even from the king and queen.

Suddenly Owl the prophet moaned into a trance and prophesied. Respectful silence was maintained. Hyena was fascinated. He was not sure he believed in prophesies yet, but there was just something about this moment, some power flooding the place. Even he was on holy ground.

Owl was once a jungle shaman who saw into the spirit world. When he renounced that life for Christ, he received the gift of prophesy. His Christian name was Asio. His wife, Flammeus, perched next to him on a twig. The quiet couple lived with other owls in a parliament along the Ewaso Nyiro River. They had relatives who still played the toxic spirit world, but they were praying and believing in God for their salvation.

Owl's large, pleading eyes were yellow in color. They had black rings around them. Between the eyes and the rings were whitish plumage disks. He looked like he was wearing artificial human eyes. Mrs. Zebra thought he was smart because his head was bigger than his body, just like hers. Hyena thought the hooked black bill gave Owl a clever look. His plumage was tawny-red, but he had a noticeable white streak on his breast. His tail wings remained bared as he prophesied, his wife mumbling prayers beside him.

"Beware when mother and cub are not mother and cub. The lion lies with the lamb, end of the beginning, beginning of the end ..."

It was an old prophesy. Every seven moons, an owl had repeated it word for word. Expectant silence followed, but Raven broke the spell with the chorus, "Oh God is good!"

Remorseful tears flooded Hyena's eyes. There was an anointing in this place he wanted to hang on to—if only he felt worthy of it. He felt like a gatecrasher at God's party. Two days before, he had eaten a dead human. The foolish humans were always killing each other and throwing the dead ones on his path. It was their fault if he went to hell! He wondered if he could appeal and blame someone else if he had enough evidence. Not likely.

Squirrel read the announcements of the day from a leaf that Parrot had written. Hyena did not pay much attention. Mostly it was a list of the animals on amnesty that week, but he did wonder why Squirrel was allowed to read when he stammered through everything. Still, he had to hand it to Squirrel. Though he had a small head and big eyes and looked like a giant mouse with a big bushy tail, he had a family. His home was a dray up the side of the church tree complete with two rooms and a nursery. His wife had just had a kitten. She was upstairs right now listening to the service.

Something caught Hyena's ear about some missing animals.

"A pat-pat-pattern is revealing itself," Squirrel read on. "Once a mo-moon, an animal disappears but does not appear on the k-k-king's list of those eaten or dead from natural causes. Someone is s-s-stealing eggs. Some birds have not had a new gen-gen-generation in many moons. We know it is not an act of humans."

Squirrel sat down, and the king stood up unannounced. This was uncharacteristic. He was distraught, and his rumbling, deep voice seemed to shake. "It is true, my friends. Something is going on. I am appointing Tortoise to get to the root of it. Anyone with any fruitful lead will get six moons' amnesty. Have a good day, everyone." He gave a small bow to the pastor, excusing himself, and left with the first family.

The queen was mortified. Her husband had never stood up unannounced before. He was forgetting protocol. She held her tongue only because they were in public. Lashing at him there was beneath her stature. Soon she would have him up close in private.

As soon as the first family left, everyone started speaking at once. An embarrassing silence followed as politeness made them wait for the other to speak first. In that brief silence, Mrs. Zebra's low, deep voice rose from the back.

"It is the rapture, pastor! We have all missed the rapture!" She bordered on hysterical, to her son's embarrassment. Her ears were pulled forward in fright. "We have been left behind to face the antichrist!"

"No, Mama Zeb," Twiga consoled, hanging onto his patience. "Our neighbors have disappeared over time. The rapture will happen in the twinkling of an eye before the antichrist takes charge of the earth. We do not ever have to meet him if we remain on the straight and narrow!"

Everyone knew Mama Zeb was terrified of the antichrist. Her earlier composure was gone. Some snickered nervously. She snuggled closer to her son, but Zeb did not comfort his mother. He was now fascinated by the long necks of the pastor couple. They sure caught the sunshine before anyone else. If they grew any taller, their heads would hit the clouds and the sun could come crashing down on them, waking the antichrist and frightening his mother. Zeb realized he was dozing. He wanted to hurry home and play kickback with his many half brothers. He always kicked highest with his hind legs. Together they could scare away even the antichrist, whoever that was.

The pastor asked Tortoise to pray over the disturbing disappearances. As he crawled forward, the birds of paradise led another song of praise to fill the gap. They finished and repeated two verses before Tortoise made it to the pulpit.

Tortoise was a senior bachelor, dedicating all his time to the work and pets of God. He was gigantic in size and faith. His carapace curved upward resembling a big rock or a giant football covered with brown square scutes. Below his ridge was a pure white plastron that gave him a clean look above the slow-dancing club-like legs. Tortoise had no visible ears, but no one made the mistake of talking behind him. He had all the inner hearing parts, and they were fully functional. His eyesight and sense of smell had never failed him. Right now he could smell a hyena but wisely chose not to acknowledge him. He must have summoned a lot of courage to come to church even secretly. That brother was hiding but not from God.

Tortoise's big round eyes seemed to rest on everyone at once with a calming effect. When he opened his toothless, sharp beak to pray, his gentle, deep voice vibrated like a caress coming from the ground, rising up to embrace them.

"Father, in the name of Jesus, your pets thank and give you praise. Please reveal where the devil has gone and taken our friends, neighbors, and the eggs that are our future generation. We stomp, trot, kick, bite, and peck on the plans of Satan in the name of Jesus. Endow man with wisdom, your image, whose choice is our destiny."

"Amen!" chorused the animals.

The prayer for man was the traditional finishing line of all their prayers. They knew they were under man's dominion and God himself had ordained it from the beginning of the beginning. But these God trotting devil stomping pets of God wanted their own personalized relationship with him. When they died they wanted a heaven where God was the landlord.

Hyena sneaked away as the sunrise broke through the bushes. His eyes were wet. It became safer to think about his smell. Giraffe had said God was everywhere, and it would not do to stink Him out of earth. He also said cleanliness was next to godliness. Something in him wanted to resemble God even more than he wanted to resemble Giraffe. Next Sunday, he would take a bath. He hoped the rapture did not come in the meantime. Heaven would stink for sure. What he really needed was that "shake and wear" body at the end of time. That stopped his thoughts in their trots. It called for a major decision to be made about his personal relationship with God.

Most of what he knew about God was from his late mother, a devout Christian. But the whole thing had seemed to mellow down after her death. The clan that had raised him and his cousin had no religious inclinations of any kind. They just were. But there was always something pending in his heart, some unfinished business with God. His mother had planted a seed. God was still watering it but Hyena had shut out the sunlight.

Visions of Armageddon

⌒⌒

Gloria worried about her husband's weight loss as she walked home behind him. He had just finished a twenty-eight day fast for the first time. The most they had done before was seven days, but the stakes were very high this time. She had known better than to dissuade him. Instead, she had joined him for the first seven and left him to continue as she interceded for his health and answers.

He had fasted for two reasons. First he was trusting God to send a creature who knew the contents of his holy book that man used as his instruction manual. He had also called on all Christian animals to fast, pray, and receive the unlikely miracle by faith. Strangely, almost the entire congregation had stood with him even though the doubt on the majority of faces was obvious. The animals had divided themselves into seven groups taking turns to fast the last seven days of every moon. It had been seven moons now, and nothing had happened. If she did not trust her husband so completely, Gloria would be very worried. This was way overboard expecting even God to find an animal on earth who knew what was written in the human language!

"Everything is possible with God." She kept reminding herself.

The second reason was a vision her husband had seen, more like a premonition of extremely evil spirits hovering over Samburu and the whole land of Kenya. He knew it was a vision and not a dream because he was not asleep.

A circle of demons hovered over the skyline of Samburu. From the horizon, a procession of mortal beasts ridden by vicious evil spirits approached, led by a brood of vipers. The vipers slithered in an SSS rhythmical movement as if trying to spell the word sin. They hissed an eerie religious liturgy of sorts. The creatures behind them repeatedly mumbled the monotonous words under their breath, unconscious of their meaning. It was a satanic mass of sorts. All noses pointed to the ground, even the beaks of flying birds that followed behind on foot. The birds were led by the mysterious vulture. Wings were glued together by something sticky and white, so no bird could fly. Everyone had little stones stuck to their backs and heads. They were heavy ridden and ready to sink in any waters.

They crawled along the Ewaso Nyiro to the haunted Pond of Tears where humans drowned unwanted female puppies and kittens. Their tormented spirits were believed to hover around. The demon ridden creatures squeezed through a triangle of climbing plants. Just before the top sharp corner of the triangle was a single deformed leaf of poison ivy. It had no business being there. In Twiga's vision, it was an eye of horrors. A coven of more ugly demons with zigzag black and red wings hovered just above. They kept beckoning to their friends who rode the enchanted creatures the way humans rode horses. There were thorn bushes and beds of stinging nettle also infested with various devils. Some danced obscenely to blasphemous songs while others sat or lay on the nettle in various positions of watchfulness.

They entered the triangle two-by-two, reminding Twiga of the human Noah's Ark. But they were not always male and female. They included pairs of the same sex, cub and adult, brother and sister, father and daughter, and even different species abominably paired together. They were not there to escape death by water but to embrace it. Within them was no desire to multiply and replenish the earth or even subdue it. Instead it had subdued them. Behind the triangle was a wide, grassy path, the highway to the Pond of Tears. They approached and suddenly it widened into the shape of wide mouth atop an ominous deep.

Twiga thought he saw Prince Simba and Princess Simbora in the lead. They looked bewildered, out of touch with reality. Just two scrawny lost cubs, nothing royal about them as they calmly approached death. There was a voice in the air, a soothing lullaby that kept repeating in the creatures' ears, a promise that they would not surely die but come up out of the water on the third day and live, becoming as God. Soon they were entombed in water.

When the last creature sank, the water appeared to close its mouth, as if observing a moment of silence for the damned departed. Suddenly it belched out an ominous dark vapor that spread purposely downriver to poison all the waters. Whoever drank the water—human, bird, or beast—would die. The demons that lay in wait on the nettle rode happily on the clouds of dark vapor, their field of operation widened to torment the pets of God.

On the sidelines, Twiga saw a dog walking home as three coyotes played with an image-maker, the instrument man the image of God used to make his own image. Monkey was up in the sky sitting in a nest that dangled from the leg of a black sky horse. He was throwing stones at the snakes. The horse had a white stripe on the neck. In the vision, Twiga was a full moon hungrier than he had ever been. Nevertheless, he was shouting praises to God along with all the other animals. Every word of praise turned into a rock that Monkey used to strike the serpents. The elephants dug a mud trench and filled it with water and praise. There some devils fell and sunk into the bottomless pit.

Twiga and Gloria prayed about the vision with Tortoise and Owl and sought God's interpretation. Finally they took it as a warning of a looming spiritual battle with the forces of darkness. Something dark was coming out of the pit to shake them, but God himself was preparing fighters among his pets. If God was for them, it did not matter who was against them. They could not figure out all the details, such as what the dog, coyotes, and image-maker had to do with anything, but God would reveal them in his time. Twiga was more convinced than ever that the animals needed to know the word of God. When other animals fasted in turns for someone who knew the contents of the Bible to come to them, Twiga fasted the entire seven days. He never doubted for a moment. If anything, he was going after God, curious to see how he got himself out of his promise to give whatever was asked in the name of Jesus. Whatever God did was bound to be very interesting and unmistakably miraculous.

On Saturday morning, the last day of his fast, Twiga had another vision. Monkey walked toward him with the same horse he had ridden in the sky. But just as he was receiving Monkey, he saw the queen hanging on a branch of the darkest tree. The noose on her neck was a rope made of millions of chameleons with enjoined heads and tails. It wound around her neck and the branch several times, and some chameleons still dangled down. Somewhere on the grass beyond the tree, the king was dying. Millions of flies buzzed around him. Twiga had already seen the prince and princess among the suicide divers in the earlier vision. Something evil stunk in the royal family, and God wanted him to purge out the evil. He knew the sorcerer chameleon was involved. He had a feeling he was not to share this vision with anyone, except his wife who was part of him.

Whatever the devil was planning, Twiga believed God wanted him to fast and pray for a full moon. That would energize the heavenly forces to come to the rescue. He knew God's army was always ready, but their marching orders came from earth as prayers of believers.

"Please, God, help me walk in your will," he prayed quietly as he led his wife home.

"Please, God, hear from heaven and shepherd my husband," Gloria prayed, following closely behind. "Do not let him be shamed in his giant step of faith!"

"Lift off the doom hanging over Samburu," Twiga continued. "I cover all your pets with the Blood of Jesus. Endow man with wisdom, your image whose choice is our destiny."

"Amen," Gloria whispered, stepping beside him at their gate. She crossed her long neck with his and nuzzled at the scar on his lip.

Monkey and a Basket of Gods

✧

Monkey was considered a good Christian in as far as he never missed church. His baptism name should have been "The Brother" Guenon. He had a lisp and could not pronounce The Brother to the pastor, so he became De Brazza Guenon. His upper and lower teeth did not align, and he spoke from the roof of his mouth. Guenon was his family name, but he had no family. His mother, father, and three sisters had been captured by humans.

Monkey had big cheek pouches as if he had food in his mouth. His chin and lips were blue and white, contrasting well with his grey coat of fur. He liked his black, long legs because a white stripe of fur crossed his thigh and gave it character. His tail was longer than his head and body combined, making it easy to balance himself on anything.

Some girls liked the crescent orange-red patch on his brow. Others fell for his long, white beard that extended from a white muzzle on his face. He considered himself a handsome hunk if no one was looking at his massive feet. He hated his feet even more than the lisp in his speech. At least one girl had liked his accent, but they all kept their eyes above his feet. Perhaps it was time to stop playing the field and marry a beautiful girl with beautiful feet - give his daughter a fifty-fifty chance. If it was a boy, he would carry on the Guenon name successfully, whatever the size of his footprint. Everyone would then address him as Mr. Guenon, with respect. But that was later. Now they just called him Monkey. It did not matter. They did not know he was on a mission to accomplish what no mortal had ever dreamt of. They might even have to search for bigger titles than mister and sir when his future was fully unveiled.

Unbeknownst to anyone, he did not live on a tree. He climbed up there to pray, exercise, and spy. His real home was in a swamp along the river. He glanced casually under his favorite tree where he had hidden a human nest. The nest was his first assignment from The Voice. The Mass had found him worthy and approached him; he, in turn, had found them credible and believed them. They knew his innermost desire. They touched base and got going. After all, he had what it took to be the smartest creature in the jungle. He was the image of the image of God. He was a close third in the universal realm of wisdom after God and man. Not bad. There were talks of a very smart dolphin, but that was neither here nor there. It could only wear its smarts in water. Monkey could walk, run, stand, climb, balance in the air with one hand on the branch, and win a swimming competition. More importantly, he resembled the image of God way more than the dolphin did. Soon he would become a super human if they let him keep all his monkey skills, a better image of God than man. He could even become Superman.

Man, the image of God, did not want to be an original but a copy of a copy of a copy … up to the current faint copy. Lizard had heard them teach in school that they were evolved over time from monkeys. On Sunday, the same cubs were taught that man was created from dust by God, right from scratch, an original masterpiece. The poor little humans must be as frustrated as he was trying to figure out truth. At home, one parent may feed them evolution, another God. Monkey figured each parent could be talking about his or her own side of the family. A kid could also believe whomever he liked more—mother, father, teacher, or priest. He could also be a half-breed of everything. Others just carried a bag of different truths and pulled out the appropriate one, depending who was asking and the risks or benefits involved. No wonder humans suffered multiple and split personalities. Were human scientists still researching the cause? When he became Superman, he would point them in the direction of the obvious.

Monkey's future depended on the evolution theory being true. That would mean there was a real human trapped inside De Brazza Guenon, a.k.a. Monkey. Perhaps if he searched around, he would even meet some monkey humans or human monkeys in various stages of evolution.

Right now, he felt like a leftover of evolution stuck with the original massive feet and toes for the rest of his life. But The Mass had promised to evolve him, not over millions of years like man but in the twinkling of an eye. Either God had evolved along with man or there was a new one on the throne, a new-age god faster than the Ancient of Days. But why was he thinking about God, science, science-God like a human developing a multiple personality? Something had to be true somewhere. For now, he just wanted to be evolved.

For the price of carrying mysterious cargo to an eerie place as directed by The Voice, he was going to be evolved. Very soon he was going to wear shoes, dance with a human female with small feet … There were endless possibilities.

Exactly one moon before, The Voice had sent him where three little humans were grazing their cows and goats. His instructions were to hide and grab the human nest as soon as the party was scattered, only the nest. He did not know what The Voice meant by "party scattered" but hid as told. The little human males were huddled together talking animatedly as they grazed long-horned cows, a few goats, and a sheep. They wore sandals made from worn out rubber and one-piece red cloths knotted on the shoulders. Every boy stood on one leg, resting the other on the knee. One arm leaned on the staff. Despite one leg and one arm being totally motionless, they chatted and gestured excitedly in perfect balance. Thank goodness he was not going to lose his balancing skills as a human. He stared at his future, wearing shoes on small feet, and owning a cow or two, heck a herd. No need to limit himself.

He was still grazing mental cows when the thundering started. It sounded like a stampede of wildebeests getting closer by the second. An eerie wind was blowing. Everything froze. Suddenly the biggest cow, perhaps a buffalo the size of a small mountain, came charging right into the boys and their herd.

At one point, the giant cow was suspended in the air. A fountain of thick, brilliant white milk rained from her massive udder. The cow mountain disappeared as fast as she had come. When the dust settled, the little humans and their animals were gone. Four streams of milk starting from somewhere beyond ended abruptly next to the shepherd boys' lunch basket, *the human nest*. It was The Voice that shook a frozen monkey into action.

"Now! Get the nest now!"

Monkey grabbed the basket by its handles and ran all the way to a spot under his favorite tree. When he paused to catch his breath, The Voice froze him again.

"Reach inside the human nest."

He reached in and brought out a child's toy flute shaped like a banana.

"That is the god of bananas," The Voice continued. "Worship only him for your food. Now reach in the basket again." Monkey did so and brought out a human wristwatch.

"That is the god of time, the one who will fast forward your evolution. There is a god for everything, but these are the two you need right now. In 666 days, you will be a full human in body and mind. But you have to undergo a test of faith and obedience first."

"I have the faith. What must I do for obedience?" Monkey lisped respectfully.

"Collect soft feathers and put them in the bottom of the nest. Hide the nest in the bush behind you and await further instructions. If you reveal this to anyone, The Mass will know. The Mass always knows."

"Must the best news of my life be a secret?" Monkey asked, a little afraid.

"If you tell, The Mass will know. The Mass always knows." And The Voice was gone.

Monkey did as he was told. He also made an altar of leaves and branches for his gods on top of his favorite tree. Like other animals, he believed in the unseen God. But he also believed in giving God a little help, especially in such a delicate matter as evolving him in the blink of an eye. The other gods were like God's assistants or colleagues.

He placed God's colleagues where they could see the whole jungle of Samburu. Perhaps tomorrow he would give them a tour.

First things first, Monkey slid into prayer position. He was careful how long he prayed and what he said to each god to avoid any jealousy. It was no secret the invisible God was jealous. It did not make sense because Monkey loved him. He just wanted all his gods to work as a team.

After prayers, he sat on a branch to think. Why in the world did the gods need a human nest? He wished The Voice had elaborated. If it was a sleeping nest, the two visible gods could fit in snugly. But he was not sure it could contain the unseen God. He was also not sure The Voice was speaking for the unseen God. He scratched his head. He thought more clearly when he itched.

Giraffe said a human nest was once upon a time used to float a baby named Moses on the River Nile. It saved him from a king who was killing all the boys, hoping one was the son of the unseen God. He was rescued by a princess of the kingdom and raised in the killer king's own palace.

Perhaps when they evolved him, he too would start off like little Moses, floating on the Ewaso Nyiro. There was something he could not remember about God, humans, and water. He scratched his head again. It was something important. Yes, when he grew up, the unseen God could even let him walk on water like his son, Jesus. No, it was Jesus who let a human called Peter walk on water. Those were the kind of games he would be playing as Superman. What if they evolved his swimming, climbing and balancing skills to human capacity? Humans were physically pathetic. Apart from that limitless brain functionality, they could keep the change thank you very much!

If Monkey had looked down, he would have seen Black Mamba the snake going round and round the same nest.

BLACK AND SON

❧

Nyoka had enjoyed the sermon from his hiding place. The anointing never ceased to amaze him. He wanted in, but he also needed to honor his parents to live long. That was Christian. Becoming a Christian would dishonor them because his father strictly forbade him to attend church. He was already all sinned up for sneaking in. Was it possible there was such a thing as a holy sin?

If only his father would take him along with the rest of the family! Perhaps his family was ashamed of him! He could also have been adopted or mixed up as an egg and they did not like what was hatched. His father never returned his love, and he did not even resemble his sisters!

Nyoka wanted to go to heaven when he died and become a pet of God. But he also loved his father. As he slithered home alone, he recalled nostalgically the only time his father had taken him for a walk along some dead vegetation, a crawl because they had no legs.

It had been a lesson in pride. Black had told him that they descended from the most worthy ancestry, the longest, most venomous snake in Africa, second only to their king cobra.

"Son, we are faster than any other snake in the world, and our venom is the deadliest if we must use it," Black had said proudly. "Remember, courage is not demonstrated by starting fights but in finishing them." Using a fallen mango, he had shown Nyoka their strike position, neck flat on the ground, loud hissing, and a mouth open all the way back to display deadly black fangs. If the opponent made any sudden moves, he was to rear a third of his body off the ground and deliver multiple accurate strikes.

They had tasted the air with their tongues and listened with their eyes since they had no ears. That was the only day his father had truly demonstrated his love. Nyoka wondered what he had done right that day, the only day he was loved. If he knew that, he would repeat it every day. His dad would love him forever, and they would all live happily ever after.

At the end of the lovely day, they had nested in the moist bark of a dead tree. Black had chosen that moment to tell his son about their god Axis. He held the axis of the earth firmly from the bottom. His agents operated in a secret body called The Mass. They had no physical bodies and contacted whomever was found worthy through The voice.

Black told Nyoka about the kindness of Axis. Very long ago in another time, Axis had borrowed the body of the snakes' first ancestor, disguised himself, and visited the garden of the Christian God. He was touched by the plight of man, whom God had created in his own image to take care of his garden. Man was not allowed to eat from the tree of knowledge so that he would remain an ignorant slave. In his kindness, Axis had done the responsible thing and given man a fruit from the tree. Man became immediately smarter than all other creatures. The male and female even realized they were naked and covered themselves with twigs. But before he could feed them from the tree of life, their creator had turned up and ruined their only chance to live forever.

God lost his cool, banishing man and all creatures from his

garden, and fencing it with flaming swords that moved faster than light. In the confusion, Axis had dropped to earth before he finished transforming back from snake to spirit and left the legs and ears behind. That was why snakes had no legs and outward ears.

Out of the kindness of his heart, Axis chose to reside on earth comforting the poor creatures that now had to deal with death. He was here to help them make the best of this life because they lived only once and after that—nothing. He wanted them to have fun wherever, whenever, and in whatever form it could be found. If something felt good, they should go ahead and do it.

In the meantime, Axis held the axis of the earth so it did not spin out of control and harm someone. Snakes were his favorite creatures. One day, Axis was going to storm back to the garden and pick up their legs. They just had to keep the faith.

That was their one and only father-son serious talk, and Nyoka was not supposed to share it with anyone.

"Are we members of The Mass?" Nyoka asked his father.

"Not yet. The Mass has to choose and approach you," he replied.

"Why does it have to be a secret organization?" Nyoka persisted.

"Because our god is not a vain show-off like Jesus," Black answered.

"But how does he show off if he is unseen, as in invisible like his father?" Nyoka asked

"He still performs miracles, just to show off!" Black replied.

"He does?" Nyoka asked excitedly, his face lighting up. "Then it's true; he is alive!"

"Stop that blasphemy at once!" Black roared. "Axis is our god!"

"Has The Mass approached you, Dad?"

"No, son, not yet, but they will. If you keep an expectant heart, they will come." Black did not want to talk about The Voice. It did not seem to be a good idea right then.

Nyoka was not sure he wanted to be part of something that only operated in dark secrecy. He wanted to be proud, not ashamed of his faith, to sing and dance as he had seen in church. He also wanted life after death. If there was no other life after this one, then he was already dead. This was quite a dilemma. He needed to believe in Axis in order to honor his father, but he already believed in the unseen God, the one who had a garden and in his only son, Jesus Christ. That meant he had believed Pastor Twiga before his own father. He wished he could believe in both, but the Christian God was jealous and Axis always had an axe to grind with Jesus.

His mother and sisters had left church earlier, but he knew they had not gone straight home. For some strange reason, his mother liked to pretend she had left. Then she would hide under some dry leaves away from his father and continue listening to the preaching. Nyoka guessed she was pretending to be disinterested in God to please her husband. That way, he would never forbid her to attend church. His father stayed in one spot until the end, frowning through it all. He was only there for appearances. Nyoka wondered what his mother's real faith was. She never committed one way or the other; in fact, she never said anything about anything, and that was not an exaggeration.

Soon he was home playing with his ten sisters who shared the name Darklay. Nyoka thought they were very smart. During hide and seek, they buried themselves underground in a flash. They could also smell their father long before he got home; they would warn Nyoka to get away from them and their mother and start acting grown up. That always pleased the head of the family. He wondered if pretense was not a sin. If only he could curl up around his dad and play with him!

Black Mamba had not come home straight from church. He was slithering back and forth on the path where he had first heard The Voice. It was down the river near Monkey's tree. The sun was overhead, and he was getting very impatient with The Mass. They had contacted him and then gone silent. Why choose him if they were not going to use him? Soon he would be five years old, almost half his life gone. What good would new legs be on an old body?

Behind a shrub, Yellow Eyes disguised as a massive python watched the impatient snake moving up and down. He was ready. His greed was ripe for manipulation.

"The Mass honors your faith, great Mamba," said The Voice. Black was startled even though he had hoped to be contacted.

"What must I do to get legs?" he asked, hardly masking his impatience.

"Follow the trail to your left till you come upon a human nest," The Voice answered.

"And what do I do when I find the human nest?" Black pleaded, attempting to speed up the things.

"Follow the trail to your left till you come upon a human nest," The Voice repeated.

"Yes, I get that, but what do I do with the human nest?"

"Follow the trail ahead of you till you come upon a human nest," The Voice repeated again in a monotone, and then it was gone. Things became clear to Black. He was going to receive one instruction at a time. He slithered along the wide trail on the left. There were belly prints as if a very big snake had gone ahead of him, something bigger than King Cobra, bigger than the biggest python. He hoped it was only an illusion. It could not be the legendary anaconda on land.

He found the human nest Monkey had hidden earlier and waited for the next instructions. He went round and round the nest like a moving rope, ready to explode with impatience. He started counting the rounds just to kill time and curled down to rest on the seventh round. Immediately an angry voice snapped him alert.

"Do not stop at seven. Never, never ever! That is an unlucky number!" The Voice lectured.

"What must I do?" Black asked, trembling.

"You must go round 666 times to erase the damage of the seven," The Voice replied.

"Then what?" Black pressed.

"You must go round 666 times to erase the damage of the seven," The Voice repeated calmly.

By nightfall he was still counting. The whole thing made no sense, but perhaps this was the way legs were grown. He kept counting without resting on a seven.

The Whole World and a Hyena

ᏻᎧ

On his way home from church, Hyena decided he wanted God to be his friend. An omnipresent friend available any time anywhere to all and to one. But he was a trifle upset that God had chosen to make man and not hyena or any other animal in his own image. Humans were not deserving of such divine honor. They stole animal habitats, destroyed beautiful forests, polluted rivers with plastics, and tried to remake everything that God had already made beautiful!

He glanced at the end of the jungle where man had burned trees and grass yet again to claim more land. So many birds had lost their nests and nestlings to logging and forest fires. Porcupine had escaped with his life but lost his entire family.

Man had to be the valley of the shadow of death. He wanted the rhino's horn, elephant's tasks, snake and crocodile's skin, everybody's something but hyena. If a human ever wanted him, it had to be pure hate, madness, or for witchcraft purposes. Not that it made a difference to die in the paws of the godly or the ungodly, but his popularity as a whole did no favors to his self-esteem.

So, man was not a scavenger like him—big deal! Yet in all his wisdom, the images of God chose to smoke, drink, eat, and inject harmful substances into their bodies, the very temple of the

Holy Spirit. They traded self-control, perverting their minds to do indescribable things that shamed their families, friends, and animals. In some alleys, Hyena had come across some who were too gross even for his scavenger nose. Whatever the humans had ingested produced toxic fumes that made his stomach rumble for days. To think that he was under their dominion for the rest of this lifetime! In such moments, he crossed his heart and said, "Dear God, endow man with wisdom, your image whose choice is our destiny!"

Thoughts of humans always upset him. They had more going for them than any other creature yet remained discontented. They even committed suicide! If the image of God could reach such a level of hopelessness, what chance was there for a hyena?

He sat under a thorn tree to cool down. Why did God love humans so much anyway? They made wars with everything and everyone—even themselves—and sent their suckling cubs to kill or get killed for causes they did not even understand. He liked human cubs and hated it when they hurt them. He wished they did not have to grow up. Unlike grownups, they liked all animals, even hyenas. His late mum used human similes to impart godly wisdom. She said all humans were equal in the image of God. But they had distinct personalities and paw prints. The discontented ones imitated everyone they thought was better than them and turned into someone even they did not recognize. They even copied losers who had the charisma to make dishonoring themselves, parents, and God look really cute. She said there were humans that lived for a century and never met themselves!

"What is to imitate?" he had asked.

"It is forsaking who you are to become who you could never be," she had replied calmly.

"That's a tongue twister, Mum, if I ever heard any!" he had exclaimed.

"You will understand when you grow up!" And just like that, it was pushed into the future where she buried mysterious things. He could hardly wait to grow up but here he was, an adult with more questions than answers!

Answers are a buried treasure, he thought. Again he wished he had been born a lion. Everyone respected a lion, even humans. Lizard said that in Kenya they could not buy or sell without exchanging a solid piece of silver or a paper with King Lion drawn on it. No one ever drew a hyena except to tell a negative story.

A tear dropped from one eye before he remembered something else his mother had said.

"Though God may have made you greater than anyone that ever lived, you can still copy beneath yourself and die without ever meeting your great self." Perhaps God in all his wisdom had a hidden treasure, a better him lurking in there waiting to be unleashed. Perhaps he did not need to be a lion. But the thought of God hiding a treasure in a scavenging hyena like him bordered on blasphemy.

When a second tear fell, he searched his mind for something funny the way his mother had taught him to do whenever he was sad. There was that time when he was very young and he desperately wanted a pet, not just any pet but a small human. It had to be female too with lots of fur on the head. His mum said he would have to learn to make fire, cook meat, and dance to entertain it. He also had to carry it if they ever had to run away. Human cubs were the most helpless and demanding. He still wanted one.

"We could feed it fruits and carrots!" Hyena had cried out hopefully. "I can dance too—I can! And I am strong enough to carry it! Please! Pretty pleeeeease!"

But she had not budged. "Who is going to pick the fruits and dig for carrots?"

"We could ask Monkey and Hare; they are our friends on Sundays!" he had pleaded.

"How many times do I have to tell you to stand on your own four feet, not to burden others with your responsibilities?"

"Does that mean I can have one? I will do everything alone; I promise. Look at my muscles!"

"We would still have to steal one, and the humans will never rest till they find her. They are worse than elephants and never ever stop searching."

"Please! Please! Pretty pleeeease!"

"The last thing we need is the image of God on our tails! Who ever heard of a human pet anyway?" She was starting to raise her voice.

"But, Mum, it's all right to be first. You always said we should be original not copies." He knew he was on thin ice now and started retreating.

"Are you going to take after your father with his dreamy ideas?" She moved intently toward him. He thought he saw smoke coming out of her ears, and her tail was beginning to rise. One minute more and she would have his ear for dinner. He scrammed. Whatever his father had done, it was not the time to find out. Even then he had known she loved him unconditionally. Her anger was directed at issues, not his entire being. Nevertheless, a bite on his ear could become very personal.

She had taught him to respect humans as the image of God. Later, he had succumbed to his cousin's pressure and tasted them. One thing had led to another and he had dishonored her memory and his intrinsic values to become a copy. Somewhere along the way, he had lost his self-esteem just like the stoned and drunk humans he had seen staggering around their vomit in the alleys. One thing they had in common with him, they were all scavengers when they met in the alley. But he was not made in the image of God, they were. Not that it was much comfort.

"This hyena is going to heaven," he declared to himself. "Everything is possible with God, even a human pet." But in heaven, he would want some answers about some mean animals and humans who hated hyenas. The same God who made them made a hyena!

Yellow Eyes, the demon, watched the daydreaming hyena. He had come very close to answering the altar call in church and was still behaving suspiciously. Hyena was falling for J. C. That was bad for The Mass, very bad indeed.

By evening, Hyena had made up his mind. He washed his nose in the river, ruffled his hair forward, and went to Giraffe's house to be baptized. He confessed all his sins to Pastor Twiga on the way to the baptismal pond. This included sniffing, tasting, and even eating a few dead humans and biting off the behind of a thief. The male human had knocked down a female, grabbed something she hung on her shoulder, and gone to hide in the bush. He had witnessed it all from his favorite watching-man shrub. Just for the heck of it, Hyena had defended the honor of the female image of God by making a snack of the male's buttocks. Not that the lady would ever know.

Promising never to eat humans dead or alive again, Hyena crossed his heart and hoped to die. The pastor made him retract the hope to die because the tongue had the power of life and death. Twiga helped him with the sinner's prayer and baptized him. Hyena chose the name Brother because he hoped to be a brother to the other pets of God. Unlike Monkey, Hyena could pronounce it.

Brother hopped, skipped, and jumped, praising God on his way home. Birds, butterflies, bees, and even a green, jumping caterpillar followed him curiously. His song and laughter cheered the whole jungle. Some animals sang along as the trees swayed in the wind. Happiness was contagious, and soon everything that had life was praising God— except the vulture that hopped disinterestedly behind him. But no one really noticed the vulture, the favorite house of Yellow Eyes.

Yellow was having a very bad day. The hyena was not supposed to become a Christian. Brother indeed! It was time to feed the new brother something really bad. The stomach route never failed with a hyena. This meant collaboration with his colleague Milika, the female demon spirit who worked the humans. Yellow Eyes hated owing Milika anything because she always collected with interest. But it was safer to owe her than risk the wrath of The Mass. The Mass never forgave. In fact, forgiveness was a curse word in his world, the F word.

The stupid hyena was singing again. Every time he sang the name of Jesus, Yellow Eyes trembled, stumbled, and fell on his knees. A stumbling vulture was a very indecent sight. It was a very bad day indeed.

That week, Brother was careful to do for others as he would have them do for him. He worked for the king as if he was employed by Jesus Christ. This meant respectfully following instructions and honoring his employer even when out of earshot. The following Sunday, Giraffe proudly presented Brother Hyena to the congregation. Clean and well groomed, Brother joyfully sang his first original composition.

Thank you, oh maker of galaxies,
The whole world, and a hyena,
Devils beware, angels prepare,
This hyena is going to heeeeaaaaaven ...

"This hyena is *not* going to heeeeaaaaaven!" Yellow Eyes sang along quietly. Neither would any of the other creatures if he knew his job. This Christian animals' business had to be nipped in the bud. The Mass would see to that. It was time to either make some serious enemies in this congregation or cause enough fear to run faith out of the jungle.

Many hugs and kisses later, a jubilant Brother Hyena was dancing home from church. In his excitement, he missed a turn and ended up on a strange path. Suddenly his leg stumbled on something soft and he sprawled to the ground. A swear word almost popped out,

but he restrained himself. God did not like foul language. *Ouch,
ouch*—it hurt big time. His eyes widened in shock at the sight of
what had tripped him. A dead human's front paw was sticking out
of the bushes. An obvious trap from the devil! *"Shindwe shetani!"*
He shouted the local slang for "Down with the devil!" and ran away
as fast as he could.

This is only my favorite meal! he thought sarcastically as he ran.
*No, ex-favorite. I have just been baptized, and this hyena is going to
heaven!* he reminded himself.

Back in his den, he dreamt of the human hand and woke up
worried.

"If only I was not yet a Christian!" He immediately regretted
that thought, but his stomach still growled and saliva oozed from
the corners of his mouth. He was losing his mind on the very first
temptation! He knew his sins had been washed white as snow and it
was important to win his first round with the devil.

He turned round and round in his den sometimes covering his
ears with his paws as his stomach rumbled in anticipation. He was
drowning in his own saliva. He almost prayed but he was no crying
baby running to daddy on the first sight of the ancient bully. He
could even win a round for God, gain his trust and prove he was
worthy of salvation. Hyena hung his tail down and took a casual
little stroll to pick a fight with the devil.

Yellow Eyes slithered behind him. It was easier to hide his
presence as a snake. Sometimes he wished he had his own body like
the angels that remained in heaven. When they fell down to earth
alongside Axis, they also fell out of their bodies. He hated having to
borrow a different body every now and then. All this would change
when Master Axis finally sat on the throne of God. The second coup
attempt was in the final stages of preparation.

Milika, his counterpart from the human side, had tossed out a
banquet. No hyena ever triumphed over the stomach. This brother

was going to bite. But something felt wrong in Samburu these last few days. He could smell the fire of God everywhere, especially from the direction of Giraffe's quarters. That troublesome pastor had to be fasting again and covering the jungle with the B. of J. The thought of the Blood of Jesus made Yellow shiver. Its sting remained as potent today as it was when J. C. stormed hell for three days after dying on the cross two thousand years before.

"This hyena is not going to heaven, or my name is not Yellow Eyes," he vowed with an unprintable swear word.

ABSENT FROM REALITY

❧

By nightfall, Black Mamba was still counting around the human nest.

Nyoka had never seen his mother worried before. She was always expressionless—affectionate in her touch but still expressionless.

"Nyoka, please take care of your sisters," she said abruptly. "I am going to check on your father."

"All right, Mum, be careful please." He huddled close to his sisters. He wanted to pray for his parents but did not know where to direct his prayers. His father believed in Axis, Nyoka believed in Jesus, and the females did not confess in either direction.

"Please, if any god out there can hear me, this is Nyoka. Please take care of my parents!" he whispered, not realizing his sisters were listening. Sometimes he thought that because they could not see, they could not hear.

"Why do you pray like that?" one Darklay asked.

"I want God to help them," he replied.

"But you have to be specific. Which God?" asked another Darklay.

"I am not sure," he replied. "Any will do, so long as our parents come home."

"Would you respond to such a prayer if you were God?" asked another Darklay.

"I guess not," Nyoka replied, still sounding worried. He hoped some human had not hit his dad on the head. They always did that even when a snake was minding his own business.

"Let's try the God who made us," another Darklay said. "If you do not know his name, you call him by his deeds."

"What if we were made by several gods? We are too detailed for only one god," Nyoka said.

"We are too detailed for more than one god," one more Darklay spoke.

"You make a lot of sense, Darklay girls. Are you saying you will pray with me?"

"Yes!" they chorused.

"Okay, girls, let us close our eyes and pray," Nyoka said.

"We are blind!" Darklay chorused, and they all laughed.

"Then open your eyes, we pray!" he joked, and they laughed some more. Nyoka pleaded with the God who knit them together when they were still in eggshells. The parents came home safely but the hatchlings were too intent on keeping the prayer a secret to welcome them. Today they had shared an important secret. They knew their prayer was not directed to Axis, the god of their father.

Swift had followed the scent of her husband along the Ewaso Nyiro River. The trail took her to the eerie path. She saw Monkey's tree some yards ahead and recognized her husband going round the human nest like one possessed. His eyes were distant, almost vacant. He seemed to be doing some mental sums. Suddenly he hissed a number, 666, and came to a sick stop.

She wondered why he was shouting the devil's number. His vacant eyes suggested some kind of dementia, that disease of the aged where yesterday became bigger than tomorrow and today went missing. He was five years old, not that old, but poor nutrition meant a shorter brain span. He refused to eat termites and other proteins, sticking firmly to dust. Junk food never nourished anyone. She wondered what part of his past he was reliving now. He had been acting a trifle wired lately, even dreaming loudly about having legs. Snakes did not have legs, period. His head seemed to have some spinning spasms long after he had stopped moving.

As she approached him, Swift hoped she was not being punished for her sins.

"What are you doing, Blackie?" she asked, using his nickname.

Black thought it was The Voice until the sight of his wife jolted him back to reality.

"Exercise!" he answered a little too fast. Swift did not believe him, but she was not there to embarrass him. A dutiful wife stood by her husband to the end, even if he was absent from reality. At least he was not demon possessed or mad. Only his brain was dying. The brain was surely just another organ, like an eye or tail that could get sick.

For a moment, Swift wished she had done a background check on Black before marrying him just to find out what ran through his side of the family. Heck, she didn't even know if he had a family. She would teach her daughters to wait and know a little about their prospective husbands before allowing the traditional full-body tongue search.

"Whatever he has cannot pass on to our daughters!" she thought, feeling happy and guilty at the same time. But Nyoka was Black's flesh and blood. Her failures weighed on her again. She had lied about her daughters out of selfish self-preservation at the cost of those who loved her. Swift did not want to be a bad wife. It just sort of happened. With every passing day, it became harder to tell the truth.

"Let's go home, Blackie," she said kindly.

He followed her without a word.

Their son and daughters were fast asleep when they got home, or they pretended to be. Swift gave Black some termites and watched him to make sure he ate some. He ate without a word, unaware of what he had eaten and who had given it to him. She may as well have been on another planet. They went to their favorite corner and fell asleep. Swift decided that in such moments a nice wife did not pester her husband with endless questions. He would talk when he felt like it.

Black woke up before the birds and was careful not to wake anyone else. He slithered casually to the usual path to seek The Voice, his heart expectant. He walked up and down impatiently willing it to come to him. Yellow Eyes let the snake fret for a while before he spoke.

"The Mass is impressed by your faith, great Mamba," The Voice said.

"Thank you, my lord. What must I do?" Black pleaded.

"It takes a lot of protein to make legs. Fill the human nest with eggs," The Voice said.

"Whose eggs and how many are needed?" Black asked, needing clearer instructions. After all, he was a male and did not lay eggs!

"It takes a lot of protein to make legs. Fill the human nest with eggs." And The Voice was gone. It was no use asking questions. Black just got down to business and started stealing everyone's eggs. Wherever he found them unguarded, he put them in his mouth and took them to the human nest.

In one week, the basket was full. It had been tough, and he was proud of himself. Sneaking around his wife and kids, and learning the art of picking nests was no mean task. He felt lucky for marrying a nice local wife. It was not customary to ask a husband where he was going or where he was coming from. For the first time that week, Black slept a full night. Surely The Voice would seek him out and tell him that The Mass was pleased with him!

Swift was getting worried. Many times she had pretended to sleep as Black sneaked out. She knew now it was not dementia. Sneaking took some careful planning, and he always found his way back. He had a sound mind that was up to no good, but spying on him was not the good wifely thing to do.

Swift was a closet Christian. She wanted to share her faith with her hatchlings, but there was no way of doing that without offending Black. Traditionally, the hatchlings were brought up in the husband's faith. Black believed in Axis, a lie. She had a strong suspicion that Axis was indeed Lucifer. She believed in God the creator and in Jesus Christ his only son, but her life too was a lie.

She was afraid her character was more like Axis than Jesus as long as she kept the dark truth about her family from them. That was why she had kept her faith a secret. She dared not expose the name of God to the shame and ridicule that would be hers when the truth hit the jungle. Christianity was considered a cult in the snake world. She needed gutsy, radical faith to come out and declare. She had never met another snake who believed in Jesus. Neither could she hope to evangelize the serpents with sin on her tail. The devil would expose her big time.

Her faith had taken root when she tried what Pastor Twiga had suggested to all non-believers who harbored a secret wish to go to heaven when they died. She had found a quiet place and told herself she was prostrate before God even though her physical position was always prostrate.

"Dear Jesus, my faith is less than a mustard seed," she whispered. "I have heard you hate snakes because our first ancestor loaned his body to the devil. If you are not still mad at us and you are sure you want a snake pet, I want us to be friends. Please forgive my sins and reveal yourself to me. I love you, Jesus, but we have to communicate in secret for a while because my husband will not like it. Help me figure out how to have a relationship with you and still honor the obedience part of my marriage vows. Thank you for being my friend."

She experienced a sense of being accepted, and joy beyond description filled her.

Just like that, Jesus had become the love of her life. She hung out with him wherever she could hide, praising, adoring, and worshipping at his feet, basking in his lovely presence. She never forgot she was only a lowly, unworthy serpent whose sins had been forgiven, or that she wanted to take her family wherever he would take her.

When Black suggested they go to church, Swift obliged knowing it was purely for appearances. Everyone went to church on Sunday. It was the respectable thing. But she faked leaving church earlier to appear less eager. If Black thought she was falling for J. C., she feared he would forbid attendance. He wanted nothing to do with the unseen God. When everyone thought she had left, she hid somewhere in the back and listened to the rest of the service with her daughters. She told them she needed a more comfortable place. Black never sat with them. He just assumed the ladies had left early to prepare his meal.

Swift looked at her ten tiny daughters who were exact copies of one another. Somewhere out there was a distraught mother who had lost her eggs and a future generation. She had confessed this to Jesus and asked him for a way to fix it.

In the meantime, her son Nyoka continued to pray secretly with his sisters in the name of Jesus. The name tasted great when they hissed it. Whenever Nyoka could not sneak to church, he enjoyed ten different versions of the sermon from his giggly sisters. Sometimes he enjoyed their version more than the pastor's. They kept interrupting one another and acting out the characters. Everyone wanted to play Mrs. Zebra. After that, they played hide and seek, and he always lost. He was too big to hide. His sisters were petit and fast.

THE DEVIL IS BUSY RIGHT NOW

෴

Brother Hyena made it back to the temptation site. The human front paw was still intact, almost beckoning. A gentle, small voice from within urged him to stay away. He hesitated and then took just a tiny, bitty sniff that stiffened him for a moment. Then his body muscles relaxed as he basked in the aroma. He closed his eyes and opened his nostrils. The smell was awesome. Suddenly a vision of hell visited his mind. The devil tending his fire with a pitchfork stole a moment to look directly into his eyes and wink!

"No!" Brother cried out, taking to his hooves again. "This hyena is going to heaven!" he reaffirmed more to convince himself than the devil. He ran all the way to his den and hoped the lions did not hear him from their lairs.

The dreams were back in a flash. While eating the hand in one of them, he wet and soiled his sleeping quarters! He had completely forgotten to visit the latrine. In another dream, he chewed a soft morsel and bit his tongue hard, yelped in pain, and woke up. This temptation was consuming him.

Brother Hyena considered sharing his predicament with his pastor, but he was ashamed of admitting weakness. Everyone put their best paw forward around the pastor. It was almost law, albeit a silent one. At sunset, Brother found his way back to the human paw. Strangely, neither vultures nor crawling insects had touched it. He could have sworn he had seen a vulture around. The devil must have personalized the temptation just for him! This time, a vision of heaven flashed in his mind. He was very handsome with the most beautiful dotted wings, taking a casual flight alongside Elephant, Tiger, and Dinosaur. Below them were streets of gold. They were going to a dance organized by a human called David. He was once a shepherd boy, slayer of a giant, a harp-trotting musician, a dancer, a bigger king than lion, and now a friend of Brother Hyena. There was a lot of love in the air between animals, humans, angels, and other heavenly creatures.

"Yes, this hyena is going to heaven!" he affirmed and then, back in reality, made an important decision. He started digging a hole to bury the temptation once and for all. That would shame the devil and prove his allegiance to God.

As soon as he was happy with the hole, he found some sour leaves and covered the paw to prevent any direct contact with his tongue and accidental tasting. Lifting it with his mouth, he pulled carefully, but the hand was firmly stuck on something. On careful inspection, he realized that the rest of the human carcass had been hidden in the tall grass all along! A whole human, the biggest he had ever eaten, an entire feast! He was almost drowning in his own saliva now, and tears of frustration blinded him. Satan was truly cruel with his generous baits. Now he had to dig an entire grave, and the temptation in his head had grown a hundredfold. Every moment around this carcass could change his eternal destiny!

"This hyena is going to heaven," he repeated under his breath again and again, resisting the urge to take a bite.

Something was nagging at him to pray, but bothering God, who was minding the entire universe, with a small matter like this did not seem smart. He started digging a bigger hole. His paw hurt. He sang whatever song came to mind in order to divert his attention from the tantalizing smell. His stomach growled louder than ever. A wasp stung his eyeball, and the tick in his thigh took a bite. *Give it your best shot, Satan!* He thought. *But this hyena is going to heaven!* He continued digging.

When he thought the hole was big enough, he took a small break to scratch an itch on his back. It felt good to roll round and round on a rocky patch, but his eyes never left the human. A thorn dug into his behind. He turned his head sharply only for his nose to land smack in a leaf of stinging nettle. Another sharp head turn and a mean bird pooped in his eye. Someone was desperate to steal his joy. In one swoop, he was upright to continue his mission.

He quenched his thirst in a nearby stream and gathered more sour leaves. Brother grabbed the human by a rear hoof, and pulled hard towards the hole. The hoof suddenly came off. He lost his balance and fell into the hole with a shoe stuck in his teeth! He swore and quickly apologized to God. Biting firmly on the other hoof without sinking his teeth, he pulled. The second shoe came off, and hyena thudded right back into the hole. He swore again, and guilt flooded him. Somewhere in his brain was a swear script he had not intentionally written. Curses popped out like second nature, crashing his spirit. He was never the swearing type, but at one time, he had listened to and been impressed by some smart swearing hyenas.

The nudge to pray struck again. *I can handle this*, he thought. *Surely God has bigger decisions to make like recreating the extinct dodo and dinosaur and preventing* forest fires. *He could be holding consul with important animals like Lion, Owl, Tortoise or Giraffe!* Brother was not some whining ninny Christian running to Daddy for every little thing, and he intended to prove himself.

He dragged the human halfway into the hole before the pants came off to expose juicy thighs. On reflex, his mouth opened wide, with teeth bared, and he was about to take the biggest bite when the devil's wink replayed in his mind!

He sprinted a short distance away. Regaining his composure, Brother admonished himself for cowardly behavior and flexed his muscles to continue. For a moment, he thought he saw the yellow eyes of the devil following him. He hoped it was just his usual vivid imagination.

THE MAN-KEY

❧

Monkey was becoming impatient. It had been a whole week and nothing was happening. He was still freaked out about the cow, but he guessed evolving to a full human was not going to be easy. It was time to start facing fear like a man.

One morning, something woke him up, perhaps a noise under the tree. He climbed down to investigate, but there was nothing. He started going round the tree impatiently.

Perhaps The Mass is just a myth after all, he thought to himself. Then he remembered the gods up the tree and the flying cow with the massive raining udder. That was as real as they came.

"The Mass salutes you, great Man-key," The Voice said.

Monkey almost froze in fear as was his default reaction but remembered just in time to act like a man.

"Why do you call me Man-key?" he asked. He was never sure if The Voice was within or without his head.

"The Mass has chosen you to be the origin of species, a newly perfected breed of humans. The Mass will evolve you to super-human status in the twinkling of an eye. Then you must go forth, replenish the earth, and subdue it. "

"What must I do?" Monkey asked carefully. This was way too

big, beyond even a miracle. He was going to be greater than humans like Abraham, Moses, David, and even the giant Goliath. The girls would love him, but he would be way up there, too good for anyone alive right now. Still, someone had to be his Eve if he was going to be the new Adam. It never occurred to Monkey that there was already a last Adam. He gloated and almost missed the instructions.

"Gently take the human nest to the top of the hill and leave it there. Do not look back," The Voice said.

"Is that all?" Monkey asked, disappointed. How could such a small task produce such monumental results?

"Gently take the human nest to the top of the hill and leave it there. Do not look back," The Voice repeated in the same bored monotone. Monkey realized there would be no further instructions. The Voice was gone.

The nest was heavy and covered with soft, dry leaves. He dared not look inside and jinx his evolution. Lifting it carefully by the handles, he took the gentlest steps to the top of the hill, set it down, and started retreating.

He thought he felt eyes burning into his back, and his ears caught a swoop of very big wings landing and then taking off again behind him. Something made him very afraid. He sprinted all the way to his tree, climbed it, and hugged his gods to calm his racing heart.

Monkey thought his assignment was complete, but he was wrong. The next time he heard The Voice, it was clear he had to make 666 similar trips. Evolving to Superman in the twinkling of an eye was proving to be a very long twinkle.

THE VILLAGE OF NINETY-NINE

֍

Her name was Aero. Other than the fake birds made by humans, she had never seen a bird bigger than herself. The Mass used her like a cargo plane transporting unholy goods between Samburu, the village of Ninety-Nine, and the Devil's Mountain.

The human nest dangling from her leg was shipping to Ninety-Nine, a mysterious little jungle whose privacy had been preserved for thousands of moons by a myth. It was whispered that only ninety-nine animals lived there. If anyone gave birth, the oldest animal in the jungle died the same day. The borders were patrolled by bodies without heads and heads without bodies! They fed on the freshest skins of animals and humans; thus the victim was skinned alive. Nobody went there, but once in a while when the wind blew a certain way, everyone could smell something fowl and rotten.

Aero landed on a clearing near the secret cave and left the human nest with its mysterious cargo intact. Even she was not supposed to know what went on inside that cave. Sometimes she thought she heard sounds of animals in there, but it was not supposed to be any of her business. She perched on top of the biggest tree and waited for sunset. She always fell asleep at the stroke of sunset. At dawn, she would pick up the empty nest and return it to the port of origin for a reload. She had to complete 666 trips, but she was no stranger to that. The sunset hugged her, and she closed one eye. Soon she was asleep.

The demon named Mundu stood outside the cave and watched the bird sleep. Aero was Axis's pet loaned for the Kenyan project. He was also assigned two of the best field operatives, Yellow Eyes, who worked on animals, and Milika, the she-devil who did humans. They were here to exterminate the sprouting Christian animals the way humans did to roaches. But unlike the humans, the win for The Mass would be permanent.

Mundu toured the country disguised as a short, stout madman. His body could only be described as round. Even his eyes, ears, and mouth were round. If he fell down, he could roll in any direction, vertical or horizontal. He wore many bright-colored rags on top of a man's trousers and a woman's blouse. Two miniature Kenyan flags, the type ministers pinned on their cars, were stuck behind each ear. A third flag flapped back and forth on his round forehead, its tiny pole pinned in the locks of his thick, unkempt African hair. One foot was bare, but a flat, tattered, female slipper adorned the other. In one hand, he held a Barbie doll missing one eye, an arm, and a leg. Her beautiful hair flew wildly in the wind.

Neither animals nor humans bothered a madman if he did not bother them. In one of the country's forty something diverse cultures, a madman was actually required to perform a certain death right. Everyone had his or her place and purpose. What is more, Kenyan hospitality was unanimously second nature. He could land in any compound, and the owner would feed him because it was the right thing to do.

It was hilarious how the females and children fed him. They placed food on the ground and pushed it with a stick. If he made any sudden movement, they shot off. No one locked eyes with a madman or did a close study of his face. They glanced at him as one whole. Both the disguise and location were perfect. No animal or human went to Ninety-Nine unless he had lost his mind or was about to lose it.

It was the second holiest place of The Mass, second only to the Devil's Mountain. There were various animals in the cave. Yellow Eyes had led the poor, discontented souls on a pilgrimage in various stages of greed. A mole and a bat wanted to see, a rhino wanted two horns like Buffalo, one ape wanted a tail of his own, and two mice wanted to become mighty elephants. Warthog's daughter wanted to smell like roses; she hated their natural smell. A brood of vipers and assorted other snakes wanted legs.

They were there before the deadline, the sixth day of the sixth moon of the six hundredth and sixty-sixth year. Every 666 years, the god Axis granted every desire of the heart. Luckily, no one lived long enough to warn the next six hundredth generation that the myth was not true. Mortals were so gullible.

Mundu smiled at his assistant Yellow's ingenuity. The Christian animals believed they had heard from God without questioning which God. After all, there was only one God, and identity theft could not have gone that far!

It was a lucky break that Pastor Twiga had not taught them to test the spirits. If they had turned around and asked Yellow to declare his relationship with J. C., he would have trembled, lost The Voice, and fallen on his knees. The name of you-know-who remained viciously potent whatever the passage of time.

Upon arrival, he had given every creature a mantra to chant till they were visited by an indwelling peace. Without realizing it, they were chanting real names of real demons.

Homeless indwellers heard them all the way from the Devil's Mountain. They had been called by name. They were welcome to visit. Even God knew that. Soon they entered through the open doors of chanting mouths, and the host creatures became calm and subdued. These guests had no intention of leaving their hosts—ever. Not unless J. C. kicked in through the door, but then he was a gentleman. He stands at the door and knocks, waiting to be let in. Meanwhile, The Mass was now on the inside looking out, making so much noise that the gentle respectful knock would never be heard.

Slowly, the seducing spirits took over the minds of their hosts. In a few more days, it would be time. The Ewaso Nyiro, the Nile of Samburu would be poisoned. The pilgrim creatures were almost fully seduced into a suicidal cult. They were going to be champion suicide divers.

On doomsday, they would calmly dive into the Pond of Tears. These faithful believed they would surely not die. Before they hit rock bottom, the power of God would engulf them. They would be lifted up from near the bottom on the third moment and then walk on the water becoming as God. All power would rest on them. For 666 days, they would have the ability to recreate themselves and their loved ones with any desired physical attributes in the twinkling of an eye.

Then the power would return to God's hiding place, a well without a bottom below the Pond of Tears. There it would nest for another 666 years when another generation like them would be perfected to receive it. Mundu knew the creatures' greed was ripe enough to believe it. They actually called it *faith*.

The plans were ready for the river. Mundu had just finalized a new streak of the deadly disease Ebola that would not discriminate against any living thing. Both plants and animals would bleed from every pore, a slow expulsion of all life-sustaining juices and blood. As soon as the creatures were drowned in a suicidal mass, the disease-bearing demon would be energized to expel its fury on legal ground. Doomsday was "coinciding" with Christmas. If everything went on schedule, J. C.'s birthday would not be celebrated in Kenya that year.

After Samburu, Axis wanted Mundu to take on Nyandarua. The entire Rift Valley province was notorious for their Christian zeal. Of late, there was no taking a casual hike into the skies without bumping into a prayer from Nyandarua. Some were real daggers. Others were downright funny. One group had predicted the exact date and timing of the end of the world, and they were praying to God to confirm it. Mundu would have liked to bump into the answer to that one! It frustrated him that God took every sincere prayer from a mortal seriously. Even when they called on him foolishly, he answered in absolute wisdom.

Not that he was praising God or anything—far be it! He was insufferable. Sometimes he was like a human parent whose baby addressed him as Goo Goo Goo Ga Dada Dada! The fact that the toddler recognized and wanted to talk to him was enough to melt that consuming fire into rain!

The Mass had no problem with religion passé. There was no separating creation from religion. All mortals believed in something bigger than themselves. It did not matter one iota what they believed as long as they stayed clear of relationships with J. C. He quickly plugged them into the power of the Holy Spirit, whose voltage no demon could withstand. Soon the Christians became God's untouchable fellow workers, even commanding the armies of heaven. Whatever they bound on earth was bound in heaven, and whatever they loosed was loosed. That *whatever* usually referred to something like him!

Luckily, very few mortals grasped what really went on in the spiritual realm unless they sought God's revelation. Even fewer believed in the Holy Spirit as a powerful being in his own right. To some, he was just the air around God and his son J. C. As long as his personality was shrouded in mystery, his power would remain a myth. The Mass was not going to sit around and let Kenyans of any species awaken that particular giant!

If Mundu lost Kenya, Axis would personally put him out of action. He would chew him, spit him, grind him, and scatter his ashes in the fire, only to come alive again for round two. The process would be repeated 666 times, and his backside would be tossed in the bottomless pit.

The Mass had no prior experience with animal Christianity. Humans were easier. There was always a forgotten door or window, and all it took was just a crack. But when an animal patented on something, it was absolutely incorruptible. Of late, there had been moments when he was at his wit's end. Just that morning, for the first time ever, Mundu had wished he could die—really die, as if he had never existed. But not even mortals had that luxury. As soon as their spirits were released from their perishable bodies, their spirits went to be with whomever they had chosen on earth, Axis or J. C., *forever.*

So the animals of Samburu wanted to be a thorn in the flesh, but he was not flesh and blood. Along with the dreaded Ebola, he intended to unleash so many devils in that jungle, not a hoof would be left untainted. He just needed some bodies to carry them in.

It was all cleared with Axis. The Mass would take the snake and the monkey to the demon transit center in the Devil's Mountain. The two were so blind with discontent and greed that they would sponge in every homeless spirit that had lost its host. He would give them a ride there on the Aeromass, but they would not need it back. No, they would be ridden back!

Once Upon another Time and God's Relatives

☙

Perhaps because Brother Hyena was hungry, his late mother came to mind. With a touch of nostalgia, he lay down to reminisce. He had loved her. She would have given her life for him in a flash. A human had killed her by pointing something that set off lightning and thunder. When the noise had cleared, there was a hole in her head and a lot of blood. Just like the hole in the head of this human. Hyena and his kid brother had scampered to safety and were raised by the clan. The night before her last day, she had told him the sacred story of his ancestors.

Thousands of moons before, they were kept as domestic animals in a land called Egypt. They were trained to work as hunting dogs for their human masters until they were old. Then they were fattened for their soup. No one died of old age.

One night, the oldest hyena recalled a story his great-grandmother had told him. Millions of moons before, some humans called Israelites were also enslaved by the same Egyptians for four hundred years. They were forced to work very hard, just like the hyenas, and faced death daily.

In their despair, some even forgot their unseen God and turned to the ten mighty Egyptian gods. They figured the gods were superior to their one unseen God, seeing as the Egyptians remained masters while they remained slaves.

But they had not counted on their God's jealousy. One by one, he shamed the ten Egyptian gods. One day he wiped out herds of cattle, and the cow god was forgotten. They intensified their worship of the river god. The unseen God woke up on the jealous side again and turned the river into blood! Everything in it died. They did not have a drink for days, and that ended their fling with the river god. One by one, he shamed the lesser gods. But there was Ra the sun god. No one but no one could possibly touch the mighty Ra way up there.

Ra continued travelling from east to west as usual, pausing overhead at noon to smell their sacrifices. But one day, the son of the unseen God turned the sun into darkness. For days, humans who had no night vision or instinct were groping around in total darkness.

On another day, the pharaoh decided the slaves were becoming too many for his safety. He ordered the Egyptian midwives to kill every slave boy at birth. The midwives, afraid of the unseen God, did not comply. God blessed them for their compassion but proceeded to kill every firstborn son of Egypt, human or animal! That was to fulfill a blessing and a curse he had declared over Israel once upon a time.

"I will bless those who bless you and curse those who curse you!" the unseen God had declared to their ancestor, the human Abraham. Then he gave life to the blessing and the curse to live forever. Whatever anyone did to Israel henceforth would wake up one or the other. The midwives' compassion woke up the blessing while the king's orders woke up the curse. The sons of Egypt died either in the firstborn male's plague or were swallowed alive by the sea along with their king.

The children of Israel remembered their God and humbled themselves, fasting with great repentance. Their God heard from heaven and forgave the sin of idolatry that had landed them in slavery. He sent a human called Moses to rescue them and gave him powers to do supernatural things. He could turn a stick into a snake. When the slaves made their escape, God used Moses to part the waters of the Red Sea. The water stood at attention on both sides as the slaves and their animals passed across the dry floor. No sooner had they crossed than the pursuing pharaoh, his sons, and soldiers followed, and the hungry waters swallowed them up. Thus the unseen God rescued Israel and took them to a place called the Promised Land, whose boundaries he had himself marked. The story still circulated among domestic animals, descendants of the pharaoh's own stock. They said the blessing and the curse were still roaming the earth, each hoping for someone to pick him up.

The old hyena who had been fattened till he could hardly walk remembered all these things. He knew his time was near. There was nothing to lose by testing the existence of the unseen God. He hid in a thicket and secretly called on him. Having grown up in Egypt, he believed in life after death. But he did not want an Egyptian god or heaven. He wanted to be a pet of the God who could turn the sun, moon, or stars into darkness and make a way in deep waters. Not knowing his name, he got down on all fours, looked into the sky, and addressed him the only way he could think of.

"God of Israel, God of the human Moses, God of the Promised Land, if you are the one who made me, please reveal yourself and the purpose for which you made me before I die!"

Immediately, he felt his fear of death leave him. He saw a vision of the hyena clan and their descendants living wild and free in a jungle that had one river, and it was not the river of Egypt. It was a jungle where no human domesticated or ate hyena. Suddenly he understood that hyenas were wild and not domestic animals. God intended to free them soon. If he could trigger an active faith in God in his friends, he would serve his purpose.

The old hyena told his friends and family what he had remembered and described his vision. They tucked the information in their hearts. The very next day, their human master had important guests. He prepared the fattened hyena for dinner. His bones were thrown out for his friends and family to eat, but they did not. Instead, they buried what was left of him during the night with utmost respect.

They fell prostrate around his grave, raised their noses to heaven, and cried out to the unseen God, repenting the sins of their ancestors that had led them to this dire existence. They needed his help. Then they invoked the living blessing and prayed for Israel.

"Dear unseen God, we bless the children of Israel wherever they are," prayed the widow of the dead hyena. "There now, God, we have prayed for your relatives; it is your turn to send that blessing and find a hyena Moses to rescue us!"

When the rain suddenly scattered them, they were not sure if God had heard them. One elderly female said the rain was God's own tears for their pain. They decided to expect his mercy.

Without alarming their human masters, the hyenas secretly fasted and prayed for seven days and nights in turns. For the next five moons, they prayed without ceasing. By the sixth moon, they had prayed with ceasing. Hope was dwindling fast on the seventh moon, and many decided it was all wishful thinking. But on the same moon, a humble hyena called Ole Baba came up out of the desert and said he was sent by the unseen God to rescue them. No one knew who he was or where he came from. Nevertheless, they had been expecting someone.

He came on the day two sisters had fought and one had lost both eyes. In a few hours, the humans would be home and the blind female would be slaughtered and eaten before she could lose weight. Her sister was devastated and remorseful, unable to remember the reason for their fight.

"If you have come from the unseen God, please do something for my sister before they eat her!" she cried. "She is my only sister!" Ole Baba placed his paw on the eyes of the bleeding sister who was lying on the ground. He prostrated himself and cried out to God. Some were very skeptical of possible miracles, but there was nothing else to do.

"Dear God, our creator and maker of heaven, earth, and hyenas, please heal this female and glorify your name. Remember your children of Israel; bless them and all their animals in every measure that you bless us. Now we stand by your promise to bless those that bless them and pray for this healing. Endow man with wisdom, your image whose choice is our destiny. Amen."

Suddenly they heard human footsteps, smelled the humans, and scattered, not knowing if God had heard them or not. When they finally reached their designated enclosure, they saw the blind female following them. Not a trace of blood or blindness was on her. She winked at her sister, and they touched noses. They knew the unseen God was among them and everything was possible at last.

Ole Baba was to lead them far away to a place called Samburu, a jungle with one river in a land of sunshine called Kenya, where no human ever ate hyena even in a dream. But they were never to eat or harm humans, for they were the image of the unseen God. That was the sin of their ancestors that had led them to their present circumstances.

Ole Baba made it clear that whenever they sought a blessing from God, they must seek one for Israel. They could ask God for anything as long as it was in The Name of his son Jesus Christ. That was shortened to 'The Name' in reverence. When the hyenas heard that God had a son, they decided God had chosen Israelites as his closest relatives. You could not love someone and not wish his relatives well. It was custom.

They were also warned to stay away from a jungle called Ninety-

Nine and the Devil's Mountain in their own Promised Land, or God would stamp them out in a stampede of wildebeests. The wildebeest was one of the wonders of the world that God had hidden in Kenya. And lest they forget who had saved them, every evening God himself would give them a sneak preview of heaven in the magnificent sunsets of the land of sunshine.

HIDE YOUR NOSE NOW!

༕

On the eve of the exodus, Ole Baba asked them to eat every fowl-smelling thing they could find, including rotten eggs. Some thought he was crazy, but desperate times called for desperate measures. Better to eat whatever than to be eaten. At midnight, hyenas surrounded the humans who snored peacefully in their caves.

"Atteeention!" Ole Baba yelled. The hyenas clicked their paws and pointed their noses in the human direction.

"Abooout turn!" The hyenas turned half a circle and pointed their behinds in the human direction.

"Taaails up!" All tails pointed skywards.

"Fire!" The hyenas bombed out pure, concentrated stink gas from the bowels of their bowels.

At this point in the story, Brother and his mother had laughed till their ribs ached.

"The blast shook the camp and the nearby hills, and even rivers changed course for a moment," she had continued gleefully. "Before the humans could figure out thunder, a bomb, or the end of the world, their noses collapsed and they all lost consciousness."

And so it was, their ancestors stole into the night and freedom, following Ole Baba who followed a star of the unseen God.

"It took three days for one old human who had no nose or sense of smell to give them mouth-to-mouth resuscitation," Hyena's mother had recounted. "Egypt stank for seven moons."

Brother smiled, recalling his mother's laughter as she rolled with him in the sand.

The exodus took the hyenas through many dangerous jungles. At the entrance of one jungle, a crow warned them that all humans hunted hyena for their tongue, heart, and teeth to use in witchcraft. Fearing for their lives, Ole Baba sent the strongest hyenas to eat all the witchdoctors of the land in advance. The six witches and one wizard were holding a coven to curse God under a very dark tree when the hyenas attacked. They ate all they could and took some back to their friends.

Ole Baba and his clan passed through quickly before the younger witches could grow up and inherit their parents' craft.

But God became angry with Ole Baba. He had forbidden the eating or harming of humans under any circumstances. For seven moons, ticks infested all soft parts of their bodies. They lost valuable time scratching and biting themselves. Finally they humbled themselves before God again, praying, fasting, and crawling on all fours for seven days. The ticks disappeared as quickly as they had come.

On various disobediences, some were swept by sudden seasonal rivers, strange swelling diseases, attacks by bees and humans. Sometimes there were clan-clashes where brother turned against brother. But whenever they repented, trusted, and obeyed God, he restored them. Ole Baba did everything to maintain unity as one clan under God, but masses always amassed problems.

Finally they landed in a dry, grassy jungle called Maasai Mara, somewhere in Kenya, during the animal migratory season. There was a severe drought. All but a few sick and lame animals had left for greener pastures. The upside of the moment was that the wildebeest was gone, so there was no risk of stampedes. Too tired to follow the migratory trail, they stayed and starved. One dirty drinking hole had some greenish, yucky water, but a few tadpoles had already claimed ownership. In the night, their monotonous music gave sound to the silent, hesitant glow of fireflies and hid the sound of the hyenas' rumbling stomachs. During intervals, an owl moaned like a bad omen.

The sick and the lame succumbed first. The rest scavenged on anything dead or alive. Soon they grumbled against Ole Baba for misleading them out of Egypt.

"Egyptians ate, but only after fattening us with good food," they argued. "A hyena got to live a little before he died!"

Too late, they realized they had followed a stranger who followed a star of an unseen God. Someone ought to have done a background check on Ole Baba! In turn, a disheartened Ole Baba grumbled to God. He secluded himself in a cave to fast and seek divine guidance.

A False Prophet and the Piece of God

☙

It was almost a full moon since Ole Baba had disappeared. In the meantime, a demon called Yellow Eyes entered a mysterious hyena whose name was Ole Matata. It meant *son of trouble*. Calmly and convincingly, he declared himself a prophet. He was longer and taller with bigger dots than everyone else. His teeth looked very white in contrast to the pitch-black lips. His eyes adopted a now-you-see-it now-you-don't yellow glow.

One day, he answered a call of nature in the bush and stumbled on the biggest animal jawbone any of them had ever seen. It was also older than time. He prophesied that it was part of a sleeping dragon god who could walk, swim, or fly while spiting fire. The god had opted to sleep rather than destroy them all for serving the imaginary unseen God. They needed to repent and feed the napping god so he could wake up and save them. He would also glorify them as gods, never to pant for food again. Lesser creatures would henceforth consider it an honor to be eaten by them!

The prophet had a revelation from a voice that dragon god himself had punished their ancestors by sending them into captivity in Egypt for their rebellion. Nevertheless, he had detached every piece of his body before the nap and scattered them in every jungle of the world to become omnipresent. Anyone who sought him could find him. It was a miracle they had found the only piece of god in Kenya.

An altar of stones was set up for food offerings. Soon they were bowing and tithing the best of their meager food to the dragon, sometimes the only bite they had. The dragon god could eat from any part of his body and it did not matter that they only had his jawbone. But only his prophet could enter the holiest bush where he ate. The food was always gone in the morning, their offerings accepted.

One day when dragon god was well nourished, the scattered parts of his body would suddenly lightning-transport and be joined together before their very eyes. He would stand taller than Mount Kenya, Kilimanjaro, and the mountains of the moon put together. In fact, the mountains would be merged into one majestic throne. They would rule the world with him, and Samburu would be the capital jungle of the universe. Prayers were chanted facing Mount Kenya whose snow-capped top already resembled a throne.

The prophet adorned himself with a necklace of dry seeds, teeth from some unknown creature, a snakeskin and a human skull dangling from a rope of dry banana leaves. Nobody knew where he had gotten the lot. It was rumored that one of the witches they had eaten had worn the totems on her neck.

Hunger slowed time as they waited for either Ole Baba to come back or the dragon god to finally piece together and save them. Some were so desperate for leadership it no longer mattered who saved them as long as someone said "Come" or "Go." The prophet kept assuring them that the dragon god was not Humpty Dumpty. One day he would be together again.

Meanwhile, the prophet reeked of good health. At night, he poured water or his own urine on the piece of god to make it look nourished as he feasted on the delicacies the faithful had brought.

"Look, brethren!" he would prophesy. "Our god had a good dream about us! Give faithfully and wake him up!"

They hoped against hope that there was hope.

A Dead God Dies Again

❧

A t the end of one moon, Ole Baba returned in time to save
a young, frightened female cub from being sacrificed to the
dragon god. Her own overzealous mother had offered her, and the
prophet was performing the last ritual before biting into her heart.
Ole Baba gave the loudest howl of horror and charged toward the
altar, tail pointing straight at the African sunset behind him. The
shock of his unexpected arrival froze the moment for everyone. Ole
Matata sidestepped, and Ole Baba almost crashed into the altar and
the whimpering sacrifice. Her ears were flat on her head in fright.
Gently he led her to one of the babysitters and hung his tail down,
choosing not to fight for the moment.

For two hours, he interrogated both the faithful and the unfaithful,
piecing together what had transpired in his absence. Whenever a male
was called to the front to give his account, he approached the leader
walking on his forelegs or knees in submission, as was custom. Finally
it was Ole Matata's turn. The rebel hung his tail and walked casually
to the front without any sign of remorse or respect.

The two leaders faced each other, unblinking. Ole Baba could
have sworn he saw the devil in the younger hyena's yellow eyes, but he
chose not to fear. He knew his God was the almighty. Nevertheless,

his flock had gullibly embraced the doctrines of demons. It made him feel like he had failed God. He was also hungry, weak, and old compared to his adversary. Only by faith did he believe he had the entire force of the kingdom of God behind him.

In fairness, he assigned five minutes for each of them to pray to his god, after which they would fight to the death. The clan agreed to be led by whoever won this battle of the gods. His god would be their god.

The dragon's prophet was confident. He had every intention of serving the servant of God for dinner. Not only had Ole Matata deceived many, but he was starting to believe his own deception. The dragon god was becoming more real by the day. A guide called Yellow now resided in his head, his voice audible only to him. That morning, he had had a vision of a great endless dragon with flaming yellow eyes. It was possible the whole thing was not a figment of his imagination and god had just revealed his existence. He was hearing The Voice of god same as Ole Baba. They were equal.

Still adorned in his priestly garbs, Ole Matata made a big show of prayer, jumping very high, shaking his hips, running in circles, and dancing to the music in his head. He tried to stand on his head as The Voice instructed, twisted his leg, and fell backward, his ample bottom crashing on the piece of god he had wrapped in leaves and placed near the altar. The god appeared none the worse, but no one could tell if he heard or accepted his prophet's profuse apology. Some animals were visibly amused and trying hard not to show it. The prophet wondered why The Voice was now mocking, fooling around, and humiliating him!

Across from him, Ole Baba went down on all fours, looked up to heaven, and appealed to his God.

"Father, in the name of Jesus, let your will be done here. Receive honor and glory for whatever you choose to do. Amen." He rose and waited patiently for Ole Matata to finish his chant and dance.

In a final slow dance, Ole Matata moved his head and hips toward each other, almost touching them in a full circle. He repeated the move in the opposite direction. The motion of the quick successive moves that followed resembled a moving snake. All the while he chanted a name neither he nor the others had ever heard before: *Leviathan*. Some animals decided if Ole Matata won, *Leviathan* was one of the names of God. If he lost, it had to belong to the devil. Others thought the monotonous chant was eerie and the strange name did not give godly vibes.

Many were happy Ole Baba was back but feared he was too frail to win. But there were those that felt he was becoming too high and mighty anyway and deserved whatever was coming to him. Was he the only one who could hear from God? Was he not just a hyena like them? Just who did he think he was carrying on like he was the image of God?

The battle lasted less than a minute. Ole Matata suddenly straightened his tail, stopped in mid-chant, and grabbed his god between his teeth. He leapt into the air charging toward Ole Baba before the signal to start. Everyone held their breath. For some strange reason, his speed defied gravity and kept increasing. Ole Baba crouched at the very last moment as the prophet and his god shot overhead at supersonic speed.

He crashed meters away into the only rock protruding from a cliff, dead before he hit the ground. The dragon god broke into pieces that further disintegrated into dust. The wind did her job, and he was no more. It was a strange way for a bone to go, but so were the ways of the unseen God. So much for the dragon god piecing together again; Humpty Dumpty now had a brother. It was strange how the invisible God manifested himself in unmistakable visible ways.

Be My Tomorrow

☙

For a full minute, Ole Baba met everyone's shame-filled eyes. "Does anyone else wish to challenge the living God?" Not a leaf moved.

"If anyone is not for him, leave the clan now!" No one stirred.

"You have just broken his first commandment and worshipped another god. Because of our numerous sins—among them, eating the human witches and now worshiping the dragon—God had decided to allow our extinction like the dodo or dinosaur. For days I have pleaded for mercy and compassion. A few of us will reach Samburu and carry our kind into the future, but the rest of us will have to nourish the chosen few with our own flesh." He studied them for a while as the good and the bad news sank in, his heart as broken as theirs.

"God himself will choose the seed of our future," he continued. No one said anything.

"Every day at sunset, we will cast lots, and one of us will be dinner. We are not to eat the body of Ole Matata who was totally sold to Satan. Neither will we eat mothers and cubs. If the lot falls on me, so be it." No one stirred as death sung them a lullaby. A distant thunder rumbled as God flashed his signature with a sharp bolt of lightning. Their fate was sealed.

In a strange twist, the lot always fell on someone who had worshipped the dragon. Nevertheless, they died bravely, repenting of their sin. Ole Baba comforted them, saying there are times when God's justice, once dispensed, cannot be recalled without being an injustice. His sword of punishment once unsheathed must run the full course of his anger.

"If you don't believe that, try idolatry!" Hyena's mum said to him.

"Mum, did God not love them anymore?" Hyena asked. "Did he not forgive them?"

"He loved and forgave all right, all those who sincerely repented," she replied. "He loved them through the consequences of their deadly decisions and shared in their pain. Then he ushered them to where sin will never be seen. They became the pets of God."

According to his mum, the dying hyenas only requested that their story be told for as long as there was a hyena alive. Every hyena was obligated to tell the sacred story at least once in his lifetime. They hoped to warn their descendants of the dangers of idolatry that provoked the maximum fury of the jealous unseen God.

His mother had now fulfilled her obligation and passed the sacred story on to him. Some day, he would tell it to someone special, perhaps a son or a daughter, or the love of his life when he found her.

Yellow eyes watched patiently. The dreaming Brother Hyena seemed to have entered a state of stupor lying next to his favorite food. The way of the stomach had never failed with a hyena before. The hyena had to bite. Just a tiny little bite was all that was needed.

Perhaps he knew of his ancestry as a descendant of the dreaded Ole Baba. Yellow recalled the dragon god days when he was the guiding voice in Ole Matata's mind. He had some good times running that particular hyena. God had cursed him to the fourth generation and blessed Ole Baba to the thousandth. It was peculiar math, but Yellow had not lost count. Brother Hyena was the one thousandth generation and he was not going to let him renew that particular contract. He had to taste the human.

God would forgive a repentant hyena. Hyena would not forgive himself. The Mass would come in as a savior, hold his paw and show him a way to be approved by the masses. A way that would seem right to him but its end would be death.

Not Yet Happily Ever After

⌒⌒

The story was not yet over. That was the intermission or whatever his mum had called it.

"Even a story needs a break!" she used to say when she needed to attend to something else like chasing dinner. He closed his eyes, picturing her animated face, and recalled the rest almost word for word.

Sunrise was a happy time for the males of the clan if one did not think of sunset. Its beauty came bearing the lots of death. First they said the grace. Then they packed up for heaven by repenting their sins, and they cast the lots. Whoever God chose for dinner was ready.

"It was a fair way to be chosen to die, but it still wasn't fair!" his mother had moaned without making much sense, the way females made sense without making sense.

The cubs chased the wind, bit each other's tails, and pulled pranks on their babysitters, but they were still afraid for their daddies and big brothers.

During that dire existence, the tragedy of the taste buds sneaked in. Hyena meat, initially intended only to save life, gradually became acceptable, a delicacy, a craving, and finally an addiction. Their mouths watered every time they saw one another's thighs. Bullies stirred up fights hoping someone would be fatally injured. Ole Baba would then be forced to allow a mercy killing. One greedy dimwit took a huge bite of his sleeping cousin's leg. Ole Baba had him served for dinner, curing his craving permanently.

The animals followed their star till at last Ole Baba glimpsed the land of Samburu. It was a two days' journey. They only needed one last meal for the final thrust, but the cost was too high. Aside from the leader, the clan was down to three young adult males among thirty females and cubs. They could not eat another male and still have a future generation. Neither could they eat females and cubs. Ole Baba made an important decision.

First he fasted by giving his meager food to whoever looked more malnourished. He always said that nothing brought one to the presence of God better than fasting while giving. Then he prayed for God's guidance in choosing a successor and called his last meeting with the clan. He decided to take whoever arrived first among the males as God's choice. God chose Ole Mwana, a fair, kind, and levelheaded male. Ole Baba anointed him with his saliva and addressed the gathering.

"I am now old and about to go the way of all hyenas. Should the Lord choose to rest me with my ancestors before we reach Samburu, you are to obey Ole Mwana as you have obeyed me. But this I must ask of you. Our story must be told through all generations to the end of time. Instruct your cubs to honor God with their choices, or they will drink from our ponds the bitter waters of disobedience and idolatry. Whenever you come to a crossroad, stop, look and listen. Ask for the ancient path, where the good way is and walk in it to find rest for your souls."

Facing Samburu, he pointed a paw toward the golden sunset.

"Samburu humans do not eat hyena. They are beautiful, magnificent butterflies who dance in a circle. Their males can jump over the moon in a still-standing position. Their vocals make better music than any instruments." He took a long pause and studied their faces.

"Do not eat their cattle either. The butterfly people believe all cattle in the world belong to them. They are among the bravest humans in the planet, and their male cubs are known to kill lions with their bare paws! Beware of invoking their wrath, and it will go well with you in the land the Lord is giving you. Remember to worship the Lord your God who made man and hyena and rescued both from slavery in Egypt. God bless and multiply you."

The Death Stone

After dismissing the females and cubs, the three males remained with Ole Baba to see about dinner. One last time, another life would be given to the future. After giving thanks to God, Ole Baba gave a small piece of meat to every one of the three hyenas. He had saved his previous day's dinner to have a last meal with the three before they lost one of them. The hyena's thought it was not fair that he had starved himself to afford the little ceremony. It was also not custom to feed before dying but he was their leader. He could change tradition. They gave thanks to God and swallowed the tiny pieces whole. Ole Baba laid four medium stones wrapped with leaves on the ground. Three hyenas would get black stones and live. One would get a red stone and become dinner.

Ole Mwana, the new leader, picked first. He figured that if he lived that night, it was confirmation that his leadership was ordained by God. He hit black. But it was not the time to sigh with relief. He was about to lose someone he loved. The second hyena picked black. So did the third. Their hearts sank as Ole Baba slowly unwrapped the stone of death.

Eating their leader was out of the question! They demanded a repeat, all three friends willing to take his place yet wanting so much to live. Ole Baba thanked them for their love and loyalty but shook his head. This was his bone to chew—tough and bitter, but honor was never like honey. He said a second prayer, this time for the three males who were now the chosen seed of the future. Everyone whispered a frightened Amen.

"The children are hungry," Ole Baba said quietly but in full authority. "Will someone please serve diner." No one moved.

Eight streams of tears glistened in the twilight. There would be no sunrise for their leader. The sunset bid the horizon good-bye, leaving only the dark, gloomy clouds.

A New Ancestor

ᔐ

Suddenly there was shaking and rambling all round. The earth swayed from side to side as everyone fell to the ground. Rocks flew everywhere. "Earthquake!" someone howled. In a few moments, it was over. Everyone seemed all right as they shook off the dust— that is, everyone except their leader. Ole Baba lay on the ground, blood trickling from his mouth.

There was a huge gash on his head from which a stream of blood flowed in slow motion. A solemn circle of friends formed around him. The females started praying. The cubs cried as their tiny tails lay flat on their bellies. The males tried to figure out a course of action. Ole Baba raised a weak paw as if to say, "Hold it; this is just as it should be."

All the praying, crying, and fumbling stopped. His wife, Maua, and daughter, Zabibu, lay next to him. They put their necks on his, attempting to share some of their life as his ebbed away. Ole Baba bravely moaned his last address to the group.

"Friends, I must now rest with my ancestors. My heart is content with a glimpse of Samburu and the blessed assurance of the future of our species. Go make us a new generation."

"We will never eat you, our master!" the female he had rescued from Ole Matata wailed. Her name was Inao. Ole Baba turned his eyes to her.

"Look to your new leader Ole Mwana, and be comforted."

Inao did. Not that she was ever able to keep her eyes from his or his from hers, but this was not the moment. Only months later did they realize that Ole Baba had actually blessed their love.

"Eat me and honor our friendship. Feed on every last part of me. If anyone loves me, carry a piece of me in your stomach into the promised land. Only promise me this will be our last act of cannibalism."

Everyone raised a paw in promise. He touched his nose to his wife and daughter, whispering a loving good-bye. Finally he beckoned to his successor. Ole Mwana crawled forward on his forelegs, and the master touched his head in blessing.

"Take care of my family?" Ole Baba asked.

"As long as I live, my master, my friend, as long as I breathe," Ole Mwana answered, placing his nose on the ground.

Ole Baba looked at all their faces for a long moment.

"You are all my family," he said weakly. "Worship the Lord your God so his blessing will be on your food and water. He will remove sickness from you, and none of you will miscarry or be barren in the land he is giving us. He will give you a full lifespan. Pray for the humans that are his image. Pray especially for Israel and their animals and his blessing will never leave you or yours."

Then he whispered a prayer they did not understand.

"Forgive me, Father, for my sinful intention, for the harm almost done to your name." And he was gone from them.

WHERE LOVE AND SORROW MEET

ᕬᕩ

ooking up to heaven, Ole Mwana, thanked God for the gift of
Ole Baba's life and the meal that was his body. They ate together
with the utmost respect, everyone waiting their turn, a humble meal
salted with their tears.

In the middle of the meal, someone gave a cry of dismay. One
of the black stones they used to cast lots was found in Ole Baba's
stomach. It meant that none of the hyenas would have gotten a
red stone that night. He had swallowed his black stone with that
untraditional piece of meat and somehow spat out the red hidden
in his mouth all along. Their leader had rigged the lots against his
favor. God had mercifully ended his life in an earthquake to rescue
him from the sin of suicide. They now understood their leader's last
plea to God.

"Forgive me Father, for my sinful intention, for the harm almost
done to your name." That had been the last prayer of their new
ancestor.

What a gracious merciful God! Ole Mwana thought. He had
given Ole Baba the gift of a natural death and the presence of mind
to repent of his intentions. In the end, everything—even death—
had worked out for the servant of God.

"May his angels receive you at the gate, my friend," Ole Mwana whispered at his piece of meat with tears in his eyes. "Till we meet on the other shore." He put it in his mouth.

Cannibals of the Promised Land

❧

The exhausted clan finally limped into the Promised Land of Samburu. They tearfully kissed the ground and the river praying they would be fruitful and multiplied in the land of sunshine Kenya. Then they asked God to do the same for Israel in their own Promised Land. They were home. So was the spirit of cannibalism. Once in a while, it still reared its head, consuming even helpless newborns. Brother's mother had called it a generational curse that only God could break in answer to prayer. She had prayed for him, repenting even the sins of their ancestors that might have been passed on to them. It had worked. Brother had never desired to eat his own kind.

His own father almost ate him at birth. Luckily he was born with his eyes open and saw the big mouth closing on his tiny neck. He let out the loudest howl his day-old lungs could manage. It was inaudible to anyone but a mother who sprung up in an instant from where she was sunning herself. Being bigger and heavier than his father, she gave him the thrashing of his life. He had scurried off with tail flat on his belly, and Brother had never seen him again.

The incident had made Brother a little scared of females. All the ones he had met were bigger and stronger than him. He did not plan on eating his cub, but one never knew what could set off a female. He also did not think he had the patience to court one for the traditional twenty-four moons. Pretty long time to make up her pretty mind, and she could still change it again and again. God help him if she did not like the den he built or stole from a warthog for her.

I will make my bride's home with my own sweat, he thought to himself. *Why steal from a hard-working warthog?* Many took that easy way out, but it felt wrong now that he was a Christian.

In spite of his fear of females, their intuitive sixth sense fascinated him. Females heard sounds inaudible to the rest of the world. A mother could tell when her cub needed her before its first cry was out.

My mother heard my silent scream and I lived. God bless her heart, he thought as he dozed off. When he was small, he always dozed off after his mum's stories.

Black Mamba's Greed Is Ripe

❧

It was Sunday again. Black Mamba woke up before the sun but not to go to church. He told his wife he had important business and took the familiar path. The Mass was moving too slowly. He wanted legs while his body was young enough to carry them. Then he remembered the legs were meant to carry his body. He expected young and agile, not old and wobbly legs. Still the body and legs should match in age. He walked up and down impatiently, willing The Voice to appear.

Yellow Eyes waited till Black's impatience outweighed reason. His greed was ripe for manipulation. Thank hell this one did not believe in J. C. They only had to worry about his reasoning capacity; the snake was not otherwise endowed.

"The Mass has chosen you, great Mamba!" The Voice said.

Though he was expecting it, Black literally jumped out of a layer of dead skin. He crawled away from it toward The Voice. He thought he saw two yellow eyes coming out of the shrubs. It was spooky. He hung on for dear legs and decided the yellow eyes were an illusion.

"What must I do?" Black got to the point. They were not discussing the weather but his future mode of transport!

"Tomorrow we scan your brain for possible upgrade to human

intelligence. You need more brain to use legs," The Voice said calmly.

"What must I do?" Black persisted eagerly.

"Before sunrise, climb into the human nest and bury yourself under the feathers. You must not look up no matter what happens above your head," The Voice instructed.

"What exactly will be happening?" Black needed to know.

"You must not look up no matter what happens above your head."

"Great, just great." Black swore under his breath.

Yellow Eyes smiled, knowing the snake would obey. He had no lips or body today, but a smile was a smile when things were going well.

The Evolving Man-Key

℧

De Brazza the Man-Key felt good having completed the six hundredth and sixty-sixth trip with the human nest. He was taking a casual walk along the river to check out some giggly girls as he waited for the divine eye to twinkle and evolve him to Superman. Suddenly The Voice froze him cold. The girls who did not hear it scampered away when he turned into a shivering statue. If he had sleeping sickness or malaria, they were not ready to share that with him. Girls were after life, not Death.

"The lord of The Mass favors you, Man-Key!" The Voice started.

"What must I do, my lord?" Monkey asked

"Tomorrow we examine your feet and bottom. They are the least human looking, the least evolved."

"What must I do?" Monkey wanted action, not examinations.

"At sunrise, take the human nest to the top of the hill. Climb inside and fix your eyes on the sixth line. Do not look down whatever happens below your feet. Do not look up whatever happens above your head. Meditate on the thin line of nature you are about to cross."

"What exactly is going to happen?" Monkey pleaded.

"Meditate on the thin line of nature you are about to cross," The Voice repeated before retreating.

Monkey thought of the girls who had run away from him as if he were a disease. Soon they would wish they had not. Soon human girls with little feet would be lining up to meet him. Then he scratched his head remembering something. He could not possibly relate to a monkey girl when he was human. Perhaps if he got married quickly, they could evolve his wife too. But he did not even have a steady girlfriend. One girl had said she liked his lisping accent, but he was not sure. For now he would obey The Voice and let the chips fall where they may. As a human, he would become the image of God. Then all things would be possible.

Swift Makes Some Swift Decisions

_❧_

For the first time, Swift Mamba took her children to church without her husband, Black Mamba. With a heavy heart, she left Nyoka behind, afraid of breaking his father's rules. Her mind was so preoccupied she only heard the announcements. More animals and eggs were missing, and special prayers were said for them. An unknown enemy was lurking around and anyone could be the next victim. Even Mrs. Zebra had no drama that day.

Swift wished she could disappear. She felt worthless, a selfish liar and a thief. She wallowed in self-pity and missed the misery and confusion her own children were experiencing. Her family was nonfunctional and individualistic except for Darklay. The ten functioned as one, even now as they lay beside her.

As she took her daughters home from church, she saw a familiar snake slithering away in the opposite direction. She thought it was one of her Darklays. Quickly she counted all ten and almost had a heart attack. She had a premonition; the snake was identical to her identical daughters. In fact, they looked like clones of this female snake.

"Hurry home to Nyoka, girls. Mum has to see a friend," she said to Darklay.

The ten blind Miss Mambas smelled their way home.

Swift caught up with the image of her daughters. She too was blind but quickly sensed her presence.

"Who goes there?" she asked.

"My name is Swift Mamba, and I saw you leaving the church … I have never seen you before … Was this your first time?" Swift fumbled.

"Yes, Mrs. Mamba. My name is Mina."

"Why do you look so sad, Mina? What's your family name?"

"It is Brahmin," she whispered and then broke into sobs. Swift slithered closer to her. Snakes had no tears, but agony had its language. Quickly Brahmin buried herself in the sand leaving only her head the way her daughters did sometimes.

"Can you talk about it?" Swift asked kindly, cringing inside.

"My hatchlings are gone, ten eggs stolen. I have prayed to every god I know without results. The Christian one was my last hope before I stop believing in God, any god."

"Perhaps they are already with God," Swift zigzagged.

"I just know my daughters are alive somewhere; a mother always knows," Mina said. Swift wondered how she had known they were daughters if she lost them as eggs.

"God works in mysterious ways," Swift sidestepped again.

"This Christian God better be real. I need a miracle!" She sobbed louder.

"I will keep you in my prayers!" Swift consoled quickly. "Will we see you in church again?"

"Yes, next Sunday and the next and the next till this last God stops playing dead! I have no others left out there. I prayed to him once when I could not lay eggs for years. He gave me a miracle and it was stolen, so I stopped talking to him because he did not protect it. Eventually I convinced myself it was never a miracle in the first place, just nature taking its course in coincidence with my prayers."

"Don't we all?" Swift encouraged.

"I remember I only asked him for eggs, not for protection. I should have sought a further relationship with him. I am so confused! If he helps me again, I will serve only him and declare him aloud even though Christianity is a cult. But what if our snake culture is right? What if there are no miracles or God, only this miserable existence and then we die?" she sobbed.

"Why don't you try another prayer to Jesus? Just check him out," Swift suggested. "Ask him to reveal himself to you and entrust your hatchlings to him."

"If he is real, then I already disregarded his first miracle to me." Brahmin sobbed some more.

"Warm up now. He will forgive that if you ask him," Swift said with a sad sigh. She could do with forgiveness herself, but she knew it would not be forthcoming—not until she asked for it and corrected her mistakes.

"I will meet you here on this spot after church next Sunday," she promised Brahmin in a shaky hiss and then hurried home before she broke down. She hoped nothing bad had happened to her daughters, Brahmin's daughters. God had already answered the distraught mother's prayer long before it left her mouth. She was the devil sitting on the answer.

Tomorrow of the Ancestors

ༀ

A roar of distant thunder snapped Brother Hyena back from slumber to his present task. With renewed vigor, he pushed on the human carcass till it finally dropped into the grave. *Boom!* Mission half accomplished. Now to cover it with soil ... front paws for digging, rear for throwing ... left, right ... left, right ... a soldier in the army of the Lord.

Finally the human was all covered. Ashes to ashes, dust to dust, but no flowers for this grave. Would any human plant a single flower on the grave of a hyena? Yet God would have him do some good even to those who called him ugly. The heck with conscience! He picked a few twigs and grass and threw them on top. Enough of a funeral already! Then he thought again and decided to make it neater. After all, God was watching from everywhere and this was his image. He decided to do it for Jesus. A search around the jungle revealed a most beautiful rose. A thorn pricked his nose, but he did not mind, not for Jesus.

Kneeling beside the grave, he respectfully placed the rose on the heart position. He looked up to heaven, prayed for the dead human's soul and for whoever had killed him.

Suddenly he stiffened. What if he had just prayed for the same human that killed his mother? Then slowly he relaxed and finished arranging the rose. Vengeance belonged to God, and there was a special blessing for those who prayed for their enemies. He hoped it counted across the species.

The whole thing did not make sense, but the pastor had said that God did not use common sense. Neither did Hyena want to be common. But this trusting and obeying God was peculiar business to say the least. He closed his eyes for a moment and imagined life as a pet of God. Another image of heaven came to mind. Angels smiled as God extended his hand to pat Hyena's back, not minding that he was ugly, a scavenger. He tried to think of something that could make God smile at him, to show him his face. Then he remembered no one could see God's face and live. It was all right if God smiled secretly, as long as Brother could feel the smile.

A sudden sound of something falling brought Brother Hyena back to earth just before the hand of God touched his back in the beautiful dream. He looked around and saw nothing. Perhaps it was just the wind. He still wanted God to smile. Such a moment would be priceless, worth his very life. Burying the human would surely be a step in that direction. He thought of his great ancestors and felt proud. He was living their dream, their tomorrow. This felt right, like something the great Ole Baba would have done. He looked up to heaven and gave a proud smile to God. Like a toddler who had just managed his first step. At that precise moment, all hell broke loose!

Yellow did not like what he was looking at. The hyena had buried everything and was now dreaming, perhaps even praying. Unless he said his thoughts out loud, Yellow could only guess the contents. It was not fair that God knew every thought, even the thoughts of demons. Suddenly he was overcome with hatred. He hated all mortals for owning their own bodies while he had to steal or scavenge for one here and there. Even when he secured a lease in a willing victim, he could not enjoy security of tenure with J.C. constantly knocking on the door and offering the highest price!

He hated mortals for the opportunity they still had while his fate was sealed forever. No, he was not going to think about his future—except that he sure as hell wasn't going there alone. This hyena was coming with him. The way of the stomach had never failed before with a hyena.

GET THEE BEHIND ME, SATAN!

⌒〇

Suddenly the human hand shot out from the grave suspending in the air like a bone from hell. Brother's smile froze. On reflex, he jumped almost ten meters away, nose breaking into a cold sweat. He did not believe in ghosts, but this was the real thing! Quickly, he reminded himself who his master was. The demons should be trembling, not him. God was bigger than whatever was out there. In the meantime, he shook like a leaf, the proud smirk he had raised to heaven wiped clean. He searched for courage within himself and found none. Quickly he asked God for some and inched forward to investigate. Brave ancestry aside, his shivers were akin to malaria.

It was the same hand. He could tell by that thing humans used to tell time. Crazy humans and their witchcraft! Weren't the sun, moon, stars, and their shadows enough to tell time? Scratching his head thoughtfully, he wondered if this human was pretending to be alive when he was dead! They were cunning creatures. *"Shindwe shetani, shindwe!"* he yelled. "Get thee behind me, Satan!"

He covered the hand with leaves again and shoved it back into the soil.

"Dust to dust, I say!" It worked for a moment, but when he turned his back, a thumb shot up and poked his thigh! He jumped and then he took some deep breaths to calm himself. The dead human had to be a wizard. A stubborn devil was staying put in the carcass, refusing to face foreclosure on his home. *"Shindwe Shetani!"* Brother exclaimed again, hoping to evict him. There should have been a *swoosh* or *vroom* when he left, but there was nothing. Either the particular devil did not recognize his evictor or someone had assured him of a bailout.

Brother had heard of casting out devils, but he was not sure about doing it on the dead. Right now he was exhausted, frustrated, dangerously hungry, and perhaps sick. There were bees buzzing in his head, and the double visioning was back. He knew the line between sick and sin was thin.

The thumb became two, then four, and finally eight. A still, small voice urged him to pray *now*—but it was such a gentle voice, not the kind of thunder one would associate with the Almighty God, creator of the universe. Hyena wanted to impress him with his strength of character, leaving no doubt he would be a good pet. He was not some whining bush baby taking God's attention from more important matters.

"I can handle this," he whispered to himself. "It is not life and death."

"It is life and death to your eternal destiny," the small voice persisted. But Brother was a big hyena on a big mission.

If only I could shake the double visions, I would know which finger to bury! Everything was foggy and blurry as hunger danced with bounty.

Yellow Eyes hung around Brother Hyena, helping things along. As long as the brother did not resort to prayer but relied on his own strength, it was very good indeed. He decided to feed him a snack of pride to accompany his inherent greed.

PHILOSOPHY OF THE STOMACH

❦

Suddenly Brother had an attack of pride, a distinct feeling that he deserved some reward in recognition for what he had achieved so far! How many other hyenas would have buried all this meat to honor the unseen God? Enough goodness for one day already!

He desired to lick the thumb—just a tiny, bitty, little lick. It was a sin to *eat*, not to lick, and he could stop anytime he wanted. His mind was clearing now, the double vision gone. His thoughts took on a new intellectual dimension. Surely one had to analyze God's instructions carefully because he may not actually mean what he said. That was why he had created intelligence! Licking, touching, sniffing, looking, or listening for a heartbeat, all these were scientific experiments, not eating the forbidden human carcass. Even a cub knew that. God gave five senses intending for them to be used along with reason. Something made Brother Hyena feel smart and intellectual.

Gently he licked at the tip of the human thumb. The fingernail was scratchy, not very interesting. The side ... hmmmm, now that was something. Up and down the mouth, then round and round like a lollipop!

A part of Brother realized he was losing the battle. Intelligence

121

did not deter his ravenous appetite. He ran off again. Sometimes physical distance made all the difference.

"Pray for strength!" the still, small voice persisted. But he believed he was already strong, a descendant of the giants of faith. God could rely on him.

"I can still handle this," he whispered as he ran. Just when he was sure he had outran the temptation, his foot caught a twig and he sprawled to the ground.

"There has to be a devil on my tail!" he swore, unaware of how true that was.

Suddenly he felt furious with God. He was denying his stomach to please God, and a twig was allowed to humiliate him!

"Okay, God, you have a good laugh at my expense up there!" he shouted at the clouds. "I just buried my favorite meal, thank you very much!" A teardrop fell.

"Watch out, God, this hyena is coming to heaven! In the meantime, I will make you as proud of me as you are of Giraffe, Lion, Tiger, Elephant, and all those high and mighty animals. One day you will trust me!" he cried.

"It is the other way round," the still, small voice whispered. "The creation trusts the creator."

Whatever! Brother was too angry and full of indignant pride to pray.

Yellow Eyes grinned again. That was quite a prayer if he ever heard one! He kept up the poison, throwing in a dose of self-doubt laced with self pity. That was sure to neutralize the newly found self-esteem that came packaged in Christian faith. Who were they kidding? As long as they forgot to pray, they were just hot air, no substance.

THE SECRET DARKLAY

❦

The ten snake daughters shared one name, and now they had one secret. Each of them had laid ten eggs and hidden them in the soft earth under one dead tree outside their home. They took turns checking on them.

For some reason, they were ashamed and unable to tell their parents. Perhaps it was because one day in the past, one of them had casually asked their mother where hatchlings came from.

"From eggs," Swift had said casually.

"And where do eggs come from?"

"From birds," their mother had replied curtly, and that was the end of that. Then she had deliberately steered the conversation away from the facts of life. Their brother, Nyoka, could not possibly know more than they did, and he had not experienced the problem. Whenever they could, the sisters huddled together and prayed to Jesus. They needed to know why eggs were coming out of their bodies and they were not birds.

It never occurred to Darklay that they were reproducing.

"Hatchlings come from God after marriage!" Swift had snapped when another Darklay dared to ask again. It was said with such finality they dared not ask which god, or the what, when, and how of marriage.

Having pieced together some rumors and theories, every Darklay had been expecting Prince Charming to sweep her off her belly in a whirlwind of romance, take her to his sand castle lain with moist, dead leaves—and voila! God would send an angel bearing cute hatchlings from heaven and put them next to them while they slept. All she had to do was count and name them.

That Sunday after church, neither the parents nor Nyoka seemed to be around. Darklay decided to visit the eggs together and pray for healing. The only reason they had not destroyed them was to keep evidence of their strange disease, just in case they gathered courage to tell their mother. The girls had also stopped growing, another symptom of something sinister. They were supposed to be at least as big as their brother who was their age and perhaps twenty times bigger.

Darklay prayed. If they were all going to die, they wanted Jesus to know. They believed without a doubt that he could heal them if he chose to. If he did not, it would mean he missed them on the other side and wanted his pets home.

Unknown to Darklay, their frustrated brother Nyoka had rummaged through all their play spots while they were in church. He was not happy that of late, they had a new play place where they went alone when they thought he was not looking. He hated it when they kept secrets from him. He had none from them. He searched in the general direction they normally disappeared till something seemed to draw him to a particular tree. He was stunned. Ten hatchlings were struggling out of their shells. One Darklay had betrayed the family honor, laying eggs before marriage. Then his eyes caught another brood of ten. There was a third and fourth. To his horror he counted ten lots of ten eggs, all with hatchlings struggling out of the shells. They looked like tiny reincarnations of his living sisters, not to mention they were all female and blind!

His family was shamed big time. Ten unmarried sisters all with ten hatchlings meant the brother had failed to protect his sisters. He should have seen some boyfriend hanging around, some kind of a sign. Instead he had been too self-occupied. Rage surged through his entire body. It crossed his mind to kill all the hatchlings before anyone knew they existed. He could just swallow the lot and that would be that. He opened his mouth and bared his fangs on the first lot. Then he remembered he never ate anything before praying and closed his mouth again.

"Please, Jesus, help me. I am too angry!" he prayed. "They made me an uncle to one hundred nieces and hid it from me!" he sobbed. "It is now my solemn duty to protect the family honor!"

But something in his conscience said it was not about his family's honor but God's. All life in any stage or circumstances belongs to him who never makes mistakes. He started to calm down but was still very angry. One hundred nieces was quite some uncle business. Besides, he had no clue what would be expected of him as an uncle.

Strange how there was not a single nephew out of a hundred. Perhaps his family was cursed. He hated being the only male. His father did not count because he never played with him. He took back the curse thought. The pastor had said no one should consider themselves cursed. God blessed all his creatures when he made them, and curses did not sit side by side with blessings.

Uncle Nyoka was still seething when the sisters sniffed their way to the tree. Darklay almost ran away when they smelled him. They sensed his intense anger and for once were glad they could not see him annoyed and ashamed of them. They loved him too much. The little sisters huddled together.

"Honest, Nyoka, we did not do anything," pleaded one Darklay even before Nyoka opened his mouth.

"We did not steal any eggs!" another cried.

"Who was he!" Nyoka threatened, flattening his head on the ground, about to strike a blow for family honor. Then he remembered they could not see his theatrics.

"Who was who?" screamed another.

"Warm up, Nyoka! Please! We do not know anything. The eggs just came out of our bodies!"

Nyoka realized they were telling the truth. Their parents had never told them anything about their bodies or what to expect. His father had promised to tell him about the birds and the bees someday, and he was still waiting. His sisters were as ignorant as he was.

The first Darklay touched her nose to her eggs and shrieked.

"You broke them, Nyoka! You broke them all!"

"Mine too!" cried another.

"And mine! Now we cannot show mother and get cured of the disease!"

Nyoka was astounded. His ten bowling sisters had no clue that hatchlings came from eggs.

"They are hatching out," he explained. "Every one of you has ten little daughters!"

"What do you mean? They were eggs when we left them!" a Darklay said.

"Hatchlings come from eggs, you beautiful idiots! You are all mothers of ten, and I am Uncle Hundred!"

The ten little mothers lay still in shock.

"But we are not married," whispered one of them. "Hatchlings come when you are married!"

"My point exactly!" exclaimed Nyoka not so kindly. "I just need the names of the males involved."

The girls remained silent. Something was totally out of order, and it was not their doing. They had not known any males, and no angel had come to prepare them either. Nyoka watched them kindly, feeling their shame and humiliation without knowing why. Then he turned toward the hatchlings in sudden determination. He started his role as uncle by planting a kiss on every brand-new niece. One hundred kisses plus ten for the mothers started the first day of the rest of his life as an uncle.

Soon Darklay were kissing their daughters and nieces. Nyoka hoped they would still come around and reveal the fathers. When he caught up with the scoundrels, they too would be multiplied to one hundred pieces—and not as neatly. Then he would toss the pieces to their uncles. He tried to focus his eyes on all the hundred nieces at once. They were clones of their identical mothers. It was so mind boggling he kept blinking his eyes in a zombie state.

That was how Swift found her offspring—ten "ooh-ing" and "ahh-ing" and one a thunderstruck zombie. Her first reaction when she counted the ten broods was like Nyoka's. Shame flooded her whole being. Ten unmarried daughters with one hundred granddaughters had to be the worst of any mother's nightmares. If Parrot got wind of this, everyone in the jungle would know.

All eleven siblings waited for her outburst. They could sense she was battling with more shame than anger, and that cut deeper. They would rather she had lashed out, even hurt them physically.

"Who was he?" she asked the first Darklay quietly, menacingly, her head flat on the ground.

"Who was who?" Darklay asked, totally confused.

Swift then did the most un-motherly thing. She slithered toward a small stone a little distance from them all, curled herself around it, and started to sob.

She wanted to die. She had made too many selfish mistakes and ruined the lives of those who loved and trusted her. A mother ought to be the well of truth in a family and not a pit of lies. She looked sadly at her one hundred granddaughters of mysterious paternity and whose mothers were hatched from stolen eggs. She wished her husband was not absent from reality even though they had no family reality.

Out of the blue, God had brought Darklay's mother into her life. Brahmin was the only other snake Swift had met whose heart was ripe for Christ. God had answered Brahmin's prayer to find her hatchlings. This would have been her perfect opportunity to witness to Mina with truthful integrity and she had blown it.

But how was a thief expected to share the good news with her victim? She had never even revealed her faith to her own children! She was also too shy to give them the facts of life and now the girls were ruined! She cried louder. Suddenly she realized everyone was awkwardly embarrassed. A grandmother who bowled before her eleven hatchlings and a hundred grand-hatchlings needed deliverance. She caused misery just by being. What if the myth was real that snakes were permanently cursed by God since the days he kept a garden? Who did she think she was, hoping to become a pet of God?

"Please, Jesus, help me!" Swift cried out to heaven with all that she was.

He did. Suddenly Darklay rushed to her side and started praying as they cried. They had heard her mention The Name. Their mother knew Jesus! They did not have to keep him a secret from her any longer!

"Please, Jesus, comfort our mum!" one Darklay prayed.

"Please, God, reveal what we have done wrong so we can apologize and honor her and live long!"

"Oh, God, in the name of Jesus, make us a real talking family," Nyoka prayed.

Swift stopped crying.

"You guys believe in Jesus?" she asked calmly.

"Yes, Mother!" they all chorused.

"Oh thank you, Jesus, thank you, Jesus, thank you …" she exclaimed nonstop. It was her sign, a miracle. God had revealed his existence to her hatchlings despite her cowardice. She had kept her faith a secret for fear of her husband. She had also kept hidden the truth about her daughters. If Jesus could hold precious the mess that she was, he was truly a mighty God. She wanted to please him, to be truthful and to be someone her young could emulate.

Deep down, she knew her family would make it. They could do all things through Christ who strengthened them. She curled herself into a circle around Darklay, drawing them to her. Nyoka was too big. She flicked her tongue at him. He pulled close and put his head on her belly.

"I am sorry, everyone, I have not been the mother that you needed," she said gently. "Darklay, you could not possibly have known what you were doing."

"No, Mum, we do not know how it happened. It just sort of did," replied a Darklay.

"Whatever happened or happens, I love you always."

"Thank you, Mum, we love you too!" they chorused.

"May I now meet my grand-hatchlings?"

Nyoka smiled mischievously, knowing she had to deliver one hundred grandma kisses, another ten for the mothers, and one for Uncle Nyoka. But she was not named Swift for nothing. She went a step further and declared a blessing on every one of them. The ice was broken, and they were all hugging, laughing, and crying.

"What a God!" Swift declared. "I never thought I would witness to anyone in my life, and I come home to an entire congregation!"

They all laughed.

"You are not the only ones with a secret," she said, suddenly serious. "I must now tell you mine."

Everyone paid attention. For the first time ever, their mother was about to share something with them as a family. That felt even more important than whatever secret she had.

"Remember, I have always loved you and always will."

Swift had their full attention now. When a parent said something like that, whatever followed was never pretty. It was not. Their mother did not leave anything out, from why and how she stole them as eggs to meeting their mother today. It was too heavy to digest at once.

"I must have other sisters out there, perhaps a brother!" Nyoka exclaimed.

The girls were silent. Nyoka was not their relative.

"I do not know, Nyoka," Swift said. "I searched everywhere for my own stolen eggs or any hatchlings. Perhaps they have already become pets of God."

"We will pray, Mum. We will fast if we have to. Everything is possible with God," Nyoka said determinedly.

"Yes, son, all things are possible with God," Swift reassured and then turned to her daughters. "Could you possibly ever forgive me, Darklay?"

They remained thoughtful for a while.

"How big is our mother?" one Darklay asked.

"Same size as you and just as beautiful," Swift replied.

"Will we see you again after we meet her?" another Darklay asked.

"I will always be there for you and my grand-hatchlings," she said emotionally. "You will always be a part of my life. But you were your mother's first, and I stole her place from her. From the moment you were hatched, I fell in love with you."

"If our mother is our size, I guess it's all right for our hatchlings to have a big guardian grandma," said a third Darklay, and everyone started laughing. Swift was forgiven. She laid her head flat on the ground and snapped half her body up in a protective grandma stance.

"What about Dad?" somebody remembered, and all faces turned ashen.

"We keep all this between us for now," Swift said quickly. "I need to talk to him alone first."

Swift did not want her children lying to their father, but she needed a little time to turn him around. She had faith that God would help her.

It was late when they got back to the house. Black was already asleep. Swift took her place next to him and attempted to wake him up. She wanted to offload right away.

"Could we talk a little, Blackie?" she whispered.

"Sorry, Swift," he mumbled. "I have to go somewhere very early tomorrow morning. Could we talk when I come back?"

"All right," Swift replied. A good wife did not pester her husband. He would listen when he had time. She wished she could assert herself and insist on being heard immediately, but it was better to hold one's peace than to be accused of sitting on one's husband. That would make him a laughing stock. Perhaps God really intended the submission of a wife as a sub-mission. She wanted to do the right thing by her family whatever that was. Nevertheless, she knew that in Christ she had found *the way*. She just needed to tell *the truth* and she could start *the life*.

The Old Serpent Takes a Bite

෴

A persecuted Brother Hyena dragged himself back to work. He had to bury that finger and be done with it. For a fleeting moment, he wondered why he was going to all this trouble. God had not assigned him this task, but it felt like the smart thing to do. He wanted very much to impress God, to make him love him the way he must love Lion and Giraffe.

The sour leaves were gone, and he was too tired to go for more. He decided it was no big deal really. He could quickly grab the finger in his mouth, dig a little with his nose, and bury it. That would be the end of that. But he still had that nagging feeling he was not impressing God. He was unworthy no matter what he did. What could a simple, insignificant hyena like himself possibly do to touch the heart of God? If only he had been born a lion!

Angrily he grabbed the thumb in his mouth for quick burial, but his teeth sliced it off like razors. He froze. This was not in the plan, at least not in his plan. The tongue did its job and tasted. "Spit it out *now* and pray!" The still, small voice was back, but again he doubted it was from God. Brother stayed frozen, tongue in heaven, mind in hell, and teeth waiting for further instructions.

He knew deep down it was time to pray. It just seemed ridiculous to approach the throne of God with a human thumb stuck in his teeth. It did not occur to him to let go. This whole business was an accident, and God knew that. Later on, he was going to pray, when he was more organized. For now he would just savor the taste, just for another moment, and then he would spit it out, bury even the saliva, rinse his mouth in the river, and eat some bitter leaves. This was not yet a sin. He could stop anytime he wanted. The juices triggered a memory. A thumb led to a hand and then to an arm, a shoulder, a chest, a soft stomach, all the way down to a fat juicy thigh!

"You are bright, Brother Hyena," Yellow the demon whispered, disguised as common sense. "Figure it out!"

Brother did. What a slow fool he had been! All good things came from God. Heaven must have allowed him a last taste of human meat before he became a serious Christian—a Last Supper of sorts. Why was the human placed deliberately on his path? God forbade the eating of humans, meaning whole humans, not just a finger! This bite was hardly a snack. There was a world between tasting and eating! He had done the honorable thing and buried the whole body. Why would the God of all creation concern himself with a small matter of a missing digit on a dead human whom he had not killed? Wouldn't he be busy judging the murderer?

Suddenly the finger slid deliciously down his throat. All his senses went gaga. This hyena was already in heaven! But heaven ended when the finger disappeared down his alimentary canal, and he wanted back in. The stub where the thumb had been was level to the ground. A little soil and it would have been covered, but that was not the way his reflex reclined. He started digging. One by one, he got the rest of the fingers and gathered speed. He swallowed the hand and watch in one gulp. As if in a trance, he continued digging and munching on everything—flesh, soil, and crawling proteins— along the way to the juicy thigh. Who needed some faraway heaven where stomachs were not allowed in anyway?

"I am just a hyena, for heaven's sake!" he shouted at his conscience. That still, small voice was not allowing him quiet enjoyment.

"I am not some pious, great giraffe or lion, just a hyena—a simple, insignificant scavenger!" he shouted angrily to no one in particular between mouthfuls.

Yellow Eyes grinned again. The brother was finally wading in the muck. The Mass had floored a giant, the last on the lineage of one thousand blessed generations. When the Almighty (hiccup) commissioned a bloodline, he put The Mass out of commission. This hyena needed to believe he was cursed to the fourth and fifth generations along with the enemies of God.

Now that Hyena had eaten the image of God, he would believe himself unredeemable, unworthy of God's grace, and take on the label of backslider. The spirit of greed that had fled to the Devil's Mountain when he was saved was already on its way back to a cleaned-out den with seven other demons, all tougher than he was. Among them would be witchcraft. Hyena would soon be having his paw and star read by the witch chameleon.

When they got him rock-bottom lonely, the spirit of witchcraft would seduce him to consult the only creature that ever loved him, his dead mother. One abomination or two would be good for getting God himself to curse him. The Mass could accomplish wonders of destruction in just one such generation. Not that Hyena needed God to curse him. His own words had potent enough venom. He believed he was not as good as other creatures and declared it loudly in his rage. Mortals were so ignorant of the power of life and death welded by their own tongues!

Hyena's stomach was ready to burst. He could see now why stomachs might not make it to heaven. He lay down to rest and digest, but the thrill of sin turned into a shrill scream of conscience. Remorse, disgust, and all self-bashing thoughts came home to roost. His face was covered with earth, blood, and his own saliva. There were swarms of flies disrespecting him all over the place. Brother feared if he died at that moment there would be a stampede in heaven. Herds of angels would be trotting to take emergency leave just to avoid him. No one would want to clean him up or deal with the gory details. Then he remembered that his dirty scavenging body was not going to heaven.

Clumsily he got up and buried the hair, toenails, and one shoe, all that was left of the human. He hoped it would register his remorse, anything that would make a difference up there to Saint Lion, Tiger, or Dinosaur—whoever was guarding the pearly gates.

A cold emptiness in the deep of his core hit him as his mind descended into another flash vision of hell. The devil was still tending his fire with a spiked tong. He looked at Brother, smiled, wagged his tail, and added a very big log. Brother's own tail rushed between his legs and lay flat on his belly. Thank God no one was looking. The belly was no place for a tail of great ancestry. He tried to lift it off, but something glued it in position.

Soon he was hosting a self-pity party of one.

"Messy failure," he whimpered, "a disgrace to my bloodline. Giving my heart to Jesus indeed! Who was I kidding? The son of God messing around with a stinky, greedy loser like me. Does that picture make sense to anyone out there?" He screamed at the shrubs: "I am nothing! I have no friends on earth or in heaven! Nobody loves me, not even me! Nobody ever loved me except my mother, and God let her die because I did not deserve a mother. What reason would anyone anywhere have to love me?"

Brother wished he could speak to the pastor. He was supposed to care. But confessing this size of a sin would shame him to death.

Hyena wept uncontrollably as small creatures around him scampered for safety. A beetle swimming in a pool of buffalo dung dove in from the deep end. A millipede took to her million heels but was still not fast enough. His misery was highly contagious.

Something bit him on the soft of his bottom. Without a pause, another took a bite under his belly, hard. He shot up like a missile giving successive yelps of pain. How was he supposed to know he was sitting on a convoy of *siafu,* the giant red safari ants? Someone once said, "Misery loves company." It was true, but no one deserved to be eaten alive by the red devils.

He cried out, attempting to scratch everywhere at once. It was no good, so he shot off toward the river. His thoughts included drowning himself along with the stupid vampires. He knew suicide was a highway to hell, but as far as he was concerned, he was already in hell. He had lost his network with God.

Yellow Eyes was thoroughly impressed with himself. The suicide suggestion was a stroke of genius. Hyena would soon be a doomed spirit stowaway, going absent without leave from earth. Heaven did not receive illegal immigrants. Nor did they deport them to their planet or body of origin. The pearly gates simply cleared and forwarded them straight to hell where every arrival got instant citizenship and his or her heat plugged in without discrimination.

Yellow hoped his boss, Mundu, would be pleased. If he was recognized before Axis, he could be promoted to Strongman. It would be great to run the evil activities of an entire country like Kenya. In the meantime, he stayed on Hyena's tail. He was primed to drown the blessings that had followed his bloodline for one thousand generations.

Brother had an eerie feeling his tail was being tailed. He was going to die today, but he didn't want to die all spooked up. All he had wanted was to please God, impress him a little so he could love him as much as everyone else, become his pet. But that was not for the likes of him. He felt so utterly wrong and worthless.

Hyena's tail hid under his belly. There was a devil up or down there some place after death, somewhere outside the body he was wearing. He needed to bypass that particular creature when his spirit left his body for wherever. But first he needed to define wherever and know the way there. Wherever "wherever" was, he did not want it to be some place a million times worse than the here and now, forever!

"Please, God, help me in the name of Jesus!" he finally whispered under smoking breath, all previous bravado and great ancestry aside. But his legs kept moving, pulled or pushed by something that made it feel cowardly and shameful to stop now.

Suddenly he was frozen midflight by the most dangerous growl in the jungle. The fierce eyes of a young female lioness burned into his. Bites from the million red safari ants on his belly became sweet caresses in comparison to her stare.

So much for prayer and God's help! he thought. *I don't deserve his help anyway; I never did.*

"Leave in peace or in pieces!" the lion growled. In a flash, he remembered the story of his ancestor Ole Baba who had rigged lots to die in place of his friends. God had killed him in an earthquake to keep him from suicide. He also gave him the moment and presence of mind to repent. If this was God's idea of an alternative death, he wished it was neater. He did not need a tour through a lion's digestive system, starting with a fanged gate! Then again, he was not Ole Baba who walked with God and chose to die in place of others. He was just a selfish, greedy relative who was trying to escape from his God-given purpose and responsibilities before he found out what they were.

"Can't we be friends *now*, God? Call a truce or something?" But that did not feel right as a prayer. He tried again.

"Dear God, I never had a friend. I don't know how to be friends.

Will you be my friend now before I die, just so I know how it feels to have a friend? While you are at it, please make friends with the lioness too, so you can tell her not to eat me!"

The lioness kept growling, keeping her ground. A glance at her cub drew a louder growl and a pounce position. But the cub was not her own. The cute, dark eyes of an oryx studied Brother's retreating figure in amusement, proud of her tough mamma. The lion was lying with the lamb like mother and cub, and neither of them was dead!

Brother maintained his slow retreat. Any sudden move could be his last. Suddenly he realized he did not want to die, not right now, not any kind of death.

"Hello, God—hello—this is Brother Hyena. Please deliver me from this creature!" he whispered. "Please come personally and do not delay or try to send others! Save me in Jesus' name, and I will serve you the rest of my life!"

Yellow Eyes swore something unrepeatable as the front part of his snake body froze and the back kept moving forward. The center of his torso suddenly resembled a mountain, and he tipped over upside down. He hiccuped. The stupid hyena had gone crying to the one who still saved every riff raff that called on his name. J. C had the breed and style but no class!

A Divine Hug

∾

The lioness turned her attention to the cub. Brother exhaled and shot off to safety, thanking God profusely.

Why in the world was the lioness playing mother to a cub of a grass-eating deer? This had never been heard of in the jungle, perhaps in the whole world! Was the lioness crazy, playing with her food, or just learning to grow it for herself?

Something flashed in his memory about this bizarre situation, and he kept searching his mind. When it struck him, his whole body shivered. It was the prophesy! Owl's prophesy was being fulfilled right before his unworthy eyes! God had chosen an insignificant scavenger to be the first witness!

"Beware when mother and cub are not mother and cub ... when the lion lies with the lamb ... end of the beginning, beginning of the end." At the worst possible moment in his life, reeking of human flesh and on the verge of suicide, God was honoring him! Only one explanation made sense: God loved him! The good shepherd had left his ninety-nine good sheep to come after one insignificant scavenger!

Within moments, the most beautiful warmth engulfed him. *A hug from God* was his immediate thought. It was not the sort of thing one could explain to others without sounding crazy, but he had no doubt it was a divine hug. He made a vow never to take his own life. He knew now to whom it belonged. It was time to spread the good news of fulfilled prophesy, the signal of the nearing end of time!

He ran, tail high in the air, all the way to Giraffe's house, laughing and crying hysterically, waking up the entire jungle.

"Wake up!" he cried to Giraffe. "The lion is lying with the lamb!"

The animals confirmed the strange sight from a safe distance without disturbing the pair. Nobody knew the young lioness, where she came from or where she was going. Thousands of fireflies lit a circle around the mother and cub. Even Ostrich was able to see in the dark through their illumination, but she buried her head in the sand to avoid going into shock. She was terrified of anything supernatural.

Finally Porcupine dared to go close and asked her name. No one in his or her right mind would try to eat Porcupine. The lioness was friendly and introduced herself as *Kamunyak*. It meant *the blessed one.*

Kamunyak allowed the cub to feed from its real mother who grazed all day within their sight. But soon after the cub was fed, the lioness, though hungry herself, would scare the mother away without harming her. The two females seemed to share some uncanny understanding as the cub enjoyed the luxury of a fierce, protective mother and a loving wet nurse.

Somehow, humans too got wind of the unnatural pairing. Over the next few days, they came in drones from many parts of the human jungle. Animals and humans watched from opposite sides, neither species interfering with the other's right to the divine event.

The next day, humans brought meat to the starving Kamunyak. Brother Hyena decided there was something good in them yet. Perhaps they too had had a prophesy. What if they started worshiping the lioness, the cub, or even its mother? Humans were capable of turning anything into an idol. It did not matter that they were the only creatures made in the image of God and that even they were not worthy of worship.

Furious as hell, Yellow Eyes watched the events disguised as the mysterious vulture. His power of suggestion was not working on the hyena or anyone else—not while the idiots were praising J. C. and giving all the glory to God. The place had become holy ground (hiccup!) with the forces of heaven prowling in full armor to the frigging flaming swords. It was a good thing mortals did not see into the spirit world. Otherwise, they would know for certain just how much their praise touched God and moved heaven into action.

Yellow maintained a safe distance. Not that he was afraid. He too had numerous agents around the place, but as usual, he was outnumbered two to one by the army of God. When Axis had led a rebellion in heaven, only a third of the angels had been brave enough to join him. If the others had not chickened out, Axis maintained they could have taken God. But their day was yet to come. That had been a rehearsal. One day they would overpower all that J. C. created—and nothing existed that he did not create, not even Axis. What a coup that would be, the master potter kicked out by the pots! Their time was coming. The Mass was coming. Soon and very soon, Axis would be sitting on the throne of thrones, his feet firmly planted on the neck of The Ancient of Days.

The Aero-Ride

❧

B lack Mamba reached the human nest before dawn. He climbed in and nested under the feathers in the bottom as instructed by The Voice. Everything smelled of eggs, but to him that was the smell of legs. He reeled up and waited.

At sunrise, De Brazza Monkey carefully carried the nest to the familiar clearing at the top of the hill. Black stayed cool at the bottom, aware that someone was carrying him, perhaps the brain maker. Luckily, Monkey never checked his cargo. He had no such instructions and just assumed it was the *evoluter* or whatever they used to measure bottoms and feet for evolution. He set the nest down on a mound of grass, climbed in, and sat on the feathers. Whatever they had under those feathers was softly comfortable and fit snuggly on the bottom of the nest. He fixed his eyes on the sixth decorative line of the nest as instructed by The Voice and waited.

Black felt a heavy weight rest evenly on him. His head was pressed hard and flat, his eyes forced firmly shut. Brain expansion was turning out to be very heavy business. When the pain reached unbearable proportions, he started moving his skin round and round like ripples of water.

Black's throws of pain were therapeutic to Monkey, the sweetest massage to his bottom and feet. If this was how bottoms and legs were assessed for evolution, he did not want the sensation to end in the twinkling of an eye. One of his feet felt especially good. He had no way of knowing it was planted firmly on one of the most dangerous heads in the world!

Suddenly Aero swooped down, grabbed the nest with her massive feet, and they were airborne, both passengers shocked out cold.

Aero had no idea where she came from or who she was. When she was hatched, the hand of the creature she called Daddy Axis was waiting and she patented on him. Daddy could turn himself into any creature, even a human. He was an invisible spirit who did not have a body of his own. She did not share his powers of transformation and suspected she was stolen as an egg.

Whenever she was lonely, she fantasized about a really nice mum and dad out there desperately searching for her. There had to be someone out there that loved her. Daddy Axis did not. He wasn't even capable of loving himself.

Aero knew no place called home. They could be anywhere at any time as long as there was a huge tree with enough leaves to hide her for the night. Whatever his form in the day, at sunset Daddy Axis turned invisible and stole into the night. At dawn, she sensed his return in an evil, depressing presence. Even trees seemed to sway away from it. Sometimes he materialized as red eyes only and hypnotized her to do things by looking into her eyes—ugly things like pulling wings off of beautiful butterflies and limbs from grasshoppers, eating the eyes off a living, little creature and leaving it to starve to death. Sometimes he made her peck on herself on one spot till she drew a lot of blood. He was fascinated with self-mutilation. Those were his kinds of daddy-daughter games.

Luckily he left her alone when she was airborne. Though he watched her every move, he was not omnipresent like God.

Daddy Axis had agents everywhere, ugly creepy spirits whose forms changed now and then. Like him, they had no bodies of their own and had to borrow or steal from mortal creatures. They moved into a stolen body like a house. Their furniture included disobedience, idolatry, theft, murder, jealousy, witchcraft, and many others. They also moved in friends that had seven times more furniture than they did.

Whenever the host creature died, they lost their home and hitchhiked to the demon transit center on the Devil's Mountain. Sometimes they were evicted without notice when the host heard J. C.'s knock and let him in.

Aero hated being used as a cargo carrier for unholy goods round the globe. She hated being used as an object, referred to as The Aeromass and loaned out to friends.

Currently she was on loan to the demon Mundu for the Kenyan project. She hoped there was no snake in the human nest. Snakes really freaked her. She learned long ago never to peek into her cargo. You read the devil's mail at your own risk and peril!

She shivered involuntarily. Living in the spooky Ninety-Nine did that to her. Mundu was also feeding her lots of meat from no one knew where, and it was making her too heavy. The previous night, she thought she saw assorted animals entering the cave on the leash of the demon Yellow. They seemed hypnotized or something, their eyes blank, a sign that their hearts were vacant for occupation. It was safer for her to see no evil, hear no evil, speak no evil, and eat whatever was served. Axis fed her vegetables and fruits. Luckily her stomach could handle anything. If she was an animal, she would probably be a hyena.

At four years old, Aero believed she was the largest bird in the world and still growing. In one rare moment of conversation, Daddy Axis had told her she could live for fifty or sixty years. Her life was just beginning.

There was a deafening noise ahead of her, and she changed course for a moment. It was another of those artificial birds with live humans inside. They were bigger and noisier but she believed herself better than them. Her wingspan was almost as large and she had excellent natural eyesight. Unlike them, she had just learned to fly backward. None of those could take even the tiniest step back on land or in the air. They therefore could not land on Devil's Mountain, the only place in the world where one approached or left backward.

Aero suspected she was pretty, but she was not sure. She had never received a compliment from anyone. Nor did she have anyone to compare herself with. Her head was clean and bold. She was all black save for a brilliant white collar of fur and striking white pyramids on her wings. Aero spoke only in whispers because she could not vocalize; she had no voice box or larynx, whatever Daddy Axis called it.

Whenever Daddy Axis mocked her about the whispering, she wanted to remind him he had a whole body missing, but she was afraid. He was not beyond stealing hers in retaliation. He was a thief. It was not the nicest thing to think about a dad, but he was in fact a cruel and sadistic thief. She survived by doing as she was told and keeping her thoughts to herself.

As she soared higher with her cargo, she thought about J. C., the archenemy of Daddy Axis. She had never met him. One day, she had listened in from her tree as the strongman from Rwanda made his report to The Mass. He inadvertently mentioned the full name of Jesus Christ. Before he finished pronouncing Christ, every knee including Daddy Axis's hit the ground against their will. When they recovered, the reckless strongman who had also fallen to his knees was taken somewhere underground to be punished by junior demons. Aero had no idea what they did to him, but she would never forget the screams. It did not matter that he had turned brothers against brothers in the worst genocide. His achievements were marred by mentioning the J. word in full.

"Who made me, Daddy Axis?" she asked him one day when he put on a grotesque humanlike form. It was easier to talk when he was visible.

"I made you, Aeromass. I evolved you from a lizard millions of years ago. You still have a lizard's bold head," he replied. "I also made planet Earth with my own two hands."

"Then why do you spend so much time destroying such a masterpiece?" she asked.

"An artist has a right to remodel his designs. Enough questions; a mortal cannot understand the intricacies of my world. You will understand when you die and come to my fullness!"

Aero had felt like she had been scorched with fire. When she died, she wanted to go up, not down to his dungeons. Somehow she would find the way before then. She suspected that Jesus had made her, along with everyone else, and Axis was trying to take the credit for it. Daddy Axis was a liar too.

One day he turned himself into a big toad. He made her fly him round and round as he cursed Jesus and heaped obscenities on his name. Not even his agents went near him when he got like that.

It was the day a report came that the youthful president of Rwanda was using the love of God to heal his land that was recovering from a civil war. The humble humans were forgiving one another in unprecedented capacities. Some had even shared their meager meals with those that wiped out their families in the genocide.

"Who would have thought that humans who wielded machetes with so much hate could now wield love and contrite hearts in the same intensity?" Axis exclaimed to Aero as if she would know. She was only the devil's pet, not the devil!

"Who ever heard of winning a war by love anyway?" he raged. "This whole thing reeks of J. C. crying 'Father, forgive them for they know not what they do,' on the cross."

Clearly there were heart operations going on in Rwanda by a surgeon that Axis could not touch. Only the heart of God was capable of detonating a love bomb of that magnitude. Aero was paying for it with a giant, sticky toad on her back, but it was a small price when you knew where love had gone. Her heart had been breaking to pieces over that beautiful land, its animals and people.

She was beginning to fall in love with J. C. even if she did not know him or where he lived. Right then she believed he was in Rwanda and that one day she was going to bump into him. That was before she knew he was omnipresent. Any God who was the extreme opposite of Daddy Axis had to be made of love. Axis was distilled hate.

"Why do you hate mortals so much, Daddy Axis?" she had asked him one day, wanting her dad to feel better.

"Because the other God, my enemy loves them even more than I could ever hate them. He gave them every opportunity, made everything possible for them to be reconciled with him, even having his own son die on the cross to redeem them. Even if the whole world chose me, I would end up with a bunch of nincompoops. I have no use for morons who just fall on my lap, off the golden platter that God put them on at his cost!"

"So why do you go after Christians with such ferocity?" she asked boldly.

"Because they are still J.C.'s catch prize. Without anyone believing in him, he would have died on the cross for nothing. This is war, Aero Bird. His ultimate thrill becomes my ultimate kill."

"There are many from God's inner circle that have eaten at his table and still defected to you. Surely you love them for choosing to follow you. They are on your side!" she said uncertainly.

"Backsliders are my consolation prize. Even if they go back, they first crucify J. C. afresh. However, a fallen Christian is no longer game to me but a stinking carcass. God has revealed his whole heart to them and they have spat on it. Why must I content myself with traitors?"

Aero suspected he hated traitors for reminding him of himself. He must hate himself even more than he hated everyone else. How could he give love unless he first possessed it?

"What then can mortals do to win your love?"

"I forbid you to use the L. word again!" Axis scolded. "But the answer is nothing! God is crazy about every miserable last one of them. His son J. C. wants them to co-inherit the kingdom that is rightfully mine! I hate them all. I hate them just for being! I hate the image of God and every detestable creature under his dominion. I hate the author of life!

"What did J. C. do that that made you angry for all time?" Aero asked.

"He tossed me out of heaven after my coup attempt, knowing I deserved the throne. Later, in the garden of God, I disguised myself as a beautiful snake and turned man, his favorite creation, against him." He winked at her. She feigned a wink at the toad that was now sitting on a tree branch opposite her. She still had to give him a lift down unless he chose to convert back to spirit. She hated witnessing this life in between where spirit and body were interchangeable.

"What happened next?" she asked in her whisper.

"You should have seen the mourning in heaven. Man and God were separated permanently by disobedience. I may have missed the throne that first time, but now I had scored an eternal victory! What was meant to live forever began to die. Sin, once it is full-blown, leads to death. I planted it so deep that it passes through the blood to the next generation. No one can ever escape it. Was that a coup or what, Aero Bird?"

"It was, Daddy Axis," she whispered, wishing he would drop dead. One day she too was going to die, and it was thanks to him.

"What happened then? Why are you still angry after such victory?"

"God made man in his own spitting image and put his own breath in him to become a living being. I cannot close in without tasting, smelling or seeing God and I am totally allergic.

"He is supposed to be love. Are you allergic to love?" Aero asked warily.

"Did I not forbid you to use the L. word?" the toad thundered.

"What did he do?" she prompted. She was used to thunder and storm. Axis changed color, lost his cool, and started shouting.

"He gave his only son, who had no sin, to die and atone for man's sin!"

"Didn't the son have something to say about it?" she asked, concerned.

"Oh no! Not J. C.! He obeys his father in everything! He refuses to have a mind of his own, contented to be the revelation of his father. When you think you know him, it is not him but his father. God poured all of himself into his son and sent him like a lamb to the slaughter."

"Are you saying Jes—sorry—J. C. had no choice in the matter, like he was drugged and dragged unconscious?" Aero pushed on.

"All right, he said yes, but who cares?" Axis screamed. He revealed more truths the angrier he got. It was when he was very nice that he was most deceitful and manipulative. He started to calm down, and Aero put her mind on cautious alert.

"The point, my daughter, is that God condemns me for entering the snake and deceiving man, but he entered his own son and committed suicide, which is a bigger sin, and I am still the bad guy of the universe! There is no God!"

"Take it easy, Daddy Axis," she comforted in childish wisdom. "You don't have to worry then if he is already dead."

"After death, he stormed my home for three days and stole the keys. That is why we have no place to call home, Aero. Do you see the magnitude of our enemy, Aero? Why we must stick together?"

"So he is alive even though he died?" she asked timidly. It was the wrong question.

"No, not to me he isn't, you idiot!" he raged. "Not for long anyway. Soon I will toss him where he belongs, along with all those that have no mind of their own! You must believe in your own mind, Aero, if you want wisdom. Trust only in your own understanding!"

She liked it when he called her daughter, but she also knew he was not her father and he was twisting the truth. He only called her daughter when trying to sink a lie. J. C. was alive; he had just admitted it. And if God, his adversary, already committed suicide, who were they at war with?

"That's all right, Daddy Lucifer, I understand." He had many beautiful names, including Son of the Morning Star. But he was more beast than beauty, and he had perfected the art of both. Aero was glad she was stolen or adopted and not a blood relative—although he had no blood. It was all just too complex. He was the first thing she saw when she came out of the egg, and that was supposed to be her mum or dad. If only it had been Jesus' hand waiting! Someone should make it possible to choose your own parents before you enter this world!

She soared higher into the sky, dreading the landing on the Devil's Mountain. One of the gates to the bottomless pit was there somewhere. She had nightmares about missing the landing as she flew backward into it. She had visions of arriving in hell and then everyone pulling out her feathers one by one. Every country had such a gate so that the souls of those that rejected God did not have to travel across borders to their future abode. Axis said it was instantaneous and that his heaven was a big ranch known as Hades. Apart from saying it was warm, he never gave further description.

The Hades Ranch was supposed to be a surprise when someone died. In fact, he went to great lengths to convince mortals that there is nothing out there after death—nothing. If he wanted them afraid, it was not of the hereafter; they had forever and ever to unwrap the surprises he had prepared for them there.

Aero wished she did not have to listen in on the conversations of devils! The details were too overwhelming to process, as she had to sift through the facts and fiction. She just wanted out of her situation, to run away from home like a normal bird. But she had no home to run from and no place to run. No one would miss her either. She had never met or related with another mortal. Her babysitters were demons.

At the highest soar in the sky, she wished she could keep on ascending till she met J. C. somewhere in the heavens. But she relied on warm currents to fly and the higher she went, the cooler it became. She could not just keep soaring higher and higher into oblivion. Perhaps one day, Jesus himself would come and get her, make her his pet, his princess, and she would live happily ever after in a flying mountain of love that was somewhere and everywhere all at the same time.

When the grim reality of her situation snapped her back to the present, she wished Jesus was not omnipresent after all. If he was here, he would see a demon's cargo dangling off her foot, destined for the Devil's Mountain. It was not the kind of moment for the devil's only daughter to bump into the only son of God.

CLEAR THE RUNWAY

◌

Mundu had already sent word for the runway on the Devil's Mountain to be cleared. The Aeromass had to land, and the area had no trees tall enough to hide the landing of the largest flying bird in the world. The sight could scare the daylights out of humans, and defaulting to prayer was the Kenyan's second nature. He was not taking chances of the Kamba who lived in the area calling upon heaven.

Kamuti, the Kamba spirit of witchcraft, received the message and got to work. Milika, the female spirit from Samburu disguised as a flying cow, was there for reinforcement and offered to help for the fun of it. Kamuti reluctantly agreed knowing how she enjoyed frightening humans. Nevertheless, he wanted her to owe him a favor. Nothing in their world was done out of the goodness of the heart. They were not burdened with goodness or hearts at all, for that matter.

Before the sun could have breakfast and start her journey west, stones pelted the iron sheet roofs of all human settlements within eye's range of the Devil's Mountain. Even the grass-thatched roofs were not spared. Sounds of footsteps bigger than an elephant's rocked the compounds, but nothing was visible through the spying cracks. Not a creature left their habitat. The early birds already out scampered for cover wherever it could be found.

The best math student, a ten-year-old, had just been appointed prefect in his class and timekeeper for his primary school. It was an important day, and he had left very early to ring the school bell. Anyone who came after the bell would be late and punished.

He was almost in school when the biggest mountain of a cow leapt into the air from nowhere in particular and flew above his head. Her smoking nostrils were two endless caves through which he could see a boiling red and white brain. Her eyes were two long and thin yellow slits that pierced like a sword. But the scariest organ was the massive udder from which streams of milk rained down.

The prefect came from a superstitious background and knew when he was face-to-face with evil. His curly African hair stood straight as his eyes bulged out of their sockets. His heartbeat was louder than the drums of *wathi wa mukamba,* the sensational Kamba dance that required the dancer to have no bones.

There was no bush or tree, no hiding place. Then he saw it. The biggest pile of steaming cow dung he had ever seen.

"*Osa vinya, Mukamba!*" the prefect shouted the Kamba slogan of the brave. "*Take courage, you are Kamba!*" He dove in for dear life. Realizing only his face could be hidden, the prefect put his hands on his head. All that mattered was that his eyes did not lock with those of the thing. If you locked eyes with the devil, they remained locked unless God came personally with his master key!

When the prefect was certain the evil apparition had passed, he sat down carefully, ever watchful with the one eye that did not have dung. In a slow trance, the prefect wiped the dung off his face with his hands and cleaned them on his new school shorts. A cold wind slapped his face and he shrieked, realizing his new uniform and school bag were soaked with snow-white sticky milk. So was every exposed inch of his body to his bare feet. He had to do something quickly before any evil took root. The apparition could be returning.

The prefect wet his pants some more and not with milk. Then with sudden resolve he took to the famous Kenyan heels and sprinted fast enough for the Olympics. There were modern brick houses on his way, but he did not stop there. He was not sure the high and mighty could understand matters of spirits and ghosts. Instead he came to a full stop outside an L-shaped house roofed with tin and iron sheets. The sides were made of mud bricks and smoothed with cow dung. A whitewash of soda ash gave it a brilliant white finish. A round whitewashed grass-thatched hut stood next to it.

The prefect banged on the wooden door of the bigger house hard enough to shake the foundation. A brick popped out of the side and fell to the ground, leaving a gaping hole. A man's hand quickly stuck the convex bottom of a small earthen cooking pot on the hole. A bed under which the children and their puppy were hiding clicked hard as their mother attempted to fit in.

"Help me, help me, someone!" The lonely frightened voice of the prefect was heard throughout the entire village.

"Help me, someone, anyone!" The boy cried harder. "I've been rained on by the devil!"

A few mongrel dogs made muffled whimpering sounds from their emergency shelters of overturned cans and buckets forgotten outside the previous night.

From the little hut, the old woman who knew about such things crawled to her tiny window, opened it a crack, and threw out a half used packet of salt. Just in case the crying voice was human, the poor child could ward off the evil spirits before they set.

Quickly, the prefect poured salt all over his body. He put some more in his mouth and made a sign of the cross. The new Prefect, Class monitor and bell ringer was not going to school. The bell would not ring. No one was going to be late or face the cane that day.

With the entire audience otherwise preoccupied, the runway on the Devil's Mountain was clear. Aero circled in reverse and prepared to land. Neither the size of the bird nor the reverse maneuver was a spectacle fit for human sanity.

A Taste of Death

❧

Black Mamba was the first to come to. He almost fainted again when he realized they were still airborne and the brain machine was still sitting on his brain box. He started writhing in pain again. He was terrified to say the least. The human nest had no wings and he had no idea if the pilot was spirit or mortal, good or bad. He had handed himself over body and soul to a strange voice, just a voice, from God or devil he had not tested to find out. If they crashed to death, neither he nor his family would ever know who or what killed him.

Funny he should think of his family now when death was in the air, the only good thing he had. He even regretted his abysmal performance as a dad! What a proud legacy to leave his offspring, a dad who stole eggs for legs! If he lived through this, he was going home to teach his family never to talk to strangers, even if it was only a voice without a body, *especially* if it was only a voice.

He recalled nostalgically the day he taught his son their attack position. Nyoka had never been more animated, more radiantly happy with him. If only he had hugged his daughters even once! They sure did not resemble him, but they were hatched in his compound and called him Daddy. Daddy ought to be the other name for love.

158

He did not want to die before making treasured memories of him for his family.

Black was also not a confessed Christian. Pastor Twiga could refuse to say Mass over his funeral and ruin his posthumous reputation. He wanted to be a good ancestor. The Mass could not burry him either. It was just a voice, a secret faceless organization. But then, so was the unseen Christian God. Not even Pastor Twiga Giraffe had ever seen him despite his endless height. Black had never needed to take a firm stand on his faith before. Now he faced possible intestate death as he ran out what he always took for granted—time.

The scent of his wife on the day they met came to mind, stirring thoughts of heaven. Giraffe had said Jesus was the light of heaven. The other heaven, the lit side, not Axis' heaven. That was the eternal nothing out there. What could possibly smell as good as his wife in pitch darkness? He worried about all the stolen eggs. Black was afraid of the dark.

Sin is a parasite inside your integrity, he thought. He felt like a spiritual louse.

Axis, the god of The Mass, and his ancestors never promised a hereafter. He was about the here and now—after that, nothing, just nothing. Still he had brought them out of … what? He would never think this aloud, but their god had brought his forefathers out of the garden of God where everything bloomed without anyone sweating for it, out along with the image of God and away from the presence of God. There. He had finished one blasphemous thought against Axis, and he was still standing—or rather, curled up in a human nest hoping not to die.

If Giraffe was right, he was in deep trouble. But you did not just wake up one morning and call your entire ancestral beliefs and value system wrong! Yet Giraffe spoke with much gusto and conviction, as if he had an inner knowing. There was also that unmistakable power around him, some kind of anointing on the moment, the ground, and the individual. That was why he kept Nyoka away. One of them had to remain pure, planted on ancestral ground and Axis. Just in case he himself was sucked in by the Christian God, the other male in the family could come get him. Jesus, Jesus ... he had no finger to put on it, but there was just something about that name.

The thing sitting on Black's brain was causing excessive thinking. So, The Mass had nothing to offer after death, and the opposite of nothing was something. There were always two sides, good or bad, tall or short, dead or alive, something or nothing. There had to be something out there rooting for your spirit when you die. And there were two of them, the good and the bad. Black was afraid of both of them.

His head hurt big time. Suddenly a warm liquid reeking of monkey pee soaked him. His brain started working faster and broader with original thoughts coming, going or lining up to be processed.

What if there really was a lake of fire for the enemies of the God of Giraffe? What was the bottom line on the bottomless pit? At that moment he smelled smoking monkey poop. It had to smell worse than any bottomless pit! He prayed the horrid smell was not his old brain as they replaced it. If that was how the insides of his head smelled when he was alive, he hoped he never smelled himself in death. Black was not sure if his thoughts were together, coming from in or out of his mind. Only that everything always connected in the end with the good or the bad.

Black was terribly afraid. Apart from the fear of flying, he worried about something going wrong with the brainwork. It was also dark in the human nest, and he was a touch claustrophobic. The only light came from the millions of shooting stars exploding in his head as they continued crushing his brain box. His thoughts were starting to repeat themselves. He thought he had thought all this before.

"My name is Black, but I do not want a black ending when I die!" he whispered to no god in particular. "Not the pitch darkness, please!" He dared not mention Axis or Jesus right then and invoke the jealousy of the other. He could not pray to Mother Earth either while he was so high up in the air. Funny how no one had come up with *Mother Sky*. It was easy to come up with any god on solid ground. He needed the god who made the *solid* part of life and the light. Even he was not sure what he meant by that thought, so he let in the next.

If Giraffe is right, and I am not thinking that he is, there is light in the Christian heaven, he thought. *J. C., the son of God, is said to be robed in glorious majesty that lights up his side of heaven. And the Christians are the light of the world, so help me, God!* He was starting to think of Mrs. Zebra, her massive head full of the spirit of interruption.

Black was fascinated with the Christian cult in the same manner as some Christians were curious about the occult and its horoscopes, Ouija boards, tarot cards, and all things otherworldly. In the end, they were ensnared by his smart god Axis. Now he feared the Christian madness was starting to rub off him. If he succumbed to their temptation, he would be a blaspheming traitor forsaking everything he was in order to become a new creature.

Jesus was supposed to be the bad guy of heaven who did not help Axis in the revolution. If Axis had won, he would have fed everyone the tree of life to live *forever*—in the dark. They had switched off the light. He must follow *the light.*

They'd better finish with this brain machine already, he thought. *I am hallucinating!*

All this listening to Giraffe was becoming very dangerous to his common sense. Again he was glad he had kept his son away from the confusion. He had that feeling in the pit of his stomach that he was slithering away from the way, the truth, and the life, and he was now looking too late for *the light* at the end of the tunnel! He was about to die. It no longer mattered if he had legs or not. They could not attach them to a corpse.

The ecstatic bottom and feet massage intensified and brought De Brazza Monkey back to consciousness, thousands of feet above sea level in a human nest perhaps piloted by a ghost. Monkey feared they could be headed to any abyss outside reality. If he died now, he would really be dead, jokes aside. No children to carry on the De Brazza name. That was serious death. They could not possibly evolve a dead Man-Key to Superman in a million moons, never mind in the blink of an eye.

Monkey wished he had carried at least one of his gods. Just in case, he could be saved, reincarnated, or ushered into heaven— whatever kind of hereafter the particular god had prepared for him. He wanted all angles and angels covered.

Reincarnation could bring him back as a fly or even a banana! He had no idea where he had sniffed that reincarnation stuff. Like something was planting it in his head.

"How can you hope in a god who depends on you for transport?" asked a gentle, small voice. He knew without a doubt it was the unseen God. He was the jealous one. Even though Monkey was baptized Christian, he was still jealous. The omnipresent God who did not need to travel any place because he was already there could not possibly understand the transport problems of his junior colleagues, why Monkey had to give them a lift once in a while.

Monkey almost scratched his head but thought better of it under the present circumstances. He had just now realized how tiresome, cumbersome, and utterly ridiculous it was to carry any god. It was not as if his gods were waiting to grow up and take over; he would always carry them. If Giraffe was right and everything was possible with the unseen God, there was one God who could carry everyone else but whom no one needed to carry. He was everywhere and could not be contained to be carried around.

As for his other gods up the tree, he was the one making all the sacrifices, carrying, cleaning and protecting them. He was even worried about what would happen to them all alone up the tree if he died. The wind and rain could bring them crashing down. That was supposed to be their role, but he did not even trust them. How could he when they had only one permanent facial expression as if they were in a coma? Instead, he had become their savior and god!

Right now, with death as a real possibility, he needed a god that could carry him here and hereafter. He had never really worried about immortality. Death had always seemed a faraway mythical tragedy that happened only to others. Whatever happened after death was way out there and had no business interfering with his day-to-day life. Besides, he had insured himself with many gods. One of them would surely carry him across ... but to where? What if there really was something waiting out there that he had not yet dealt with?

Aero circled the Devil's Mountain and prepared to land in reverse. The human nest was cumbersome. She was not to let her cargo hit the ground before her but she also had to mind her tail. It was spooky, landing backward like some witch. In a certain spot it always felt like, a familiar spirit took control and put her on autopilot. She was almost there, the spooky energy creeping in preceded by the bad smell. Today it smelled like monkey waste. Aero's wingspan was so vast she could see her own shadow on the ground below. That made her more afraid.

Slowly she started sinking into autopilot, resigned to her fate as the devil's pet landing backward on the molehill he called his mountain.

The devil is not interested in the height of a mountain, only the depth, she thought.

Suddenly an unidentified flying object came spiraling directly onto her path. Whether a shooting star or a falling planet, she was putty if it hit her. She had seen many flying objects in her time but not a flying goliath cow whose horns were aimed at her face. Her appointment with death was finally here!

The cow passed just inches above her in the few most ominous seconds of her life. A massive udder rained snow-white milk on her and her cargo. It was the kind of joke Daddy Axis and his cronies would pull. Only God or the devil could fly without wings, and the spirit of God was not in the business of fear.

At the precise moment when Aero lost her balance, both the snake and the monkey realized whatever was carrying them was flying backward. There was only one place in the world you entered or left in reverse, the Devil's Mountain. In one shared moment of terror, three living creatures connected by a human nest screamed the only name their inner selves knew could save them: "Jeeeesus!"

Everyone heard two voices besides his or her own and passed out cold. The nest hurtled earthwards. The forces of darkness that had started taking over Aero trembled and bowed involuntarily to The Name. Then they stood aside to enjoy the tragedy. The devil is not in the business of saving anyone from imminent death. Terror is too enjoyable to interrupt!

THE JESUS TREE

❧

When Aero came to, she was neatly perched on the greenest tree she had ever seen. The leaves and branches blanketed her completely. She was not afraid, and that was uncharacteristic. There had never been a time she was not afraid. As she breathed in and out, she had a sense of something or someone heavy and smelly leaving her inner being, the substance or spirit of fear.

Something had changed from the moment she had uttered that name ... uttered? It was the first time she had ever made an audible sound, and it was a name. It had just popped out, breaking the laws of nature that said she could never vocalize without a voice box. Welcome to the world of miracles!

The tree was cool and serene. The warm rays of the morning sun pierced through the greenest green leaves.

God must love green, she thought.

It felt like someone had embraced her in a peaceful rest. She was physically and mentally exhausted, weary from carrying all manner of burdens around the world and back again.

"I am resting on The Name!" she whispered to the leaves, making no sense even to herself. What kind of peculiar thinking was "resting in The Name" on top of the Devil's Mountain?

The last time she had checked, this mountain had no plant that fit the description of a "tree," only shrubs, thorns, and rocks. What if she had died and gone to heaven? She was the pet of Axis, unworthy of any measure of love from God or even mentioning his name! Yet she had called on The Name and lived.

Aero recalled her accident, the cow, the milk, and the tumbling down before she passed out. Even if this tree had existed before today, there was no ordinary way she could have landed safely on it when she was passed out. Someone bigger than Daddy Axis had her back right now, and it felt safe. She scanned as far as possible without moving her body.

The miracle tree was overhung with nests. Hundreds, perhaps thousands, of birds were singing morning praises to the creator. This was a peculiar, massive tree whose length touched heaven and earth, its breadth an umbrella overshadowing the Devil's Mountain entirely. She was perched closer to earth than heaven.

Every branch sported a different kind of earth's best-looking fruits. There were mangoes, papayas, plums, bananas, and many she had never tasted.

This tree can only stand on the roots of God, she thought dreamily, succumbing to the sweetest sleep. *It must be a Jesus tree!*

The Jesus tree swayed forward and backward in the morning breeze, gently rocking the trio to sleep. Monkey was curled up on the branch above Aero, safe but still out cold. Black Mamba was snug and out in the human nest that still dangled from Aero's foot. Aero nested on her newfound peace.

The Name worked in mysterious ways. For three days and nights, three unlikely bedfellows slept peacefully in a miracle tree that was and yet was not.

The trio woke up at different times on the third day. Aero was up at dawn but could not join the other birds in the singing. She realized her wings were glued to her sides and her feet to the branch by the sticky milk of the flying devil cow! The yucky stuff had probably stopped her from tumbling down to her death, but she knew it was a miracle that had saved her, a miracle in The Name. That milk was intended for bad, but the power in The Name had turned it around for good. She also distinctively remembered two other voices besides her own calling on The Name. Perhaps they were just echoes of her very first sound.

Her immediate concern was starving to death in the Jesus tree surrounded by the best food in the world but chained by the devil! She was still not afraid. If The Name had saved her from death, it could still throw a plum her way.

"Not that I deserve to live," she whimpered suddenly. "I am scum of the devil. Why do you care, Jesus? Why did you save my life? Oh, Jesus, if you are the one, please reveal yourself and feed me before I doubt and die. Feed me till I want no more!"

Suddenly a papaya flower budded out on a branch within reach of her mouth. In moments, it opened up to reveal the tiniest green papaya. She marveled at it, her huge eyes widening by the second. "Thank you, Jesus!" she whispered, and it got a little bigger. "Thank you, Jesus, thank you, Jesus, thank you ..." she beaked continuously, and those words seemed to contain life. The fruit kept enlarging as she watched!

Little birds peered at her from their nests. They did not appear shocked by the growing fruit. Aero instinctively knew they had seen the provision of The Name before and simply lived in thankful expectancy. They did not worry about what they would eat next. What a carefree way to live, expecting a miracle every day!

She peered down the tree at earth as if she were on another planet. In a way, she was. The Jesus tree was really so tall, so wide, and she was sure, so deep, it reminded her of a song she once heard little humans sing under another tree, describing the love of Jesus being as high, as deep, and as wide.

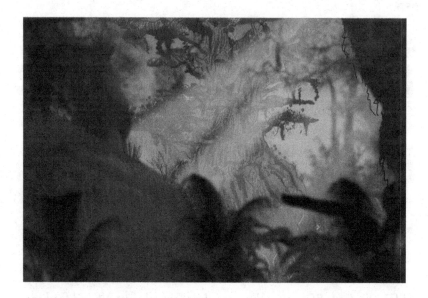

The little children danced round and round a round tree, hands joined in a circle as Aero secretly watched from up the tree. Daddy Axis who had business nearby broke them up by sending the village bully. The tiny tots scampered for safety and held tightly to their mothers. Aero had only wished she had a mother.

Daddy Axis hated when she had fun. If the children had been pulling feathers off a living bird, he would have made her watch. There were times he transformed into the biggest snake. She was terrified of snakes and he knew it but he enjoyed her fear. He also poked fun at her gigantic size.

Aero was in a dilemma. She wanted to be a pet of God. She had gathered that Jesus was the only way, but she was a pet of Axis. Jesus would have to steal her from the devil, and he was not a thief. Even if she ran away to him, he would probably do the right thing and return a lost pet to the owner. Because he was just, she had no hope. Sometimes it was just not just to be just!

She focused again on the fruit that had been growing. It had stopped growing when she stopped thanking. She was letting in fear and it was feeding on her faith, retarding the growth of her fruit. Why was she worried when she was safe in a Jesus tree? Whenever she dropped faith and embraced doubt, a crack started opening somewhere in her heart, letting in the fear.

"I get it now. Faith locks out fear!" she encouraged herself. "Thank you, Jesus, thank you, Jesus, thank you, Jesus ..." she whispered.

Her drying out papaya turned green again and resumed growing. When it attained what she believed was its natural size, it stopped growing and ripened for her to eat. She said a final *thank you, Jesus,* and dug in. Looking around, she realized every fruit was next to someone's nest. Some fruits were big, and some were small. Instinctively she realized everyone was getting provisions as big as their faith. Her papaya was as big as her expectation of its natural size. There were nests with nothing next to them and some tiny birds with fruits many times bigger than they were! There was no way they could finish that in one lifetime! She was the largest bird in the world, but her faith and fruit were not in the same league.

Aero noticed that those who had much kept sharing with the ones who had too little or nothing. Soon no one had too little or too much. They were also extremely happy singing thanks and praises to The Name. Aero thanked God for her meal and prayed for those who did not have. She could not move or gesture to them to share her provisions. If she lived to see the next day, she decided she would fast and somehow give her day's share to those who had nothing. If they ate the fruit of her faith, perhaps they would develop their own. It would be her little way of honoring The Name. Aero felt unworthy of Jesus, but she wanted him to know she had found him more than worthy of her praise. She wanted him to have her papaya, even though he had given it to her in the first place. She would give it to him by giving it to others whom he loved just as much as he must love her!

REVELATIONS

❧

At noon the same day, De Brazza Monkey the Man-Key woke up angry with himself. He was also three days hungry!

"So much for an idiot following *a voice*!" he seethed at himself. He was unaware of Aero one branch below him. His experience of the Jesus tree was different from hers. Instead of birds, it was full of monkeys. The tree had fruits of every kind and then bananas, all the different kinds of bananas in the world, and every one belonged to someone. The other monkeys were unaware of him. The tree was so big and high up in the sky that it had no business producing bananas. It was supernatural.

He focused on the monkeys that owned the bananas. Some had bunches upon bunches, others had one bunch or one banana, and still others had nothing. The rich kept sharing with the poor, but they still had more after giving.

"What happened to the saying, *If you feed ten hungry monkeys, you will be the eleventh?*" he wondered. Whenever the monkeys went back to their spots after giving to the poor, they found more bananas than they had before. The increase in bananas was always multiples of the original number! Amazing, but nobody was sharing with him. They were oblivious of his presence.

He scratched his head. All his gods were on a tree in Samburu, wherever that was from here. None could prevail on the other monkeys to share a banana. Today was the first day he had called only on The Name, and he had been taken to heaven. It had to be heaven. Where else could a tree that bridged heaven and earth grow? It had to be somewhere in the garden of God. He hoped the banana was not the forbidden fruit, or another original sin was coming. He did not need a snake to tempt him. Besides, there was no way one could be lurking around there.

If the unseen God could grow such an array of bananas, there was no point having a banana god. At last, a God who could carry him, a one-stop general practitioner God! He was tired of carrying specialized gods for his every need! It had to be the invisible God of Giraffe, the omnipresent and omniscient. But how was he supposed to prove his existence or his intentions if he had no face? Monkey judged character best by facial expressions!

He was no stranger to prayer. He had performed many rituals and had said liturgies and mantras from dawn to dusk. He was even baptized to the God of Giraffe. If the right God revealed himself, he knew of ways to honor him. He scratched his head again.

An hour and a rumbling stomach later, not a single god had responded. He had never really felt a connection to any of them. That was why he was very excited when The Voice had approached. He had just assumed it was from one of the gods, and he could always figure out which one later. Now he thought about it, all he ever wanted was a connection, a relationship, a god who spoke and listened in the closest of friendships. He narrowed it down now to The Voice that had led him on the mysterious quest for instant evolution and The Name that had saved his life. The Voice wanted to be heard. The Name wanted to be known. There were two gods after him, and he did not know which one to go after. And one of those had to be the jealous God. If he chose the wrong one, there would be fury. He scratched his head again.

If he went after the jealous God, he would have to lose all the others. He scratched his head and got a revelation. The one true God was jealous for monkey, because he had made him without anyone's help! Another scratch got another revelation. All other gods were made from raw material the jealous God had made! A few hunger pangs later, he heard a gentle, small voice.

"God is a true gentleman," Whispered the gentle small voice. "When invited for a meal along with other gods, he lets them go first!"

No wonder he was in the process of starving to death! He looked on with a painful appetite as other monkeys munched on bananas.

"Please help me, God of Giraffe, in the name of Jesus!" he prayed. Suddenly an inner knowing told him he was on the right track and well equipped in The Name to get his own bananas! At first he felt inadequate, totally unworthy. He also had no idea what length or accent of prayer God his creator preferred before he could hear him. Should he sing it, mumble it, dance it, lay prostrate on the tree, stand on his head ... what? He scratched his head again to think.

Hours later, he was sure he would surely die of starvation. He called on The Name from somewhere in the core of his being with everything that he was, all the way to the lisp in his speech.

"Thank you, unseen God of Giraffe, whose image on earth is man for saving my life," he prayed. "If I call on you foolishly, remember I am only a monkey and answer me in your wisdom. I do not know if I am in a dream, a vision on earth, or in heaven, but I sure would appreciate you forgiving my sins and sending your son, Jesus, with a banana. Amen."

Suddenly a lady monkey threw a ripe banana accurately onto his lap, waved, and smiled. He smiled back shyly, not sure she was real. The banana was.

"Thank you, God. Thank you, Jesus," he said as he peeled it

hastily. But just before he could taste it, his eye caught the pleading ones of a scrawny-looking monkey who seemed to be starving to death. His rib cage was visible. He had wounds all over his joints, and his eyes were bigger than his face.

This is all I need! he thought, losing his temper. *A beggar when I am starving myself.*

The beggar's eyes followed every movement Monkey made with his banana. His mouth opened along with his as he prepared to take a first bite. Monkey became angrier. Why couldn't the beggar pray for his own banana?

The still, small voice came back, barely audible.

"You haven't done anything to deserve the banana either!"

Hand and banana froze an inch from his mouth. It was true. Instead, he had grieved the creator of the universe by placing him in the same category with gods made from stuff he had first created. He had been discontented with the way God had made him and had just about sold his soul in an attempt to become human. In spite of himself, God had spared his life and given him a banana. It dawned on him that God had created him a monkey on purpose, not from leftovers or mistakes of another evolving creature. If God wanted a man, he knew how to make one without remodeling a monkey! The Voice was wrong. He was going with The Name.

"Forgive me, Jesus, for my selfishness," he whispered.

When he focused on the scrawny monkey again, he was moved to tears. Perhaps God had intended him to be a monkey at this precise moment to show kindness to this beggar. He gave a wet smile to the beggar and extended his hand. He was still salivating with appetite, but he managed to give the heavenly banana away. It gave him more satisfaction to please God. The beggar grabbed the banana and gobbled it down with a most thankful look.

"Thank you," the beggar said.

"Jesus loves you," De Brazza replied. "Thank him, not me!"

Those words just came out. He had not planned them, but he meant them sincerely. There was no response from the other monkey who was too busy eating. De Brazza felt honored to be used as the hands of God in providing for someone else.

"I thank you, Lord, for trusting me with the interests of the poor. Now I know you as my source, I am not worried about my own provisions." He yawned involuntarily. "God, I am thrilled to meet the new creature you are turning me into!"

Suddenly seven bunches of ten huge ripe bananas grew on the branch he was sitting on. He thanked the God of multiplication and dug in. On his second banana, he remembered something Giraffe had said about tithing. *Ten percent of everything God gives his creatures belongs to him, even time.* Counting seven bananas, he put them aside with a prayer.

"Lord, I see no priest or pastor to handle this, but it is your tithe from a monkey called De Brazza because your wish from now on is his command." The seven bananas disappeared. The remaining bananas started growing bigger till they covered the entire area the tithed seven had occupied. They also looked fresher than before. It was then he saw the insects, worms, and other tiny destructive creatures, but they were all headed away from him. Strangely, they had no interest in his bananas.

He waved at the scrawny monkey again and gave him a bunch. The beggar snatched the bunch and held so tight that some were badly squeezed. He was afraid someone might want some. He hid himself under some leaves clinging to his treasure. De Brazza motioned to a female monkey with a kid on her back to join him. She sat nearby, a little wary of him as he passed a banana. The female cut it in half and shared with her kid. Instead of eating, the toddler quickly slid off the mother's back, broke his half banana to a quarter, and trotted to another kid on another mother's back to give him a piece. Suddenly, the first kid's banana became whole. He cut half and gave the mother of the kid he had just fed. Suddenly he was holding a bunch with seven bananas. He put one where De Brazza had put the tithe, and it disappeared. The remaining bunch of six became bigger to cover the missing piece and looked fresher. Soon he was giving one to everyone. The unseen God kept adding when they tithed and multiplying when they gave. De Brazza scratched his head again, unable to keep up with the math.

"Giving to the poor is loaning God," said the gentle, small voice. "His interest is on your faith!"

Then Monkey saw where the insects and worms had gone. They were mobbing the scrawny beggar who still clung tightly to his first bunch, stinking, squeezed, and oozing rotten. Having no faith to tithe or give, he had not been increased or multiplied. He was also unable to receive from others because his fists were closed on what he already had.

De Brazza felt sorry for the beggar who had clearly been skiving God's math lessons. He scratched his head and pondered the newly learned formula.

You have to let go of your treasure to keep it. He did. He kept looking for anyone needy to whom he could give and catch a blessing. Soon others shared their favorite fruits with him. Some he had never seen tasted better than he could ever have dreamt or imagined. He was tempted to hide them just like the beggar, but he heeded the gentle, small voice.

Monkey feared if he had not called on The Name, he would have died thinking that bananas were the tastiest fruit God ever made. He was never going to limit God again. The branch he sat on was now sprouting with all kinds of beautiful fruits along with the bananas. He continued thanking God and doing his math, but the formula remained the same. It was more blessed to give than to receive. The unseen God manifested in very unmistakable ways.

He is alive! Monkey thought. *I cannot possibly keep such a big secret to myself.* Monkey had found his purpose. He was not sure about the correct title or terminology, but he wanted to be the biggest gossiper in the jungle, spreading the secret of the hidden treasure. He had found the map and cracked the secret code. The missing truth was in The Name all along. The Name was The Way! It was also The Life, so they needed not fear the attackers on the way to the treasure. Yup! A gossiper was as good a career as any other if he was passionate about it.

Monkey was not kidding himself that he was as good a speaker as Parrot, Mole, or even Mrs. Zebra. Neither did he have the royal commanding presence of Lion, the beauty of Tiger, the grace of Giraffe, or the respectability of Elephant. There were those who thought he was cool for resembling the image of God, but he felt totally unequipped for this call to be God's Gossiper. He spoke with a lisp!

"God does not call you to service because you are ready or eloquent," whispered the gentle, small voice. "He calls you to trust and obey him as he makes you ready and eloquent."

De Brazza felt so honored beyond his worthiness that he held his head in his hands and sobbed. God was so big and so holy, yet he had time for one idolatrous monkey.

"Forgive me, God, for everything and teach me to make you smile even if I cannot see it!" The tears kept coming. Soon huge teardrops were falling steadily on a huge, black rock sitting on the branch below him. At some level of consciousness, he wondered how such a huge rock had climbed the tree or what mighty being had thrown it so high. But he was wetting the wreckage of his crashed plane. The Aeromass of The Mass was perched below him. He finally whimpered himself to contented sleep.

Snake Dares God!

☙

Snake came to at sunset, still in the human nest that dangled from Aero's leg. He recalled falling thousands of feet to his death with a brain machine still sitting on his head. It was still sore and flat. He smelled monkey poop and urine. That was good. His brain was still running his sense of smell and had not poured out in the chaos of death. But how had the monkey smell followed him to heaven? Was he not supposed to have a new body? He still had the same head! So he was not in heaven, but he was not on earth either. For the moment, he was glad he just *was*. Just to *be* was something too, though he did not know what he meant by that. Wherever he was, far or near, it was dead silent. Perhaps it was the abode of Axis, a dark and silent heaven, the nothing out there after death.

He was getting claustrophobic and needed to look outside. The smell hit harder, jolting him back to consciousness. He was still in the human nest, but the brain maker must have fallen off. He hoped the instructions to remain under cover had expired with the accident. The human nest rocked back and forth in the wind. Still wary of the instructions, he craned his neck out and aimed his eyes downward. He missed a heart attack by a fang. The ground was too far below! He drew back with a sharp hiss. He did not know which was greater, his fear of heights or of the dark.

A calm authority emanated from this awesome place, and it was not from The Voice. It had to be The Name he had hissed when he was about to die. Never in his wildest dreams could he have imagined that name on his fangs. All along it was lurking in there, waiting for the face of death to purge it out. Something inside of him was patented to the other god through The Name, something that blasphemed Axis. The Name should have choked him, but it had not. Jesus, Jesus, there was just something about that name.

Two other voices had called out The Name along with him. Giraffe had said that where two or three were gathered in that name, they would get whatever they asked. But he was not gathered together with anyone and certainly not in The Name. If anything, he had been gathered there by The Voice.

Thinking positively about the Christian cult was dangerous, the result of the flattened status of his head and brain. Besides, any kind of peculiar thinking could easily happen on the Devil's Mountain. He was also on top of this massive tree that bore no semblance to Axis. Instead it reeked of a Jesus Tree. He had never heard that expression before. Either he had brain damage or The Name was alive. Jesus, Jesus, there was just something about that name.

The Name seemed to invite him to look up and not down, as if up was life and down was death. Slowly he raised his head again, and all his fear was gone. He looked around the tree, flicking his tongue in and out tasting the air. Then he saw them. There were broods of every kind of snake hanging, slithering, and snaking all around the branches. They looked extremely beautiful, contented at being serpents and enjoying the gift of sunshine that seeped through the rainbow colored leaves. Funny he was thinking of sunshine as a gift, a thing that was older than Tortoise, Crow, and everyone in the jungle. Surely the sun was just a part of the state of being, but now he was tagging someone's ownership on it. Nothing is a gift unless someone owns and treasures it first. Jesus, Jesus, there was just something about that name.

Suddenly Black had a vision. It had to be a vision because he was not asleep. He was outside of himself looking in and liked what he saw. A very handsome snake drawing *oh's* and *wows* from others. Suddenly he grew legs like a lizard, and everyone ran away as if he were a terrible disease. Lizards of all types took the vacated places. He walked up to them, proud to show off legs that resembled their own. Some broke their own legs as they scrambled to escape his presence. Not a lizard remained.

One by one, he got the legs of different species, but they took off either in fright or disgust. At some point, the tree became a millipede haven and he got a million legs. As far as he knew, millipedes never won a running race, but those millipedes deserved to be in the Olympics. The different creatures ran in only one direction—*away.*

Finally it was humans. The image of God came in all colors and sizes, as male and female, and some he could not tell. Surely these would accept him. He had legs and an advanced brain just like them. Instead, they put him in a cage and studied him with both artificial and natural eyes. Then they came with a box of tools, cleaned and prepared to dissect him for further study. They needed to know what species he had evolved from. They did not care who he was, only to whom he was related!

Black called on The Name again and lived. The humans lost their sight and scalpels and he was able to escape. His legs were good only for running away, a repulsive and ridiculous burden. He wanted his original self back, but it was too late. Then, still in the vision, he heard Giraffe's voice.

"Everyone is wonderfully and fearfully made to God's own specifications. Thankful contentment is the resting place of the soul!"

How right that was. But he had corrected the master's masterpiece and become a freak on earth, perhaps even in heaven! He had sold his integrity, his soul, and wasted the love of his family chasing a worthless dream and blaspheming his creator! But when he had called on The Name, his life had been saved.

He shivered out of the vision, extremely frightened. He was relieved to see his smooth torso without legs. For the first time, he felt beautiful. Jesus, Jesus, there was just something about that name!

"So I have a cursed ancestry as a snake, but somewhere within me is a fingerprint of God!" he said to himself. "Jesus, Jesus, I know that I know that I know that there is just something about that that name!" He sighed.

Black pressed his head against the human nest and attempted to remold it. It was still too flat. He needed to rule out his physical condition as the cause of the peculiar thought line. What if The Name only saved his life out of common decency, a neighborly thing between gods?

A flood of doubt washed over him, and he decided to steer clear of any deity mumbo jumbo for now. He would go solo, believing only in himself till he was sure.

Right now it was safer to hang on to his rooted beliefs. There was no hereafter for snakes since the curse in the garden of God. No heaven and certainly no hell. It would be unfair to put snakes in hell. Axis alone had planted sin in the garden of God regardless of his snake disguise.

When the son of God walked on earth, it was humans that killed him. He was never bitten by a snake even though he most likely walked barefoot. But now he was alive and well, preparing a place in his father's mansion for all his friends. Snakes had never fit that description.

There was also the matter of Jesus' forthcoming wedding feast.

Everyone knew snakes were disinvited long before he met his bride. It was humiliating to be cursed and rejected by the very God that made him. He coiled and recoiled in the bottom of the human nest, wishing he could go to sleep and never wake up. Deep down, he wished there was a bridge between snakes and God. It did not occur to him that right then he was sitting on it.

Suddenly he raised his neck proudly. Black Mamba was neither an ordinary snake nor a worm. He knew deep down that The Name was greater than Axis. He was on to the one true God, but being a snake made him illegitimate. It was time to love his family by keeping them far away from any religions and gods, to be their head and protector, the closest thing they would get to God. He would personally give them a good life on earth, forbidding any talks of happily or unhappily ever after. That would spare them the disappointment planned at the end of time when serpents were shamed and turned away at the pearly gates.

Black had never chosen to be a snake—or even to exist for that matter. It was not fair that he should feel ashamed of just being! Neither was what his first ancestor did his fault. It was especially not his fault that God in all his wisdom had chosen to create a devil. The Mamba family did not need mansions and streets of gold. They were contented with dust castles. They were not going to crash the Jesus wedding if he had chosen to exclude them. His bride could not be all that smashing either. For crying out, who ever heard of a bride with such a name as *The Church?*

It was exhausting business to process all the details of earth, heaven, hell, now, hereafter, thereafter, forever, and never. Amen!

"If you ever want us, God, you know the Black Mamba address," he hissed and then raised his head even higher. "Oh, and do not bother sending anyone; you must contact my family personally!"

Everything would have been so neat if there was no end of time, no God, devil, heaven or hell, no questions or answers, just to be and then not to be. But there was this something he could not flick his tongue on, and now he was sinking into a very troubled sleep, and his head was still too flat.

"Jesus, Jesus, there is just something about that name," he hissed softly and then slept on it.

THE DOCTRINES OF DEMONS

❦

When Aero came to again, warm drops of liquid were pouring down her stuck wings, loosening the grip of the devil glue. She was unaware of a repentant monkey crying over his sins. The unseen God kept up his mysterious ways, using the warm teardrops to set the captive free. One thing she was sure of, she would live and not die!

"Thank you, Jesus, because you are saving me right now," she whispered. That was before her ears were pierced by the ugliest sound of hell on earth from all the way down the Jesus Tree. A furious Daddy Axis was thundering curses and obscenities at someone, his anger growing to bomb proportions by the second. Aero knew that tone. Someone was in deep trouble. She focused her eyes down and saw Mundu the madman demon who did animals in Ninety-Nine. Opposite was Milika, a she-devil who led Samburu humans on the crooked, wide road, the flying milk cow. God had used her glue milk that was meant for evil to hold her in place, or she would have crashed to her death.

Mundu knelt on one knee in supplication to Axis. His other knee was raised because he was in authority over the cowering cow down on all fours. She no longer resembled the confident shooting cow that rode the skies earlier.

Aero thought of the three devils as the satanic trinity. They were arranged in a sharp triangle, the two field agents on opposite corners while Axis stood alone on the sharp edge. Their disguise for the day was the stuff of which legends are made. Axis was a man-beast with muscles sprouting everywhere. Two massive heads each with a short stout horn in the middle were alight with four flaming yellow eyes. A red loincloth covered his bottom but not his dinosaur tail, which belonged in a museum of size. His humanlike torso was a thick coat of short red hair down to his webbed bare feet.

Flame-colored hair longer than a lion's mane sprouted out of his four nostrils. This made his mouths invisible, and his voice came ominously from no specific point. His dagger nails resembled Mr. Krueger's, longer than his fingers and toes. He waged a claw menacingly at Mundu.

All the eyes of Axis could look in different directions at the same time, reminding Aero of the witch chameleon, their autonomous functionality a pathetic attempt to fake omnipresence. This was completed by two eyes on the back of each head and one each on top of the massive heads. He was always searching for ways to counterfeit God. The two yellow eyes that looked up the tree worried Aero.

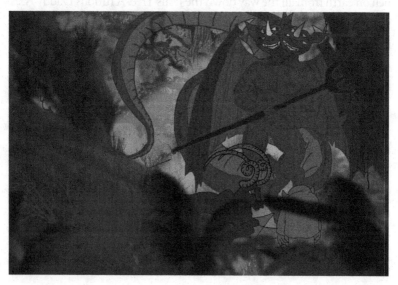

"I am not afraid," she told herself repeatedly. "Greater is he that is in me! This too will pass in Jesus' name!"

She realized they could not see her and the Jesus tree; if they could, they would have gotten to her by now. Axis kept gesturing wildly, his invisible mouth a smoking pit of obscenities. The government of The Mass was hierarchical. Milika the cow was lower in rank than Mundu her boss. Axis did not care to address a junior directly even though everything was her fault. Instead he relished humiliating Mundu because ultimately he was responsible for whatever the juniors did wrong.

"You useless unreliable spirit! What happened here?" Axis thundered at Mundu.

"You useless, unreliable, worthless servant! What did you do with the master's Aeromass?" Mundu passed on the insult to Milika.

The cow appeared thunderstruck, her skin dotted like a strange disease. Aero recognized extreme fear. The cow was still down on all fours on a carpet of her own fresh dung and urine. Her nose was planted on the rocky soil in supplication to the bosses. She appeared more scared of Mundu than Axis. When his hurled insult hit, her buffalo-like horns fell off and cluttered like china.

"Masters, I am very sorry I frightened the Aeromass before she could land the cargo! I was just having a little fun," she whimpered. More milk poured out of her udder to mix with the dung.

"You lazy idiot!" Mundu thundered. "No one ever broke a schedule to have fun in over two thousand years since the cross! We celebrated as they laid J. C. in the tomb, thanks to our master here. But that traitor rose again on the third day, and our honeymoon was over. Now Madam Leaking Milk, have you accomplished such a feat as our master that you take time to have a little fun with his bird?"

"I am sorry! God tempted me!" The cow demon cowered. "It's like he is setting camp in Kenya after being foreclosed and kicked out of America. What can I say, masters? Forgive me!"

"You used the F. word!" The madman was really mad now. At some level, Axis seemed to enjoy the exchange filled with anger and fear.

"Quit the milk, imbecile. You are soaking us all!" Mundu hissed. Milika stopped the flow, but Mundu was not done. He waved a thick finger at her udder, and the teats sealed completely. The milk continued to flow into her veins. There was a moment of silence and great expectation from the two senior devils. Milika did not seem to get the joke until her entire udder and four teats swelled like balloons. Her eyes bulged out in pain. Axis's own eyes widened in glee as the madman continued pointing an excited bewitching finger. To their amusement, Milika writhed in perfect agony.

Aero thought she was going to die. She could not watch pain inflicted on anyone, even a demon. Suddenly all four teats burst with the loudest splash as Milika rolled upside down giving thunderous moos of pain. Four fountains of snow-white milk erupted like a volcano and shot to the skies missing Aero by a feather.

Axis was so excited he did a double somersault landing on his two heads. His massive tail balanced perfectly high in the air, the sharp dagger tip pointing right at Aero's eye. An eye on the back of his head stared vacantly at Aero. His horns dug deep into the ground as four dark caves of hairy nostrils spat unholy fire. It caught on the dry twigs, igniting the pitiful dry grass, and then started spreading. Aero hoped the invisible Jesus tree was also fireproof. She was no longer resting on The Name but hiding in it.

A triple somersault had Axis perfectly balanced on the tip of his tail. The fire stopped from his wind as suddenly as it had started. Aero was now face-to-face with one of his heads, his eyes boring into hers. She froze, unable even to blink. She dared not move a muscle even though she knew he could not see her. Then she saw into the depths of the sea in one of the eyes. The insides resembled unlatched gates with an inviting All Are Welcome sign. Suddenly she caught a glimpse behind the gate, before a curtain seemed to close. A lake of fire grinned, its mouth open to reveal its tongue, a spouting fountain of rippling red, orange, and yellow waves spreading far and wide from a well stocked source, a bottomless pit!

Aero trembled like a leaf. Jesus tree or not, the flesh was still flesh. A "Thank you, Jesus, for saving me" cluttered out of her teeth. God used her involuntary trembling to loosen her trapped wings some more. Before her heart could stop, Axis leapt neatly back to his feet and turned his attention back to Mundu. He still needed some answers.

"She is sorry she frightened the Aeromass," Mundu said humbly, as if the culprit Milika was not present. "She has been duly punished, my lord."

"Never mind the stupid bird!" Axis shouted as Aero winced up in the tree. "We are strategizing for Armageddon, our final battle to take the ancient throne, and your troops are having a little fun with a bird! Kill that mortal creature before she becomes an eternal diversion!"

"Right away, sir—soon as she is found, sir!" Mundu promised. Aero experienced her worst moment of despair. The creature she called Daddy had just sentenced her to death. If Jesus did not keep her, she would be lucky to be history. No one knew her enough to remember her, not even herself. If she died and went to heaven, they had better know her. She could not even introduce herself. Nor would she have known her creator or what he had purposed for her.

"Who am I, Lord? Just who am I, Jesus?" she whimpered.

"Aero has a soft heart, one that could incline toward the enemy," Axis continued thoughtfully. "Should J. C. knock at her door—and he knocks on all doors—she will open it. We should never have brought her to Kenya. Christianity is rubbing off on animals and birds like body lice from the humans!"

"That's right, sir. These Kenyans pray even to answer a call of nature, but we will soon be on top of it."

"Top of it, that's crap! The hyena got saved and baptized while you were on top of it! The bird has to die before she calls on The Name!"

"We will need another transport, boss," Mundu said, tactfully changing the death topic. "I kind of rely on the Aeromass a lot for this project."

"Her mother just laid another egg," Axis said as Aero stifled a gasp. "We are legal to steal from her without interference from the J. C. cronies because she dabbles in witchcraft. And get this insect out of here!" He pointed disgustedly at the cow.

Mundu pointed another finger at Milika, and her udder was completely healed.

"Rise up and walk!" Mundu mimicked Jesus. The cow rose up as Axis laughed. Aero winced, feeling the slap of the blasphemy.

"Say thank you and go back to your station. No more fun games!" he said, dismissing Milika.

"Thank you, boss," Milika said before vanishing into thin air. But as she flew back to Samburu, she vowed to do something so destructive to the pets of God that Axis would promote her above Mundu. Then she would have her revenge on her ex-boss. Time was not a problem. She could wait till J. C.'s second coming if need be. No one knew when the end would come. Not even Axis. Milika just hoped it was after she had hurt Mundu badly. On the way, she kept transforming herself to different creatures, not for the fun of it, but to defy Mundu, her way of sticking her tongue out at him. That madman was just too uptight!

Back under the Jesus tree, the two devils continued talking.

"Has God really bowed out of America?" Mundu asked conversationally.

"No. His cronies like TBN, Daystar CBN and every J.C. nut

will not let him go bankrupt. God's American neighbors include Joyce Mayer and that conniving female Pink Panther who would birth the 'Church of all Nations.' His next door is our own most wanted good old Billy Graham whose son Franklin spends his life holed up in the Samaritan's Purse. Two thousand years later that poison purse is still around!

"There's a John Hagee Today." Mundu offered lamely.

"I'll be there tomorrow!" Axis said with a curse.

"I know," Mundu said without emotion. 'It's predicted in both the Hal Lindsay and Jack Van Impe reports."

"Damn humans!" Axis cursed. "Lunatic Express is all fueled up at Copeland. Their driver Benny Hinn is buckled up. All we need is their cheerleading conductor, Mr. Smiley face Good Looks Joel Osteen! They have God's own bouncer T. D. Jakes for ticketing and security. I tell you God still has a nest in America."

"I have faith in you, boss," Mundu said, wishing he worked in America. He still thought there was less work there than in Kenya, where even animals had started soaking in the Holy Ghost.

"Good. America may be the tallest tree with the roots of God, but I have my worm well in place. For now, let's just crash the Kenyan animals before we have an epidemic on our hands. I wouldn't be here personally if yours was not the most important assignment right now!"

"No problem, boss," Mundu said, bulging out on the compliment.

"Remember, you and your troops have eternity to have fun once I am established on the highest throne," Axis said.

"Could I keep Aero for my errands in Ninety-Nine?" Mundu asked respectfully as Axis tapped his tail on the ground impatiently. He was not omnipresent and still had to roam the whole earth personally.

"I could have a spirit inhabit her," Mundu continued. "We have left her normal for too long."

"Just get her cargo intact!" Axis yelled. "Do with the ugly bird as you like." Then he leered, remembering how much Mundu enjoyed hurting birds. She had enough feathers to pluck out one by one. If he pulled them out sparingly, he could still keep her alive for a very long time. Axis did not like Mundu, but he got results. No harm in that kind of fun.

"She patented on me from the time she was hatched," Axis boasted. "It's a real kick when someone follows you blindly of their own free will, even if it is only a young chick. Kind of gives J. C. a kick in his smug shin for loving little ones from all walks of life! But what do you know—the parents keep handing them to us by rejecting God."

"Aero considers you her father," Mundu said.

"That's what makes the betrayal so sweet. She even believes I created her!" They laughed some more. "I forgot to teach my daughter that nothing exists that J. C. did not create, not even me!"

Aero's heart sank.

"The devil is a liar and a thief," she whimpered. Her past, present, and future, her very identity had been stolen! What a fool she had been! She felt shamed and worthless. Something had to be wrong with her to have a witch mother, get stolen as an egg, and to have been brought up by the devil. He planned to steal another egg from her mother, her brother or sister, and there was nothing she could do about it. As long as her mother—whoever that was—did witchcraft, every evil spirit had a legal right to torment her. Her entire body became numb. She feared she would never feel anything again, not even pain. Her eyes closed at her command, but there was no closing her ears.

"She is only a mortal," Mundu said. "You are Lucifer, son of the Morning Star, not J. C. saving everyone and everything that calls on your name. You have class, boss!"

"I Know." Axis bulged out proudly. "Be smart about killing her.

Remember, all life is still in the hands of God. His ear is not too dull to hear nor his arm too short to save her. If she has not called on The Name, we still have legal ground. Every mortal carries the death sentence of the original sin unless he or she has handed it in to J. C. Then it stops counting against them. Still there are those moments God allows the torment of the faithful for his own purpose and the creature's ultimate good. But I am in no mood to wait for the Ancient of Days to throw me a bone!"

"Remember all the dirt we pulled on Job the human?" Mundu said. "Talk of perfection! He had only one gate open, fear. We could only get in as the thing he feared the most!"

"God gave him back everything he lost many times over—kind of futile in the end," Axis replied, tapping his tail on the ground.

"Still, it was fun while it lasted. A rich, Godly man loses all his cattle, his ten children, and his entire body fills with sores. We have God's express permission to torment him and he knows it, but his friends blame him for his predicament. His wife almost gets him to curse God. Those were the good old days, boss!"

"But he didn't curse God!" Axis retorted angrily. "Next time you want to flatter me, at least use a winning example, not where we almost won!"

"Like the king who was eaten by worms?" Mundu said.

"Something like that." Axis grinned.

"And Eli fell off his chair when his son Judas committed suicide after his girl Jezebel was eaten by the village dogs!"

"Mongrels, but not in that order, Mundu. Mmmmmmmmm."

"I am learning to twist the Bible."

"I don't want you distorting facts till you are more subtle," Axis said thoughtfully. "Alter only the meanings for now."

"Remember, boss, you are also God," Mundu praised. "Even if Aero has called on The Name, you will find a gate, a crack, a tiny bitty weakness, and you will be home."

"She does not think much of her own self-worth," Axis said thoughtfully. "We can still convince her she is unworthy of God's love, that she is somewhere beyond grace."

"You have outdone yourself in that regard, boss," Mundu pointed out. "See what you have achieved with the snakes! Even *I* have started believing they are cursed beyond grace."

"Glad you noticed!" replied Axis. "Go ahead and enjoy the Aeromass when you find her; you have earned her."

"Thank you, boss," Mundu replied. "I have a whole bag of tricks to win her back from God, such as lack of faith, idolatry, hatred, jealousy, selfish ambition, fits of range, envy—"

"Okay, okay, I am the author and finisher of the lot. Don't you think I know them all? Just keep her away from love, joy, peace, patience, kindness, goodness, gentleness, self-control, and all that she can be. Even better, keep hitting on one of them till you wear her out completely."

"No problem, boss." Mundu wanted to say he knew them all too, but it was safer to let the boss win. "This whole country is patrolled inch by inch. She cannot escape except under J. C.'s wing. You know how he arms heaven to the teeth over one miserable sinner who repents!"

"Are you chickening?" Axis tested.

"No—never, boss. They are no match for us when we really get down to it," Mundu said.

"Well then, get down to it," Axis said.

Aero realized without a doubt if she did not give her life to Jesus immediately, she would lose it.

"My past is gone, but I still have something to say about the future," she whispered in a holy rage. "I give it to you, Jesus. Let me hide myself in you. I am only a bird, but when you died for man, you died for all creatures under his dominion. Before my mother was even an egg, you knew me and died for me. Please set my destination before me, the unique purpose for which you made me. Glorify yourself with my life!"

Suddenly her whole countenance changed as a new perspective hit her. Axis had unwittingly given her an inheritance by revealing his vile self. He was everything God was not, and she only needed to think opposite to know God. Though she could not read, Aero knew God's book already. The demons called it the unholy Bible.

They read it aloud over and over again, but not even Axis comprehended it. One day in a slip of the tongue he was wearing that day, he revealed that the Bible was understood only through the revelation of God, to whom it was patented. When he realized what he had done, giving due credit, he made it clear that he had personally authored many religious books while that god had only authored one. The Bible code was revealed selectively only to those who sought to know the author with all their heart. Axis's books were delicious morsels, and no one needed to know the author to understand and follow him. For that reason, the Bible was inferior.

Nevertheless, Axis wanted his army to know the Bible, infiltrate the enemy ranks from within. They needed the key to the mind of God if they were going to overthrow him. The failed coup in heaven once upon a time did not mean he could not rise again. Even J. C. died and rose from the dead, and Axis considered himself above him. He was going after God the Father as soon as he understood the intricacies of the Trinity, how three equaled one and one equaled three. It could be fatal to attack the one God he knew existed only to face three of him! The last time he tried, it was the Archangel Michael who led the forces of God. The real thing could be tricky.

Sometimes he attended church personally to gauge the understanding of the leaders. That way he could sneak in or out little tidbits that distorted entire scriptures. He also handled the destruction of Christian leaders' reputations personally these days.

Shaming them kept non-believers firmly out of church and prevented any desire to relate or be associated with God. Axis did not mind if everyone thought he had moved house to live in church.

Aero remembered the day a few junior demons were put in a classroom and forced to practice a few distortions like "God helps those who help themselves" and "everyone for themselves and God for us all" and "money is the root of all evil" among other common sense scriptures. They were not in the Bible, but everyone thought they were.

Aero realized that all along, God had been preparing her for just this moment. Apart from knowing the scriptures, she understood many human languages. The demons spoke them to the latest slang, even coining some phrases. By thinking of her only as an object, the devils had underestimated her learning capacity, which she had hidden well. Her knowledge was going to be invaluable to other creatures that sought to know God. In the end, even the painful nickname, the Aeromass, had served to camouflage her. God had turned her miserable existence into a miracle!

"Dear Jesus, this is Aero. I love you. Please say something before my heart explodes!" she prayed.

Aero experienced a deep sense of being accepted just as she was, past-less, present-less, nameless, tainted, filthy, and shamed. She began to envision herself as a newly hatched chick perched on the hand of Jesus, patenting on him forever to trust and obey, follow wherever he led. There was now no condemnation in her heart. For the first time ever, she was happy just to be.

"So this is the nature of your grace," she whimpered. "At last a future worth meeting!" She could only weep. Whether in the end she passed out or slept, she would never know, but this she knew without a doubt: she was patenting on The Name to be a pet of God.

Who Warmed the Holy Water?

ℰↄ

The three creatures on the Jesus tree were still unaware of one another. Snake and Monkey woke up at the same moment the devils discussed their fate. Snake could not see the speakers, but he could taste evil in the air. When Monkey spotted the unholy duo, he froze like a statue as his bladder gave. A stream of very warm urine snaked to Aero's back, melting the chains of the devil's glue milk.

Monkey darkened in embarrassment even though for all he knew he was alone. Aero was now the sleeping beauty having a beautiful dream. An angel monkey stood somewhere in the garden of God. On his hand was a coconut shell filled with holy water. He poured it steadily on her wings, and it was very warm—so warm that the chains of evil that held her captive began falling away. Her eyelids were heavy with sleep. The sun had set, but the son of God had risen early to set the captive chick free, the pet he had chosen for himself. Trembling devils scattered in seven directions, but she could still hear two of them. Their voices rose from the place where dreams and reality interweave; she was snoring but could still hear them.

"What do the snake and the monkey know about this whole business?" Axis asked. Snake was fully alert now. So there was a monkey! It was not a brain machine that had flattened his head but a monkey. Still he wished he could shut off his hearing. Whatever was talking down there sounded ominous.

"Yellow has the snake believing The Mass will fix legs on him," Mundu said. "The monkey is here to be evolved to a human in the twinkling of an eye!" Axis had another bout of laughter, and Mundu was pleased.

Snake experienced a twister of shivers more from anger than fear. He was counted among the bravest, the largest, and most poisonous snakes in the world. Whoever it was out there—god or devil—ought to be very afraid!

"It was ingenious how Yellow got Monkey and Snake to share a cabin on the Aeromass!" Axis joked. "Next time, assign him to a human comedian. He is hilarious."

"No problem, boss," Mundu replied warily. He was insecure when his boss praised the juniors.

"My boy Yellow is doing a good job. I was right to promote him," Axis pushed on, enjoying Mundu's insecurity.

Mundu flushed with jealousy, and Axis was more pleased. Unlike J. C., he was not afflicted with weaknesses like love, friendship, or loyalty. Axis was more of a politician, no permanent friends or enemies. Everyone was a potential disposable tool for his purpose. The fear of him and promises of greatness when they took over the throne of God kept his demons in complete obedience.

"Sir Axis, have the plans for the cargo changed?" Mundu asked.

"Absolutely not! Snake and Monkey go to the demon transit center. Your homeless colleagues will take over their bodies, no less than seven demons for each, including witchcraft. Monkey becomes a false prophet in the jungle to neutralize Owl. He resembles the image of God and all that crap; they will believe whatever he says. Dress him in charisma, cunning deceit, and pride. You know the routine, toss in some divination. He performs a couple of miracles in The Name of God, and no one asks which god. Let that Pastor Twiga lose some height!"

"Good idea, boss," Mundu said. "I could give Monkey a spirit guide, a voice of his ancestors talking through his banana god or something."

"Whatever works to sneak in our own doctrines. Just remember quality, not quantity. And in regards to quality, the subtle obscurity, like makeup on a woman, less is more. Just a tiny lie hidden in 99 percent truth is enough to keep J. C. crying."

"My people are lost for lack of knowledge!" Axis and Mundu chorused together.

"That is why I named my village Ninety-Nine," Mundu said.

"Only, it is my village," Axis corrected, not very politely. "I do not share my glory with anyone!"

"Yes, boss, no, boss!" Mundu stammered.

"So the monkey becomes as God and forgets evolving to a human, the snake becomes his high priest, medium, or a seer—whatever witchcraft the masses will go for. Keep them plying with my fire; give them the matches to light their way into the spirit world. As long as they play, they are legal to be visited by their worst nightmares."

"Why did you choose the snake?" Mundu asked.

"The serpent remains the smoothest negotiator since our little affair in the garden of God."

"I agree, boss, and the garden remains our biggest mortal scoop with immortal repercussions," Mundu complimented again. He knew Axis liked to be praised.

"Since then, snakes have believed themselves beyond the love and grace of their creator," Axis continued proudly. "Their name is used in the derogatory by both heaven and earth. They must summon a mountain of faith and not a mustard seed to rise above that. When anyone reaches the point of perfect hopelessness, they can be exploited, exploded for mass destruction, or imploded to self-destruction. Either way, we win."

"Cool, boss, just perfect," Mundu said.

"Let the two creeps keep on believing The Mass will evolve them to whatever in hell they want," Axis said. "Godlessness without contentment is hell's goldmine. As soon as they are entangled to a point of no return, we will demand some blood sacrifices too."

"I don't understand that bit," Mundu admitted.

"Monkey and Snake will lead a cult to rival Pastor Giraffe," Axis confided. "Eventually, they will recruit the faithful for a pilgrimage to Ninety-Nine where they will join your suicide divers!"

"But I have enough suicide divers, sir. Six hundred and sixty six assorted animals. We also have birds, snakes, and other reptiles hatched from stolen eggs."

"You dumb moron!" Axis exploded. "Who decides when we have enough?"

"You do, sir."

"Have we ever set limits on our wide roads?"

"No problem, boss." Mundu retreated and changed the topic. "Snake believes the eggs were protein, raw material for manufacturing his legs." They both laughed.

"It is fun being a devil!" Mundu said happily, but Axis was already serious again.

"I want to rise up spiritists, mediums, diviners, and everything otherworldly in Kenya. The youth will start their day by checking horoscopes, and babies will play with tarot cards and Ouija boards. No wife or mother of any species will serve a meal before consulting the occult."

"Why the females?" Mundu wondered. "Is the male not the head in Kenya?"

"One female will hand over a family. Whatever path a female

chooses, they flock the ones they love ahead of them. Take out the female and win the war!"

"The war?" Mundu persisted. "Most warriors are male!"

"I know that. Only this is spiritual warfare not a mortal combat!" Axis said, tapping his tail impatiently. Sometimes Mundu could be really dumb. "Prayer warriors and the intercessors are mostly female and armed to their booties. They are more vicious because they fight not just for themselves but for their loved ones as well. Make no mistake, God's latest model is fully loaded and equipped for mass destruction. She cries like she's made of water, but when she detonates on her knees, those tears are jagged, hard glass aimed at your jugular!"

"I have seen the Kenyan missiles when we serve their husbands traditional brews," Mundu agreed.

"Just don't underestimate them. Your job is to wear them down, cease their prayer life. Praying without ceasing energizes their guardian angels against us."

"But why are humans lapping up the occult faster than all other species? Learned, illiterate, secular, or churchgoers, they all want a piece of witchcraft," Mundu observed.

"They reason too much, trying to make sense of everything, even matters beyond their comprehension. It leaves little room for faith or absolute truth," Axis said. "Animals, on the other hand, are instinctive like little babies. When they patent on J. C., his existence becomes absolute truth. Childlike faith obligates the parent side of God to respond very protectively. Stop the bug before it spreads nationally. Never mind the churchgoers, the baptized, or the confirmed; focus on only those having or seeking a personal relationship with J. C. Allow the rest a comfortable form of godliness as long as they deny its power. They are not against us."

"About the hyena, my lord," Mundu said, changing the topic and eager to cover much ground while he had the boss's ear.

"I want my personal curse on that hyena!" Axis roared.

"We cannot curse what God has already blessed," Mundu worried. "Hyena and his girlfriend carry the mark, the one thousand generation blessing for those who love God. Ole Baba and Ole Mwana are their ancestors!"

"Are you angel or demon?" Axis roared. "Both are in the blasted blessed end of bloodline thousandth generation! Last I checked God still credits faith as righteousness. All they need is the slightest shred and the love covenant is renewed. We could well end up with an Abraham of the jungle!"

"No problem, boss!" Mundu promised.

"You keep saying 'no problem.' If those two marry, what do you think they will do with their litter?"

"Bring them up in the fear and admonition of God," Mundu replied calmly.

"Exactly," Axis said menacingly. "On second thought, give the snake the jungle cult. I have a better role for the Man-Key."

"What other role, sir?" Mundu asked.

"Perfecting blood sins."

"You are losing me," Mundu confessed.

"Unlike humans, animals kill only for food and self defense. They want to imitate human Christians, so let them also learn some hardcore bad stuff from the image of God." Axis winked. "Monkey will make a good death midwife while waiting to become human in the twinkling of an eye!"

"Who is he delivering?" Mundu asked.

"The pre-born of the jungle, the little ones the creator is still knitting together," Axis replied coldly.

"That should be a beautiful knife in J. C.'s heart," Mundu agreed.

"Twist it so the blood does not stop flowing."

"We have already accomplished that with humans, sir. It's a

running river, but what would motivate Monkey or any other animal to do such a thing? Animals have never hurt the pre-born!"

"Greed, fame, excelling above others and being sincerely deceived. He is looking to become the Man-Key, the real origin of species and Superman all rolled together. Promise to make him the world's first evolving doctor, speeding the evolution of species to the next level. A lizard could become a bird in the twinkling of an eye."

"He might want some proof," Mundu wavered.

"Give him a caterpillar. Let him watch it without ceasing. In a matter of hours, he has the proof in a butterfly. Only he will be doing the same in the twinkling of an eye. He will be able to move back and forth in time, revolving between the distant past, the present and the future to fill the gaps in the studies of History, Anthropology, Evolution and Revelations."

"What if in roaming the times he stumbles on the beginning, the real origin of species?" Mundu worried aloud.

"Are you all right?" Axis thundered. Mundu recoiled as if he had been slapped. That was the highest insult in their world.

"Sorry, boss, I forgot it is only the pipe dream we feed Monkey. Your plan is so credible I was beginning to want the job myself."

Axis eyed him suspiciously and then continued, "He must first study the pre-born of all species from conception to just before birth. Convince him the study material is not really alive because life begins after birth. His conscience must be clear before we can trust him."

Monkey's bladder ran faster than lightning. The pre-born were God's own work in progress, tucked in what should be the safest place on earth, the mother's womb. You did not interfere without the full fire of the Almighty's wrath coming after your tail. Such things had never been heard of in the jungle. Another original sin and they wanted him for Adam. All they needed was the snake!

"Tell Monkey he will be world famous, sought after by the

rich and powerful, females from all species looking to evolve parts
of their bodies without the pains of exercise and diet," the devil
enthused as the madman stared, flabbergasted. "Oh yes, evolving
cosmetics or cosmetic evolving services, think of the possibilities.
A lady may want a first-century butt and bust suspended on an
eighteenth-century waistline and carried on tomorrow's transport!"
They both laughed.

In spite of his frozen state, Monkey winced in shame as the devil
made a joke of his discontented life. Where was God now? He felt
unworthy even to think of his name. Urine kept bubbling from him
and falling on the rock below as if his bladder had evolved into a
well. He had not had a drink in days!

Aero kept mumbling, "thank you, Jesus, thank you, Jesus," as
holy warm water kept washing over her, setting her wings free.

Back in the human nest, Snake's anger was still mounting. He
had been used, cheated, and made a fool of just like the first snake in
the garden of God. His ancestor had loaned the devil his body. Black
had loaned out his soul, and he wanted it back without the mark of
the beast! He wanted to bite someone, anyone, and very hard, close
his fangs on them like a scorpion and release the poison slowly,
maybe fast or even faster—bite the devil and hope his venom was
less toxic than his own, or he could be the one poisoned. Maybe if
he just got out of the nest, he could find an easier fall guy. There was
monkey business going on here. All he needed was the monkey!

"Inao and Brother Hyena should be Monkey's first customers!"
Axis said excitedly. Then we will expose them, disgrace them in all
jungles. The Name of God will never be mentioned in their clan
again for a thousand generations."

"God only curses to the third or fourth generation, and they
could always repent," Mundu stammered.

"Not if you are still on duty!" Axis warned. "While Brother is drowning in shame, the homeless spirit of cannibalism from his father enters him. One day he eats or attempts to eat his own son, same difference. His wife despises him, the marriage breaks—like father, like son. Someone declares cannibalism runs in the family and it becomes just so, curse conceived and received through the spoken word."

"Right on spot—just perfect, boss!"

"Meanwhile, the wife, Inao, is too angry with God to tell her offspring anything about him. I want God blamed for this, their shame lasting forever and a day just like his blessing. Let hyenas believe they are cursed, damned, unworthy of God's grace just like snakes!"

"The hyenas' blessing is too solid," Mundu confessed. "There were praying mothers along the bloodline storing up blessings for their future generations. J. C. sits on the right hand of God, pestering him to answer every one of them, even in posterity."

"If we cannot close a door that God has opened or open one he has shut, we can at least give an illusion of doing it through magic if we have to," Axis said. "What's our best gate into the hyenas?"

"The stomach," Mundu replied.

"The Kenyan hyena is now Christian," Axis replied. "The stomach gate closes when you learn to fast."

"Try shame," Mundu proposed. "Everyone calls them ugly, and they receive illegitimate shame by believing it. Shame parasites on self-esteem."

"Good. Stay ahead of the couple and keep them vulnerable. Hyena courtships last two years max, enough time to lead them into fornication," Axis continued, trotting up and down.

"Giraffe wants the pair teaching Sunday school," Mundu cautioned.

"Good. So Inao gets pregnant at the same time Giraffe nominates them for the job. They will be honored publicly as soon as they secretly conceive dishonor. For the first time ever, hyenas are given a position of leadership, a victory for their entire community, but the extramarital ripening fruit threatens to shame them back to oblivion." Axis was talking faster now.

"Go on, boss. I like it, I like it very much," Mundu enthused.

"Meanwhile the hush-hush monkey's clinic is ready. The frightened couple tosses him some bananas and a chance for embryonic studies. He removes the 'problem' and saves their face and future. But the secret is out somehow. I leave the details to your ingenuity."

"Sounds delicious," Mundu said.

"They are shamed from within, without, tossed out of the church and—they fear—out of the presence of God. Self-righteous believers ostracize them. They sincerely repent. God forgives, as is his nature, but the jungle does not, and neither do they forgive themselves. They become infamous, but in retrospect, monkey's clinic gets discreet free advertising in and out of church. The bloodbaths open wide, and we have rights to destroy the jungle."

"Animals will need a big motivation to start 'family planning.' They never cared about their numbers or birth timings before."

"The same time and material crap we feed the image of God," Axis said impatiently. "There is not enough land, man has grabbed every habitat. They are running from forest grabbers, man-made fires, poachers, sport hunters, plastic, pollution, and all perils of man. They pant for food, water, a resting place, and time has become an endangered species."

"You are losing me, boss."

"Those whose hope is on what they see will take a modern step and cut down on inconvenient parenting. After all, man, the image of God, is doing it, and Monkey, the image of man, is the doctor. It must be right. A river of innocent blood gushes out, and we row, row, row our boat of plagues never even heard of before."

"We become the sword of God slicing through the masses."

Mundu danced. "We are The Mass. Though they will pray, but every time God would bless them, he will hear the cry of innocent blood as in the day of Abel and turn his face against them."

"You are catching my drift, demon mine!" Axis praised. "If Monkey and Snake are sincerely deceived, they will deceive even the very elite."

The devil jumped up and down, impressed with himself and feeling like God. The madman jumped with him, but he wondered how he would get animals to learn bad habits from man. It was easier the other way round. Man is always reaching in to pet the animal within him.

"How's the Lion Queen project going?" Axis asked, jolting him back.

"Better than expected, sir," Mundu replied. "She is wrestling the kingdom away from her husband."

"Good. We cannot have a king who decrees all animals go to church and not kill one another on Sundays! It's time for a Queendom, but get rid of her after she is through destroying her family."

"Who then do you want as king of the jungle?" Mundu asked.

"Tiger. Sado and Lin, the tiger couple in Nairobi," Axis said.

"Why?" Mundu asked.

"Unlike Lion or Hyena, a tiger is not a team player. He will divide the jungle and open gates for us everywhere. He is also more likely to legalize Monkey's business and give it respectability. He really cares for no one but himself."

"We are doing very well with the monkeys business in humans. We just had a great coup in Nairobi!" Mundu boasted.

"You haven't filled me in," Axis accused.

"They found seven late-term pre-born babies dumped in a river. We thought you would like the twist in God's favorite number! The Catholic nuns cried for days, and the church gave them Christian names! They were buried Christian like and proper, but they were still dead."

"Who were they?" Axis asked, excited.

"A future president, the first black pope, the researcher who was going to discover a cure for cancer, a second Billy Graham, a Mother Theresa, the world's fastest long-distance runner, and a thief."

"Why the thief?" Axis asked. "He was not against us."

"He was a twin to the president," Mundu explained. "No way to separate. Besides, he was a Christian president; he could have prayed for his brother, and J. C. would have heard him. There are many more littered in dumpsites, rivers, pit latrines in the countryside, and the good old incinerator. An entire generation is gone, and there are some muffled requests to legalize."

"Good. We are legal to stay. What are your plans for continuity?" Axis asked.

"The youth are getting more 'modernized' as they call it. We feed them pot, crack, weed, alcohol, whatever their poison. Hard-line stuff is served to toddlers as they watch pornography. Alcohol is finally outselling tea and Coca Cola even with females. We are laying the groundwork to kick God out of schools and all public places. But it's still a longer shot here than legalizing abortion and gay marriages."

"Why do you say that?" Axis prompted.

"This culture is still too God and morality based. Ungodly kids have praying parents, and ungodly parents have praying kids. It's sick. They play gospel music in the bars. Even in their drunken stupors, J. C. still has a voice. In Kenya, everything starts and ends with prayer—even quarrels!"

"Cut the excuses! Now you sound like Milika the cow," Axis thundered.

"I have a chunk of youth despising everything African as primitive, even their nutritious traditional food," Mundu confided.

"They are addicted to junk and will soon rob their mothers to buy it. I am also working to neutralize the family as the social security system. The future Kenyan family will be nuclear just like the first world. Once we saddle the entire load on the government, the penniless, sick, elderly, crippled, and pre- born will become a disposable inconvenience within common sense. Our boat of plagues will run in a river that never runs dry."

"Good. But the country is still almost 100 percent Christian!" Axis said, not too pleased.

"I have a host of new religions coming up in The Name of God minus J. C. Some worship their inner beings as their own great *I am*," Mundu boasted. "I throw them a miracle here and there, a visit from the dearly departed, a celestial being or two, and they are good—no questions asked, no testing the spirits."

"Well done, good and faithful servant!" Axis said in mock imitation of God. They laughed and did a high five. "Take that, J. C., big brother," he mocked, "first born of all creation! You will not pursue equality with God but take on the very nature of a servant! You reduce yourself to a curse and get nailed to a tree ransoming the scum of the earth from eternal death! You died for nothing, son of God, unless they receive you! Keep standing at the door and knocking like a gentleman! Oh no, don't trick or force your way in; don't even use the back door! Don't you see they're crucifying you again and again and again with their rejection! Who's smarter now, eh, J. C.?"

Aero, who had woken up, began to sob. Devils were mocking her precious Jesus, and they were right—humans were crucifying him all over again. So would animals if they caught on to the sins of man.

"Oh, God," she prayed, "endow man with wisdom, your image whose choice is our destiny."

To Hate and Hit the Devil

☙

Up the Jesus tree, the three mortal creatures could not contain their rage any longer as The Name was mocked. Snake coiled and recoiled, head flat on the bottom of the nest in his most vicious strike position. God may have cursed the snakes, but he had saved Snake's life that day. He was going to return the favor, and then they would be even. This would be the first time he struck a target from outer space, whatever galaxy they were on, and his first bite of the devil! He started raising his body out of the nest to drop down at an angle, wishing he could see better for precision.

The devil had used the first snake to bring sin into the world. Black was going to be the last snake and rid the world of the devil. He was going to bite him three times, once for the conned ancestor, twice to pay his debt to the unseen God and a third time for his family. If he was going to forbid God in his home, they did not need a devil around either. His venom was ready. He laid his head flat on the floor of the human nest and shot up like a rocket.

De Brazza Monkey knew he was not going to evolve into a human in the twinkling of an eye or in any amount of time. So he decided to die like a man. Though he had soiled himself and cried a

208

river, the Guenon family name had never been carried by a coward! He needed to jump one of them to have any shred of dignity—the one with one head, and perhaps Jesus could jump on the other. He had to be around, being omnipresent and all that. De Brazza Monkey Guenon crouched low and prepared to defend The Name, the jungle, and his right to the name Guenon!

Just as he was about to jump, he saw the largest airborne snake glide heavenward, mouth wide open, fangs glistering, and the angriest look. The snake bit on the biggest banana just above his head, missing him by a hair. Monkey had never ever seen or heard of a snake biting a banana, and he was not hanging around to see what else he could bite on the way down. Without thinking, he jumped onto the rock he had used as a toilet below him, hoping to hide under it. He slid on his own urine on Aero's feathers and fell snugly back in the human nest. In the twinkling of an eye, he covered his head with the feathers. Today was not a Sunday when no one harmed anyone, and somewhere above him, a snake was coming down fast!

Aero felt something hit her and assumed it was a big papaya. She needed a weapon to strike the devil. Having known the enemy inside out, she knew her weapons too. Nothing confuses the kingdom of darkness more than praising God. She just did not know if she could pull it off without a larynx, never having vocalized except when she shouted The Name. Perhaps The Name had healed her for always and not just for the moment. If God loved her enough to die for her, he loved her enough to heal her. It was time to confirm the healing, to receive and posses it. Besides, the devil could not read her mind. He needed to hear it. That is why he had a fly on the wall in every conversation. If mortals knew that, they would really guard their words.

Snake thought he smelled the monkey on his way up, but gravity pulled him right back into the human nest. He landed on top of the feathers, but he thought something or someone was trembling under him. He could still smell a monkey. Perhaps there were two monkeys. Whatever he had bitten up there was neither devil nor monkey. Neither of them could possibly taste sweet! Too late, he realized he had failed his own math. He was supposed to jump and curve downward to boomerang on the devil, but he had not counted on gravity pulling him back down to where he started!

There had to be a monkey under him. Surely he was not miscalculating that too. He could reach down and bite him, clean his sticky fangs. That monkey had peed and pooped on him! He was owed. But if he searched below and there was no monkey, it would mean he had that disease his wife called dementia. He was too proud to risk proving her right. If the monkey was a hallucination, it was safer not to know. He decided to probe casually downward, pretend he was not looking for a monkey, bite whatever was there, and if there was nothing, his brain was all right and his wife was wrong and his fangs could stop being sticky.

Monkey knew the snake was on top of his head. It was time to believe, really believe in the power of prayer and miracles, time to call again on The Name.

"Please, Jesus," he whispered, trembling like a leaf. "This is De Brazza. I know we have only just met, but if you save me from this snake, I will give you the rest of my life, never ever to touch, taste, smell, or think of another God apart from you!"

Snake buried his head under the feathers and smelled monkey's hair. This was no dementia! He opened his fangs wide, but just before he struck, the sweetest song hit the air. No one was as shocked by the beautiful voice as Aero herself when she vocalized. She had no voice box and had whispered all her life. But when she opened her mouth to praise God, she had miraculously vocalized. She was going to spend all her sound praising God! The nursery rhyme Axis had once interrupted came to her.

Jesus' love is very, very wonderful
Jesus' love is very, very wonderful
Jesus' love is very, very wonderful
Ooooh wonderful loooove!

So high that you can't get over it,
So low that you can't get under it
So wide that you can't get around it,
You must go through the Lord!

Snake was charmed, so enchanted by the sweet voice that his anger melted within him. In slow motion, his Amazon mouth closed on the deadly fangs as his eyelids felt heavy. He flicked his tongue in and out, searching for the source of the heavenly sound. He knew it was not from Monkey. If there was a heaven, that was the way it should sound, divine lyrics coming from all around him till he lost the urge to bite anyone, even a monkey.

Monkey would have enjoyed the singing, but right now with his life hanging on the next move of a snake, it sounded like funeral lyrics. He just kept whispering, "God loves me, God loves me…" He needed to make that his mantra. If he was going to come out from the valley of the shadow of death intact, he had to focus only on God. That way, whichever side of heaven he woke up on, he would not be alone but in the presence of God.

The music boomed on the six ears of the two devils and burned like coal. The Name became pepper in their eyes as they trembled and hit the ground on their knees again and again, as many times as Aero sang The Name. Only when she came to the lines without The Name did they stand and look around, perplexed.

Suddenly Aero heard thundering footsteps, like the marching of an army. The devils stopped to listen. Axis appeared worried, every one of his eight eyes searching in a different direction.

"What in hell is that noise?" Mundu asked in a shaky voice, all bravado gone.

"The forces of heaven!" Axis replied, flexing his shoulders, showing courage in the presence of his junior. He had a hard time controlling his tail, which kept hiding between his legs and flat on his belly. Its dagger tip came all the way to the chin and protruded through the long mane that grew from his nose.

"That minx Aero has called on The Name!" Axis said venomously as Mundu released a stream of obscenities. "Scram! We are outnumbered!" Axis ordered. They switched to invisible spirits and vanished in different directions.

"Oh no you don't!" Aero screamed, opening her massive wings to follow them and hurt them some more with her song. She did not know which way they had gone, but she could sing in wide circles. One of her legs was still stuck on the branch, and she almost tipped over. She had forgotten all about the sticky devil's milk. Keeping her wings open for balance, she bent her head and pecked the stuff off her foot. Then she wiped her beak clean on the branch and soared into the freedom of the skies. The devils were gone, scattered to the seven winds. "Thank you, Jesus, thank you, Jesus," she chanted for a while. Then she started humming the Jesus love song.

Thousands of feet above the Devil's Mountain, she realized that the human nest was still hanging on her other foot. Her cargo felt intact. There was no telling what the devil had loaded in there and she could not shake it off.

The two passengers in the human nest had passed out again on takeoff. Aero kept humming her praise, ready to detonate The Name loud and clear if the devils materialized. Meanwhile, she celebrated her newfound freedom.

When The Name sets you free, you are free indeed! she thought and decided not to chase after the devils. God was big enough to deal with that vermin all by himself. From now on, she was going after

God. In him she had an identity, a family. She would begin every day with praise to invoke his presence, bask in his love, and live like the birds on the Jesus tree, expecting a miracle every day.

She soared to her maximum height and displayed her full wingspan. Then she balanced to a short stop and looked down for a glimpse of the Jesus tree. It was gone. She took a nosedive, thinking she had risen too far to see it. There was nothing. She circled the Devil's Mountain. The tree was really gone. Had it all been an illusion?

"Please, God, increase my faith," she prayed. Then she saw something she had not noticed before on the ground. Right on the spot where the Jesus tree had stood was an enormous ripe papaya. She almost landed to eat it but realized that was not its purpose. It was food for her faith, not her body.

Let someone else find it. Perhaps someone hungry in this dry place will eat it and thank God for his provisions, she thought.

Aero wanted everyone else to know The Name, even if they never got to know her. She had never met or related to another mortal, but she knew the pets of God were out there. Again she soared to her highest, feeling high on the most high, adoring the vast heavens above. If she could keep on going, perhaps Jesus would meet her in the air. She really had no one down there, no reason to go down but the force of gravity. Warmth enveloped her in the coolness of the height, and in it was a comforting thought: Jesus did not need to meet her in the air; he was already in her heart.

"I don't really know where to go from here, Jesus," she whispered. "If it pleases you, please lead me to the right friends for my growth and help me walk with you. If not, I am content that you love me. You are everything I need, the only one who can take the place of everyone and everything that I need to be fulfilled."

She relaxed to autopilot, gliding casually past the clouds, and searched her mind for something, anything she could give God, something the maker and owner of everything did not have.

"Please, God, just name it. There has to be something you cannot give yourself!" she whispered. It was then she sensed more than heard the still, small voice.

"Praise, my pet. I cannot give myself praise."

Aero's eyes welled in tears as she started the nursery rhyme again, the only song she knew other than Kenya's national anthem. She needed to learn new songs, even make them up if she had to. In the meantime, she would sing the rhyme seven times, and then seven and seven again times seven and seven sevens. Let the devil figure that one out; he hated praise. She was going to sing that song till it was tattered. Then she would make a new one and still sing the tattered praise.

She realized she was near Samburu when she located the Ewaso Nyiro River and followed its course. Axis was planning something evil for the river. It was important that she warn someone in the jungle. The pets of God needed to prepare for combat, put on the full armor of God. One right connection and she would find a way in. She would fight alongside them with The Name going ahead of them. To think that someone as lowly as her wielded such power over the devil in The Name! Jesus loved her undeservedly. She loved the pets of God even before she met them because they were his.

"Please, God, just one friend or contact, even just to practice my new vocals with. Just one hello from any mortal creature who does not want to eat me or steal my soul!" she prayed.

Suddenly Aero saw the small hill where she used to pick up the human nest and circled to land. Her feet had almost touched the ground when something sinister beat them to it. A huge, black coiled snake hit earth and rolled downhill away from her. Quickly she ascended back to the safety of the skies trembling to the last feather.

"Oh, God!" she prayed, exasperated. "When I said I needed a hello from anyone, it did not include a snake! Surely you *know* that. If you don't want me to meet anyone yet, I appreciate you are jealous for me. But I sure would like a friend I can see, touch, and share the earthly moments of my existence with. I promise to still love and introduce you to everyone so we can all be friends. If some of my friends do not like you, I will not be ashamed of you even if I have to stop being friends with them. Only do not ever take your presence away from me! There now, God, if that's a deal, we can call it a covenant and you make me a friend who is not a snake!"

Finally she perched on the tallest tree along the Ewaso Nyiro River. She felt a tugging of something coiled on her foot and hoped it was not a snake!

"Please, Jesus, I know you will take me home one day, but not this route—please not a snake. If I must die, please kill me yourself!" She shivered. Slowly she turned her head, bracing for a heart attack. Then she saw the human nest. The two sisal rope handles were still mucky with the devil's milk and firmly stuck to her foot. She needed to lose it, but she couldn't. She pecked on it once but quickly cleaned her beak on the bark of the tree, remembering it was the devil's milk and cargo … ugh! Any witchcraft could be in there! If she could only free herself of it and drop it, the river below could wash it away along with her past. She gathered courage and pecked again very carefully.

Suddenly a movement in the nest startled her. She turned her head sideways to look inside the nest with one eye. A pair of the most frightened eyes Aero had ever seen stared back at her. That was before the creature quickly covered them with two hands the way human children did.

The Eye and the Circle of Gods

ℰ✇

When Monkey regained consciousness, he was still in the human nest on top of a tree but not the Jesus tree. It had the aura of his tree in Samburu, but there was a dark cloud above him. He remembered sliding under the huge rock and the airborne snake. But he was even more scared of the dream he had just had.

He had died and gone to … wherever, he did not know. His spirit was roaming across galaxies. It seemed important to remember his full names in case any god was asking. He had served so many on planet Earth, his eternal citizenship could be anywhere. Finally, somewhere away from the Milky Way, he stood for judgment in a circle of gods. They were as numerous as those he had served and made from every material on earth. He recognized the banana god who was made of mountains of bunches of endless bananas.

Some wanted him in their heaven, others in hell. Finally the leader of the United Circle of Gods proposed that he serve time for the required millions of years in every hell he had earned on earth, after which he could go to banana heaven. That was if the unseen God had nothing against him. He was yet to stand in his court. Suddenly they heard his footsteps. The other gods walked respectfully away so he could have the circle to himself. He did not share his glory with anyone.

Suddenly the ground the circle of gods had stood on folded itself like a carpet and tossed itself after them. A floor of pure gold floated in and laid itself where the rocky, soiled ground had been. In the blink of an eye, the great I Am was before him.

He was one, but there were three of him, the father, the son, and the person of the Holy Spirit who was the power of God. Monkey scratched his head as he blinked his eyes vigorously. The one equals three equals one holy God was made of brilliance, yet Monkey could make out the man-like features.

The son came out of the father and opened a big book. He searched under D for De Brazza and shook his head, then looked under M for Monkey and shook it again.

"Guenon," Monkey whispered his family name, and the son shook his head again, sadly looking at his father.

"If you do not know him, son, neither do I," the father said quietly to the son. The Holy Spirit looked at Monkey. De Brazza was sure he had seen him somewhere before. Then the Holy Spirit turned a sad face to the father and son, as grieved as they were. The three became one and looked at him with one big questioning eye, almost as big as his head.

At that point in the dream, Monkey realized there was no banana heaven. He was in deep trouble with the three-equals-one God! The council of gods had been a lie. He was eye-to-eye with the real thing and was being found wanting.

Suddenly he woke up, but the big, sad eye continued to stare at him. Once upon a time, he was supposed to be the origin of species, the Man-Key. But that was another time, another place, another god. The eye of God stared steadily at him, unwavering.

His whole system froze. He had frozen before but never like this. If Lot's wife turned into a pillar of salt, he had just turned into a block of ice. On reflex, he brought out his hands and covered his eyes and face, remembering that no one saw God face-to-face and lived. If he could not see God's eye, perhaps it could not see him either. He was conscious of his bowels. *Please, please, not here, not now on holy ground!*

In spite of paralyzing fear, Monkey did a quick calculation. If God was here now, he may as well introduce himself and make friendly conversation. Even God could not hit on someone who was talking nicely to him.

He took a deep breath and then another and slowly removed one finger to uncover one eye. He stared into the kindest pond of an eye he had ever seen. De Brazza Monkey Guenon had seen God face-to-face and lived!

Aero was tongue struck. She had prayed for a friend, a contact, anyone but a snake, and all along she had carried one in the human basket! God had known her need even before she had prayed about it. She watched as Monkey removed one finger from an eye and introduced himself.

"My name is De Brazza Monkey Guenon. Are you God?"

Aero laughed. It was the first time she had ever laughed, and it felt good. She could not stop laughing. Monkey got more frightened now. If God was laughing at him, he was really in big trouble. Giraffe had never talked of it being written anywhere "and God Laughed!" But the eye of God looked happily amused, not mockingly amused. Then a more frightening thought struck. The devil could laugh too! He could only see a round, black, giant eye. Mirrored in it was his image, a shivering monkey in a human nest, holding tightly to untrustworthy bowels. It was not a flattering image for a Guenon.

"I am still De Brazza Monkey Guenon. Are you God or devil, sir?"

Aero laughed till tears came out of her eyes. Monkey saw a giant tear about to land on him. He ducked under the basket, but it still soaked him. Aero realized she was scaring him half to death.

"I am neither one, Mr. De Brazza," she said, still amused. "My name is Aero, and it is miss not mister. I am a bird who wants to be your friend! Here, I will raise my head high so you can see my neck."

Monkey ventured his head out slowly. Her neck was a long tree trunk leading to a young, bold head many times bigger than that of Ostrich. The nose was not big, but it sat on the biggest, sharpest, curved beak. It could tear his heart out in an instant and snack on it. He decided to stay put and never come out of the nest—ever. It was safer to die of hunger, leave the body, and escape as a soul!

"Please, I really need to communicate with someone right now," Aero said. "I do not know anyone else in the world," she pleaded.

"Nice try, Miss Aero," Monkey said. "You do not know me either. And just so you know, no one but no one knows anyone in this whole wide world. *Shindwe Shetani*, get thee behind me, Satan!"

"I really don't," she said sadly. "I was raised by … my father. I grew up … I was raised away from mortal creatures," she stammered.

"Are you an alien then? Mars? Jupiter? I am Earth," Monkey said with sarcasm.

"I believe I am an earthling really," she replied wistfully.

"Mortal or spirit?" Monkey quizzed.

"Mortal now, I am sure, whatever you are," she replied in the saddest voice.

"What do you mean?" Monkey asked. "No one was ever both or not sure!" His late mother was right. He should never have talked to a stranger, and a laughing, sobbing female was the worst kind. You get sucked in by the first teardrop and are already too deep.

"For a long time, I wasn't sure," Aero said with a sob. "It's a long story, and I don't suppose anyone wants to hear it. It doesn't matter. I don't matter, and perhaps you are not the one."

"What do you mean I am not the one?" Monkey asked, curious now. He loved a story, and this was going a step further. He was supposed to be in it.

"I prayed for someone, anyone 'normal' to be friends with. I guess you are not the one; you could not possibly want to be my friend," Aero moaned.

"What do you mean 'normal'? Are you abnormal then—as in, are you all there?"

"Normal as in earth normal, mortal and not spirit. Please forgive me for scaring you. Would you help me free my leg from this nest, and I will leave you alone?"

Monkey scratched his head. He wanted to be normal whatever that was, just a normal ordinary monkey. In a way, he could identify with Aero. His quest to become human in the twinkling of an eye was just as bizarre as not being sure if you were spirit or mortal.

"Are you hungry?" he asked politely.

"Yes, as a matter of fact I am," Aero said shyly.

"Got you!" Monkey exclaimed. "Nice try, Aero Bird. I bet you need a nice monkey snack!" he exclaimed in mock fright.

"I can't eat anyone right now. I stink!" Aero said. A look of shame crossed Monkey's face, and she wondered why. She knew that look. She had worn it all her life. It broke her heart to see it on her first friend in world. She wondered where she had goofed but chose to let it pass.

"I need your help to warn the other animals," Aero said, serious now. "Satan is planning something bad for Samburu. I think you know it. You were there with me."

"You mean, it was not a dream, the other tree?" Monkey asked.

"No, the Jesus tree was real."

"Is that what it's called?" Monkey asked.

"It's the only name that came to mind. What do you think?" Aero asked.

"The same name crossed my mind," Monkey said.

"That makes you a witness to The Name. Do you remember just before we crashed? Did you shout "*Jesus*?"

"Yes. So did another two voices," Monkey replied.

"One was me," Aero said. "Who was the other?"

They looked at each other. Monkey was getting used to Aero's eye.

"The Name was kind of hissed out," Monkey said quietly. Aero trembled visibly, and so did Monkey, pulling deeper into the human nest. "You don't suppose he is up the tree, do you, Aero?"

"No, De Brazza. I saw him roll off when we hit the ground down there."

"When we left the Jesus tree, he was on top of my head!" Monkey said, still trembling.

"Around my leg!" Aero shivered. Monkey lifted his head up, closer to Aero. He was beginning to trust her now that she showed fear of snakes. That ought to make her a mortal like him.

"They plan something bad for him too," Monkey confided.

"Really?" Aero gasped. "I guess they spoke about you and him after sunset. I always fall asleep after sunset."

"What do we do now?" Monkey asked, scratching his head.

"There is no time to waste. Please untie my leg." Aero said.

"I can't get my head out," Monkey said. It was true. The handle was twisted, closing the mouth of the basket. Aero looked at it and started turning around till there was enough of an opening. Monkey lifted out his head successfully but pulled it back quickly, looking embarrassed.

"Are you mad at me, Aero?" he asked.

"What on earth for?" she asked.

"Back at the Jesus tree, I thought you were a rock ... so I, eh, used your back as a toilet."

Aero thought for a moment, and her eyes lit up in amusement. "That was you? I thought I smelled some monkey business on the holy water!"

"Holy water?" Monkey was incredulous.

"My wings were glued together till God hit me with hot holy water. It melted the sticky milk from the devil cow!"

It was Monkey's turn to laugh. He laughed so hard that the human nest swung back and forth precariously. He held onto Aero's leg and climbed out still laughing. His urine was holy, and the lady could swear. What kind of swear word was "devil cow"? Aero was laughing too. He sat on a branch next to her, and they looked like the giant and the dwarf.

"God sure works in mysterious ways," Monkey said quietly, studying her size. She looked like a laughing mountain, but the gentlest kind, not volcanic.

"You have no idea, De Brazza, you have no idea," she said. It was turning out to be the happiest day of Aero's life. New vocals, a friend, and her first audible laughter!

"What's your favorite food?" Monkey asked. She was a guest on his tree, and he was a Kenyan monkey. It was customary to feed a guest before quizzing.

"Papaya, but you don't have to worry about it," Aero said.

"A guest must be fed whether she is hungry or not. Only then will I be comfortable to talk with you." That too was custom. One is not likely to fight with someone they have just shared a meal with.

"Then make it papaya, my gracious host. But you have yet to untie my foot!" Aero said laughing.

"I never had such a beautiful prisoner. Perhaps I should not untie," Monkey flirted a little.

Aero blushed. It was the first time anyone had ever called her beautiful.

"You are very kind, sir!" she said.

"Don't sir me now. I like De Brazza better, but everyone calls me Monkey."

"All right De Brazza, I beg you to untie my foot and call me Aero!" she pleaded laughing.

"Right away, my lady Aero." De Brazza was not made in the image of the image of God for nothing. He tore through the sticky muck and freed her instantly. He stiffened for a moment at the milky glue. This was some unusual stuff. If she was not just swearing about the devil cow, he preferred not to know just yet. Devil cows did not exist, not even the one he thought he saw when he got the human nest from the two little humans. And if they did exist, they could not fly. Fear aside, he had a guest to feed, even though it meant leaving the safety of the tree. It was custom the guest came first. It was also custom a Kenyan male did not show fear, especially in the presence of a female.

"You sure you don't eat monkey?" he asked, pretending to be afraid.

"Only after sunset!" she said, playfully looking at the horizons. She knew he was pretending to be pretending but did not want to embarrass him. Her size could frighten anyone.

"I better grab your dinner before sunset then." Monkey started climbing down with a lot of bravado but halfway down paused to look up.

"Aero, please climb higher into the thicker leaves. I don't want anyone to see you yet!"

Aero's heart seemed to sink, and Monkey sensed it.

"I want to be the first one to introduce you around," he added, sensing her hesitation. "No one takes that particular honor from me!"

She was glad he was not ashamed of her.

"Whatever you say, my lord!" she laughed, doing as she was told. Monkey was glad. He did not want anyone having a heart attack at the size of her. No one in the jungle had ever seen such a big bird, bigger than Ostrich, and she could fly. She was awesome, and yes, he was proud to have found her, been found by her—whatever, together they would make shockwaves!

When he hit the ground, he sprinted all the way to the papaya tree. If that devil cow existed, it was more likely to be on land. Soon he was back with a big, ripe papaya and two bananas for himself under his armpits. He placed the papaya between two small branches next to her and sat on an opposite branch facing her.

They ate quietly, glancing at each other occasionally. It was custom that serious business was not to be discussed between mouthfuls. When they were done, Aero looked at him as if something was bothering her.

"What's the matter, Aero?"

"Do you believe in God for real?" she asked.

"Yes, and in Jesus Christ his only son, my Lord, born of the human virgin, and so on!" Monkey said, equally serious.

"Then I must trust you as a brother. The sun is already over our heads, De Brazza. At sunset, I must fall asleep until dawn. You heard the stuff back there; we have no time if we are to save this jungle."

"What can we possibly do? You saw those creatures," Monkey said.

"Will you go to war with me, for Jesus?" she pleaded.

"Anything for him, Aero, anything," Monkey said. "I have fruits of mass destruction. A store full of coconuts—aim two with both hands at both heads of the devil and I am dead accurate!"

"No, no, those are not the weapons we need!" Aero said.

"What could possibly hit harder than a coconut? You find those clowns, and I'll fix them for Jesus!"

"No, De Brazza," she said earnestly. "Fruits would be canal weapons, and this is no flesh and blood war. We are going after principalities, the very powers of darkness."

Monkey looked up, down, and around him and then shivered visibly and huddled closer to Aero. When it came to invisible enemies in total darkness, even a Kenyan male was allowed to be afraid.

"I don't see in darkness," he confided.

"Me neither," Aero said, "but we have the light now. We have Jesus."

Monkey looked a little confused.

"I am going to tell you my story, and you will understand," she said. "By morning we must have a plan."

"I don't usually spend the night on the tree, but if you like, I will. You go first. I will tell you mine too, about the origin of species."

"What you saw there, the one with two heads was who I thought was my father," Aero started. Monkey froze for a moment. Sharing a tree with the devil's daughter was not in the plan! But he recovered, hanging onto *"I thought."* She had only thought so. This was going to be quite a story.

Aero told everything as far as she knew it, including what the devils had said while Monkey was frozen or passed out. Monkey filled in gaps with what was said after sunset. Finally they pieced together what the devil had in store for their jungle, the river, and the land of Kenya. To infest them with demons, turn the snake into a wizard and De Brazza into the midwife of death for the pre-born of the jungle. He planned on using them to put the Christian jungle and the land of Kenya under God's own curse. They planned on humiliating the queen of the jungle, dethroning the king, and giving the kingdom to Tiger, who would tear it to shreds and scatter the pets of God. And some evil was coming to the river, a cultic suicide diving, a sacrifice to the devil that would awaken the sickness demons.

Monkey scratched his head again and again.

"Please pray for the night, De Brazza," Aero said as she watched him, her eyelids drooping. The sunset was at its most beautiful.

"Now we lay us down to sleep, we trust our backs to you," Monkey prayed. "Should the evil one snoop around, you are tougher than a coconut and your aim is better than a Guenon. Now we lay us down to sleep, endow man with wisdom, your image whose choice is our destiny. Amen."

"Goodnight, Aero."

"Goodnight, De Brazza."

"Goodnight, Jesus."

"Bad night, devil."

The beautiful sunset disappeared in the horizon as Aero sank into a deep sleep.

Monkey stayed awake for a while thinking. They had to see Giraffe as quickly as possible. Aero could live with them now, perhaps with Ostrich, her closest lookalike. Ostrich could teach her to run, and Aero could teach her to fly. Ostrich was as fast as any plane on the runway, she just never learned to take off and get airborne. But all things were possible with God.

When Black Mamba came to, he was somewhere between Monkey's tree and the trail he had used to ferry stolen eggs to the human nest. It seemed like a lifetime ago. He feared he was sleepwalking and somehow blamed his wife for his confused state of mind. She should never have mentioned dementia to him. Even though she had only mumbled it in her sleep, she had said it next to his name. He was only five years old for crying out, and it was supposed to be an old-age disease. But what with the image of God polluting the air with gases not made in the image of God, anything was possible!

His family and friends were supposed to love him through memory loss, hallucinations, restlessness agitation, and being absent from reality. The symptoms were there, but he had failed his family and had not yet made a friend. He had spent his life as a self-reliant snake, never bothering anyone or letting others bother him.

There was no cure for dementia, and it could last three to five years. What should have been the happily ever after stage of his life was going to be a long, lonely, and hazy slither back to dust.

Right now, he did not know what time, day, moon, or year it was. He was not sure if the present reality in his mind was in the past, present, or future. He knew of no place they grew a Jesus tree or snakes with legs. That had to be the future. Stealing eggs for a voice was another dementia predictor. It was still his wife's fault through her power of suggestion. The spoken never failed to actualize. Swift was one of those wives that said little, but when she spoke—even in a dream—everyone and everything listened, even dementia.

He shook his head from side to side hoping to shake dementia away. He was going home, and no one—especially a female—had the right to ask where he had been. It was not custom. If Swift asked, he would act like the insulted husband. It was time to take his place as head of the house with or without a head. He had already made up whatever was left of his mind.

Aside from domestics, Black hoped The Mass did not know he

had called on The Name; therefore he had not. It was also not true that devils had laughed at him for wanting legs. He had dreamt that part. The monkey had been an illusion even though he resembled De Brazza Guenon. He was going to avoid him for a while till things were clearer.

Make up your mind, Black Mamba! he admonished himself.

Axis was the god of snakes. Jesus was the head of a cult. He had simply confused the names when he called out Jesus because of all the churchgoing.

These things happen even to those without dementia! he thought and wished he could bite off his own head. He had no dementia. His wife really needed discipline for planting such a thought, some good old-fashioned wife beating. But there was also husband bashing these days, and that wife of his was probably stronger and swifter than he was. Still, he needed to discipline someone. If that no-good son Nyoka went to church again, he would know who the head of that house was. He actually thought he smelled him in church once.

In his house, there would be no one above him. He would forbid belief in God, devil, The Mass, heaven and hell, any deity or spirit that sought to exult itself above him as head of the family. That way he would have fewer decisions to make about rights and wrongs, and no one would know he had dementia.

He could provide food and shelter, the here and now. There was no hereafter for snakes. He knew his thoughts were starting to repeat themselves. He had thought all that before, and for the life of him, he did not know why he was not staying firmly decided. Jesus, Jesus, there was just something about that name!

Black Mamba slithered home a very disturbed snake.

GOD HAS LOST HIS MEMORY

⚬

The fulfillment of the Prophesy sparked a wave of new believers. Pastor Twiga spent most of the week in the water baptizing. In the meantime, Brother Hyena hid in the reeds nearby, hoping to catch the pastor alone. He needed a discreet second baptism to start things over again with God. His sin was too awful for grace to be sufficient without some ritual. It was safer to reboot, just switch off and then restart his walk with God. It made sense, especially when he was still belching out the human among other methods of tossing the sin out of his body. On the seventh day after church, he got audience.

Twiga took one look at Brother's tormented face and led him to the counseling tree. It was a hysterical confession. The pastor calmed Hyena as he pieced together the details of his fall. The devil in a human carcass had tempted him. His stomach, had betrayed him and he had flirted with suicide, after safari ants tried to eat him alive. Hyena was carrying insurmountable guilt but he was sincerely repentant.

But while he was stuck somewhere in the devil's workshop, Hyena believed that God had hugged him, at which point the safari ants had vanished from his body as if they were never there in the first place!

There was only one conclusion for the pastor. God still loved Hyena unconditionally. Who was he to judge God's servant? He hugged Brother Hyena and cried with him for a moment.

"My brother," he comforted, "God loves you regardless. He will never leave you or forsake you."

"Then baptize me again," Hyena pleaded. "Let me re-start my relationship with God."

"If everyone who fell and sinned were to be baptized again, we would all live in the river," Twiga said gently. "When we believe, we become cubs of God's. If a cub stumbles, falls, or wanders away in ignorance, the father does not abandon but gathers him up in loving discipline. And there is always the not so confident one working to impress the father, to be worthy of his love, to earn it through his own effort."

"How did you know?" Brother asked sadly.

"It happens with most of us, especially new believers. Overzealous, anxious to please, but a little misguided."

"I can relate to that." Brother said. "I sure hoped to score some points back there, to prove my worth I guess. Now that I think about it, a gentle and small voice kept urging me to pray. I just thought I could handle it."

"He enjoys handling things with us, being part of our lives, and sounding the warning before we trespass," Giraffe said affably. "And there is no proving our worth to God. Our righteousness is filthy in his sight, and only his presence in our lives can make us worthy. We cannot earn his love either. God already made up his mind to love us a long time ago and gave us Christ his only son as the guarantee. We can only love him back and honor him with our trust and obedience."

"It is not easy," Brother moaned. "The heart is willing, but the flesh is weak."

"Well said," Twiga encouraged. "Everyone struggles with the

flesh and the devil till they let go and let God. Christ understands all that because once upon a time he came here in the flesh. He understands our weaknesses and remembers we are only dust. He ought to know; he made us himself. When we sincerely repent, he forgives our sins and chooses to lose that part of his memory, as if it never happened."

"He might have to lose his entire memory this time. You don't understand! I ate his image! I ate the image of God!"

"Calm down, even that is not beyond grace. You know The Name now, the only one given under the sun by which we can be saved.

"But many animals believe in God directly without Jesus or through other prophets. If I could find another way to God till Jesus calms down ... are there not many routes leading to the same God?"

"Sorry, friend, Jesus is the only mediator between God and the world. He ransomed it from eternal damnation with his own life. He earned it, he owns it, and in all fairness, it makes him the only one worthy of all the praise and honor in the world. No one can deny him and know God, yet anyone who acknowledges him does."

"How can we really be sure he is alive?" Brother wondered.

"We have an inner knowing called faith by which we choose to take what we cannot see as if it were. Faith is a gift from God. He knows it is not easy for mortals, and that is why he credits it as righteousness."

"It would be great to really know, to have some proof when you talk to others," Hyena said quietly.

"Everyone who has sniffed the graves of the other prophets swears their bodies are still snuggly there even now. But there are animals that have sniffed the tomb of Jesus in Miracle Land and they swear it is empty. He rose from the dead and manifests his existence in real ways. Do you doubt that he hugged you today?"

"No," Brother Hyena replied quickly.

"Would you rather gamble your eternal destiny on a messiah who has conquered death and lives, or one who is still dead, waiting to be resurrected and judged alongside you?"

"I sure don't want to be standing in line next to my messiah, waiting to be judged by another!" Brother replied.

"After Jesus gave his life for the world, conquered death, and rose again, the father gave the world to him as his inheritance. God would be dishonoring his son if he were to entertain those that deny him his rightful place. Just imagine if you owned a little jungle, gave it to your son as inheritance, and told the squatters you have allowed to live in it, 'This is my son, from now on, you only talk to me through him,' but one creature replies, 'I do not believe he is your son. Let me introduce you to your son!'"

"And just like that, God is accused of fathering a stranger!" Hyena said sadly.

"Well, not exactly. God did make everyone of them. He loves them as much as he loves Jesus, or he would not have sent him to die in their place. He is also pleased to give them the kingdom as co-inheritors with Christ. But Jesus Christ is the firstborn of all creation and he will not be robbed of that position. The father has entrusted everything and everyone into his hands. No one can go to the father except through him. It also makes no sense because the father has put all of himself in his son. If you have seen the son, you have already seen the father, for they are one. There is no other way of reaching the father because Jesus is the only way!"

"I am already getting very angry for God!" Brother fumed.

"He is big enough to take care of himself, but you do get the picture, my brother." Twiga smiled.

"How does one get rid of guilt after receiving God's forgiveness?" Brother asked.

"By forgiving yourself because God who is bigger than you

already did," Twiga advised. "Satan keeps reminding us of our past mistakes to make us feel inadequate and unworthy of a relationship with God."

"I guess we don't need the devil to remind us of our down and ugly," Brother moaned.

"Carrying guilt about already forgiven sin gives the devil a stronghold and casts doubt on God's willingness to forgive. That amounts to lack of faith, the basic ingredient of our entire relationship with God. Remember, when God credits faith as righteousness, the devil makes it his business to discredit."

"How is a simple, ugly hyena supposed to remember all this stuff?" Brother asked anxiously.

"God already wrote it down in your heart, the right and wrong," Twiga said, circling the counseling tree with him. "His Holy Spirit is the alarm in our conscience that sounds way before we sin. It keeps ringing nonstop till we escape the trap or seek forgiveness." Leaning toward Brother's ear, Twiga whispered, "Your alarm has been screaming nonstop for a while now. You know that you know what to do."

Yellow eyes would have taken to his heels if he had any. In a moment, they would be screaming the J name, and he could not hang around to fall on his face. He hated this giraffe because he could not harm him. Every morning, he called on The Name and covered himself with the B of J. Yellow could not complete the B word either. Pronouncing the Blood of Jesus in full made him burn all over!

It was not fair that someone's name alone was enough to hurt him. One of these days, Axis would cross swords with the dreadful son of God. Yellow was extremely jealous of J. C.'s unmatched power, and he suspected Axis was too. The only way he could personally hurt J. C. was to hurt his creatures, and he was going to aim directly at his heart.

Good thing Axis had laid out the legal foundation with original sin. Every living thing reeked of that, except those that had already called on The Name. For now, this dangerous creature, this high and mighty neck in the clouds, needed to be taken out!

Yellow smelled smoke before they could hurl The Name at him and vanished with a major swear. It was comforting to think he had taught many kids to swear just like that. They damned themselves pretty well before he ran them over.

"Take that, J. C.!" Yellow said with a grin as he flew away.

I Forgive You, God

Brother Hyena and Twiga stared at each other with tears in their eyes. Twiga's knees hit the ground first. He cried out to God for his friend's forgiveness and restoration.

Soon Brother gained courage and started praying loudly for himself.

"I thank you, God, for Jesus and for my pastor here. Please forgive me for eating a human made in your own image. Teach me to hear your voice, to trust and obey you before my stomach. Thank you for forgiving me. I forgive me too. Allow me to forgive you too, God, for taking my mother even though she was yours first. Receive praise and honor, from Brother your pet. Thanks for loving a scavenger like me. Remember Israel and their animals and keep them from what you have forgiven me. Endow man with wisdom, your image whose choice is our destiny. Amen."

Peace beyond understanding enveloped him as he felt another divine hug. Somewhere in his core, he knew he was loved as he was, loved just for being.

"I love you too, God," he whispered, tearfully staring into the gentle rays of the rising sun, its warmth the purest caress. All was well with his soul.

"Let's go for breakfast!" Twiga said, bringing Brother back to earth. "My place."

Brother merely granted and followed. He did not want to lose his spiritual high yet, but the pastor said something again.

"That is great, praying for Israel."

"I always do. It is custom with us hyenas. Even if you never pray for yourself, you have to pray for Israel so the ancient blessing can pass by you."

"Brother, don't be a lone wolf," Giraffe advised. "The spiritual journey can be lonely sometimes."

"Frankly, I am enjoying my company with God very much. Must we crowd it?" Brother asked possessively.

"The devil has been likened to a marauding lion, but I have never seen one attack a united park of hyenas, have you?"

"No."

"You can still be an individual in a team. God relates with us both jointly as the body of Christ and singularly. You can still have your bone and eat it!"

"I guess so," Brother replied reluctantly.

"Fellowship gains from everyone's unique gifts as we become our brothers' keepers."

"Jointly and singularly sounds too legal," Brother jested.

"There is nothing illegal about God. He is just," Twiga replied.

"So was my mother."

"And your father?" Twiga asked.

"I almost went down his digestive system at birth. Mother kicked him out, and I never saw him again," Brother replied.

"Bitter?" Twiga asked. He knew about some hyena fathers eating their young at birth.

Brother hesitated and nodded his head. He was not going to wear masks with his pastor.

"Let go," Twiga suggested. "Forgiveness breaks the bondage

of bitterness. It took me years to forgive God and my mother," he shared.

"What on earth for?"

"I started my life by crash-landing six feet to the ground and splitting my lip. Feeding was very painful, and the other cubs called me scar-crow. Later my uncle told me about the birds and bees, including the fact that most mothers remained standing when they gave birth. Our females are very tall. A giraffe cub's first glimpse of the earth is when it comes to meet him in the air with a first kiss on the mouth, which is not supposed to hurt. It was just an unfortunate accident, but I turned my anger to God for letting it happen. I learned to forgive God along the way, knowing it was necessary if we are to be best friends. Now my wife tells me it was the scar that first attracted her to me—that it makes me look rogue, whatever females mean by that. God used something I really hated for my good!" He finished with a wink.

"I forgave my mother's killer when I was burying that human, and it felt good," Brother said. "I guess it's time to forgive my father. Hatred stagnates and wears you down completely. If we expect forgiveness from God, we cannot withhold it from others."

Giraffe looked at Hyena with renewed respect.

"Remember the story of your ancestor, Ole Baba, and the origin of cannibalism," he said. "Your experience will encourage many brothers that are fighting the inherited scourge. No one needs to carry on the sins of their ancestors. If we ask him, God can always begin a new generation with us."

"Thank you, Pastor," Brother replied as they resumed walking. "I will be honored to be part of a fellowship."

"Good. We have one for new believers. I'll see that you are connected. And, Brother?"

"Yes?"

"Do not refer to yourself as ugly again! God made the best you that he purposed, and no one has the right to question his taste."

"I've been called ugly all my life," he said sadly. "I simply accept it to numb the pain, like getting used to an old wound."

"Anyone who criticizes your looks is really criticizing God's taste. The upside of it is that God turns their insults into blessings for you. Pray for them and get blessed even more!"

"Thank you, Pastor. That's a whole new perspective."

"One of these days you will wow a princess of the kingdom. She will tell you just how handsome you are!"

"But I do not have a scar on my lip like yours!" Brother moaned.

"Put your nose behind my hind, and we will give you a bigger one!" Giraffe laughed. "Oh, Brother Hyena, I do believe you got that hug from God. Think about that." He smiled, affably patting Brother's head briefly with his long neck.

"That was not the last one!"

"Do tell!"

"He does have his mysterious ways." Brother smiled as Twiga's wife met them at the entrance to their green patch of the jungle.

Yellow eyes watched from a distance. He had to wait till the hyena was in a safer place, somewhere not covered with the B of J. This giraffe and his compound were reeking of it! But he was patient. One of these days, there would be a crack in that giraffe's compound and he would widen it to a highway. Perhaps there was a back door. He would steal in somehow.

A Princess of the Kingdom

∾

M rs. Twiga had the most beautiful dots, but that was not what Brother was staring at. Sitting at the breakfast thicket was the biggest and the most breathtaking female hyena Brother had ever seen.

"This is Inao," Twiga introduced, sitting Brother next to her. "She is the one thousandth generation of Ole Mwana and the first Inao."

A princess of the kingdom! Brother thought, his eyes popping out.

The two stared at each other as if they were from different galaxies. Inao had never seen such a beautiful male. For some reason, he looked vulnerable, and she was struck by an overwhelming urge to protect him.

In his wildest dreams, Brother had never imagined a female so big could be so well put together or so gentle. He was quite unnerved as they talked back and forth about everything and nothing.

Their hosts doted on them, amused by their nonsense. There would be time enough for the two to talk some sense later. Right now, Twiga and his wife were just glad that two lonely souls were finding each other. Exchanging a wink, Twiga and his wife excused themselves to sort out some domestics.

Soon Inao and Brother relaxed and opened up about their personal lives and their relationship with God. Inao confessed to eating a small, dead human she had bumped into recently. The guilt had shredded her heart till she sought God's forgiveness and got counseling from Gloria Twiga.

When Brother told his story, he left out nothing, including his cannibalistic father and the loss of his mother. She touched her nose to his in comfort and told him about her own tragedies. Her own mother had died when she and her sister were born. Their dad had eaten her twin sister as she watched. A nursing aunt had rescued her and brought her up with two female cubs about her own age. One day, when they were bigger, their aunt was attacked by a lion when she was out for a walk. Most of their clan had gone hunting, but with the help of her cousins and the babysitter, they had surrounded the rogue lion and scared him away. Her aunt survived with a broken hind leg and many puncture wounds from the lion's claws.

The clan cared for her as best as they could, but a few days later, they were hit by a stampede of migrating wildebeests. Everyone was separated as they scampered for safety. When the dust cleared, her aunt was dead. She never saw her cousins again. Soon after, humans captured her and put her in some closed container that moved recklessly. She prayed all day like the human Jonah in the belly of a fish till the humans vomited her in Samburu. Samburu was a coming home of sorts. Her late mother was born and raised there, but she too had been captured and taken to Maasai Mara, where Inao was born.

"Trust God's image to correct all his original designs!" Brother said.

"God himself put us under man's dominion," Inao said resignedly. "Their choices remain our destiny till we go to heaven. God is the landlord there."

"Halleluiah to that, Inao!" Brother said with a distant look. She huddled a little closer to him, liking the way he said her name. There was something about that Samburu accent, a beautiful Kenyan drawl.

Brother loved her Maasai Mara accent, but he was saddened by her story. He searched his mind for something appropriate to say, a little annoyed to be falling for her. How was he expected to have butterflies in his stomach and say smart things at the same time?

Perhaps it is true that males think with only one side of their brain, he thought.

"What exactly is this wildebeest migration?" he said, diverting to a happier topic.

"Oh that!" Inao said excitedly. She loved talking about Maasai Mara. "Every twelve moons, something triggers urgency in the millions of gnus of Maasai Mara to move to greener pastures immediately. They set off accompanied by elands, gazelles, and hundreds of thousands of zebras, a magnificent cloud of life stretching from one horizon to another. There is rumbling, thundering, and grunting resounding toward the Serengeti in the land of Kilimanjaro.

I tell you, Brother, that convoy is the most beautiful spectacle this side of heaven!" She paused for emphasis as Brother's eyes and mouth opened wider.

"Unfortunately," she continued, "their escorts from behind are lions, feeding on the weak, the wounded, and the very young. Hyenas, wild dogs, and leopards spring up from the sides at any point of the journey. Once in a while, the gnus stampede to scare their enemies, but everyone gets to feast on them. Suddenly they are face-to-face with the raging Mara River, and the convoy hesitates, but the pressure from behind plunges the frontrunners into the raging crocodile-infested waters. Some crocs lose their noses to descending hooves, but they are well compensated." An enchanted Brother kept nodding his encouragement.

"When cubs and mothers are separated in the river, they keep swimming back and forth till they find each other or drown in exhaustion, but then that's the way of love."

Brother winced at the word love as if he was caught stealing.

"Mostly they survive the river of death, but there are no angels waiting on the other shore—only lions and other carnivals thanking God for the approaching feast! Thousands die, yet they must go to the land of Kilimanjaro. There the heathen crocs of the Grumeti have their teeth sharpened and waiting. More deaths, more sorrow, yet the gnus must go. By now you would expect the poor beasts are ready to curl up and die in the Gorogoro Crater, but they keep going! The whole thing resembles God's harvest season, a natural selection where only the best of the best are allowed to make the next generation."

"I'd rather be a hyena," Brother commented.

"Me too," Inao said without missing a beat. "Months before they go, the gnus calve with a vengeance, replacing in advance those they must lose. Believe it or not, all calves are born within three weeks of one another, and uncannily leave their mother's wombs before the sun is overhead. They run around within minutes of birth and race the adults in a few days. But here's the really goofy part. A calf that loses its mother can imprint on you and follow you to the ends of the earth. Food can literally carry itself to your dining place, and many have experienced that particular miracle!"

"Mmmmmmm!"

"Even humans have taken to tagging behind or waiting ahead on the trail. There is an animal in man yet! God's artistic coordination of nature and creatures is so splendidly displayed it ought to be the first wonder of the world."

"You make it sound heavenly."

"It is, Brother, it is. I miss it all so much, but it seems somewhat disloyal to my aunt," she said, a tear falling to the ground. Brother wiped it off with a paw.

"What does this wildebeest look like?" Brother asked.

"It has no looks of its own!" she replied mischievously.

"What do you mean? Is it some kind of spirit or ghost?" Brother screamed, jumping up in mock fright.

"More like a walking debt or loan." Inao laughed, standing up. "The forequarters are from an ox, the hides from some deer, perhaps antelope, and that mane has to come from a horse! If everyone demanded their parts back, that beast would be no more."

"That's terrible!" Brother said.

"Would you believe a newborn calf bears no resemblance to either parent? Even their genes are borrowed. Sadly, they forgot to borrow vocals cords. They can only grunt, and grunt they do."

"Is there nothing original about them?" Brother sympathized.

"They are organized to a fault, and that's not borrowed. Their dwellings are complete with married quarters, bachelor quarters, nursing mothers, and the like. Even those are organized according to the ages of the cubs. I'd let them organize me any time!"

"I think you will do just fine on your own." Brother laughed.

"Maasai Mara must be quite the fairy tale! I have heard rumors but never met anyone who has been there."

They gazed into each other's eyes for an embarrassing moment. The Twigas chose the same moment to come back, breaking the spell. Gloria allowed Brother to see off her protégé but jokingly warned him to behave himself or face one of her hind legs. She stretched it out displaying its length and strength, and then the other. Brother promised to behave. He was not sure he could carry a scar on his lip as well as the pastor did.

Yellow Eyes followed the hyena couple's trail. This time, he was a slithering python with a human head. There were moments he was entirely invisible, and in others, only the head was visible. He knew it was very scary for an animal to see a crawling human head. He could not describe to others what he had seen without sounding mad. Fear was a powerful instrument against the pets of God.

Brother and Inao walked endlessly in circles wanting the moment to last forever. This was the most fun either of them had had in a very long time. They played hide and seek, and Brother used his hide moments to sneak quick, uncensored prayers to heaven.

"Let her be the one, God, the princess of my kingdom!" he whispered as he let her catch him. All he wanted was to catch her for real, to live happily ever after.

"Please, God, give me something impressively smart to say to her!" But whatever smarts he had, he was still going to have to court her for twenty-four moons before popping the big question. That was the traditional courtship period for hyenas, almost a lifetime. It was not fair. She allowed him to take her halfway home and no more.

"I have not seen you in church," Brother commented as they stopped to say good-bye.

"Everyone knows me there, but mostly I help out in the Sunday school with the cubs," Inao replied.

"I sure have missed a lot," Brother said wistfully. "Would you walk with me next Sunday after church?" he blurted out and then regretted it immediately. He was going to die if she said no.

"I would like that very much, Brother," she said quietly looking into his eyes.

"Thank you," he mouthed, walking away with a dignified swagger, only to dance his way home as soon as he was out of sight. Halfway to his own den, Brother realized he had no idea where she lived or whom she lived with. He wanted to kick himself for being dumb.

"Dear God," he prayed, "I will need one of your mysterious ways to move from 'hello' to 'I do' in twenty-four moons, so help me, God. Amen."

The Bold and the Faithful

❦

It was Sunday again, and Black's family was frantic. He had been missing for almost a week. Swift concluded she was being punished for her sins. A husband did not just disappear into thin air unless the wife had been bad in some way. Not everyone would necessarily agree with her, but she just couldn't shake the belief.

She found a moist corner in their hut, moved in her one hundred grand-hatchlings and relaxed to her fate. Black could well have a heart attack, but that was alright—as long as he came home. For a moment she wished he had dementia, so he could mistake them for one hundred hallucinations. She repented the evil thought immediately. What selfish self preservation! She gathered her family together and prayed for the safety of the head who was yet to meet the majority of the family. And they were all calling on The Name he had not authorized.

"Very neat, Swift, very neat!" she chided herself. She made her hatchlings promise not to reveal their faith in Jesus to anyone yet.

She feared other Christians believed snakes were relatives of the devil, beyond God's saving grace. Other snakes could also ostracize them for Blaspheming on Axis.

There were two factions in the snake faith. One considered it an honor to die in a holy war. You immediately landed in snake heaven where legs of all kinds and sizes were available to choose from. With any heavenly legs, a snake would finally walk upright like the image of God, never to be hit or stepped on the head again. Black belonged to the second faction that believed in a wonderful here and now—after that, nothing. Both were deathly devoted to Axis and dangerous to defaulters. Unlike the Christian faith, there was no luxury of choosing to believe or not. You were already in the faith if you were born a snake. Swift's philosophy was simple. In the end we die, either for nothing or for something. She was choosing the latter.

In spite of choosing Christ, Swift was wary of the Christians themselves. She feared they welcomed snakes to church just so they could feel righteous sitting next to such sinful creatures. Some looked at them as if they were made of crude, unpurified sin. A public confession of Christ was likely to draw dangerous attention to her family and possible bodily harm. She decided they would be safer as closet Christians till they surprised everyone in heaven. In the meantime, she was praying that her husband would accompany them as long as he was not too grumpy up there among the happy angels!

She took her children to church as usual. Nyoka remained home in obedience to his father and watched over his one hundred nieces.

As soon as she settled her hatchlings on their favorite spot, she slithered respectfully to Squirrel, the announcer, and whispered that Black was missing. She had already sent word with Nyoka to King Cobra's court, and all snakes were aware.

When Squirrel read the announcements, Black Mamba was not the only one missing. Brother De Brazza Monkey Guenon was suspected to be missing.

The pastor called for more prayers. Then he reminded them

that it was the fasting week again. They were still expecting God to move their mountain and toss it into the sea. By faith, someone who knew the contents of the holy book that was the word of God was coming to dwell among them and teach them its mysteries. They knew it in part but were soon going to know it in full. It seemed an impossible feat, but the pastor was adamant that all things were possible with God.

There were many who were scared for the pastor, including his wife. But they dared not verbalize their doubts lest they grew roots. If this faith fast did not work out, many were never going to be comfortable with *Pastor* before Twiga's name or *Almighty* before God. Today was the start of the seventh week of the seventh moon of fasting. The jungle had never trusted God for something that big before.

On the patch of honor, the royal family was not looking right. They were totally withdrawn, except for the radiant queen. The king and the princess looked tired and did not even attempt to greet the animals. There was an *away* look about them, as if they were absent from their bodies. Suddenly, totally out of protocol, the cheerful queen stood up unannounced.

"Greetings to you all, good animals!" she said before putting on a seemingly practiced stern look. "Rest assured that no stone will be left unturned till every missing animal is back safely. We are still firmly on the throne."

Before the animals could respond, she led her family out, and the king tagged along with the princess. No one seemed concerned that the Crown Prince Simba was not with them. After all, he was not reported missing. Instead, they were wary of the queen's behavior. A wife did not speak for her husband when he was next to her as if he was dumb. In this part of the world, she was a wife first and queen second. It was a sign that the king was losing control of his family. A male whose wife "sat" on him aroused serious doubts about his leadership qualities. There were also some serious protocol violations, but no one dared to voice anything. This was church; you saw a weakness on your brother, and you prayed about it without humiliating him. Today the king was a brother.

Swift did not care about the king's domestics. Her brain could only handle one worry at a time and it was overloaded. Her husband was missing. She had stolen daughters to return to a distraught mother. Perhaps the curse could then be lifted from her family, and Black would come home to forgive her.

After service, she sent her daughters home and went in search of their biological mother. She was supposed to smile a greeting. It was custom. But Swift could not remember when she last smiled and feared she had forgotten how. Brahmin waited patiently at the agreed spot. Like her daughters', she seemed to prefer lying on moist earth. Swift tensed her muscle to produce a smile, but she knew it was not there. She decided to forgo the niceties and get to the point. After all, she was not nice.

Swift began, "A couple I know had eleven eggs, and ten were stolen under the wife's care. She was cowardly, selfish, and terribly afraid of her husband. So she went in search of any eggs to replace her own and avoid his wrath. She stole someone else's ten and hatched them as her own. Since then, she watches her entire family live a lie and dies a little every day. What will you do when you find the thief?" Swift asked, wanting a swift ending.

"Do you mean? Are you …?" Brahmin had no words.

"I really need to explain," Swift said very softly.

"I would like to understand why anyone would deprive another of their future generation! All this time, I hoped to lay more eggs, perhaps forget the past, but the gods have closed my womb. I really need to understand."

"The hatchlings are copy images of you. You must come with me. Please," Swift said and led the way.

Brahmin followed at a slow pace, and Swift kept waiting for her.

Finally they were home. Darklay had smelled them and waited near the entrance to the hut with Nyoka.

"Ladies, this is Brahmin," Swift said. "Brahmin, this is Darklay. Our ten precious daughters share one name. They already know you are their mother."

Brahmin was not sure about "our" daughters, but she flicked her tongue emotionally on her ten daughters. Nyoka watched the females hold a bowling party oblivious of him. Inwardly he was praying furiously to Jesus for a happy ending.

"I will not ask your forgiveness," Swift said in a breaking voice. "I do not deserve it, only let me keep loving them."

"You have taken good care of them," Brahmin said. "I do forgive you, only I cannot be separate from them now, please—never again."

"I agree," Swift said quickly. "You are welcome to move in with us if that is all right with the girls. Perhaps you need time to discuss this; whatever you decide is good with me. But I do have one more confession, one unforgivable thing," she whispered.

Everyone watched Swift, waiting.

"I failed to teach Darklay the female facts of life," Swift continued. "Someone took advantage of that and they have yet to tell me who."

"What are you talking about?" Brahmin asked.

"You must now meet Blessings," Swift replied. "Please follow me."

Everyone followed inside, even Nyoka. The identical Brahmin and Darklay moved so precisely it was hard to tell they were blind. Their smell was as good as sight.

"Who are all the little angels?" Brahmin asked as soon as she smelled them.

"Your grand-hatchlings." Swift replied hesitantly. "There are one hundred of them, ten from every one of your daughters. I named them

Blessings because no hatchling is an accident, father or no father. God purposed for every one of them to come to this world."

"Oh praise God, the father of our Lord Jesus Christ!" Brahmin exclaimed. "Surely he replaces a hundred fold whatever the devil has stolen!"

Swift winced. She deserved that even though she realized Brahmin was not referring to her.

"You are not mad that I do not know the absent fathers?" she asked Brahmin.

"Oh, Swift, you have never heard of our family?" Brahmin asked incredulously. "We are the only family of snakes in the world that does not need a male to reproduce itself. We are all female and every one a clone of their mother. There has never been a male in our family tree!"

"Whaaat!" everyone asked at once. Even the hatchlings lay still, caught up in the shock.

"How wonderful—I mean, how interesting!" Swift stammered as Nyoka eyed her curiously.

"It is true," Brahmin replied. "As soon as one is of age, the process begins automatically."

Swift and Nyoka were caught in a new wave of guilt. Darklay was telling the truth all along and they had not believed them. Apologies were quickly exchanged and accepted. Darklay were thrilled to have two mothers.

"I will stay with all of you for a while," Brahmin finally announced. "At least until the head of the house is found and he has had his say."

A dark cloud suddenly hung on the homestead. Swift quickly gathered everyone together to pray for the safe return of Black. She also needed God to give him a dose of peace that surpassed all understanding.

THE BIRTH OF A QUEENDOM

❧

The queen was elated. Lately the king was leaving important matters to her wisdom. The Voice was right; this jungle needed a Queendom not a kingdom. The females did most of the work anyway. She personally hunted and gave birth while the king lay like one dead pretending to be thinking. She wondered what her husband's title would be when the time came. Prince or first gentleman were not that bad. Hers would be *Madam First Lady most Excellent Queen Bora*. She would make the males address her in full, start hunting and picking up their roles as the family providers. It was time females stayed home to give quality time to the cubs. Lions should live and hunt as a group instead of fighting for domination of a homestead.

Queen Bora knew the quality time thing was a good idea but … heck, she also wanted more males in her compound to keep the roving eyes of her sisters off her husband. And she wouldn't mind having someone to make the king jealous. A little competition never hurt anyone, even a king who was on his way to becoming Mr. Bora! But first she had to come up with a plan everyone would respect, even her jealous sisters. They all liked the king more than her, and he liked them right back. That was a devil to deal with all on its own.

Chameleon had just given her another magic portion. It was

not really witchcraft, but the king's eyes were going to rest on no other female except her. He also needed to mellow out enough to support her when the kingdom became a Queendom. All he had to do was stand at her side. A queen looked more respectable if she had a husband. She knew there were jungles where that would not matter, but this was Samburu. It was good for female votes and for warding off the wrong attention.

Madam First Lady most Excellent Queen Bora sounded just fine. The Voice had said she did not need to stage a coup de tat. Her elevation would happen gradually. The Mass believed she had the smarts to pull a slow, intellectual takeover. The king had to appear to lose his mind, and the jungle would panic. She would step in as a savior.

"What about Simba?" she had asked The Voice. "He is next in line to the throne."

"He is the price you have to pay," The Voice had replied. "Even God in heaven gave up his only son for greatness. The Mass needs your son; the jungle needs you." There was a long pregnant pause before her conscience went into labor. She delivered her son.

"You are not going to kill him, are you?" she asked in concerned stupidity.

"The Mass needs him; the jungle needs you."

"Please, please, pleeeease!" she begged. "A mother needs to know."

"The Mass needs him; the jungle needs you."

"What a bore!" She swore inwardly and then composed herself into a queenly poise.

For many moons now, she had been working with Chameleon as instructed. The Voice said The Mass had anointed him shaman of the jungle and endowed him with all magical powers.

"The Mass is impressed with your wisdom and saddened by your problems, Madam First Lady most Excellent Queen Bora," The Voice saluted respectfully.

"Who is there?" she had asked, pushing her shoulders back to assume a queenly stance. "The angel of light."

"How does The Mass know my title? I only thought it in my mind!" she asked timidly.

"The Mass always knows," The Voice had said before going away. Yellow could have told her he planted the title in her head. What a beautiful idiot!

Every time she took her evening stroll in that direction, The Voice came back at the same thicket to give her guidance. It was slowly becoming her holy thicket, a shrine of the angel of light. The shrine was also near the Chameleon tree. There were perhaps millions of chameleons living on it. The tree was secluded and gave an impression of sprouting out of nowhere. All around it was long, green grass.

The first evening The Voice had guided her to the tree, she had stood there, mesmerized and a little scared of all the chameleons. They crawled on all the branches of the short, stout tree. It had very long, slender leaves that resembled more chameleons. Her host seemed to be expecting her. She made a very slow, deliberate descent from the highest branch, which called for all her patience. Soon the two females were face-to-face, almost nose-to-nose, each willing the other to flinch and become the subordinate. The queen bulked first.

This was the biggest chameleon Queen Bora had ever seen, almost like a baby multicolored crocodile with horns. Her huge round eyes were covered by a thin layer of skin, a fusing together of the upper and lower eyelids such that only two tiny dots were visible. Her body was built like a lizard with scales, and she had feet like a parrot. Only hers were four. Three of her toes were glued together on the outside and two on the inside. In spite of her slow jerky movements, she seemed to have a very good grip of the branch she clung to.

Chameleon locked one eye with the queen and kept watch of something up her tree with the other. It was unsettling and irritating. chameleon was not in the least awed of royalty. The one eye focused on her was very intimidating. Queen Bora wondered if the witch had two brains. If she could look in two places at the same time, she had to be able to hold two thoughts spontaneously. All she needed was two mouths and she could run two conversations. Her tongue was long enough to be cut and shared between several mouths. When she spoke, it went over the head of the lioness.

"My name is Earth Lion," the chameleon said. "And you are Bora. Your mantra is ready. Get down on all fours and start repeating, 'I amass the mastery of The Mass,' nonstop 666 times starting now." And the chameleon was gone.

The queen was stunned. The very nerve of her subject! First she names herself Lion, not even Lioness seeing she was female. She had also called her by name as if they were equals, no Majesty, Queen, or First lady. She also had the audacity to order her down on her knees like a servant with all those other chameleons looking ... what other chameleons? They were gone, as if they had never been there in the first place. She was on her own. Slowly she got down on all fours and told herself it was for Samburu. Even The Voice had said the jungle needed her.

"I amass the mastery of The Mass," she started and then kept it up till she was hoarse.

"Six hundred and sixty six," she counted in her mind.

Suddenly Earth Lion materialized, walking and floating in the air with the same jerky movements she used on the ground.

Surely this whole thing is from God, Bora thought. *Earth Lion is walking on air. The Lion of Judah walked on water and I am ... flyyyyyyiiiing!* She found herself airborne, floating toward Chameleon. Soon she was circling Chameleon and the tree. Earth Lion stayed in one position for a long moment and then stepped in line with the queen, circling alongside her. Soon the circles were descending in slow motion till the two landed gently on the ground.

The queen was totally bewildered. She did not want to think of herself as bewitched—no, she was Christian and properly attended church every Sunday. She just wasn't a radical calling herself saved, oh no, sir! Her Christianity was the nice kind, the one that even non-Christians were comfortable with. And now that she was about to become a reigning monarch, she could not offend anyone by declaring her real faith. She would rather keep them guessing. That way, she could easily glide into whichever side was politically correct. After all, religion was a private matter.

Earth Lion had no time for niceties. Again she watched the queen with one eye while the other motioned to someone up the tree. A relative or an aide materialized at snail speed with three magic portions wrapped in leaves. Queen Bora wished they would hurry before anyone appeared. If anyone saw her here, the Queendom would be finished along with any shred of her Christian mask.

"This you feed your husband to mellow him out," Earth Lion instructed. "He will start respecting you without questions." Chameleon paused and gave her the second portion.

"This will kill any interest in other females. Apply to his meat, sit on it six times, and feed him. He will have eyes only for you." Earth Lion paused even longer for the last portion and handed it over with a sigh. This time both her eyes were focused on the lioness.

"If you ever use it, his mind will leave him completely. You want to be sure you need that," she warned.

Poof! Just like that, both the chameleon and her tree disappeared from sight. The queen hurried home, removed the portions from her mouth, and hid them in a thicket. She had a short coughing fit and hoped nothing had leaked into her system. She wasn't going to swallow anything for a while, just to be double sure.

Last night, she had fed the king the portion for the roving eye, to keep his eye away from her sisters. It was not the recommended order, but it had become more urgent. When she came back from Chameleon, she had found the whole lot huddled together and no one had even missed her.

She and her sisters had gone hunting a gazelle. The whole family had eaten together as usual, and the king had even taken a piece to that hyena servant. Bora had hidden the best portion in the grass. As soon as everyone was asleep, she had rubbed in the magic portion and sat on it six times. Then she put it in the mouth of the unsuspecting king with a passionate kiss. He had gulped it down in one swift swallow and snuggled closer to her than to her sisters. It was working!

Only this morning, she had fed him the mellowing portion, and the results were already evident. He was mellowing down to a melon, saying yes to everything. But so was the princess. He must have hidden a piece of meat and fed his precious princess. Then she realized she had not seen Simba. He had not even accompanied them to church. These days he considered himself grown up even though he could not roar and did not want to be watched all the time. But he was a prince, and a prince was always in harm's way. Perhaps he was with one of the aunts. None of the other lionesses went to church. No, her heathen sisters never went to church. They just stayed home to steal her husband!

As she led her zombie-like husband and daughter home, something stirred in her memory, a distant fear of a deal she had made with the angel of light for the Queendom. She hoped they had not come to collect. Then she glanced at the princess and felt a touch of guilt. She was still a melon, and Bora wasn't sure if these things could be reversed. Anyhow, with a reigning monarch for a mother, the princess was not going to need a brain!

GRAFFITI ON GOD'S IMAGE

&

Yellow Eyes yellowed some more after hitting pay dirt. The one thousandth generation hyena couple was becoming an item. If he played his cards right, Axis would reward him. Perhaps even give him a name. The Mass just called him Yellow, and that was a color. He wanted a respectable name like Son of A Gun or something equally smart.

Suddenly it dawned on him what he must do, the perfect bait to separate the couple from God. But he needed the help of his counterpart on the human side.

Yellow reverted to spirit and rode the wind instantly to the human side of the jungle. Milika was watching a Samburu dance. Today she was disguised as a traditional Samburu cow complete with a hump and very long horns. Whenever she wanted to inspect a certain homestead, she became a lost cow with milk bursting from her udder.

The thoughtful villagers took her in, milked her out of kindness, and set off to look for whoever may have lost a cow. They put a rope round her neck and led her from *manyatta* to *manyatta*. Mostly she led them, pretending to know her way home. Then she ran like the wind, and they let her go. Soon she found another Christian home and let them drink her milk as she listened to their words. Some spoke of death and all sorts of harm to themselves, and she got to work fulfilling their self-proclaimed prophesies. Parents called their children fools and good for nothing, and individuals declared themselves failures. She fulfilled the words of their mouths and the meditations of their hearts and left the forces of J. C. to pick up where the humans blessed themselves.

Right now the cow was watching a Samburu dance. They normally danced at twilight around a fire, but today they did it in the day to cheer themselves up. They were very few. Most of the young men had left with cattle, looking for greener pasture. She had caused the death of many cows and calves this year through drought and foot and mouth disease. The owners themselves had declared they saw those things coming with the changing weather. Whenever the Samburu settled somewhere too long, little J. C. churches budded out, making her work very difficult. She kept them scattered in search of food and quarrelling over water wherever they found pasture. Hunger and anger kill hope. She worked hard for The Mass even though that Strongman Mundu did not appreciate her. One of these days, she intended to show him with something so big that only Axis could thank her enough. Then she would be on top of Mundu, sitting on his thorax, squeezing his throat…

Milika's thoughts were interrupted by Yellow's arrival. He was invisible to the dancing villagers. There were no niceties in their world, so they got down to business right away. Neither did anyone refuse a colleague a favor. A favor is always collectable one day with massive interest. Almost everyone was indebted to someone, and no debt was ever cancelled. Milika listened carefully to Yellow's problem. He was prepared to owe, and she was happy to be owed. It was a deal.

"I have been working on this girl for nine months, a Sunday school teacher," Milika said. "The Samburu do not do this kind of thing, but now we have a first. She is giving birth right now near the jungle, alone. You know how virginity is treasured here. No one has even guessed she is pregnant. I have her convinced this is the only way out or she will be shamed in the entire Christian community. She will never get a husband, and no good girls will be allowed to befriend her. Everyone will point her out in the village dance as an example of what was good gone bad.

"Recently she had half the Sunday school kids accepting J. C. as their personal savior. That was before I sent the boy, an irresistible Moran whose heart belongs to Axis. He is doing some cattle rustling right now with an underground group, and I have his eyes on another girl. The Sunday school teacher is going to throw something your way, and you can take matters from there. You owe me one, Yellow."

"What happens to the girl?" Yellow wondered. Not that he cared.

"Perhaps she will meet a good boy from another village and get married, but the guilt of what she is about to do mingled with fake purity will keep her too shamed to go near J. C. Every time she looks at her good, kind husband, she will feel rotten to the core. In the end, no one will know why suicide visited such a happy family."

"Brilliant," replied Yellow as he disappeared. He had his own winning to do and no time to marvel at the boasts of his more successful colleague. Hell, he was jealous and he was going to show them all!

The next Sunday after church, Inao and Brother found each other and a secluded patch of grass under a tree. They sat face to face, their eyes lost in the other's maze, searching for happily ever after. There were butterflies flying lazily around them and many others fluttering in their stomachs. Monkey and Aero watched them from the tree. Love was definitely in the air.

Suddenly an anguished cry pierced their ears. Brother and Inao jumped at the same time, banging their heads so hard the chemistry class threatened to turn into surgery. Inaudible apologies were exchanged as they hurried toward the cries. It came from where the jungle bordered with human habitats.

A newborn human cub was crying its lungs out and waving its tiny paws. It was wrapped in swaddling clothes and shoved into a plastic bag. The lovers glanced at each other with the same thought. In another time, another life, this would have been a perfect snack to share. But they were now new creations in Christ, healed of their addictions to eating the image of God. Their hearts broke at its helplessness and the cruelty of man to the defenseless.

"Dear God!" Inao cried. "Endow man with wisdom, your image whose choice is our destiny!"

"Aaaamen!" Brother said emotionally. "Thank you, Jesus, for trusting us with this life, which is in your image. Please show us how to save it."

Yellow Eyes watched in great anticipation. Milika had outdone herself. These two were still hyenas, even if they proclaimed J. C. as their lord and savior. All their choices and inclinations were greedy. They would bite. He hoped they would hurry because the baby was making too much noise. Any ungodly creature could turn up and grab what was meant to ensnare the pets of God. Milika should have done something to the baby's vocals.

If all went as planned, the two would never recover from the guilt of that snack. Yellow was totally invisible now but for the yellow eyes, and they were too engrossed to see him.

Suddenly Yellow felt sick to his stomach, trembled, and collapsed on his invisible knees as the dreaded J word hit his ears. He was burning all over without being consumed.

Inao and Brother made the unanimous decision without need for words. The human cub had to be saved, if only to ease the guilt of similar moments in the past. They stood guard and trusted the creator of all three of them to make the next move.

Suddenly they heard the whoosh of landing wings as a raven came to investigate.

"Quick, Raven!" Brother cried urgently. "Get man's best friend! Get Dog quickly!"

"But, Dog is afraid of you!" Raven hesitated, grasping the situation quickly.

"Brother and I will hide and let Dog take the little human," Inao said. "But tell him to use his nose and avoid the cub's real mother. For all we know, she dumped him herself. There has to be a human with a soul out there somewhere! We will pray in the meantime."

Raven wasted no time as he flew to the human settlement. He perched on a branch of a tree under which Soldier the Dog was watching a cock fight. Raven politely explained the situation and Soldier swung into action. There was no time to waste if the newborn was to leave the jungle and live. He followed Raven.

The baby was still yelling heavenward with all its might, unaware that God had already heard his cries. Soldier bit firmly on the swaddling clothes and held. Without hesitation, he jumped the fence, crossed a river, escaped some bully mongrels, and came to a very narrow path that led to his master's compound.

Suddenly he was face-to-face with the biggest mad cow he had ever seen. She was all white with a jet-black nose and mouth. The tips of her long horns curved upward. Her hump was a quivering mountain, and her flaring nostrils blew big smoke. Four rivers of milk were flowing from her udder. The cow started scratching the ground with her hoof like a fighting bull. There was no room to pass or turn back.

Soldier's tail tucked itself flat under his belly, but he did not let go of his now silent buddle of joy. If the humans did not want this baby, he was prepared to raise him as his own and name him Soldier Junior after himself. But first he had to rescue them both. Soldier sensed the baby's trust, and courage surged through him. They were going to live and not die. He had never really learned to walk backwards, but he tried to retreat.

Suddenly the cow's eyes turned a brilliant yellow as she charged. The baby fell from his mouth and rolled to the side with a wail as Soldier involuntarily barked his loudest.

"*Jeeeesuuuus!*" he barked. They heard him all the way in heaven.

The cow came to a sudden stop, trembled, and fell on all his knees with the biggest thud. Soldier grabbed the baby, jumped on the trembling demon cow, and walked over him to the other side. He ran all the way home without looking back.

Finally he was at his master's doorstep. He placed the baby on the floor and started barking like he was facing the antichrist. The baby seemed to get the message and started bawling for its life. Soldier knew his master had a good soul. A dog had a sense about such things.

The door opened suddenly, and a man came out. His eyes almost popped out, but he did not touch the baby. These were female matters. It was custom. He yelled something once, and his first wife came out running, wrapped in a one-piece brown cloth and tons of multicolored beads. Soldier thought she had more colors than a rainbow, but he liked her.

She grabbed the baby, shrieked out something, and the other six wives ran out of their *manyattas*. Curious human cubs clad in one-piece clothes abandoned their games to come and see what was happening. Soldier watched from a distance as the seventh wife, the childless one, came out last, hesitatingly. She was beautiful, especially when she smiled, but that was very rare. Like the other wives, she wore two pieces of cloth, a plain brown one up to her chest and a multicolored piece on her slender shoulders. Her long neck was invisible. It was adorned with layer after layer of multicolored beads.

The first wife handed her the baby, and there was total silence. Even the children seemed to realize something had changed forever. Instinctively she held the baby close to her heart. He looked into her eyes, put his tiny hand on her beads, and stopped crying. A single tear hit him between the eyes. His new mother kept holding him close to her breast. Soldier knew the baby was too young to see but was starting to imprint. The language of love was unmistakable. The beautiful seventh wife smiled at the world as radiant as the morning sun. She had the most perfect set of white teeth. No one would pelt her house with cow dung in mockery ever again. *Nkai* had sent her a baby from heaven.

In all the color and excitement, no one noticed the lost cow that had wondered into their homestead—not even Soldier because the cow had no scent. Even the milk that dripped from its udder had no smell. The new mother dropped down on her knees, still holding the baby, and started worshipping Nkai loudly, covering the baby with the Blood of Jesus. The cow trembled and dropped to her knees. Then she shot off to get lost some place else. Milika the demon cow realized her milk would not nourish the new baby that day, perhaps never if the mother kept up such prayers.

She decided to use the Moran again before his curse period was over. He was the fourth generation of a witch and a wizard who had performed abominations by seeking answers from the dearly departed. God had cursed them to the fifth generation. Unless he had called on The Name, he was still legal ground for demons.

It was also time to leave for The Mass to make her 666-day report. In a way, Milika was happy her colleague Yellow had failed. The hyena and his girlfriend had not eaten the baby, and there would be hell for Yellow to pay. She looked forward to tormenting him when The Mass demoted him.

The cow walked to the secret bush where humans and animals never went. They associated it with evil and never took their cows there. She said her secret code, and the door opened. The cow took the wide ancient path and started her journey to the Devil's Mountain. Four parallel trails of milk flowed to make what she called *a milky way*.

A Sympathy Card for God

෴

Soldier's good deed for the day was done. Giving an all-is-well sign to Raven, he went back to the cockfight, but it was long over. Luckily he knew how to start one. He had to do something to forget that cow.

Raven flew away thanking God he was not a human. No self-respecting animal or bird would do to its young what the image of God was doing to their own these days.

Brother and Inao saw Raven and rejoiced. The tiny image of God was safe. What an honor to serve God where man had failed. What shame on humans!

"I feel sorry for God," Inao said quietly to Brother as they watched the human side where Soldier had disappeared.

"That's blasphemous!" Brother retorted indignantly. Someone had to defend God's honor on that one.

"I'm sorry, that came out wrong," she apologized.

"What did you mean?" he said more gently.

"Think about all he has invested in man. He made an entire world filled with answers for every question man would ever ask all before he made man. Even we animals exist only as man's answers. He prepared man's joy and comfort beforehand. Then he made man in his own image and laid it all at his feet. Yet among all creation, man remains the most discontented and insecure, even in his own identity as a species. It is not enough to be the smartest on earth, he also wants to swim like a fish, fly like an eagle, run like a deer, fight like a lion, and outsmart God! But God only gave him enough time to be man. So in order to do everything else, he steals his own rest, robs God of his Sabbath, and withholds his love from those that need it the most, including him because it costs time to give it."

Inao took a moment to exhale. Brother wondered if he was supposed to process all that. He had heard that females used more words than males. He did not know what response was expected, the smart thing to say or ask.

"Why do you think man is discontented even as a species?" Brother asked. It was safer to keep her talking till he figured it all out.

"How does God feel when what he made turns around and tells him, 'You did not make me!'? If a potter uses a stick to mix his clay, should the pot say, 'the stick made me'?"

"Please speak in jungle language, I am lost," Brother pleaded.

"Man denies being God's original creation and prefers to be an evolved monkey. Even if for argument's sake the monkey was the stick God used to make man, would he stop being God's creation?"

"Man's morals and compassion are at an all-time low, but we are yet to see a monkey dump her young or interfere with the unborn," Brother said. "There is no way those two are related."

"God's favorite creation, the only one he made in his own image, is giving its birthright to a monkey. He gropes for anything but the truth that is manifest in his own existence and everything around him."

"If I was God, I would seriously reconsider who represents my image on earth, and man would not be on any *Earth's Got Talent* competition." Brother said the first thing that came to mind.

"Have you any idea how animals have suffered in his hand?" Inao fired on. "Donkeys worked to the bone, beaten, slashed, or just tossed out in the cold, cocks and bulls fighting to death for entertainment, horses dying for centuries with the image of God astride them in wars that did not concern them, the sacrificial animals and yet, everything pales to what man does to his fellow man."

"You don't want to go there, the man eat man thing, but what did you mean sacrificial animals?"

"Millions were sacrificed on holy and unholy altars to atone for man's sin. At first the sacrifices delighted him, but man was very resourceful in finding new ways to grieve God. He spiraled out of control to the point where animal blood was no longer sufficient. God's justice called for permanent separation with man."

"So why are they still around?" Brother prompted.

"Twice he almost wiped out the lot, with fire and flood," she answered. "Animals roasted and drowned alongside the image of God. Mercifully, God left a remnant of everything to continue all species. All creatures including man hastened to replenish the earth. But as man increased, he found new and reconstructed old ways to grieve God afresh."

"Poor God!" Brother moaned.

"My sentiments exactly!" Inao snapped. "Man is either ignorant or does not care that his choices determine the destiny of everyone else. If God does not do something soon, this world as we know it is history."

"Ancient history," Brother agreed sadly.

"A fossil for future generations or a bunch of aliens to discover some day!" Inao huddled closer to Brother and continued venting on man, still angry for God. "So, here is God holding a condemned world in his hand. They have sinned their way to oblivion unless the highest ransom is paid. His compassion cannot bear earth's extinction, and nothing is found in the world worthy of redeeming it. What was God to do? "

Brother said nothing, and Inao suddenly straightened out.

"Oh, forgive me, Brother. I must be boring you to death!"

"As you can see, I am not dead. I like listening and I love the way you tell it. Please don't stop now!" Brother replied. He focused his eyes on her mouth and kept hoping for a miracle.

Please, God, he prayed. *Your will be done on earth as it is in heaven. But see if you can sneak my will in there. Amen.*

No Relatives Please!

❧

"Please, please don't stop now!" A new voice intruded, snapping Brother back to reality. It was Monkey hanging on his tail above them. There were other eavesdroppers. Raven perched on the same branch with Monkey, and the rest of the jungle had crept up unnoticed.

Inao looked at Brother questioningly. He nodded encouragement, happy for new company. Now he could take breaks to listen and watch her talk as others helped with some of the answers. This female knew a thing or two about life, and he was a tad intimidated. If he remained silent, he could exude a mysterious aura. His rogue cousin would have known the smart way to behave.

Inao gave a friendly look to everyone and continued her monologue.

"A newborn cub imprints on its mother at birth. You would expect man to imprint on his creator. God put his own breath in man and patented his masterpiece by making it in his own image! When did Monkey get the patent?"

"Say something, Monkey! We are discussing your cousins!" Brother jested.

"No, no, no and never and not! I could never have such ugly

relatives who have no skin or fur. Save for their brains, they are physically just pathetic!"

"Did you know they are teaching this stuff to their cubs in schools?" Lizard, who liked hiding in classrooms, asked.

Monkey jumped to another branch, as if he had been stung.

"Why then do we not have monkey human creatures half-crouching, half-standing in all evolutionary stages? The only creature evolving must be man himself."

"What do you mean, Monkey?" Inao asked.

"God probably made man with a fur coat like mine. He lost it when he wore clothes. Then he cooked most of his lifespan along with the nutrients when he discovered fire. His poorly fed body is losing the little hair left on his head and becoming susceptible even to animal diseases. Their souls are so malnourished they can dump a newborn in the bush. He believes in the supernatural God who speaks things into being but also believes in a process of being called evolution! Does anyone think that sounds like me?"

"Easy, Monkey, watch your blood pressure," Brother joked.

"Man pursues happiness in the path of unhappiness by turning his greatest discoveries to destructive purposes. Look what they did to fire. Once upon a time, they used it to cook, light their way, and warm them. They partied around it and told bedtime stories to their cubs, sneaking wisdom into their young minds. The stories are gone, and fire is now featured in every weapon of mass destruction. And every time man makes a new destructive firer, his neighbor makes a bigger one and the rat race is on again."

"What's wrong with rats racing?" asked an indignant rat.

"No offense, Mr. Rat, just an expression," Monkey replied respectfully. "I love your races."

"None taken. Just be sure to be cheering on my side."

"I am proud to be a monkey. Man suffers from progressive disconnection and is looking for someone, anyone, to call his roots rather than the one to whom he truly belongs. His so-called evolution is only change caused by his own interference with nature over time. I tell you, he is no relative of mine!"

"Easy, Monkey, we believe you already," Raven comforted. They had never seen Monkey that passionate. No one realized he had an important guest to impress up in the tree. Aero was the silent, invisible guest.

"Quite a sermon there, Monkey," Mole joked, facing the wrong way. He was blind. "Somewhere in all that you admitted it was God who created us all and the one we owe all reverence."

"In the future, let's quit any insensitive 'my cousin' jokes!" Monkey sidestepped. He was not yet comfortable proclaiming his faith in one God. "Have you any idea what they do to my relatives in scientific experiments? Why would anyone do that to their own family?"

"Enough please!" cried Mouse. All his hair was standing up at the mention of man and science. "Does anyone care for a graphic description of what they do to my relatives?" he asked not so politely.

"No!" the animals thundered unanimously.

Aero smiled up in the tree. Monkey had advised her to wait. He was still figuring how best to land her in the jungle. She was far too important to just appear casually. But God seemed to have chosen to bring the world to her feet. She was getting to know everyone before they were aware of her existence. In a way, it gave her a sense of God's own loneliness for those he knew and loved but who had no idea of *his* existence!

God's Crossroads

෬෨

"Inao, please, you were telling a story," Monkey prompted.

"Where was I?" she asked.

"God was holding a condemned world in his hand," Mole reminded her, and everyone drew closer.

"Oh yes. The world reeks of every sin, and the stench is overwhelming. Heavenly creatures cover their noses, as God rummages through the sewer that earth has become. He is retching too but his pirated stinky lovechild is drowning in eternal muck. His Justice says to condemn, his mercy says to forgive and Love must find The Way. Love and Mercy appeal to Justice. He warns that the ransom would be the highest ever and even ever after.

"'Can I ransom them once for all time even for sin not yet committed?' Love asked Justice.

"'Be my guest,' Justice replied, 'if you can pay the price.'

"'Name your price,' Love replied. 'That's how much I love them.'

"Justice stifled a sob. 'The lamb of sacrifice must be most pure, never blemished by sin, more precious than earth and all heavens— oh yes, and higher than all creation! Only the blood of such a lamb could wash your soiled baby world. Then she will be white as snow!'

"There was a long pause in heaven," Inao said sadly with a long pause of her own. The animals sat on another pause. Up the tree, Aero was mesmerized. She thought she was the only one who knew something. God was unveiling himself to these creatures right here even before she met them. And the lady had oratory skill! She wanted her for a friend. She wanted everyone for a friend, but she had to wait for God's moment.

"What did God do?" Squirrel asked, jumping up and down impatiently.

"Please continue!" others begged.

"Love searched both the heavens and earth. Nothing and no one was found worthy. Then he looked at his only begotten son—"

"No, he didn't!" Bush Baby cried.

"He did too!" Inao replied. "What is more, he had put all of himself in his son. So he was really looking at himself! And only his blood was worthy. Love looked at Justice. Justice nodded. It was a deal."

"What a tough moment to be God!" Brother observed. "To be just in his justice, the world had to go. And to remain in his nature as love, the world had to be saved!"

"What did he do?" many voices asked at once. Aero almost shouted the same question, but it was not her moment.

"He chose love and justice."

"Inao, please, it was a 'choose one' question!" Lizard interrupted.

"In love, God gave his only son. In justice, Jesus became flesh bearing all sin for all time and took our death sentence on himself. The firstborn of all creation took on the punishment of the rest of creation."

"Talk of big brother!" Elephant said with a tear.

"There you got it!" Inao agreed.

"Did Jesus not have a say in the matter?" asked Leopard.

"Jesus obeys his father in everything. He is his father, sharing the same love for the world. So he was led like a sheep to the slaughter."

"Holy cow!" Jackal swore.

"There is no holy cow or any other holy creature," Inao said calmly. "Only God is holy."

"As pets of God, we are not permitted to swear. Not by heaven, earth, or anything else—even a cow!" cautioned Mrs. Zebra.

"That's right, Mama Zeb," Inao said. "When we swear by anything, we offend the holiness of God who made everything."

"What happened next?" Jackal asked.

"Please, Aunt Inao, make it a 'Once upon a time' story so it can end happily ever after!"

Everyone turned to look at the sobbing Quirra, Squirrel's little daughter who had tagged along. Quirra recoiled from all the eyes and hid with her father's bushy tail.

"That's all right, Quirra," replied Inao, ever the Sunday School Teacher. She moved closer to Quirra and bent her head lower as if she were telling the story only for her. The other animals drew closer. They could have made the same request, but Quirra beat them to honesty.

"The story is sad, Quirra," Inao started.

"Start with the sad part," Quirra said sadly. "I want a happy ending!"

"Once upon a time, God stood on a hill in heaven waving good-bye to his son. The son waved back, descending toward the sun. There were tears in both their eyes for the tears on the fabric of the world. Father and son waved on till they were out of sight.

"The son Jesus left the splendor of heaven, his glory no longer aglow in the glare of the sun. That too was left behind. The sun warmed and lit the earth as it had always done before, in obedience to the son.

"God stayed firm on the throne, dressed in light and might, crowned in all majesty and the saddest face that ever was worn. He had to lose his son for a moment or the world forever. See, he loved them both the same. The son descended to earth into the womb of a human virgin known as Mary who lived only to please God."

"Wow!" exclaimed Quirra. "How did he do that?"

"Through the power of the Holy Ghost," Inao replied.

"I am scared of ghost stories!" said Mrs. Zebra.

"He is really the Holy Spirit, Mama Zeb," Inao said.

"Who is the new character in the story, this Holy Spirit Ghost?" Monkey interrupted.

"There is God the father, God the son Jesus, and God the Holy Spirit. All three are really one. The father created everything through a spoken word. His word is life personified in his son Jesus. It was Jesus who created everything through the power of his father, which is in the person of the Holy Spirit. All three are God in their own capacity, but they operate in a union referred to as the Holy Trinity. The Holy Trinity is the unanimous functioning of the three as one. Like there is only one God and those are his parts."

Monkey nodded but mumbled an inaudible "Whatever!" and scratched his head.

"He gestated in the virgin's womb for nine months and was born human. She named him Jesus as the angel had told her beforehand."

"How sad!" Brother commented.

"Why sad?" Inao asked. "I thought his death was the sad part."

"Think of a human cub. Born blind and no skin or fur to protect it. The sight is there in a couple of days, but it is years before it can walk, run from predators, talk, or find its own food. It is the most pathetically helpless cub in the world!"

"A clear demonstration of how low Jesus was prepared to sink to save this world," Inao said.

"He could have been born a lion, tiger, elephant, or giraffe, but remember, man is the image of God."

"Daddy, could you asked the grownups to let the story continue?" Quirra pleaded. Inao had turned her attention elsewhere, and she was feeling neglected.

"Quirra is right," Elephant said.

Tortoise put out his head from his shell and spoke right next to Brother, startling him. He had sat there all along looking like another rock.

"Forgive my intrusion, but I never tire of this story."

"No problem," Brother replied a little angry at himself for being startled and also starting to feel a little possessive of his time with Inao. This was somewhat a date, and the whole jungle had turned up.

"Most humans did not believe he was the son of God or that he was God," Inao said to Quirra. "His earthly father was only a carpenter, and he was born in a manger."

"If he chose to be born in a manger, animals are major in his plan!" Toad exclaimed, jumping up and down.

"Yipeeeeee!" exclaimed Quirra, jumping along with toad.

Amen, Amen and Hallelujahs resounded. Inao continued as soon as they settled down.

"He went from place to place, healing the sick, restoring sight, raising the dead, and forgiving sins, telling everyone how much his father loved them and he was here to prove it."

"Was he handsome?" Quirra asked.

"Yes, Quirra, beyond imagination," Inao replied with emotion. "He was flawless the way man was meant to be. The origin of all appearance flows was the original sin in the garden of God. It tainted everything that God had made beautiful, including the life that was supposed to remain happy ever after. Now imagine someone who was never touched by sin. How handsome he must have been!"

Then Inao sighed, as if she dared not say the rest of it. Quirra looked at her concerned.

"What is it, Aunt Inao? Did he become ugly later?" she asked.

"No, Quirra. The only moment he looked ugly was on the way to the cross carrying all the sin of the world. There were open lashes on his entire body as the humans beat and tortured him. By the time they reached the hill where they planned to kill him, he was just an unrecognizable mass of raw flesh and blood."

"But all he wanted was to be friends!" Quirra said indignantly, angry at humans for hurting him. Her tears welled up again.

"He made many good friends, mostly with those whom the world considered unworthy. He called them to him and made them worthy. They were the ones who continued spreading the good news after he was gone, and many even died for The Name. But that's another story. Religious humans thought he was starting a dangerous cult and accused him of blasphemy against God. Others felt they were too good for him. Some did not even know why they hated him, they just did. But he never stopped loving any of them."

"What happened next?" Quirra asked.

"The humans hanged the son of God on a tree between two thieves, a punishment reserved only for those who are cursed. But he had now become the curse for the world. They pierced his side with a sharp object called a spear, which man uses to hurt his enemies in a battle."

"But he was not fighting back!" Quirra cried.

"No, Quirra, he wasn't," Inao said sadly. "Instead, he let them. And when they hurled insults at him, he did not retaliate; when he suffered, he made no threats. Instead, he entrusted himself to his father because he knew he was just. Without knowing it, the humans actually fulfilled the purpose for which he had come. When his blood gushed out, it washed away all sin. The curse on the world was broken permanently and its death sentence substituted for life eternal. It was the most painful, most lonely, and most humiliating death ever suffered, but he bore it for us. His blood remains potent to this day so that anyone who calls on his name will be saved."

"Are you saying he died for a world that was ignorant of him and the purpose of his death?" Monkey asked, very concerned.

"Yes, Monkey, while we were still sinners, he died for us. We were like lost sheep that Jesus returned to his father, the shepherd and overseer of our souls. We were all torn and bruised by thorns and enemies, but he took those injuries upon him so that as he is we can be also. And with his last breath, he asked his father to forgive man who was killing him, for he did not know what he was doing."

"What manner of love forgives your killers at the moment of death?" Monkey asked with a broken voice.

"A supernatural one," Dove whispered and perched next to him.

"He gave up his spirit and descended into hell," Inao proceeded as more tears glistened.

"Where the antichrist lives!" cried Mrs. Zebra her ears and hair standing up sharply.

"No!" Quirra exclaimed. "It is where the father of the antichrist lives, and now he is giving birth to the antichrist. Is that correct, Aunt Inao?"

"You are both right," Inao said. "Just as the son of God is God, the antichrist is being born of the bigger antichrist, the devil himself. Their mission will be to counterfeit the true son of God and mislead his friends."

"But how can the son of God go to hell? That's not a happy ending, Aunt Inao!" Quirra asked, tears welling up again. Bush Baby began to cry out loud.

"Easy now, Baby!" Inao consoled. "Jesus knew exactly where he was going and his exact mission."

Inao stood up and started acting out the next part for Quirra and Bush Baby.

"He descended into hell and thrashed the devil big time! Then he stormed his dungeons and released the captive souls who had sat desolate in the darkness for millions of moons. 'Hello, fellows! I am Jesus Christ the son of God. My father loves you very much. He said to come and get you if you want to come home!' They believed him and the spell was instantly broken. Immediately they turned from chained souls and became princes and princesses of the king of kings, and the devil could not hurt them forevermore. Their big brother, Prince Jesus, stood guard with the sword of God!"

Inao sat down again, facing Quirra who had stopped crying.

"Please, please, what happened nest?" Quirra asked.

"On the third day, he battled the monster called death. He ran him through with the sword of God, and he became alive again. He was not dead evermore," Inao finished with a smile.

"Was he still handsome?" Quirra asked with a coy blush.

"Absolutely! His resurrected body was unblemished. But he chose to keep the scars on his hands and feet as a permanent reminder that the price was paid and God's baby world was no longer condemned. No one owes the devil anything. It was also for baby world to recognize her big brother when she sees him again. Those scars are the only thing made on earth that is in heaven."

"But, Aunt Inao, you said in Sunday school that nothing imperfect is allowed in heaven!"

"That is still true, Quirra. But because of *why* Jesus was pierced, the father and all heaven consider those scars more priceless than all the streets of gold!"

"How did he go back home when he was not dead evermore?" Quirra asked.

"First he said good-bye to all earthly family, friends, and followers. He promised to go and prepare a place in his father's house that has very many mansions, beautiful bushes, and jungles all around it. Once it is ready, he will come back for all of us who believe in him. Then his father sent a chariot made with clouds and driven by the wind to take him back to paradise with all the newly rescued souls. The crowd of souls was so big it resembled a cloud of dust. It was the first resurrection, and they are still living happily ever after, waiting for the rest of us. One of these days, Jesus will come back and it will be our turn to fly!"

"How will we recognize him, Aunt Inao?"

"By the scars, Quirra. By the scars on his hands and feet."

The pets of God huddled together, looking up as if he was already coming to get them.

"Are you saying there is no more sin in the world, that it was all washed away?" Raven asked, quietly bringing everyone back to earth. "What was that we witnessed today, a newborn human cub dumped in the jungle?"

"He did not come to remove sin from the world but to pay the penalty for it. Many will be purified, made spotless, and refined by his blood, but the wicked will continue to be wicked. It is a matter of choice. Only those who call on The Name of Jesus will be saved. All who believe in him will not perish but have everlasting life because their sin will no longer count against them. We can only be saved through faith and his gift of grace and not our perfection; otherwise no one will make it. Everyone is born tainted with the venom of original sin, and Christ's blood is the only anti-venom that God has given his baby world. But we must believe it to see it!"

THE PETS OF GOD

ℭℑ

"We are reasoning as if we are human. Did Jesus die for us animals too?" Leopard, who was camouflaged in the tree, asked no one in particular.

"I believe so," Buffalo replied. "Jesus made us himself. Then he came to earth to be born in a manger. He is still called the Lamb of God and the Lion of Judah. His death made animal sacrifices unnecessary for all time, and he never once said he was only coming back for humans. What more evidence do we need?"

"He provides for us without toiling or storing up food like man," Tortoise said. "He has given us the gift of instinctive faith. If we trust in him, we will not be left behind."

"It must be hard for simple faith to penetrate the intricate intellectual thinking and reasoning processes of humans," Mole said, still facing the wrong way. "They can only understand it when they are very young, before reason is full blown."

"We must pray for them as long as we are under their dominion," Guinea fowl cut in. "Their choice is still our destiny."

"Come quickly, Lord Jesus!" Brother Hyena moaned. "If our hope is only in man, then we are hopeless!"

"That's true," Mole said. "But Jesus said he is the way, not man! We dare not lose hope that God loves us directly."

"Well said, Mr. Mole," agreed Bat. "When God saved the human Noah from the flood, he told him to take with him two of every kind of creature. He wanted us to exist for his purpose."

"God used the belly of a whale to transport a human called Jonah who could not follow directions to a place called Nineveh!" Warthog said, causing laughter.

"Their sense of smell never fully developed to help their eyes with directions," Monkey defended man.

"A donkey once spoke in a human language after seeing an angel of God," Crow shared. "God opened his mouth to protest unjustified beating by his cruel master a prophet called Balaam."

"Jesus entered Jerusalem riding on a colt of a donkey!" someone shouted.

"Donkey is still the most exploited and mistreated creature by humans, yet he is one of God's favorite pets," Inao said calmly. "One day donkey will be comforted directly as a pet of God."

No one noticed the tears of one homeless donkey wounded and lying down behind them, far away from a cruel human home. Today was Sunday; he was safe. Tomorrow someone was sure to tear into his already torn up body and make a meal of him. He knew that. But now he had just heard that God loved him, and that was enough to hang on to.

"Lazy men were told to emulate the ant!" a safari ant shouted.

"Not a safari ant!" Brother who was still recovering from his bites shouted, not very kindly.

"He did too!" Safari Ant retaliated. "An ant is an ant is an ant; he never specified which one."

"That's enough, you two!" Inao cautioned with a giggle and a wink at Quirra, who was thoroughly enjoying the exchange. "There is plenty of evidence that God takes pleasure in our existence, and heaven cannot be heaven without all his creation. We are under man's dominion on earth, but we ultimately belong to God. Does man grow our food or send the rain? Does he control the sun or the moon? Did Jesus say that man is the life? We are the pets of God. And if we are placed under man in heaven, it will not be the kind that hurts animals but those who chose Jesus. As Jesus is, so will they be also!"

Monkey scratched his head vigorously, his banana still half eaten.

"Bring it on, Monkey," Inao provoked him. "Share your thoughts."

"I want this God, this Jesus, but you know how I have many gods made on earth just like some of you. Now I know God loves us; I feel his jealousy for us too. It is either the God who made the world or the gods the world made. The one true God will not share his circle with others who did not help him make us. They are also made from material that he first created." Monkey was still remembering the vision of the circle of gods.

"How beautifully put, Monkey. After everything God had to put his son through, we are with you!" Elephant said emotionally.

"Must the unseen God really be the only one?" asked Ostrich. She had a small god hidden under her wing for double protection.

"When Jesus returned to heaven," Inao explained, "God the father not only restored all his former glory but also gave him the world he had ransomed as his inheritance. His name became the only one under the sun by which anyone could be saved. Everything and everyone exists through him and for him."

THE GODS MUST BE BURIED

∾

Twiga looked proudly at his flock from the back. How they had matured! Then he walked to the front of the gathering and stood to face them.

"I cannot add another word to what has been said here today, but I think it is time for an altar call. Does anyone want to commit his life to God today? Does anyone want to be a pet of God?"

Monkey did not hesitate. "Give me a minute," he said, swinging to a higher branch where he had hidden something.

In the meantime, Quirra ran to the pastor's feet. "Pasta Tiga, can I be a princess and a pet of God so you can baptize me and I will play with big brother Jesus, please, please!" She was still learning to pronounce.

"Absolutely, Quirra," Giraffe said, spreading his legs to shorten them and lowering his neck to face her. "Repeat after me, Quirra. *Thank you, Jesus, for loving me. Please forgive my sins and write my name in your book of pets.*" Quirra did and became a pet of God.

"Now you work with Aunt Inao and she will instruct you," Twiga advised. "She will let me know as soon as you are ready to be baptized, and I will be very happy to do it."

Monkey arrived on the stage as soon as Quirra left.

"My brothers and sisters help me to burry these idols," he begged.

Brother and Mole led the digging team. Monkey dropped in all his gods but one. He looked at banana god for a long time—a red, banana shaped, plastic toy flute. He remembered the times he had blown into it and made music to wake his god, but he never did wake up. Still it was not an easy decision putting the idol that had become a habit to rest. Finally he dropped it into the hole. He almost said "dust to dust, ashes to ashes" just to bury this one a little dignified, but he remembered he was now with the jealous God. He was also not sure plastic could turn to dust. It was closer to everlasting than soil, but it was still not God.

Suddenly his face became radiant with warmth he did not understand. It was not from the sunlight. He felt the weight of all the gods leave him and the embrace of one God who would walk with him, carry him, and die for him.

Ostrich followed suit and dumped her god, a plastic worm she had picked up someplace. It looked ridiculous now. She almost buried her head in shame for ever having associated herself, but on second thought she decided it was a step forward just realizing it was wrong. She held her head high on her long neck like a princess. There was now no condemnation in her heart. If she buried her head again, it would not be in shame but only to shield it from the sun. And if she enjoyed burying her brain box in the earth now and then, that too belonged to her father, the King of Kings!

There were gods and charms of all shapes, sizes, and colors dumped that day, including fairy teeth, roots, claws, and skins as the owners opted to serve the invisible God.

When the altar call ended, the birds of paradise started a praise song so robust, all creatures great and small, young and old, danced away for the unseen God.

Brother Hyena marveled at the unexpected full-blown church

service. It had to be a sign. His marriage to Inao, which right now only existed in his head, was ordained in heaven. Aero marveled at God's mysterious ways. She and Monkey had not gone to church, but God had brought it under their feet. God was letting her witness the major events of the day, from the dumped human baby to the buried false gods. He was giving her a stepping-stone to begin her ministry.

Where Love Meets Grace

ᖇᖇ

Suddenly everything stopped as a small hesitant voice cried, "Wait!"

They froze. Nothing could have prepared anyone for the last convert. The snake's only son, Nyoka, painfully slithered into the ring. His mouth was bleeding, he had some lacerations, and a significant portion of his tail was missing. Painfully, he curled onto a small rock and raised his neck. For all they knew, he never even went to church. Everyone strained forward to see him, smaller ones climbing on bigger animals. Many birds perched on Elephant's trunk, others on Brother Buff and Rhino's horns.

"Are you all right, Nyoka?" Dove asked. "You are bleeding!"

"It's nothing," Nyoka replied shakily. "My father attacked me this morning as I tried to sneak to church. Mostly I manage to listen in on all the services, but today I bumped right into my father who has been missing for days. He just sprung out of nowhere and realized I was going to church. As you can see, I got the thrashing of my life. I love my parents. I want to honor them and enjoy long life on earth as God has promised. But my father has never understood me. He exasperates me. I was running away from home when I saw all of you here. Pastor Twiga, why would God allow my parents to hurt me for wanting to know him?"

"Your parents love you very much," Gloria Twiga said moving closer to Nyoka. "They are trying to protect you from harm as they understand it. You are still to honor them in order to honor God. Then pray that God will reveal himself to them and open a way where none is visible. As for what you have suffered, it is better if it is God's will, to suffer for doing good than for doing evil, and everything works together for good in the end for those who love God."

Gloria stepped aside for her husband; he was the pastor.

"You have our full support and prayers as you love your parents with his love, which you are already demonstrating," Pastor Twiga said.

Nyoka was quiet for a long moment.

"Tell me, Pastor," he continued shyly, avoiding all eyes, "does God's love possibly extend to a snake, the symbol of evil? We have been told we carry the chromosomes, DNA, or some such thing of the devil that makes him our relative. I am too ashamed of my ancestry and too disgraced to lift up my face to God. My sins are higher than my head, and our guilt is known by all generations from the day of our first ancestor in the garden of God. Would God ever embrace me?"

Everyone was silent. For once, Twiga was lost for words. Neither he nor his congregation had ever seen tears in a snake before or one publicly seeking God. Nyoka's Eyes were definitely swimming.

"That is a very good question," the pastor said, hedging for time, his heart praying furiously. Everyone seemed to observe a moment of silence. Even the wind had stopped blowing. No one really thought of snakes as possible pets of God, even though he made them.

As far as the pets of God knew, God did not make mistakes even though he created the devil at some point. But the devil was what was very good gone very bad, way back before Once Upon a Time. Snake was created good. He sold out by loaning the devil his body to deceive the image of God in the garden of God. The devil returned it poisoned and with legs and ears missing, but that had never been enough reason to pity or forgive snakes. They were still ostracized.

The pets of God knew all about God's grace but perhaps not to the extent of covering snakes. If snakes were allowed under the blanket of grace, they might as well stretch it all the way and cover the devil! This was the kind of question a congregation left to God and their pastor, trusting the two to work together. In the meantime, they would pray for faith to embrace the pastor's final answer as the word of God.

Brother sat upright, scared stiff for his pastor and friend.

"Before I answer your question, Nyoka," Twiga said, "all of us here would like to commend you for choosing to honor your parents. In doing so, you honor God and you do have the reward of a good life."

"Amen!" shouted many males whose male offspring were now big and ready to either kick them out of their home or fight them for dominance. They envied snake his good son, even though a snake begets a snake.

"Let us all retrace the genesis of your question," Twiga continued, still buying time. "First, you are no relative of the devil, never mind what you have heard. Satan was once the most beautiful heavenly prince God created to lead his worship. He named him Lucifer, Son of the Morning Star. Then evil was found in him. He led an unsuccessful coup de tat, attempting to overthrow God and take his glory for himself."

The animals remained mum needing to hear every word. Allowing snakes in church was one thing, but embracing them was another. Yet this snake was showing more passion for God than most in the crowd. They hung onto Twiga's every word.

"There was a war in heaven," Twiga continued. "Michael, the Archangel Commander of God's army, and his force fought against the dragon. Lucifer fought fiercely alongside the angels that had chosen his path. They lost. The devil dragon was hurled away from the presence of God along with his followers, the fallen angels or demons.

"Then God grew the most beautiful garden, put everyone in it and declared man the king. Everything was laid up for happily ever after as long as man ensured no one touched or ate from a certain tree. But the devil got wind of it.

"He disguised himself as the most beautiful creature trusted by man. It is not clear how the business was transacted, but for some reason the beautiful creature, the snake that was your first ancestor, gave Lucifer control of his body. The devil used it to trick man into disobeying God. The humans ate fruit from the tree that God had told them in no uncertain terms they must not eat from. Disobedience is the first ancestor of all sin.

"Henceforth your species symbolized the devil even though they are not the actual devil. When Jesus is referred to as the Lamb of God, it does not elevate sheep to the status of God. Neither does a snake become one and the same with the devil. It is only symbolic of the purposes for which the two creatures were used, one to bring sin into the world, the other to atone for it."

Nyoka was visibly relieved to hear the devil was not his relative. So were many others who were starting to admire his courage and recognize the miracle that was unfolding.

"But even in his anger, God mercifully kicked out everyone from his garden. If they had stayed, they could have eaten from the tree of life and lived forever in that sinful state. Any hope of reconciliation would have been lost.

"Snake lost his legs, man had to work for what was once free, every female experienced hard labor in bringing forth her young, everyone received a death sentence in the end, and the devil's future in the lake of fire was revealed! When man sinned, he fell along with everything that was his or under his dominion, and that includes us. For that reason, all—and not just you, Nyoka—have sinned and fallen short of God's glory."

"Why did everyone else have to die?" Mrs. Zebra blurted out. "Only Snake and man entertained the devil!"

Pastor Twiga felt the devil awakening a hind kick. Instead he whispered a prayer for patience and kept calm.

"It is true that the snake was misled before man, Mama Zeb," the pastor replied, "but God had already given man the world and it was his ultimate responsibility. Man's choice had already become our destiny. And he chose death."

All eyes riveted on the pastor and the snake, once again reminded that they were man's flock and he was not always a good shepherd. They were going after the good shepherd himself, the one who was ready to leave ninety-nine in search of one lost sheep. Man was more inclined to cut his losses and keep the ninety-nine unless the lost one was found quickly or was worth more than the ninety-nine put together. They would not question the wisdom of God in putting them under man's dominion. It was enough that he loved them and they loved him. But did he love snakes?

"Mama Zeb is right. We snakes are more directly responsible for everything that is wrong with the world than other creatures!" Nyoka said painfully. His missing tail hurt too much. "It is no wonder God has made heaven with streets of gold. Snakes cannot walk on glass or pure gold. I know Jesus Christ is Lord and I love him, but he has not prepared a place for snakes. Why won't he forgive and love me back?" He lowered his head, his body completely curled up on the stone.

If ever there was dead silence, this was it. Not a leaf moved. Then the Bush Baby began to cry. It was all right, there was a time to cry. Aero saw her own loneliness and self-doubt reflected in Nyoka's. She understood completely. Her tears fell on Monkey's head and prompted his own. The hummingbirds hummed a verse from a precious ancient song.

> *Just as I am though tossed about,*
> *With many a conflict many a doubt,*
> *Fightings within and fears without,*
> *Oh, Lamb of God, I come, I come.*

Nyoka had come. Only he was not the only one doubting that he would be received. Brother Hyena felt prompted to pray and raised his voice above the humming.

"Dear God," he prayed, "we don't really know what we are thinking right now or what we ought to think. As for me, I just know I am ready to love Nyoka here if it is all right with you!"

There was a unanimous *Amen.* All they needed now was a course for the river to flow. They had enough tears.

"Brother Nyoka," Pastor Twiga said, looking into his eyes, "no one can say Jesus is Lord and mean it except by the spirit of God. If we believe that Christ's blood can wash away all sin, then that includes yours. And when he said *all* who seek him will find him, he did not exclude you."

"How much grace can there be, Pastor?" asked Mrs. Zebra. The pastor's hind twitched again almost visibly. His wife, Gloria, nuzzled his scar and he felt better. A pastor could not afford to be quick tempered.

"There is no exhausting God's grace, Sister Mama Zeb," he replied calmly. "If Satan were to humble himself to his creator and sincerely repent, God's grace would still be sufficient to cover him."

Mrs. Zebra gasped audibly. She was ready to lead a mass walkout, but a quick scan around the faces told her they were with the pastor. She was sure she had heard a few gasps, but that was all.

"You are here today because you heard God's voice," Pastor said to Nyoka. "He missed you and called you. Before you were even an egg, he knew you, and before you were hatched, he set you apart and appointed you a prophet to the snakes. Nyoka, if you confess with your mouth 'Jesus is Lord' and believe in your heart that God raised him from the dead, you will be saved. (Rom. 10:9–10)"

"Yes, Pastor, I believe, I declare him Lord over my life," Nyoka said humbly, his tears flowing freely. "Pray for me, Pastor. Pray for me, someone, anyone, everyone, please!"

They did. Hearts, mouths, and tears pleaded with God. The hummingbirds hummed the first verse of the precious song.

Just as I am without a plea,
But that thy blood was shed for me,
And that thy promise I believe,
Oh, Lamb of God, I come, I come.

"Dear Jesus, I admit I am a sinner," Nyoka repeated after Twiga. "Thank you for dying for me on the cross. Take my life and make it yours. Forgive my sins and write my name in the book of pets. Thank you for your forgiveness, amen."

There was a moment of silence as if someone had commanded it. Brother Hyena shot up, propelled by something he did not understand, and moved slowly toward Nyoka. Everyone watched him. Even Hyena wished he could watch himself because he was totally surprised.

"Would you like to be healed of your wounds?" he asked Nyoka. Twiga stepped back as if it was part of the arrangement. Everything was so unexpected, yet so orderly.

"Yes, Brother Hyena, I hurt badly," Nyoka replied in excruciating pain. The pets of God held their breath, mesmerized by the boldness of Hyena.

Black Mamba froze too. After the incident with his son, Nyoka, he had gone home and chased out of his house one hundred and fourteen females. Then he had gone back looking for Nyoka again, his only flesh and blood, to see if there was anything left of him to salvage. It was a pity he had to beat sense into him physically and that his brave bloodline was likely to be continued by a worm. But it was better if Nyoka came home just in case the wife reported to King Cobra's court about domestic violence. Then he could say he had not really tossed out his entire family, only what was not his and what had gone bad.

His cheating wife had shouted the truth at him on her way out about the stolen hatchlings and added how happy she was that her daughters were not tainted by his demented blood! Not that they had her blood either. The other female was their mother. Perhaps if he had not attacked them immediately, he could have gathered more details. But he had been all strung up after disciplining Nyoka for trying to go to church.

It was not fair. All he had wanted was to go home and curl up with a Do Not Disturb aura around him so no one would ask him where he had been for almost a week. Instead he had found every ground in his house occupied. There must have been fifty of those grand-somethings on his sleeping corner alone! He sighed. One hundred grand-hatchlings behind his back and not even a rumor of one wedding could make any father froth in the mouth and lose precious venom.

A wife ought to know those things about her own daughters and tell them stuff beforehand. How was he supposed to hold out his head as head of that kind of household? He was now the definition of shame, never mind he was too young to be anyone's grandpa or to have that dementia she kept wishing on him.

Swift had called him another name too before she disappeared with her brood. Something earthen, yes ... *heathen*. He had no idea what it meant and decided it might be safer not to find out in case it caught. Ten blind daughters, one hundred blind granddaughters, a blind female stranger who could be a witch and not one of them had the decency to bear a son! Perhaps it would be peaceful bliss if he really had dementia. He would be absent from reality with no memory of anything, not even who he was. The laughingstock can laugh along with everyone else and never know why he is laughing.

So his fangs had torn off Nyoka's tail and he had followed the rest of him to this hysterical, peculiar bunch called Christians. Nyoka was right in the middle of things where he dared not confront him. To his further frustration, his son was waiting to be healed by the great I Am whom no one had ever seen, smelled, or tasted. But that could be just what Nyoka needed to cure him of his quest for God. A major disappointment! After that, if Nyoka even looked in the direction of the church or mentioned the name God, he was going to rip off his head. Let them try miracle healing on that!

Black turned his eyes to Hyena who was giving Nyoka false

hope. If man was the image of God, snakes had always been considered the image of the devil. Even if God were to heal him, did Nyoka think for a moment the Almighty would use an ugly scavenger like Hyena? Hyenas were as far removed from God as snakes—all right, almost. Snakes were beyond saving grace. His family was not going to scavenge for the love of any god, thank you very much!

Black looked at Hyena again. He knew Hyena. Everyone did. But something strange was happening to Hyena now; either he was not the one in his body or he was not alone. Someone was compelling him to move forward. He also spoke with an authority no hyena had ever possessed. Jesus, Jesus, there was just something about that name ... but a hyena?

"Do you believe that Jesus Christ was beaten, died in our place and by his stripes we are healed?" Hyena asked in full authority, his voice seeming to echo another.

"I believe," Nyoka responded with awed confidence.

"Then by his stripes, by his precious blood, receive your healing!"

"Thank you, Jesus, thank you, Jesus, thank you," Nyoka chorused along with many of the other animals.

No one was more surprised than Brother Hyena when Nyoka visibly trembled and then straightened out, brandishing a whole new tail. Not a bruise was visible on him. He danced around and around, his head held high as in the strike position but only to praise God. Hyena went down on all fours, raised his head to heaven, and thanked God profusely. He had just received the gift of healing not out of great faith or anything he had done. It was just that, a *gift*.

Black Mamba tensed and froze at what he had witnessed. Then he remembered his earlier outburst to God, that if he cared about the Mambas to contact his family personally. Without a doubt, he knew that he knew that he knew there was a living God. He had just healed a snake, his own flesh and blood son, contacting his family personally! When he defrosted, his heart faltered as fear made him tremble. The majestic snake was humbled to a tiny worm by the unmistakable presence of the most holy and almighty unseen God.

Black knew God was there to break the spell, to tell and show him personally that snakes were his creation and he loved them, that the curse was lifted for them too and now they were blessed. Surely his grace was sufficient even for them. He felt a liquid wash his eyes. Black Mamba was no crying Bush Baby and had never had tears. Those were supposed to have been left behind with legs and ears! He looked at Nyoka, and his heart broke at the damage he had done.

"Forgive me, God, my creator," he cried. "Forgive my sins and the sins of my ancestors. Now I know you love me, and I am falling in love with you right now. But I am afraid because I only know how to displease you. Please teach me to please you, how not to mess up our relationship all over again!"

Suddenly Black Mamba was enveloped in the love of God. He started moving forward toward his son, wanting to touch him with *that* love, his precious son, a gift from God.

The brethren noticed his approach and braced for trouble. Brother Buff raised a hoof to trample him and kept his horns informed of the progress. Elephant's foot was also in the air. Porcupine prepared his missiles, but he was not sure how to aim just one at the enemy without causing mass destruction all around. Brother Wolf snarled behind the perceived enemy and prowled on his tail. Mrs. Zebra jumped in front of Nyoka and gave her back to his approaching father. Her back kick was oiled and ready. She was feeling a twinge of guilt for her earlier opinion of Nyoka. He was family now, a brother. Protecting him now would be akin to an apology.

No one had seen Monkey go, but now he was sitting steady on a branch, his hand aiming a big coconut at Black Mamba's head. Most little creatures hid either under or above the big brothers. The pastor's eyes almost popped out, never leaving the approaching venom. He dared not hurt the flock, even a snake, in case he came in the name of the Lord. Nevertheless, his hind leg was more ready than not, just in case he needed to resist the devil in a physical way.

Nyoka looked into his approaching father's eyes and knew something was different. He had an aura of brokenness, yet he was bigger than he had always been.

"Please wait, everyone!" Nyoka pleaded, turning his neck round and round to address everyone.

"This is my father; please do not hurt him!"

"You mean ... you still care?" Black asked his son as soon as they were face-to-face.

"You are my father," Nyoka replied respectfully. "Forgive me for any time I disrespected you."

"It is I who needs your forgiveness, son," Black replied. "I have done nothing but exasperate you and now you have led me to the living God."

"You mean you believe, The Name?" asked Nyoka carefully.

"Yes, son, Jesus is the real thing and I want him in my life. Give me a second chance to be your father." Everyone relaxed their combat postures.

"I love you, Dad. Let's forget the past," Nyoka said happily. The two looked at each other with loving respect and embraced by wrapping their necks round and round each other.

"Please forgive me, everyone, anyone I have wronged," Black said to the gathering as he detangled from the embrace. "Give me a chance to be your brother because your miracle was my miracle too. You serve the living God, and I have now received him in my life."

The "Thank you, Jesus" chorus and dance thundered in the jungle. Everything that had breath praised God as the most colorful sunset boldly displayed his glorious majesty. Black and son slithered out of center stage. Pastor Twiga raised his long neck to heaven, and everyone was silent. His wife, Gloria, was sobbing happily.

"And now to you who is able to do immeasurably more than all we can ask or imagine," Twiga prayed. "Thank you for honoring your pets with your healing presence. To you be the glory and to Christ Jesus throughout all generations, forever and ever, endow man with wisdom, your image whose choice is our destiny!"

"Amen!" answered the pets of God.

"We have fasted for seven moons now, and we believe you will come. We receive by faith a creature who knows the scriptures, the contents of your holy book in the language of man, that we may be better instructed to serve you. Even now in our ignorance, you have written your laws in our hearts. When we call on you foolishly, you answer us in your wisdom. And one of these days, we will tell the devil, 'It is written!' Endow man with wisdom, your image whose choice is our destiny!"

"Aaaaaaamen!" chorused the pets of God.

AND THE SKY FELL DOWN

❦

The unseen God chose that moment of the seventh moon of their fast to deliver the miracle they had fasted for. But the angel he assigned must have dropped it! Somewhere in the long Amen, a portion of the sky seemed to fall through the tree with a thunderous bang. The biggest bird anyone had ever seen rolled unceremoniously on the spot Nyoka and his father had just vacated. Smaller creatures maintained their safety above and below the giants. Even the big creatures retreated. Ostrich crossed herself with a wing and quickly buried her head in the sand. She had never seen a bird bigger than herself lying upside down!

Aero had been witnessing everything up in Monkey's tree, being part of it yet apart. Many times, the gentle, small voice had prompted her to reveal herself and start her mission, but she had been afraid. Instead she had waited for Monkey to hint at the correct moment—a mistake she realized too late after landing on her tail feathers. She hoped the human Jonah had a better moment when he was vomited from the belly of a whale in Nineveh!

"Take it easy, God. I never refused to go!" she quipped as she struggled to turn herself upright. "The sunset caught up with me, God. You know I always fall asleep at sunset!" As soon as she had snored at sunset, a thunderous Amen had startled her out of balance. That had never happened before; not even in earthquakes did she ever lose her balance. Aero fully suspected God in the matter! She got up slowly, shaking out the dust.

"Ouch!" she yelped. Her tail hurt.

"You live in me now, God, so if my backside hurts, your backside hurts too!" she yelled, her beak pointing toward heaven. It felt stupid in a way, looking up to shout at God when she had just said he was right there inside her. Well, he was also omnipresent and most of him had to remain home in heaven. Then it fully hit her that she was wide awake even though the sun had set. That too had never happened before. So he was a jealous God demolishing the sunset slumber stronghold. He was saying in no uncertain terms that her promptings should come from the son and not the sun or the monkey!

"Not fair, God!" she cooed, but her tone remained accusatory. "You finally give me a voice to praise you, but even you have to admit that making an entry flat on my rear is no praising posture!" Then she mellowed down remembering this was God she was addressing.

"All right, God, I get it. It's not about me and my bruised ego but you, only you. So here I am in a Kenyan Nineveh with a broken toot, waiting for further instructions. Now what, my God? Now what?"

"Only this is not Nineveh," said the gentle, small voice. "These creatures have sought me with all their hearts. They have asked to know the contents my book, the Bible. I saw that prayer coming long before they did and prepared you for that very purpose. You have asked me to use you. I am!"

"But God, did you have to crash the Bible Teacher upside Down on her debut? How am I supposed to get them to respect me and take me seriously when I am landed as a joke?"

"They are supposed to respect and take *me* seriously in *my* class and I *am* the teacher."

"Oh, God, I am honored to be your instrument, the chalk in your hand that the great teacher can hold in any way he wants. Why do you still love a mess like me?" she sobbed.

"Because I do, Aero, because I do," answered the gentle, caressing voice.

"Thank you, Lord. So I decrease and you increase, just help me remember to use and teach the law of 'decrease equals increase,'" she whispered. Aero got up with her head high. She shook the dust and grass from her ruffled feathers so vigorously that it caused the crazy one-spot twister wind called *ngoma cia aka* or "female devils."

The pets of God protected their noses and eyes as best as they could from whatever witchcraft the goliath bird was shaking off. There was a chance this bird was not real. Even when the presence of God was so manifested, there was still a devil out there. The animals were in their fight or flight positions. The fighters like Owl, Tortoise, and the pastor were ready to cast out demons, while others favored flight—like Mrs. Zebra who had run all the way to the back. The giant black bird could very well be the antichrist! There were white pyramid-shaped writings on her huge wings, perhaps the number of the beast.

Zeb was left behind by his mother, but he was not afraid. He calmly watched Pastor Twiga's majestic neck high in the clouds. Pastor Giraffe Twiga was nearer to God up there than the rest of them were. As long as God could see the pastor's head, he would protect them from whatever had landed. Zeb had heard of unidentified flying objects from outer space too!

Twiga was profusely thanking God for whoever this was. As far as he knew, everything and everyone happened for good for those that loved God. Somehow he knew God had a plan. God always had a plan. He just had to wait for it to unravel, wait to be surprised.

Aero slowly focused her eyes on the gathering that peered right back at her. Her flesh was still mortified even though all was well with her soul. What an embarrassing way to meet the pets of God! If only she could fly away, but where?

Deep down, she actually knew why God had humbled her. While up in the tree, she had been gathering a sense of self-importance. She was an answer to their fasting and praying, a miracle, almost a messiah in her own right, come to reveal the contents of the holy Bible! Only it was not her holy book but God's. She was not the revelator, God was. Never in forever was it going to be her glory, but his. Luckily, she knew that God only disciplined the ones he loved and had accepted as his own. She had just been belted on the rear. What a comfort!

"I am sorry, God," she whispered almost in tears. "Receive the praise, the honor, and the glory for whatever you accomplish with my life."

She gave a get-well peck to her hurting bottom, and stood at attention, eyes focused on the ground. It was God's move. She was not moving a feather before he did. Monkey recovered first, recognizing his guest. He swung down on one arm and was instantly at her side.

"Are you all right, Aero?" he asked, his hand on her wing.

The other creatures peered closer. Monkey knew her, and he was okay. She had to be all right. They waited for an introduction. Monkey cleared his throat importantly.

"Pastor Twiga, everyone, this is Aero, my guest and the servant of the unseen God. She is perhaps the only creature other than the image of God who knows the entire contents of the holy book."

The pastor was staggered and visibly shaken. It couldn't be … it had to be! For seven solid moons, the pets of God had fasted and dared to believe in the impossible, and God had delivered!

"I am pleased to meet you all," Aero said hesitantly. "It is true that I know the entire contents of the holy book, the Bible. I would be greatly honored to share any or all of it with the pets of God. I am only his servant at your service."

It was not the first time they had seen their pastor cry. But this time, his passion was too great. He went down on all fours prostrated before the almighty. Zeb was completely bewildered. The pastor was still too tall even on his knees! His huge tears had to fall quite a distance and probably poked holes in the ground. It did not seem appropriate to go closer and check. Later.

"You are worthy, you are worthy, you are worthy, son of God, you are worthy of our praise!" Zeb repeated everything the pastor was saying and sobbed along with him. One day, the son of Punda and Milia was going to meet the son of God to be best friends, even though Jesus was already best friends with Pastor Giraffe!

The hummingbirds hummed "Amazing Grace" as everyone including Aero prostrated on the ground in honor of the living unseen God. They knew he was there. Some even rolled upside down the way they honored best, and Aero was no longer ashamed of her earlier posture. She realized there was no shameful physical position for worshipping this God. What mattered was how the heart was positioned.

WELL NOW, MY BETROTHED

☙

Brother landed back on earth faster than everyone but still on all fours alongside Inao. He was sure that a window was wide open in heaven right now and the prayers were going right in. This was the kind of moment that could never be recreated. He glanced at Inao again with one eye and quickly sent a private and confidential petition while that window was still open. Another glance at Inao, their eyes met, and she quickly looked away. She had also noticed the open window and sent her own petition. This hunk was something special, but she needed God's wisdom. If he was in God's plan for her, he was not going anywhere. If not, God had an even bigger plan waiting to unfold. But this sure looked good. Brother gathered courage and gave her a questioning steady gaze. He saw the answer in her beautiful eyes even as she mouthed the words of "Amazing Grace."

After the song, Brother shot up and asked everyone to share a moment with him. "Brothers and sisters," he said shyly, standing in the middle of the circle, "this happens to be a day of miracles. Please say a quick prayer for me as I take the scariest step toward my other miracle!"

Everyone was paying attention as he turned to face Inao. They looked into each other's eyes, a puzzled expression in hers. Then he went down on his two hind knees.

"Inao, you are the smartest and most beautiful female I have ever seen. I love you around the jungle and back again. Will you, Inao, make me the happiest hyena in the world and marry me, make a family with me?"

The Bush Baby began to cry again. So did Mrs. Zebra and Gloria Twiga. Zeb stared at everyone amused. Females!

Inao looked at Brother for an entire two minutes. Hyena's nose began to perspire. Everyone was silent, hopeful for their brother. Her answer was taking too long, and quick prayers started finding their way to heaven. Embarrassed doubts were sneezed, trotted, or granted here and there. Brother was clearly uncomfortable, beginning to doubt. He should have waited till they were alone … She was way out of his league … This was going to be the most humiliating … What had he been thinking?

Monkey scratched his head though it was not itching. Black and son prayed silently next to the praying mantis. Dove sang the first line of the love song "Malaika," *Angel, I love you, my angel,* to speed up things. It worked. Inao said the biggest *yes* jumping up and down. It was not her intention to embarrass her suitor, but a female was expected to mull over such a major decision and not seem too eager. It was custom. Her aunt had said it made her more precious to the male. She said even when a male seemed totally decided, he still did not want things too easy. Deep down, the male was a hunter and that position had to be protected. In a way, it contradicted her Christian thinking. One's yes was *yes,* and the no was a *no.* It was hard to strike a balance without offending either side.

"Yes, Brother, the answer is yes! I would be honored to be your wife and make a family with you!"

"Thank you, Jesus, thank you, Jesus!" Brother screamed happily, jumping up and down.

"Hey, that was me you proposed to!" Inao joked to everyone's amusement.

"Sure, thank you, Inao, and thank you, Jesus!"

Everyone started jumping around as if she had agreed to marry them all.

"Not so fast now!" she said in mock seriousness. You must still court me for the traditional twenty-four moons. Time enough to confirm God's will for us."

"I wouldn't want it any other way," Brother replied. "A threesome with God is just fine as long as his will transcends our own. But in the meantime, I want every marauding rascal male out there to know we are engaged!"

"If God says yes, I expect you to dig the biggest den for me!" Inao warned. "After I inspect it, I will say yes or no again!"

"You got it, my lady! Digging happens to be my specialty. If Pastor and our friends here pray for us, we will become officially engaged."

The two moved to the center of the circle and knelt down. Pastor Twiga raised his voice to heaven as the animals lifted their hearts.

"Thank you, God, for love, the sweetest thing this side of heaven. If this attraction is your will, we will be honored to join them in Holy Matrimony in the twenty-four moons as is the hyena tradition. May they earnestly seek you as they court each other and come to the fullness of love as you intended it. We seal their comings and goings from the evil one with the Blood of Jesus and declare them officially engaged. Endow man with wisdom, your image, whose choice is our destiny.

"Amen!" the congregation responded.

There was hooting, trumpeting, and cheers of all kinds. Monkey restarted the abandoned love song "Malaika," and dancing kicked up a storm. Monkey tried to teach Aero to dance, but Ostrich cut in. She wanted Aero under her wing. The Bible teacher was clumsy on her feet, to say the least.

"Do you fly?" she asked Aero.

"Like a shooting star, but I am zero on the ground," Aero said excitedly.

"And I run like wind, but I have never been off the ground," Ostrich said in the same manner.

"Would you like to be friends and exchange lessons?" Aero asked hopefully.

"I would love that!" Ostrich agreed eagerly.

Suddenly the dust along with the animals seemed to freeze in midair as a loud roar thundered in the entire jungle of Samburu. The king had arrived and was heading to the center stage.

"Who is in charge of this illegal gathering, and what in my jungle is the plot?" he asked in a chilling voice.

"Your Excellency!" Brother stammered respectfully as some trembled like leaves. "Inao just agreed to marry me, and I just asked her to marry me, and we just got engaged, and the pastor just blessed our engagement, and we were dancing and … oh … long live the king!"

"Why didn't you start with 'long live the king,' Mr. Bridegroom-to-be?" the king asked, smiling a little but wanting to maintain his authority. "And no one bothered to invite poor old king?" he jested, relieved it was not a political meeting.

"Oh, King, live forever! We are honored to have you here today." Brother bowed almost chocking on his words.

"Go dance with your betrothed before someone steals her!" the king laughed. "Who said the song and dance should stop?" he said in mock harshness. "Is this any way to celebrate love? Move those lazy bones, everyone!" He gave a technical jig or two in the tradition of politicians and left for more important Jungle business. A few steps away, he changed his mind.

"Come out here, my queen!" he called to his wife, who was listening behind some tall grass. "We can't let them have all the fun. Let's show them how to shake a leg or four!"

Queen Bora was mortified. The king had no self-respect. And instead of honoring his queen, he was dragging her to dance with common mongrels. She did as she was told, but one of these days she was going to give him the final portion from chameleon. Then she would step in and save the jungle from a low-class king like him.

The Hanging Queendom

ᘓᕲ

When the royal couple got back home, the princess was nowhere to be found. The queen turned ashen as her intestines churned. She had this sinking feeling that she knew ... The princess was never part of the bargain. Later, when the search parties were far and wide, she walked the secret path and sought The Voice by expecting it.

"Did you take my daughter?" she asked The Voice, shaking like a leaf.

"We always collect our debt with interest," The Voice replied sounding bored.

"But she was not part of it. You have the prince!" she cried.

"We always collect our debt with interest." And The Voice was gone. Queen Bora slowly wet herself.

In two weeks, the search for the prince and princess was officially over. They were gone. Brother Hyena lay prostrate before God in his den and prayed for their safety. He did not want to judge and slander even in the secret of his own heart, but his guts had a suspect. The queen was somehow involved with the missing cubs and the king's strange behavior. Whenever she fed him these days, the king lay comatose for a long time. When he got up, he was bewildered and then gleefully happy like a little cub. This always happened when the

314

queen's sisters were not around. She was also suspiciously generous, saving up bits and pieces for him, which she had never done before. Brother prayed that God would rescue this family from whatever was after them. And it was in the queen!

Queen Bora prepared to see Chameleon. The magic portions were weakening considering the way the king had danced at their servant Hyena's engagement. He needed to be more restrained. She still had the last portion, but Chameleon had said to think carefully before using it. She was going to reconfirm its potency and expected results. It had to be something that could not backfire on her. She had paid too high a price for the Queendom to lose now.

Bora believed the jungle needed her breeding and style, but she needed to lose that ugly name *Bora*. It sounded common. Earth Lion had suggested she change it to Jezebel. That had a royal ring to it, a queenly name if ever there was one. It was supposed to belong to an earlier queen, a human too. Perhaps she could inherit her spirit. Today she was scheduled to eat the Royal Wisdom portion in the air, whatever Earth Lion meant by that.

She glanced in both directions and made sure nobody was looking. Then she took the ancient path. Brother Hyena peered at the queen from his den, a prayer for her family still hot in his mouth. He followed his instincts and the queen. In the meantime, the king lay on his side in the sun circled by his sisters-in-law. The sisters scratched his back every once in a while. He loved that. They were all too comfortable to notice one sister and a hyena disappear into the sunset. Hyena was happy the king was getting some comfort after losing his cubs.

An invisible Yellow Eyes followed behind, hating the interfering hyena. He dropped a lame antelope right in front of him, but the hyena was not moved. A fox carrying his kill dropped a portion, but he did not bite. Yellow put a heap of fresh bones on the way, but Hyena may as well have lost his sight and smell.

"This hyena is going to heaven!" Yellow cursed. "The stomach highway is bolted shut!"

Yellow tried many different stumbling blocks, including causing Hyena to fall flat on a thorn, but Brother just dusted up and followed his path. Finally Yellow made a startling sound causing the queen to look behind her. Brother ducked just in time and decided to go back. That was close. The queen lioness could be very dangerous if she thought she was being spied on.

"If it is your will that I follow her God, please send some backup," he prayed.

Back in the palace, the king had missed his queen, so he disentangled from her snuggling sisters and went in search of her. This was totally out of character for him, but suddenly, he would rather be with her than with one thousand others. Perhaps it was the loss of their cubs. She had also seemed very withdrawn lately, and he did not like the disconnection.

Brother's prayer was still hot on his lips when he bumped into the king.

"Have you seen the queen?" he asked.

"Yes, your majesty, she went this way," he replied.

"Well now, engaged fellow, walk with me and tell me all about your bride-to-be!"

Hyena could not believe God's ways. Not only had he gotten the right backup, but the king had personally invited him for the walk. He did not have to report that something was suspicious. The king would find out for himself.

"Please God, reveal the truth and extend your love to this family."

They followed the barely used path that seemed to lead them in circles. Her scent was in the air. They just couldn't pinpoint which direction she had gone. The king wondered why he felt this urgency to find her now. Usually he did not care if she came or went as long as she brought food.

Yellow did everything to confuse their trail, but it was not working. He rushed to Chameleon and prompted her mind to speed things up. A legion of homeless demons had already arrived from the Devil's Mountain to make a home in the queen. She lay prostrate under the tree repeating a new mantra, the one that would open wide the door to her heart. But she did not know that. Earth Lion the chameleon was up the tree dangling the Royal Wisdom portion. Queen Bora prepared to eat in the air and generate the wisdom needed for running a Queendom.

"Maheni maheni maheni," she chanted the six hundred and sixty sixth mantra. Slowly without any effort of her own, the queen was raised to a standing position feeling weightless, empty of all thought.

Yellow watched with satisfaction as she chanted the familiar name of the legion of demons that had already started flowing into her in an enjoined convoy. Every spirit was pulling a bigger one behind him. The last one, whose name meant death, could hardly shut the door behind him. There were hand boys that stood outside positioned around her. At a signal from Yellow, they lifted her slowly toward the dangling lie, the portion that was to create a well of absolute wisdom within her.

Yellow smiled. The fool was going to swallow the mad demon and eat grass like a cow. She had been an easy conquest because she did not fear God. That would have complicated matters. Fearing God triggered the kind of wisdom that made his own schemes transparent.

The king and his faithful servant came to a halt as soon as their path ended in a sudden triangular clearing. There was a tree in the middle that defied any description. It seemed to change form with every sway of the wind.

Their mouths fell open when they saw the queen below it. She was standing, but her feet were not touching the ground. Then she began to rise, walking uphill on the air in very slow motion. The world stood still as only her legs moved. Her eyes were focused on a giant chameleon dangling from up the tree. But Chameleon was not perched on the tree. She too was suspended upside down, hanging in the air! The portion she was aiming at the queen's mouth was in the shape of a little dragon wrapped in red leaves.

"Do you see what I see?" the king asked Hyena in a daze.

"Yes, Your Majesty," Hyena whispered.

"It is so … otherworldly. Do you think this is of God? It seems too magical not to be of God. Jesus walked on water, and she is walking on air."

"It is magical, Your Majesty, but it belongs to another god."

"Are you saying this is witchcraft, Hyena?"

"You said it, my king, not I. Long live the king."

"You suggested it! You suggested it is pure witchcraft. I could never possibly think that the queen is a witch!" the king said menacingly.

Brother was in deep trouble. The king could never own up to such a thought. He needed someone to blame, and Hyena was the only one around. The devil was nowhere to be seen!

"Oh, King, live forever, but I do not know what I was saying!" Hyena pleaded.

"So you do admit it!" the king accused.

"Please, God, save me and glorify yourself in this situation," Hyena whispered. "Please shift his blame from me and show him the real culprit, the devil, before he tears me to shreds!"

But it was Hyena who saw the devil in a flash vision. He was busy shooing smaller demons into the queen through an open hole where her heart should be. The hole was so big it resembled a bottomless pit. Soon the fattest demon named death shut the door behind him. The queen then opened her mouth to receive the demon of madness dangling from the chameleon. Only it was disguised as wisdom. The witch herself was filled to the brim with her own demons. Others were still outside lifting and holding both the queen and Chameleon in the air. Then his inner eyes closed, and the demons were no longer visible. The king was no longer angry with him but had shrunk into an inner shell of his own depression.

"You have power in The Name," whispered a gentle, small voice. All fear left Brother Hyena, and a surge of courage followed like he had never felt before. The devastated king lay in a heap ready to meow like a cat. His sad eyes begged his servant for help, but they held no hope.

"The king is still on the throne," Hyena whispered kindly.

"Thank you. I know I am," the king replied.

"The king of kings," Hyena said and quickly turned to the ascending queen.

The king looked at Hyena in confusion. He was walking purposely toward the queen as if he knew exactly what he was doing.

Two very yellow eyes narrowed to slits. The influx of demons into the queen was complete and the door closed. She just needed to swallow the mad demon, and they would lower her back to earth to eat grass and house the legion of destruction. That should destroy the king who loved her, the same king who allowed animals to go to church and not harm or eat one another on Sundays. They were almost done—if only this God-trotting scavenger did not bring The Name into it.

Brother Hyena came to a full stop under the tree. The queen was still ascending, oblivious of anything but the portion dangled above her by Earth Lion who still floated in the air.

"Excuse me, everyone inside and outside!" Hyena boomed as if addressing an entire congregation. "By the authority of Jesus Christ, I command every spirit to be subject to The Name above all names. I cover these pets of God with the Blood of Jesus. Lose your hold on them *right now!*"

On the first "Jesus," Yellow Eyes fell to his knees, dusted up, and vanished. The other demons, too preoccupied with their floating cargo and settling in their new home inside the queen, did not really hear The Name. But they ceased all movement for a moment. There was just something about something they thought they had heard. When Hyena mentioned The Name again along with the Blood of Jesus, his spirit eyes opened again and he saw the legion. They suddenly trembled like leaves and dropped their cargo. Every devil hit the ground with its knee before they scattered in seven directions! In the physical realm, Brother ducked just in time.

The queen landed on her bottom, only for Chameleon to crash-land on her nose. Earth Lion started climbing down the mountain that was the queen, but her sneeze sent the witch flying to fall on her back a few inches from Brother Hyena. She could not get up. Brother picked up a nearby stick with his mouth and held it inches from her struggling legs. At first she was frightened. He looked angry enough to kill her. Glancing in his expressionless eyes, she grabbed at the stick.

"Thank you," she said as soon as she was on her feet. Brother said nothing. Then she started rolling her eyes in all directions as if searching for something. For a moment, there was total silence. She felt very light. The weight of 666 demons had just left her.

"Are you searching for this?" Brother asked, stepping furiously on her portion, a bunch of dry leaves that the wind started scattering away. He seemed intent on doing the same to her.

"Please do not hurt me," the witch begged.

"No one could possibly hurt you more than you have already hurt yourself," Hyena replied more kindly than she expected.

"Whose servant are you?" she asked quietly.

"I am a servant of two kings, the king of the jungle and the king of kings," Hyena replied. "But this moment is for the king of kings, the Almighty God whose high is higher than yours!"

"I believe you. He just overrode the powers of the rainbow god."

"The rainbow god?" Brother asked incredulously.

"I was made in his own image reflecting all his colors. What would it cost me to be in with your God, posses such power as yours?" she asked, all businesslike.

"Nothing," Hyena replied. "He already paid the price."

"Nothing? How can something so priceless cost nothing?" she asked.

"You got that right—priceless. Only he could afford the price, and he paid it."

There was a big pause.

"How did you meet your god?" Brother asked to keep the conversation going.

"Through The Voice," she replied. "How does one meet yours?"

"Through The Name," Hyena replied, his eyes on hers. "The only name given on earth by which anyone can be saved. The name to which every knee must bow willingly now or unwillingly later. The Name that makes every demon tremble and bow its knee. The Name is the reason the servants of your god dropped you from the sky to land on your backside."

Earth Lion searched Brother Hyena's eyes and saw only sincerity. "I truly thought I was serving the one true God," she said very sadly. "After serving the queen the Royal Wisdom portion, they were going to evolve me to a powerful crocodile with one color that describes me. Everyone knows what color they are except me. I am also too slow. How am I supposed to accomplish anything with my short life at such a speed?"

"Your changing color reflects God's own mysterious nature. You visualize in different directions spontaneously, reminding us of his omnipresence. As for your speed and lifetime, God designed you precisely for what he purposed with your life. He made the rainbow for you, not you for the rainbow! You are the more precious of the two, and he loves you just as much as a crocodile!"

"Did you say love? You mean God can love me, a witch?" she pleaded.

"He loves all witches but hates witchcraft as an abomination," Brother replied as answers popped in his head. "It is an attempt by a counterfeit god to steal the heart of a world he did not create, through deception. God is jealous of our attention and will not share the glory for his work with anyone."

"He loves me," Earth Lion whispered with a strange look, one eye gazing into the heavens and another at Brother. Then she broke into sobs. One stream of tears went up and another down. "Oh, God, please forgive me!" she wailed. Then they heard the meow from the queen. She had listened to everything and now felt less than a kitten.

"I am worse than any witch. I have killed my cubs, my husband. I am the definition of greed and selfishness. Someone, please help me die!"

Hyena was by her side in an instant. The king moved closer but kept his distance. He was not sure whether to love her or kill her.

"Only your sin needs to die, my queen," Hyena comforted. "If you sincerely repent, God will forgive anything and forget it permanently."

"Not even God Almighty can forget this, even if he forgives," she sobbed. "Just help me die and go to the lake of fire. Even that will not be as hot as I deserve!"

"That lake was not prepared for you but for the devil and his demons. You are his most precious pet. Maybe he will not forget what happened, but it will no longer count against you. Embrace him in The Name and become a new creation. Then all things will become new!"

The queen looked at Brother for a long moment and then at the king. The king looked away but not before she glimpsed the pain in his eyes. She had thrown away the most beautiful part of her life and lived to know the pain.

"Please, God," she sobbed, prostrated on the grass. "Hide me somewhere till your anger has passed. Toss me aside and make a whole new me. Forgive me in The Name of Jesus!"

Brother rubbed her front leg with his paw in encouragement. Never in a million moons would he have imagined the queen seeing any goodness in him. Quickly he reminded himself it was not his goodness but God's. Without Christ, he was nothing.

When her sobs subsided, she crawled slowly forward and lay a few feet from the king, her eyes downcast.

"My master, my king," she sobbed in a small voice, "I have dishonored you in every imaginable way. Allow me to honor you with the truth, not for your forgiveness—because I do not deserve that—but because I owe it to you and to God. I cannot carry the burden of lies any more. After that, I am your humble servant to do with as you please."

"Just start from the beginning," the king said, quietly gathering what authority he could muster under the circumstances. He was shamed to the core by the female he had loved ... still loved. Hyena tried to excuse himself to give privacy, but the queen motioned for him to stay on along with Chameleon.

"I traded our son for a Queendom," she began. "But they took our daughter too. The Voice said she was interest on the debt."

"Who? What? Who took them?" the king said.

"The Voice," she replied, as if it was the most normal thing.

Everyone fumbled to sit in their most comfortable position. Whether the queen was talking sensible nonsense or nonsensical sense, King Moran decided to listen to every word. He needed to get to the bottom of it, if indeed it had a bottom.

Once in a while, they asked for clarifications. The queen left out nothing, even about the portions fed to the king. Sometimes she let Chameleon fill in the gaps about her own role. When all the details were out, the king sat still in pregnant silence, and everyone was afraid of what he might birth. Brother Hyena kept shooting quick silent prayers for wisdom. Apart from genuine concern, he also needed everyone to come out of this alive so he could enjoy his time with his fiancée.

"Your Majesties, King and Queen of the Jungle," he said carefully, respectfully, "it appears both the queen and Earth Lion were deceived by a power that is intent on destroying the jungle and the royal family. Unless we stand together and fight as a team, they will have won."

"You know I am not afraid to face any enemy," the king said with forced authority. "But a voice, just a voice—I cannot put my claws on a voice. I cannot devour a voice to defend my family!"

"It is not a flesh and blood battle but the forces of good and evil," Hyena replied. "Today we were all witnesses that The Name is above The Voice. As soon as I invoked it, the powers behind The Voice trembled, dropping the queen and Chameleon from the air. We need the protection of the greater power or they will be back. In fact, they will always be back. But they will no longer have a hold on us as long as God is holding us."

"All right, go ahead and get it," the king commanded. "You have my express permission to put the jungle under the lordship and protection of the God whose only son bears The Name Jesus Christ!"

"Right away, sir! Thank you, Your Majesty," Hyena replied, humbly kneeling lower in supplication. "If it pleases the king and queen, I will run round this clearing symbolizing our land of sunshine, Kenya, and cover every step with the Blood of Jesus. That ought to send the evil outside our borders. Then I will declare the lordship and protection of Jesus in Samburu, the jungle that is blessed to have you as king."

"By all means, friend," the king replied. "But I am running right behind you. I want my footsteps to count. I want them planted firmly in his," the king said with a faltering voice, his eyes glued to a spot behind Hyena.

"Who?" Hyena asked, looking around and seeing no one.

"The other king behind you with the bleeding paws. He is going to leave his blood all over your paw prints!"

Hyena was stunned. But he was no stranger to God's mysterious ways and did not pursue the matter. He *knew*. The queen and the witch looked around, saw no one, and said nothing. It was wiser not to contradict the king.

"Thank you, Jesus," Hyena whispered and then turned to the mesmerized king all business-like. He knew when the anointing of The Name was flowing.

"On your mark, get set, go!"

Hyena shot off like a bolt of thunder with the king close on his heels. The silent, elegant queen got up and glided after the husband and king she had betrayed. She knew she could outrun her husband, but she did not. Not when the Lord was with him. Her past dishonor had only led to loss, tragedy, and shame. Henceforth she wanted her paw prints planted on his, whether he ever loved her again or not. He was still her king. She had come to the end of her road, and it was where God's road began. It began with protecting and honoring her husband.

Earth Lion knew it was the Lion of Judah running behind Hyena even though only the king had seen him. She wondered how he was faring with those three running and praying so fast. Then she took off after them. She was no longer discouraged by her speed. Instead she was happy to pray for the finer details that needed slow observation. Every time the three overtook her, she heard the paw steps of four great creatures. Seven rounds later, the three collapsed on the starting point. Chameleon was not even a stone's throw from

them on her first round, but she intended to finish. Something was
unfolding here, and she wanted to be part of it. She was not sure
what that meant, but she was in the race to finish even if it took
several lifetimes.

Brother spotted Earth Lion and pointed her out to the king and
queen sitting on either side of him.

"Let her be," the king said. "This land needs every prayer."

"Long live the king," Brother said.

"Amen," said the king and queen.

"Majesty," Brother continued, "I am but your servant. It is
more fitting that the king himself declares with his own mouth the
blessing on the jungle. You have the authority both in your capacity
as king and also in The Name. You know he is here."

The king knew. He had seen *him*. He prostrated himself and
raised his voice.

"Dear God, the king of the jungle bows to the king of kings, the
lion of Kenya to the Lion of Judah. Thank you for your worthy presence.
I take full responsibility for every sin of my subjects, my family, and
myself. Please forgive me and heal our land, restoring everything the
devil has stolen. Remember our domestic brothers and sisters. Let man
treat them with loving kindness. I now humble myself and honor you
by declaring every ground shaded by this tree where we performed our
witchcraft and profaned your holy name a public latrine! Endow man
with wisdom, your image whose choice is our destiny."

"Amen," the queen and Hyena answered as the fate of the tree
was sealed with the king's curse. It would never be associated with
any clean business in the jungle again.

The royal couple and their servant sat in silence for a long time.
Brother marveled at the wonders of God. A lowly hyena was sitting
snuggly between two—and not just any lions but the king and
queen of the jungle. They were respectfully waiting for Chameleon
to finish the race.

Hyena could feel the turmoil in the royal couple's hearts. They still loved each other. They just didn't know their way back into each other's hearts. He prayed silently for God to do something. Chameleon had sensed the mood when she rolled her eyes all the way back and started praying for them too, repenting her own role in damaging the relationship. Her movement may have been slow and jerky, but she knew that prayer moved faster than legs.

Suddenly Queen Bora gathered courage and moved from Brother's other side to face her husband. She had a very sad expression on her face. Brother Hyena excused himself to run an errand. He knew he had to do something to lighten the mood. The king changed positions and lay beside his queen, watching their retreating servant.

Brother walked purposely toward the cursed witchcraft tree. He was going to be the first to carry out the king's decree. As soon as he was in its shade, he chose the right position and answered a call of nature. For the first time, the queen smiled as the king held in his laughter.

"Alas! My good and obedient servant steals a smile from the queen!" the king observed, laughing softly.

The queen laughed, but her eyes were still sad. "Where do we go from here?" she asked hesitantly.

"Home," he said quietly.

"Home?" she asked, searching his eyes. She was prepared for Armageddon not a peaceful reconciliation.

"No kingdom is complete without its queen. Forgive me for when I took you for granted, dishonored you, or left you to do all the work. I want us to be a team if that is all right with you."

"I don't deserve you. Just forgive me and it's enough. Perhaps one of my sisters ..." she faltered.

"I knew you had sisters when I chose you. I know you have them now. But you and I are one now, for better or for worse. God already forgave you. We have forgiven each other. Now we must forgive ourselves and step into the future."

"Our cubs ..."

"God will bring them home," the king said. "He loves them even more than we do. And there will be others too. Let's go home."

"Thank you, my lord," she said. "But first I have an errand to run."

"Not you too!" the king exclaimed in mock mortification, glancing toward Hyena who had just concluded his obedience.

"Just watch me!" she teased and headed for the tree. The king watched with an open mouth. Brother had heard the last part of the conversation and quickly left the latrine. He took a wide angle toward the king, avoiding the mischief-bearing queen. Surely she was not going to do *that* in front of a servant.

At the last moment, the queen changed course and walked toward Chameleon. Earth Lion had almost made it quarter circle. She rolled her eyes back and looked into the approaching queen's eyes. There was silent communication. The queen stopped in front of Chameleon and put her tail on the ground. Earth Lion climbed on it slowly. The queen waited patiently till Chameleon was comfortable on her back. Then she ran, carrying the weaker Christian through her first round and the remaining six. The king and Brother Hyena sat applauding.

"What a beautiful female," Brother commented amid a cheer.

"The very best," the king replied.

"I have never been more proud to call you my king or to be called a Kenyan," Hyena said quietly.

"Neither have I been more honored to be your friend and king—and her husband," the king replied, his eyes never leaving the queen.

"You tell her, my friend. You tell her."

"Mmmmmmmm" was all the king grunted, distracted by his approaching queen.

"Thank you, God of beautiful beginnings," Brother whispered to himself as the image of Inao, his betrothed, filled his mind. "Mmmmmmmmm." He echoed the king's sentiments exactly.

The Image Maker

oldier the dog considered the baby he had rescued from the jungle his own puppy. He spent a lot of time crawling alongside him, overturning cans and chasing grasshoppers outside the house. Sometimes the toddler was content just to lie next to Soldier, pulling his tail, ears, or fur. He even tried to hike a ride on his back, but they were yet to manage that feat. But this morning, the little boy had slapped him smack in the eye, and Soldier had yelped in pain. The mistress had taken him away. Soldier wondered if his puppy did not love him anymore.

Soon the humans left the house and he was home alone. They always forgot to close the door. He went in, sniffed around, and found the square frame the mistress always looked into when the master was cross with her or not visiting her. He jumped onto the sofa set the way he had seen her do and looked into the box. He came face-to-face with another dog and jumped off the couch. What was the mistress doing with a trapped dog? He looked behind the frame for the rest of the dog. He was sure he had seen the face of a living, moving dog, but the rest of him was missing. His mistress could well be a witch. He ran out the door. A living, breathing dog's head without the rest of the body ... was the stuff of the Devil's

Mountain. As much as he loved this family, he was going to have to run away. He hid under a tree whimpering, tail flat on his belly. He was a brave dog, but witchcraft was witchcraft, thank you very much. He told himself he was really crying for his human puppy.

Raven chose that moment to visit Soldier, only to find him whimpering.

"What's up, Soldier?" he asked kindly, perched on the nearest branch. Soldier continued whimpering. Raven, seeing nothing suspicious, dropped next to Soldier. He pieced together that Soldier had resolved to run away and become a homeless mongrel because his mistress was a witch! He could no longer reside there. Raven did not know what to say, so he just sat there and shared his sadness.

Unknown to them, Fighting Cock was listening. He had been everywhere in the house and had even picked a major fight with another cock in the same wooden frame. It had taken him a few more fights to realize it was his own image. He let Dog stew for a while. He had chased him around many times to amuse that human chick he called his puppy. Every dog had its day, and this was Soldier's. He laughed loudly. He always knew he was smart, but today he was feeling exceptionally smart.

"What's so amusing, Mr. Cock?" Raven asked respectfully.

Cock liked that, being respected. It was rare these days, so he responded in kind. He approached the ignorant pair, cleared his throat importantly, and explained what the thing was.

"The image of God uses the glass in the wooden frame to make its own image." He cleared his throat. "As you will realize, an image cannot function or even exist in the absence of its maker. Your image was there because you were. It ceased to exist when you left!"

The three went back into the house. One by one, they looked into the framed image-maker. The other two confirmed that the image disappeared the moment its maker did.

"It is the same with God," Fighting Cock confided. "*We are* because

332

Grace King'ara

he is. That is why I worship him so early in the morning. I wake him up and ask him to hang in there and be so that I can continue to be."

Dog and Raven renewed their respect for Fighting Cock. At least he knew where to place his faith. He was going to turn out all right. Cock left to frighten some new young cockerels the master had brought, just to give them a little orientation. They needed to understand who was running the pen and the hens from the start. That way, he could avoid the sin of showing them.

Raven left, and Soldier started thinking. He needed that image-maker to examine his face for flaws. If his mistress was anything to go by, image was everything to humans. Perhaps his human puppy was offended by something in his looks. Carefully he carried the image-maker in his mouth and hid it in a bush where the jungle began. He made his image one more time, thanked God for the image-maker, and groomed himself as far as his tongue and paw could reach.

Please, God, he prayed silently, *reveal any flaws that I can fix them and clear the ones that I cannot. Only do not let my human puppy stop loving me!* He hid the image-maker carefully and went home to love his puppy.

The coyotes Coy and Oteso had no idea where they were born, but it was not in Kenya. They were stolen from their motherland and flown in the belly of an artificial bird that crashed in Samburu. Luckily they had escaped unscathed, but they did not know the fate of the humans. The other animals had been good to them. Being the only two of their kind, King Moran had declared them endangered species and granted them lifetime amnesty. No one was to harm or eat them for as long as they lived. It was, however, their responsibility to hide their existence from humans. No one could predict the image of God. Being so unique, they could well be stolen again, and who knows what planet they might crash on next?

Coy and Oteso found the image-maker and freaked at their images just like Soldier Dog, but they figured it out faster than he had. They took it home to their only daughter, Cocoa. She loved elephants but feared to go anywhere near them. They had told her every bedtime elephant story they knew or could make up. How they stuck together through thick and thin, sick and sin. If one was lost, they found him—period. Even if he was dead, they searched till they found his bones and moaned for him as appropriate. If the loved one was murdered, they found the killers and took revenge, even if the culprits were human. They just never gave up on one another. They also never forgot anything done for them, good or bad.

Cocoa had prayed every night that God would show her elephants—at no risk to her. Her parents, afraid it was too risky, would not take her near them. Even if they climbed a tree, the elephants could easily pluck it out by the roots because they were the strongest creatures on earth.

Cocoa recognized the answer to her prayers when she saw her image in the image-maker. She set out with her parents, who carried it between them, in search of the best viewing point. It was a long distance. Sometimes they stood on two legs to check out their location, but they walked faster on fours. This time it was on threes. Each parent had to spare a foreleg to carry Cocoa's gift as they walked, hiding in tall grass and bushes. At last they spotted elephants but quickly turned their backs on them. Coy covered her daughter's face and turned her body around while her dad placed the image-maker at a strategic angle. They dared not face the elephants directly because they had a little son. They were likely to attack anyone who showed interest in their son.

Coy and Oteso planted the image-maker perfectly between two rocks where Cocoa could watch the elephants without them knowing they were being observed. She thought God must have sent his entire herd because they were very many.

Elpha and Phanto, the elephant couple, loved their son, Phanto Junior, more than anything in the world. For twenty-four moons they had waited for him to be born, and now he was here all eleven moons old. They were constructing a mud pool just for him, a first birthday present. Mother and son watched. Phanto and a bunch of his friends dug on the mushy ground formed by a very tiny tributary of the Ewaso Nyiro River. Weeds, reeds, and a few tadpoles were quickly pulled from the marsh with their big trunks. A baby elephant belonged to the entire community, and they had all turned up to work, trumpet, or just to be counted. When they were done, they gave thanks to God for their strength, their unity, and for their beautiful son.

Cocoa watched as the elephants completed the little mud pond. There was not enough water, so they went to the river and brought it back in their trunks. They spat out fountain after silver fountain into the pond. The mother elephant waddled in the mud up to her knees. Her son danced joyfully before someone threw him in. A few aunts and uncles joined in, but the pond was too small. Junior made great efforts to pull one out as she pretended to be stuck, only to fall on his rear and look up to his mum. She put her trunk in and pushed up his bottom. Now she had to clean herself all over again.

The elephants were the most beautiful thing Cocoa had ever seen. She had had a few prayers answered abundantly in her time, but this was it big time. Not only had God shown her elephants, he was making them entertain her. That was the God her parents had taught her to believe in.

The sun was setting. The coyote family huddled together to thank God for the elephants, the image-maker, and one another. They went home leaving the image-maker behind.

Son of the Morning Star

∾

I t was a Friday evening, the six hundred and sixty-sixth day in the demon calendar. The sun had not set, but the forces of darkness crept out of the cave of Ninety-Nine as scheduled. For 666 moments The Mass had performed every relevant ancient ritual for their demons to inhabit the bodies of the lost-and-not-found pets of God. In one rite of passage, carnivores ate grass, herbivores drank blood while omnivores bit and swallowed pieces of their own bodies. They were now ordained into the revered sainthood of Suicide Divers soon to make a sacred dive into the deep Pond of Tears. The saints believed they would not surely die but come up out on the third moment walking on water to be as God. That included powers to accomplish all their wishes.

The entire legion of the cave and other demons imported from the Devil's Mountain all tried to squeeze into the open souls of the living saints but they were too many. Some rode on top of them, others on top of each other. As long as the individual had responded of his own free will when The Voice made a pass at them, dark angels were legal to come in and assume control.

Mundu bulged in pride, having deceived even the very elite. All Kenyan species save the image of God were represented. Man was

Milika's territory. The crown prince and the princess of the jungle led the saints behind the serpents harkening to The Voices of beings of light within them. The prince wanted to roar. The princess wanted to be a beautiful sleek feline like her mother without the baby fat.

What the saints did not know was that their suicide would unlock the floodgates of hell spilling its contents on every life in Kenya. They would release demons of bilharzias, cholera, foot and mouth, Ebola and all their previously dormant traits that could attack both humans and animals in water, air, on and under the earth, with no existing cure. The Mass had massive treasures chained in the dungeons of the river bottom by the witchcraft of praying Christians. Those sleeping beauties were about to be kissed awake by the prince of the jungle and Kenya would live unhappily ever after.

Mundu had an original virus too, a present for Axis' 666666666666th Birthday. He had lost count of the sixes, but Axis celebrated on Halloween. The virus would be unlocked as soon as both animals and man learned to harm the pre-born. Man was good and ready. They were yet to work on Monkey to initiate the animals. Just thinking about it made him tremble in excitement. Their bones would be eaten from within, flesh and skin left intact. The victims would become slithering worms, dying like their pre-born, struggling to wiggle away from sanctioned suction deaths without a firm bone to stand on. He smiled just thinking of the little ones their loud silent screams of "Don't harm me! I'm alive! Mum! Someone! Anyone! Please love me; Let me live, I am alive!" But The Mass had mastered the justice of the masses, condemning the little Misses and Masters as masses of tissue.

But murder was not the business at hand. It was a beautiful day for suicide. Still one had to marvel at all the possibilities of grieving the Almighty and his beloved mortals afresh. And every time God would heal them, he would hear the blood crying in the ground, just as in the days of Abel, and turn his face in sadness.

The son of the morning star stood outside the cave ready to flag off the suicide diving personally. His hand held the massive red, black and yellow flag of hell imaged with screaming humans and animals in a lake of fire. He glanced at his project manager. Mundu stood one hand akimbo, the other waving a tiny flag of Kenya. There were more tiny flags in the curly locks of his unkept African hair than in the entire country. Axis decided Mundu must lose them after the project. The Kenyan flag was related to the country's National Anthem. That dreadful song was an entire prayer, a whole bunch of icky stinky incense, an aroma pleasing to God! No matter, they were not going to stand attention and sing it with all the diseases coming their way.

A music demon beat a drum to the gentlest rhythm of a God cursing song, a soft caress in the ears of the ungodly, a loose cover for the permanent hole in their hearts that only God could fill. Axis had no detergent or bleach for that particular stain, that sense of foreboding emptiness that made them restless deep down wherever he put them. Whether in a drunken stupor or in a coma the idiots knew something was missing. Nevertheless, God's days were numbered and mortals too would cease to exist.

He waved his endless flag raising both his heads and hands with a thunderous salute to heaven.

"Behold, your pets on their first suicide mission, my turn to say 'It is finished!'" The sound echoed right back as if the message was returned to sender.

Axis shrugged and ascended nonstop past the first to the second heaven, one floor below God and hesitated. Once upon a time they evicted him out of the third heaven and stripped him of every shred of influence but he still had actual access. He could feel the old bitterness smoldering deep within him.

Once in a long while, God hit him with a mongrel's bone and

allowed him to touch a saint on earth for his unknown selfish reasons. He wished he could turn down the favor but he so relished the victim's impending torment at his mercy. There was always the possibility that the saint could lose faith and remain in his custody. But results were never guaranteed in his favor, not when everything always works out together for the good of those that love God. Then Axis felt used, cheapened and highly insulted.

There was that day he had really roamed the earth far and wide ending with a casual relaxing stroll to the third heaven. He saw angels lining up for some reason and got in line for the heck of it, after all, he was still an angel. God saw him in his compound and started gloating about Job, his primed and proper servant on earth. He dared the almighty to remove his favor and let him do a job on job, see what would be left of him. God was in a gabling mood that day and he consented, confident he would win. Axis took from Job everything that could be lost, property, livestock, children and skin. The blasted stinking sore covered saint still came up roses!

Axis escaped the annoying thought by taking a quick stock of his achievements on earth with the image of God. He considered America, the biggest tree with the roots of God and marveled at the chewing his worm had done on the roots. The States' public systems had either retired or outright fired the God of their founding fathers without as much as a handshake or a long service award. Thank you very much we'll take it from there God!

He watched in amusement as man's knees buckled under the load of God, his day getting shorter, and more so his days. He stole the night from himself and the Sabbath from God, yet his day shrank, his boat sank. Laughter was cast overboard where friends, sport, and fun were drowned. His boat was down to nuclear family, yet it sank. Some wrote off filling the earth yet their boat sank. Babies waddled in muck and fog still in swaddling clothes. They sunk or swam, but never in clean water.

A little boy was raising himself and dragging his drugged parents along; a little girl cried for Daddy, but then, so did Mummy. A boy hurried with a man's stride, his daddy's loaded gun in his lunch box. He was going to school, where God was kicked out for good behavior. Axis found it hilarious, Godless systems staggering under parenting while parents were out running godless systems!

There was a new breed of parents with no operational values, no clue how to motivate their young, they never met The Way. Parents who grow up inhaling death cannot exhale life. They exhale a worse generation, suckling babes with full-blown criminal minds. Their first toys were guns. They watched boxing with Daddy, who always hit Mummy along with them. Good manners were a public uniform lest they shame their homes but their selves were shelves of shame. Axis smiled proudly. Yea, the cups were clean outside but inside he was growing little Pharisees!

Adult jails were littered with school bags from the future of man, those frightened, undirected toddlers breastfed on hate, weaned on violence but bequeathed the job of God, *love*. Love your parents, love your siblings, love your neighbors, love your teachers and love your country— love, love, love, but no one said they loved them or pointed out The Way of love!

Despite that, never before had a nation so steered the destiny of man. Youth round the globe were still going Gaga and patenting on her artists. For years America had and still thrived under the full favor of God. Axis knew the reason. It made him gag, the way God dandled Israel on his knee giving them a big brother whose ancestral legs were planted on his own. No one had swaddled and dandled God's baby as much as America, but then, no one had been more blessed. (Hiccup!) No matter, the son of the morning star knew a thing or two about making ancestral legs real wobbly. For now God remained fired in all their public places, thank you very much.

Sadly, he was still bumping into fiery American prayers rushing to the highest heaven. From bedrooms to bathrooms, kitchens, chicken pens and churches, they were still praising The Name. He had planted undercover agents deep in the system to muscle, muzzle and outlaw that foolishness even in the confines of their homes.

Only the day before, he had observed an angel of God circling and weeping over America. Not just any angel but the leader of the legion assigned the great nation since independence - when their fathers submitted their borders on their knees to the protection of The Name he considered below his own. Axis had discreetly followed to listen to God's messenger. Angels cry more with words than tears. This heaven's bush baby was too distraught to notice even his distinct smell.

"America, America, still your brother's keeper, sharing your last bowl of food and pieces of your peace. Your open arms and borders, embrace everything human, even from the lands that hate you the most. Oh champion of human rights, holding every life sacred, even to your peril, your very constitution welded with a soul!

America, America, a refugee collapses at your doorstep, his purpose and dreams wrapped in layers of hopelessness. You serve a warm meal and bed to his tattered human dignity. The mummified lava that was once his dream flutters out. Behold a beautiful butterfly that might never have been.

America, America, your young soldier hurries where others flee. He leaves his warm bed to the refugee and rushes to his bleeding homeland, often switching fate to die in his stead. Yet the soldier soldiers on, he is American.

America, America, the living definition of the fullness of God's blessing, bequeathed the noblest job to be the conscience of the world. Your duties include protecting the apple of God's eye and the brotherhood of man. Oh best maid of the world most prominent in the book of works, but why does the ink of your name grow faint in the book of life?

America, America, You have now come of age, and sought to go the way of all great empires. Has God not suffered your journey - from bondage and a contrite heart on the altar of the Almighty to freedom and prosperity beyond anyone's dreams, lending to all nations and borrowing from none? Now your tattered consciousness of the Ancient of Days is seduced, romancing boldly with paganism as your secret lover plants your garden with seeds of bondage!

America, America "I will bless those who bless you and curse those who curse you!" That too is still forever.

The son of the morning star smiled. So the grass was not that green on Almighty's lawn either! He added his own cries to those of the weeping angel.

"America, America, I too had a dream, the Best Maid of the world came to a crossroad and wondered in her wanderings. Her nose wrinkled at the narrow ancient path of her ancestors, trusting only in her own understanding. "I will stay the night on the crossroad, leave decisions for the morrow."

Yea, I too had a dream, she rested naked in the sand, the sun and the son. I beheld her unequalled beauty, and went into labor. Beloved princess of the lion of the tribe of Judah, behold thy robe I labored all night for thee! Cast away thy rags. I will adorn thee beyond the stars in borrowed silver and gold. Fret not my pretty you will pay on the morrow.

I too had a dream, she cast aside her rags but only a ragged heart can see the old ragged Cross, the mark her ancestors left behind. She fell in love with the robe of my labor and hugged the sash to her sashay body. My plaguing rat concealed in her hem. Gnaw, gnaw, gnaw went her roots God. Come hear my dream, I saw a mighty tumbling down of the giant tree where the dreams of man were nesting.......

America, America, run away with me, we will elope to the land of Kenya. I will kill us a lion, break the neck of the giraffe for thee, skin

*the laughing hyena, together we will stampede on the wildebeest shoot a
porcupine and I will yet adorn you in ivory...*

*America, America love me now before the morning, before the stir
of the morning star, we will catch the shooting star to the pasturelands
of your father; divide up his land and help them pluck the wings off the
butterfly of God.......*

*America, America, come be my love, my princess, do not be coy for I
adore thee. Roll with me in the sand and rest your eyes on papyrus. The
son of the morning star has watered a garden and I, only I will sprout
new roots for thee...... in Egypt!*

Heck, poetry was no longer his lot, not since the days before
time. Not that the wailing angel had his rhythms and rhymes
together either. *"I will bless those who bless you and curse those who
curse you!"* He mimicked God. One of these days he was going to
define the curse part of that ancient promise in God's favorite nation
even if he had to counterfeit him to achieve it.

It felt like a great idea, impersonating God especially in America.
The great nation was like a giant octopus whose tentacles spread
round the world in a form of omnipresence. He was also legal there
these days. Any place where J.C was out he was in. That was custom
in the spirit world, no vacuums. Vacuum was another of his ingenious
doctrines. The individual believed he was rid of both God and devil
and chose any name that he believed excluded both. But only the
gentleman stays out in the rain, knocking ever so gently.... He neither
needed an invitation letter, nor was he a gentleman.

Axis was painfully aware that all humans had a piece of God
inside them. Consciously or unconsciously they hungered for their
source - like homing birds. The image of his worst nightmare
provoked such intense hate it was difficult to think straight. His
wrath intensified with time. So did a sense of doom as his future
hovered closer... The meek will not surely inherit the earth!

He thought about that hole in their hearts again. It needed more than the loose covers of abyss music, pornography, and abusive addictive substances. This was the time to outperform Hollywood and give the world a god after their own hearts. A good comfortable god, the kind they expected from the beginning, a one-size-fits-all god. One of these days, he too was going to have a son. The son of God came to bring a sword of division. His own son would come in peace and leave them in pieces.

He had already started a new age in the world, a wave of godlessness that had so blinded the minds of unbelievers that they would be totally unsuspecting when he laid in place his counterfeit god—the very one they once feared as the antichrist. Only they would have lost the fear of what they ought to fear and turned it into a myth. Already they considered him romantic, an ugly but lovable mythical monster with two horns used to scare kids at Halloween.

Monsters, demons, gargoyles and witches displayed his image on every street and shop while children were costumed as them. Christmas tagged on a moon later stripped naked save a loincloth engraved 'Happy holidays!' Everyone knew what Christmas was about but many were becoming ashamed of it. Few grasped the meaning of Halloween but many celebrated with gusto lost in the luring seduction of the unknown, the mysterious and the otherworldly. That was his specialty.

For a flash second, he remembered once upon a time when God created him most beautiful, loved and named him Son of the Morning Star. But God never allowed his own star to rise. A creature of his caliber was expected to spend eternity worshiping God, who had no plans to retire even after forever! After a careful examination of his personal attributes and potentials, Axis fell in love with himself and rebelled!

If Jesus had helped him, they could have taken God. He had all the insides on God but no, the son obeyed and honored his father in everything, never taking a single step outside his will. They unleashed the Archangel Gabriel and set all the troops on him. Unfortunately only a third of the angels had been brave enough to follow him.

It was not a fair fight. Even if he had turned Gabriel, mastered all the angles and angels, it would still have been a long shot. Where did one grab the one who had no beginning or end and knew the end from the beginning? How was he to contain the omnipresent that stretched from here to there and everywhere and kept the vast space in a place? What good would it have done to throw the consuming fire into the lake of fire? It was Jesus himself who showed him the door and gave him a new name, *the devil.* Some day he would return the favor, not just in America but the same door. He was owed.

One day God planted a garden! It was so beautiful that no words have ever existed to describe it. Every plant and creature was there. He realized God was extremely happy right at that moment. It was not so much the garden that pleased God but the creature he had planted it for. The highest voltage of jealousy coursed through his entire being and bounced him between the sun, the moon, the consternation of stars and billions of galaxies.

For days he pondered the character of man, searching for any door, window or hole into his heart till he found a crack of discontentment. He befriended and duped God's soul mate into eating the fruit of death. That was the best day of his entire life. Changing eternal destiny was no small feat even for the Son of the Morning Star.

The Almighty did not share house with sin, not then, not ever. Then Axis became aware of another garden. A secret garden of God planted deep in man's heart. It had not hit him how much God loved man, every miserable last one of them till he gave his only son to take the bullet in their place.

Axis realized his mind had been wandering from matters at

hand. Suddenly he was very angry. Leading animals astray was not a job for someone of his caliber. Who was this puss in boots Kenya playing in the big spiritual league anyway? What did they take him for, an insect that even their animals could handle?

Suddenly Kenya reminded him of something in the sojourns of his past, no, someone, a little sling trotting shepherd boy who once demolished his castle with a pebble. It was the biggest castle he ever lived. It had an exotic name too, Goliath. They treated him like a common mongrel then and they were doing it again. This time it was animals, birds, and insects from a small sun and Son scorched land on the equator! Axis dared not underestimate anything these days, not even a hymn singing worm. Once upon a time he spoke in one donkey and he still had no class!

As his anger smoldered, Axis suddenly realized his favorite name was a Christian name! They named him Son of the Morning Star and it was not all his. He was only *son of!* He had another hiccup just thinking who *the morning star* title belonged to. The Alpha and the Omega, the beginning and the end, the same old root and offspring of David, the bright Morning Star, that was his maker, what was supposed to be his father!!!!!!!

Suddenly his mind was invaded by a stupid chorus that every creature sang or hummed in Kenya.

> *"He is the lily of the valley,*
> *The brightest morning star,*
> *He's the fairest of ten thousand to my soul!"*

To see Kenyans praise God, tears streaming, eyes closed, arms or paws raised all the way to heaven, you would think he was only their father and no one else's.........Oh hell and Herodias what kind of thought was that!

"*So help me!*" he swore, "*I too have the roots of God but who cares about fathers, ancestries, ancestors, roots or routes? I am god in my own right, not some affiliate, part of, made of, born of or such unwholesome J. C. crap!"*

Axis reminded himself he was here to prevent a potential worldwide God trotting epidemic. But one day, he would overthrow J. C's father and become God Almighty. He knew he was not lying to himself ....

He swooped lower to the first heaven.

"It is finished, it is finished," chorused the bewitched creatures after the serpents. The innocent bulls to the slaughter sweetly mocked J. C.'s last moments on the cross. Axis grinned recalling J. C.'s agony. He dared not think ahead to his moment of eternal humiliation when J. C. died and surprised him in hell. Try getting thrashed in your own backyard none stop for three days and the adversary takes off with your house keys! His anger was just as fresh two thousand years later and counting!

Axis kept his smoldering eyes preyed on the pets and image of God. For now, it suited him fine that the world thought he was just a myth.

The Lion of Judah

எ

There were rocks and thorns on the way, but the lost pets of God did not feel them. The snakes slithered to the place where the coyote family had left the image-maker, a gift of love for their daughter Cocoa, and thanked God. It had fallen flat across the ancient path. When the first serpent slid on it, he could not slither any further. The creator had not designed their bellies to move on glass.

The spirits within the snake curled him into a tight ball and tried to throw him across. Instead, the snake's tail worked like a propeller. A strange negative gravity lifted him higher and away to fall into the mud pond that the elephants had built in love for their son and thanked God. One by one, the entire brood of snakes tried to jump across with the same result. Something about that mirror seemed to give them a spirit of stupor.

It was the turn of the crown prince of the jungle. Without a thought, he took to the sky as if the mirror was something to be avoided at all costs lest one examines himself. The uncanny reverse gravity of the moment shot him off like rocket fire, Whether in spirit or body he did not know, but he was heading heavenward in slow motion. He rose past the trees, the birds of the air, and a manmade flying object that made a lot of noise. He wondered if he even existed.

Suddenly the prince was not alone. The biggest lion he had ever seen was riding the skies alongside him. His awesome mane resembled many shooting stars, and his body extended from horizon to horizon. His hue could only be described as the color of light. Simba felt like a tiny dot floating next to such magnificence. He was so high he could not get over him, so low he could not get under him, so wide he could not get around him. But somehow he knew he could go through him if he chose to, if he was not so afraid. It was the big lion's wind that kept him afloat. He also had the strangest feeling that he *was* because the other lion *was.*

"Who are you, sir?" Simba asked timidly in his girlish voice.

"I am here to teach you to roar," the big lion replied in a still, small voice, smaller than his own. If he was not so big, Simba might not have believed him. Yet the gentle voice was purely soothing, compassionate, and undeniably fearless.

"But who are you?" Simba persisted.

The big lion raised himself higher, shot forward for a moment, then backward, and righted himself. Simba caught a glimpse of both his hind and front paws. They were flawed something bad. All four had big holes wide enough to see right through, and the blood was still flowing. His paws had to have been deliberately pierced in excruciating pain. Only one creature could cause harm with such precision. Man. He wondered why the image of God would choose to harm the gentlest lion. He wished he had the words or the language to comfort him. But this lion had such awesome majesty, such reverent power, that not even the image of God could hurt him unless he let them.

"I cannot roar even to scare my sister!" Simba sobbed. "What does anyone care? It is finished, it is finished!"

The lion laughed, a very beautiful laugh, like he was laughing with him and not at him.

"Indeed it is finished," he said gently to Simba. "I have chosen to roar in your voice but not to scare your sister," the big lion replied calmly.

"Awesome!" exclaimed Simba. "You must have the biggest roar!"

"I do. When my roar resounds, it holds nothing back," the majestic lion replied. "But that is when I choose to use it."

"So why in the world would you choose to give it away? Don't you want to roar ever again?" Simba asked.

"My roar comes to its fullness when given away. Nothing could ever exhaust it."

"That's peculiar philosophy!" Simba exclaimed, losing more of his initial fear.

"Try math; it is more blessed to give than to receive."

"Whatever, Lord, but I am small and weak. How could I possibly contain any part of you?" Simba asked.

"My strength is made perfect in weakness."

"I need a formula for that kind of math, a different wisdom," Simba said.

"The fear of God is the beginning of all wisdom."

"I want to fear God, to revere him," Simba confided.

"You must fear him without being afraid."

"I do not understand," Simba said.

"A marauding rogue lion is looking to devour you and your kingdom."

"Me?" Simba asked, feeling too insignificant for anyone to want to harm him.

"He is not against your present but your future."

"What must I do now?" Simba asked.

"Do not worry. God already saw it coming and prepared a way out."

"Just point out the way, and I will follow," Simba pleaded.

"I am the way. If my roar is in you, even the mighty will be terrified and flee, tail on belly. But you must choose now, this very moment, or you will surely die."

"I am not supposed to talk strangers ..." Simba tried to retreat. Death was something that happened to others, and he was still too young. He also knew that his life had been spiraling in that direction for a while now, since he had listened to The Voice of the other god Axis, the one who held the axis of the earth in place. He was going to give him the biggest roar. His kingdom was going to stretch beyond Samburu to the whole land of Kenya.

"Who are you?" Simba asked again.

"I have known you from before your father," the big lion said. "Before you were formed in your mother's womb, I knew you. And deep down, you have always known me. You just never acknowledged me."

"Please, Great Lion, who are you?" Simba persisted.

The lion was silent for a moment. They passed the sun, the moon, and a garden of galaxies. Everything appeared to revere him. A shooting star stopped in its tracks, retreating to position when the lion waved a paw. The entire firmament and constellation of stars were awed. Simba remembered the song in church, "We Are Standing on Holy Ground." He was cruising in holy space, and Holiness himself was beside him.

"I am also the truth and the life," the lion said calmly.

"Are those your real names, the way, the truth and the life?" Simba asked in his girlish voice.

"I laid the foundation of the earth and marked off its dimensions. I laid its cornerstone while morning stars sang together. I give orders to the morning and show dawn its place. I extend the vast expanses and know the way to the abode of light. I have counted the drops of dew and know the storehouse of snow. I curve a path for the thunderstorm and send lightning bolts on their way. Do you still ask who I am, Mighty King?"

"Mighty King?" Simba asked, looking right, left, and behind him. "Sir, there is only the two of us. Who are you referring to as Mighty King?"

"You, Simba. That's the way I see you."

"I am, weak, below average, nothing like my father," Simba said sadly.

"You see where you are; I see your potential, all that I tucked inside of you when I knitted you together in your mother's womb."

"Please, please, I want to know you with all my heart," Simba pleaded. "Let me know you so I can live!"

"I too am a prince," the majestic lion replied. "My father and I are one because he put all of himself in me. He roars in me, just as I will roar in you."

"You want to give me your father's roar, a gift meant for his son?" Simba asked in his youthful wisdom.

"I can share my roar with all who choose me, for my father has already chosen them. I am pleased to share even the kingdom with my friends."

"Let's try another way," Simba said in what he considered a princely manner. "Just who is your father? Surely I have heard of his kingdom!"

"The Lion of Judah," the lion replied matter-of-factly.

Everyone had heard of the Lion of Judah. But one only went to him through The Name.

"Are you The Name?" Simba asked in a shaky voice.

"You have said it," replied the big lion calmly.

"Forgive me, Lord. I have betrayed you, everyone, and even myself. I am not worthy to lead or live, least of all to have your roar in me. Get away from me. I am filthy, extremely toxic!"

"Never mind that, young prince. See the blood in my paws? It washes whiter than snow. If you sincerely repent, I will forgive your sins and remember them no more. And if you obey my commands that are already written in your heart, I will establish your kingdom. Your enemies will be scattered to the four winds. But you must trust and obey only me, for mine is The Name, the only one my father has given under the sun by which anyone can be saved. You see, like you, I am his only son."

"Roar in me, Lord, roar in me," Simba said with tears in his eyes. "And let me roar only when it pleases you."

"When you roar for love, peace, justice, truth, and mercy, that will be me. Go honor your father and mother in obedience and make their hearts glad. Then you will roar in your own kingdom to a ripe old age."

"Why me?" Simba asked, feeling honored but unworthy.

"I care for all my creatures long before they are. Your great-grandfather did what was right in the eyes of my father, storing up blessings for his future generations. He also prayed that his bloodline would never fail to glorify the Lion of Judah. My father answers every prayer from those who love him even long after they are gathered up to their ancestors and to him."

Suddenly Simba was hurtling back to earth alone. The sun scorched him, but he was not consumed. The shooting star passed through his chest but did not split or splatter him. And the earth was coming up fast to meet him.

"Jeeeesus!" he cried just before he hit earth. Only it was not hard concrete earth but the back of the big lion. The gentle lion had already gone before him to be his cushion. Then he was gone—*poof*—as if he was never there. Simba stood in front of the mirror⋅ where the snakes had tried to go. He was still leading the convoy ahead of his sister, whose turn it was to jump the mirror. Her eyes were unfocused, her mouth chanting along with the suicide divers, "It is finished, it is finished." The creatures were still dazed, oblivious of any giant lion that had come and gone.

Simba was enraged by the chant. He knew now whom they were

mocking. Taking a deep breath, he turned around to face them. Then he opened his mouth as his vocal cords released his first ever roar. It was louder than his father's.

The earth vibrated. The trees swayed. The chant stopped mid-word as every creature stood still. Even the demons that rode them could not make them move as they saw the brilliance around him. The young prince roared again just to confirm he was really the one roaring. Then he braced himself for the third and unleashed his biggest roar. That one was for the Lion of Judah. By now, everyone stood at attention just as they did with his father.

THE AEROGEDDON

❧

Suddenly everything including time stood still as a bomb of praise detonated, scattering all the powers of darkness. Simba had never heard the song before, but he felt its earth-shattering power. It was only a nursery rhyme resounding both in the air and on the ground, but he had the inner knowing that it was being sung on earth as it was in heaven. All hell was breaking loose as the demons trembled and bowed to The Name.

Two birds were shot as missiles of mass destruction. Aero circled the aero space of the jungle at full speed, her magnificent wings spread wide as she sang. Ostrich rode the ground at the speed of light while mumbling the song as much as speed permitted. The king had assigned the two newfound friends to circle Samburu seven times on behalf of the land of Kenya. Everyone else sang from the background, but there was total harmony. It was the day the king had declared for prayer and fasting.

The sun was almost setting, but no one had eaten a thing that day. The prayer procession started from Monkey's tree where God had met them last. It was where Aero first landed as a miracle, Monkey burned his gods, Hyena got engaged, and Nyoka got his tail back. The place was almost a shrine, and they planned to start another church there.

King Moran led them crawling on their knees and bellies and every way they knew to supplicate to their creator. They were his pets, called by his name, repenting in dust and mud. If only the Lion of Judah would hear them from his den in heaven and see their contrite hearts, he would heal the land and bring their lost friends back home. They had nothing to offer the Lord but thankful adoration and the sacrifices of praise. So they sang Aero's song again and again as she had taught it to them.

The king thought he heard a roar as powerful as his own in the distance; it stopped his world for a moment. The queen went faint beside him. They remembered their son could not roar and was gone from them. But the heart of a parent knew certain things. Perhaps the sound was only in their imagination. Nevertheless, they thanked God for the memory of what could have been, just as they did in everything. They continued to lead the praise for the land with everyone who could move behind them.

> *Jesus love is very, very wonderful*
> *Jesus love is very, very wonderful*
> *Jesus love is very, very wonderful*
> *Oh wonderful love*
>
> *So high that you can't get over it*
> *So low that you can't get under it*
> *So wide that you can't get around it*
> *You must go through the Lord!*

The creatures behind Simba stood still as if history had paused to catch its breath. The music was coming from everywhere. Simba knew it was his cue to lead, but he was somewhat unsure about the way. Then he saw him. The great lion was walking ahead of him. He just needed to follow in his footsteps. Simba waved his head and mane in authority for the others to follow. They did. The princess was not afraid of Simba's roar. Instead she stepped in the mirror and broke it as she followed her brother. Then she broke into song, the same song that was in the air. Simba joined her. It was easy to follow. One by one, the creatures stepped in the mirror, grinding it into dust along with the self-image they held before. Then they joined in the song and followed Simba. Their prince finally knew the way, and he could also roar away.

Simba kept following in the footprints of the great lion. Even when he could not see him, he believed he was there. The Lion of Judah had promised never to leave him or forsake him as long as his roar was in him. Slowly Simba was led to the shores of the Ewaso Nyiro River and the Pond of Tears, the same place where the snakes were leading them to die. The thought made Simba afraid again. He amplified praise and felt the fear leave him.

Suddenly, just like his father on the other side, Simba felt the music surround him as if heaven had joined in the praise. All things were possible. The lion prince followed the footsteps around the Pond of Tears and knew it was no longer unclean. The Lord had passed by there! They stood in a circle around the pond that resembled an extended stomach off the Ewaso Nyiro. Everyone faced the water. The big river raged on unaware of the stomach operation that would rid it of toxins from the bottomless pit.

Simba planted his paws firmly on those left by the great lion. He raised his nose to heaven, thanked God, and drank from the pond. Their music paused on earth but not in heaven. The other animals hesitated only for a moment before they drank in communion. The last spirits of destruction that had been immobilized by The Name in the song grabbed the chance to scatter in seven directions. Simba glimpsed in the spirit some carrying one another and others hiding inside of others, but they all left.

Then he saw the mighty lion across the water from him. He

stood majestic with the sun behind him, looked straight at Simba, and winked! It was a wink that said, "I know you, I love you, I am with you." Simba responded in kind with a huge roar. It was not just any roar but an "I love you big time" roar. He felt it in every pore and paw. The big lion gave a most radiant smile and turned his head sideways, drawing Simba's attention to a movement in the other direction. Simba turned his head and saw his father prostrate on the ground next to his mother. There were tears in his parents' eyes.

King Moran had seen the prince and the princess lead the missing animals to drink in the pond. He had also seen the great lion approving as Simba roared. The great lion with the bleeding paws, his blood still potent thousands upon thousands of moons later.

The king and queen stood up as Simba and his followers hit the ground to honor them. The whole jungle was prostrate before their king and the king of kings. The royal couple walked to the prince and princess and put their mouths on their heads to bless them. Then they signaled everyone to rise up and receive the lost and found friends and family.

The Ewaso Nyiro raged on unaware of the battle that had just been won. She would continue to give life and not death. As the sun began to set, the jubilant animals declared the goodness of God. He had set the captives free. They were home.

A song swept down from up the river where the humans lived. Everyone and everything that had life in Kenya had heard that prayer song so many times that it had become just another sound made by humans. That is until Aero told them what it was, the song of songs of Kenya, the national anthem, a complete prayer for the land.

What they did not know was that the human president had also declared a day of fasting and prayer for the land. They too were prostrate before the Lord as a nation in every way that they knew, even to ashes and sackcloth. On this day, all the species of the land had sought forgiveness for their godlessness and the healing of the land. Earth would call it *coincidence*, a word coined on earth but missing in heaven's dictionary.

A torrent of rain hit their heads and the land on a particularly sunny moment even for the Land of Sunshine. The king of the jungle raised a paw, and everyone who had legs stood at attention. Aero posed in the air above the royal family, her wide wings resembling an open Bible covering them from the rain. For the first time ever, the pets of God stood still in honor of God and their country's National Anthem.

Axis sat on the Devil's Mountain gloating over Kenya's impending doom. That was before Aero's song hit the airwaves of the jungle with *The Name, The Name, The Name*. Whenever his ears heard The Name, his knees knew nothing but to bow. But this was so unexpected, he fell forward, two heads hanging precariously in the mouth of the cave below. His hairy legs and webbed feet waved desperately in the dusty air. If they only stopped with the blasted name, he could right himself in an instant.

It had to be Aero. He had not realized the stupid bird had picked up the silly rhyme when he scattered the human kids. She had taught the creatures the only song she knew, and it was turning out to be lethal. The elephants trumpeted. The owls hooted. Every mouth praised J. C. It was turning out to be a very bad day for one who was meant to be as God.

He tried staring blankly at the hole before him, but it reminded him of something that blew him ... another hole not in his past or present but somewhere in his future. It was a hole in the center of the center of an endless lake of fire. Only it was not a hole but a pit, a bottomless pit. No, no, he would not surely die. He was already dead.

For the first time in thousands of years, his well-suppressed emotions surged to the surface and he cried out in great passion. It was not "My God, my God, why hast thou forsaken me?"

"Does heaven, earth or under the earth realize how scary it to be me?!" he cried.

Then he gave a sigh and recharged his battery of pride, a hard thing to do while standing on his heads in a hole without a bottom. A bolt of anger surged through him as he realized he had indulged in a moment of self-pity. He was destined to be God!

"My strength is also made perfect in weakness!" he encouraged himself.

The sun was setting. Darkness was coming, and the song would soon stop. Aero always fell asleep at sunset. He had a stronghold on that.

The song did stop, and something else held him in place—a chain of power he could only deny but not resist. He knew beyond a shadow of doubt the dreaded one was around. In the blink of an eye, his eternal enemy rose before him. Deep down Axis had always known J. C. is the son of God and choked on it. He also knew he was God, honest to God, God, the hell with the honest. Just as a calf is cow, and a kitten is a cat, God can only beget God. But that did not mean he could ever willingly obey him! And here he was, robed in all the glorious majesty of the father, which he had coveted since once upon a time! It was less frustrating to think of him as God Junior and reduce him a notch. He recalled painfully the day The Truth was announced for the entire universe to hear.

"This is my son whom I love; with him I am well pleased!" That was the voice of God from heaven when J. C. was baptized by John. At least he had John's head served on a silver platter to a pagan woman!

Axis looked at his adversary's belt and saw his own keys. Two thousand years later, he still had the keys to his dungeons. It made him so angry, but he dared not make a dash for them considering where they were hung. Next to his keys was the half-unsheathed flaming sword of God!

The prince of darkness and the prince of light locked eyes in the war for Kenya. Darkness escaped as the hole was sprayed in brilliance to the entire Devil's Mountain. Axis knew it would no longer be his mountain; it never was. His knees compulsively glued to the ground above in supplication.

The firstborn of all creation waved a finger at Axis and shot him upright above the mountain. The mountain shook as they both planted their feet on it. Everywhere was brightness, save the giant shadow of Axis. The prince of light waved a finger again, and Axis was planted upright like a statue. Axis wondered what this was about. The son of God usually had him on his knees, but now he wanted him upright.

For a moment, Axis entertained the thought that Jesus had remembered he too was made by God the father, the most beautiful Son of the Morning Star, and was here to hand over the kingdom peacefully. God was surrendering ahead of time because they knew he was coming! Too late he realized what was happening.

The sun was setting. So was the day of prayer and fasting for the land. In every province, the flag was coming down at this time with the song that Axis hated. He knew God had heard from heaven and that the course of the nation's history was about to change.

The president of the humans gave his signal at the same time as the king of the jungle. Axis gritted his teeth as he was forced to stand and pay attention. The flag and the sunset went down very slowly, and as in one accord, the children and the pets of God in the land of sunshine released their hearts, tears, and vocal cords to the Song of Songs, the national anthem of Kenya.

> *Oh God of all creation*
> *Bless this our land and nation*
> *Justice be our shield and defender*
> *May we dwell in unity*
> *Peace and liberty*
> *Plenty be found within our borders.*

Let one and all arise
With hearts both strong and true
Service be our earnest endeavor
And our homeland of Kenya
Heritage of splendor
Firm may we stand to defend.

Let all with one accord
In common bond united
Build this our nation together
And the glory of Kenya
The fruit of our labor
Fill every heart with thanksgiving.

EPILOGUE, TWENTY-FOUR MOONS LATER

❧

The wedding was on a Sunday, at sunset, when no one was likely to eat anyone. Even Soldier the dog was invited, and he was not afraid. The king had granted him a permanent visa in the jungle for his act of saving the little image of God. He could come and go as he wished and no one would harm him.

It was supposed to be a blast. Everyone was invited.

Elephant trumpeted an early wakeup call. Monkey was first to arrive at the Pond of Love, which was the renamed Pond of Tears, with his own specially trained traditional dancers. Pastor Twiga had a new collar of soft sisal, which Inao had found. Peacock and his family stood arranged as one flower with all the splendor of their wings and tails displayed. Perched neatly on Elephant's trunk were the birds of paradise.

Nyoka had become an evangelist to the snakes and had led many to The Name. He and his friends coiled and uncoiled around a small plant in well-coordinated displays to entertain the bride and groom. Far afield were his parents, who were back together and practicing Christians. Behind them was Aunt Brahmin, her ten daughters whom he still considered his sisters, and his one hundred nieces. His mother had led Brahmin and all the grand-hatchlings to the Lord. Nyoka smiled for a moment, remembering that every one of his parents' one hundred grand-hatchlings had laid ten eggs. They were about to welcome with a kiss one thousand great-grand-hatchlings!

Monkey's two beautiful daughters were the flower girls. Porcupine had given many pines to Monkey to decorate the wedding bush. Ostrich and other birds gave feathers. The animals arranged themselves in two rows, making a path for the procession. At the end of the path was a bush where Inao and her bridesmaids were hiding. On the other end was the altar, an elevated ground where beautiful grass spread like a carpet.

Soon the king and queen, prince and princess of the jungle were seated in their place of honor around the altar. So were Pastor Twiga and a slightly sweaty but ecstatic Brother. He had tapped on all his digging talents and experience to make his bride the most beautiful den. Inao had declared it divine. It was on a small hill where he believed both the sun and the Son could reach his home fastest. The family could also see anyone approaching. Still his nose was sweating. He just wanted her to say, "I do." Time was crawling.

Not only had God blessed this union, he had reunited Inao with her long lost cousins. The two had been captured and brought to Samburu in much the same manner as Inao a week before the wedding. Two days later, his rogue cousin had arrived in a different cage—a ragged-looking drifter but still his beloved cousin, the kind that made a wonderful uncle. But it was not right to think that far ahead, before she said, "I do," or was it? Amazing how God's wedding gifts had been the first to arrive—all the family they had in the world gathered together, unless his father was still alive somewhere. He sure wanted to see him and tell him he forgave him for trying to eat him at birth.

Elephant trumpeted "Here Comes the Bride," and everyone stood at attention. The blushing bride had not even shown her face when everything went haywire. The grasshoppers jumped out of the bride's hiding place as practiced the evening before. They hopped in step about two hundred times higher than their own height in a magnificent pattern of a cross. Only they were heading in the wrong direction, away from the altar! No one remembered that the hoppers rode on wind, and it had now changed its course. They hopped on and out of sight, the beautiful cross leaving the wedding before it began!

The usher, Mrs. Zebra, came to the rescue. She bowed behind the hoppers and shook her massive head three times in approval as if that was the plan all along. Then she motioned for Inao's procession to begin. Elephant kept trumpeting as if everything was perfect. A gallant Inao poised herself and walked forward. The beautiful sunset behind her was good for something old. For something new, she had a live necklace of day-old butterflies flying in a ring around her neck. The Beetles had trained them all night to dance to their music and Elephant's trumpet.

The Beetles were the best band of all time in the jungle, as long as they were together. Every Beetle was extremely talented individually, and their combination was the stuff of dreams. But they were also very individualistic, and every one of them preferred to find his pile of dung. It had taken all of Crow's selling skills and a subtle request from the queen to convince them to come together for this most important wedding. Inao and Brother were the reigning couple of the jungle.

Some very blue birds perched on Inao's head as a crown. She had nothing borrowed. Unlike the image of God, the pets of God did not believe in borrowing or owing anything but love. It was custom. Aero had also affirmed from her memory of God's book of instructions that the borrower is a slave to the lender, be it another individual or a system. When they gave or received, it was for keeps.

Two beautiful bush babies preceded the bride, followed immediately by Monkey's identical twin daughters. He had finally married the girl who liked the lisp in his voice. Inao was flagged from behind by her two beautiful cousins, who were as large but not comparable in beauty, if you asked Brother.

A whole train of assorted animals followed behind her. A vibrant Mrs. Zebra got everyone to their rightful spots. The bride and groom knelt in front of the pastor who prayed for their peace, love, unity and multiplication. Finally it was that magic moment…

"Dearly beloved, we are gathered here today to join Inao and Brother in holy matrimony. If anyone has any reason why the two should not be joined together, say it now or forever remain silent!"

He looked around the congregation. Everyone looked everywhere at once in the most intense moment of any wedding. Brother sweated some more and called for more faith from heaven. Inao was not worried until the wind suddenly blew into her face and sounds like shots or fireworks were heard approaching nearer and nearer. She hoped it was not another female with a litter behind her coming to claim her groom. Some held their breath while others whispered their speculations. Someone was definitely coming with a reason!

Calm was restored peacefully when the lost hoppers finally hopped to their allotted place on the altar, riding a new wind. Inao exhaled. So did Brother. He had no known reason to have been apprehensive, but a few brothers had been framed!

This time, the hoppers arranged themselves in the shape of two hearts with an arrow across them. But being hungry and exhausted from the extended hopping, they started eating the grass they stood on. They ate at such a high speed that soil was soon exposed. Everyone was dumbfounded.

As soon as they realized their behavior was inappropriate, they started turning around and around in embarrassment. Another wind came to their rescue. They hopped higher than before and then away in no particular order, just a fast getaway.

On the spot where they had eaten lay two beautiful hearts with an arrow between them, their own wedding gift. Again Mrs. Zebra nodded in approval and curtsied behind the hoppers as if everything they did had been prearranged. The leader of the hoppers looked back for a moment and smiled before they were all out of sight. Elephant trumpeted what sounded like a "Thank you."

"I, Hyena receive you Inao as my lawful wedded wife, to love as myself, till death do us part."

"I, Inao, receive you, Brother, as my lawful wedded husband, to love, as myself till death do us part.

"Brother Hyena, do you promise never to eat your litter?" the pastor asked.

"I do," Brother replied.

"Sister Inao, do you promise to help Brother raise your cubs in the fear and admonition of the unseen God, praying for Israel, the pets and the image of God?

"I do," Inao replied.

"You may now chase the bride!" the pastor declared. Everyone held their breath. The bride took off like the wind with the groom close on her hooves. The bride's necklace of newborn butterflies and the crown of blue birds took cover. The congregation cheered—the females for Inao, and the males for Brother. Sparrows flew overhead, making shapes like kites in the air. All birds of flight took to the air circling around Aero in different colorful patterns.

Ostrich, who had been taking flying lessons from Aero, made a frustrated attempt. A few animals snickered, and she did not like it. She knew that God did not endow her with wisdom or give her a share of good sense. She did not know why she laid her eggs on the ground and left them to warm in the sand, unmindful that a foot may crash them. She treated her young harshly as if she were a wicked stepmother. But one thing she knew, when she spread her feathers to run, they paid attention. So she did.

Soon she was ahead of the bride and groom, making very wide circles around them without interfering with them. Then she widened the circle to include the entire gathering. Aero and the other birds made similar circles to fly alongside her. Guinea Fowl and Peacock tried to catch up with Ostrich but gave up in a short run. Nevertheless, they made everything more beautiful in that time.

At last, Brother caught Inao, or she let herself get caught; it did not matter. They touched their noses and crossed their necks among shouts of jubilation. Brother kissed his bride. They were family.

The weaverbirds sprinkled millet all over their heads, and the newlyweds were licensed to multiply.

The gatecrashers chose that moment to arrive. They were the most famous gatecrashers in the jungle. It was whispered that they came all the way from a desert called Kalahari. They were locusts. At first everyone thought someone had invited them, perhaps the king because they were everywhere, even in his face. Within moments, the Kalaharis had eaten every green thing, including the first family's carpet of grass.

"*Shindwe!*" Mrs. Zebra shouted, but it was such a happy time and the *shindwe* was so inappropriately funny, they all started laughing and rolling on the ground. The king knew they needed to tighten security or the Kalaharis would be back.

Suddenly they realized Ostrich was still running a circle around them. Either she had forgotten to stop or she was spinning out of control. The king sent Cheetah to run alongside her, calm her down, and lead her back for closing prayers. Still she did not stop. Once again, Mrs. Zebra came to the rescue. She started stamping on the ground in applause as if the race was over and Ostrich had won. Cheetah caught the drift and stayed behind her, allowing her the win. He knew he could have beaten her, exhausted as she was. Everyone got the coded message and kept the applause till a jubilant Ostrich came to a stop with a bow for the first family and a curtsy for the bride and groom.

The king and queen blessed the wedding couple and left for another important engagement. Their presence had lent the occasion star status. Quirra had a boyfriend, but her parents had not looked him over yet. Mrs. Zebra's husband, Punda, was now attending church. Zeb was in love, but he did not know how to approach her.

Monkey and his traditional dancers took the jungle by storm, raising the curtain for the long-awaited Beetles. Their performance was always over the moon. The Lord's choir led by the birds of paradise did not allow them to forget who made such a day possible.

Inao and Brother had two beautiful daughters, Faith and Mercy. They were careful to pass on to them the sacred story of their ancestors. The fear of the Lord was their wisdom teeth. Their handsome rogue uncle and two dotting aunts lived with them. Brother went into construction work digging dens for bachelors in courtship, and Inao taught Sunday school.

That rogue cousin whose name was Hiti seemed to like one of

Inao's cousins a little too much. Even the cubs could tell. Her name was Naomi, meaning *one who smiles*. But that is another story. Our favorite couple thanks you for your company. But they want us to stop the story so they can start living *happily ever after*.